朗文

隨時隨地說得得體、說得自然、說得漂亮

生活萬用
句典

The Essential
Handbook for

常駿躍 編著

PEARSON
Longman 朗文

DALIAN UNIVERSITY OF TECHNOLOGY PRESS
1985

國家圖書館出版品預行編目資料

朗文生活萬用句典 = The Essential Handbook for
English Learners ／常駿躍 --初版. -- 臺北
市：臺灣培生教育, 2007
面 ； 公分

ISBN　978-986-154-590-5 (平裝附光碟片)

1. 英語　2. 會話　3. 句法

805.188　　　　　　　　　　　　96014862

朗文生活萬用句典
The Essential Handbook for English Learners

編　　　　著	常駿躍
發　行　人	洪欽鎮
主　　　編	李佩玲
責　任　編　輯	陳慧莉
協　力　編　輯	官芝羽、林美妏
美　術　設　計	黃聖文
美　編　印　務	楊雯如
行　銷　企　畫	朱世昌、劉珈利
發行所／出版者	台灣培生教育出版股份有限公司
	地址／台北市重慶南路一段 147 號 5 樓
	電話／02-2370-8168　　傳真／02-2370-8169
	網址／www.PearsonEd.com.tw
	E-mail／reader@PearsonEd.com.tw
香 港 總 經 銷	培生教育出版亞洲股份有限公司
	地址／香港鰂魚涌英皇道 979 號（太古坊康和大廈 2 樓）
	電話／(852)3181-0000　　傳真／(852)2564-0955
	E-mail／msip@PearsonEd.com.hk
台 灣 總 經 銷	創智文化有限公司
	地址／台北縣 235 中和市建一路 136 號 5 樓（翰林文教大樓）
	電話／02-2228-9828　　傳真／02-2228-7858／02-2228-7852
學校訂書專線	(02)2370-8168 轉 695
版　　　次	2007 年 11 月初版一刷
	2008 年 7 月初版三刷
書　　　號	TL032
I　S　B　N	978-986-154-590-5
定　　　價	新台幣 550 元

行政院新聞局局版臺陸字第 101274 號

Authorized Adaptation from the Simplified Chinese language, entitled 【交际英语口语句典, ISBN: 7-5611-3155-0, 常駿躍】Copyright ©2006 by DALIAN UNIVERSITY OF TECHNOLOGY PRESS. All rights reserved. No part of this book may be reproduced or transmitted in any form or by any means, electronic or mechanical, including photocopying, recording or by any information storage retrieval system, without permission from DALIAN UNIVERSITY OF TECHNOLOGY PRESS. Published and distributed by Pearson Education Taiwan in the territory of Taiwan by the arrangement of DALIAN UNIVERSITY OF TECHNOLOGY PRESS.
All rights reserved. No part of this book may be reproduced or transmitted in any form or by any means, electronic or mechanical, including photocopying, recording or by any information storage retrieval system, without permission from Pearson Education Taiwan Ltd., Inc.

本書相關內容資料更新訊息，請參閱本公司網站：www.PearsonEd.com.tw/index_2.asp

序 言

許多讀者爲了學好英語，狂背單字、片語、文法等，但是到了眞正面對外國人時，卻緘口結舌，什麼話也說不出來，枉費學了那麼多年的英文。其實讀者往往忘記了學習語言的最重要目的——溝通。英語學習的最終目的不是爲了應付考試，而是爲了成功地對話溝通。因此，學習英文的最重要目標，就是要培養口說的會話能力，成功達到溝通無障礙的境界！

俗語說：「見人說人話」、「上什麼山唱什麼歌」、「一樣話幾樣說」。這裡的「人」和「山」指的是說話的「表達內容」和「對話場景」；這裡的「幾樣說」指的是一個意思有多種表達方法。學習語言若不注意說話的場景，說話不可能得體；若不注意表達的多樣性，語言就不可能豐富。這些俗語和語言學習理論的共同點，都是在強調語言功能和說話場合的重要性，與多種表達的必要性。《朗文生活萬用句典》正是根據以上理念，進而根據時代要求和讀者的實際需求而編寫成的。

本句典有以下幾個特色：

1. 將實際的口說表達根據說話者要表達的情緒意圖和身處的會話場景來進行分類；

2. 每一個分類之下包含中文表達的意思、實用的口說句型；

3. 爲各類句型精選實用的、常見的多樣表達法；

4. 爲各類句型提供了典型、精確、實用的範例；

5. 各類句型中可替換部分用 "…" 來特別標記，以方便讀者舉一反三；

6. 對可能的生字加註音標、詞性、翻譯，以方便讀者學習；

7. 對東西方的知識背景和文化差異做了適當的講解說明。

《朗文生活萬用句典》系統實用，內容豐富。希望讀者能熟記常用的口說句型，勤於練習。唯有這樣，才能在面對面的溝通中，脫口而出，準確且道地的表達自己的意思。

本書的完成，要感謝編輯韓露、徐言春等人的幫忙。由於能力所限，難免有疏漏與不足之處，誠懇讀者不吝賜教。

編者於大連外國語學院

符號說明

v.	動詞（verb）
adj.	形容詞（adjective）
adv.	副詞 （adverb）
n.	名詞（noun）
interj.	感嘆詞（interjection）
sb.	某人（somebody）
sth.	某事（something）
【尤】	尤指（especially）
【美】	美式英語（American English）
【英】	英式英語（British English）
【澳】	澳式英語（Australian English）
【法】	法語（French）
【西】	西班牙語（Spanish）
【正式】	正式用法（formal）：適用於正式發言，但是不適用於普通的交談
【非正式】	非正式用法（informal）：適用於一般交談，但不適用於正式的場合
【舊式】	舊式用法（old-fashioned）：曾經普遍使用，但現在較少使用
【幽默】	幽默用法（humorous）：一般以開玩笑的方式使用的詞語
【俚】	俚語（slang）：僅限於某一特定人群使用
【口】	口語（spoken）：僅用於或者幾乎總是用於交談的詞語
【諱】	忌諱語（taboo）：因為非常粗魯或者具有冒犯性而不應使用的詞語

目 錄

 第 1 部分　情緒意圖篇

第1章　會話技巧

第 2 章 思想溝通

第 3 章　正面表達

🎧 第 2 部分　會話場景篇

第 5 章　特別時刻

第 6 章　商務溝通

第 7 章　海外生活

第1部分
情緒意圖篇

第1章
會話技巧

① ②
③ ④ ⑤
⑥ ⑦

　　問候是人際往來的開始，它具有建立和延續人際關係的作用。問候的形式受時間、地點、場合、地位、年齡、關係親疏等因素影響。熟人相見要互致問候；陌生人在有人介紹認識之後，也要相互問候。問候是互相的，不然就會顯得冷淡。相互問候可以透過語言，也可以透過點頭、微笑或手勢。用英語問候要熟記一些用語，因為中文和英文的問候語差別極大。問候時還要注意恰當地使用稱謂。

0001	你好！ **Hello!**	002
替換	Hi! Hello there!	
範例	**A:** Hello! 你好！ **B:** Hello! 你好！	
提示	"Hello!" 為一天中常用的問候語，用於一般場合；"Hi!" 比 "Hello!" 更口語，常用於熟人之間。	

0002	早安。 **Good morning!**
替換	Morning!
範例	**A:** Good morning! 早安！ **B:** Good morning! 早安！

0003	午安。 **Good afternoon.**
替換	Afternoon!
範例	**A:** Good afternoon. 午安。 **B:** Good afternoon. 午安。

0004	晚安。 **Good evening.**

| 替換 | Evening! |

| 範例 | **A:** Good evening, sir. 晚安，先生。
B: Good evening. 晚安。 |

0005　你好嗎？
How are you?

| 替換 | How's everything?
How are you doing?
How are things (going) with you? |

| 範例 | **A:** How are you? 你好嗎？
B: I'm fine, thank you. And how are you? 我很好，謝謝。你呢？
A: I'm fine, too. 我也很好。 |

0006　您好！
How do you do?

| 替換 | Howdy! |

| 範例 | **A:** How do you do? 您好！
B: How do you do? 您好！ |

| 提示 | "How do you do?" 用於在正式場合時，初次見面的問候語。
"Howdy?" 用於非正式場合，源於 "How do you do?"。 |

0007　好久不見了。
It's been a long time.

| 替換 | I haven't seen you for ages.
I haven't seen you for some time.
I haven't run into you in a long time.
Long time no see! |

| 範例 | **A:** It's been a long time. How's everything? 好久不見了。你好嗎？
B: Just fine. 還好。 |

0008　真想不到在這遇到你！
Fancy meeting you here!

| 替換 | Imagine meeting you here.
Never thought I'd meet you here.
This is a pleasant surprise!
What a coincidence!
What a surprise to meet you here! |

範例　A: Fancy meeting you here! 真想不到在這遇到你！
B: This is a real surprise! 真令人驚喜！

提示　coincidence [koˈɪnsɪdəns] *n.* 巧合

0009　很高興在這裡見到你。
Glad to see you here.

替換　Glad to run into you here.
How very nice to see you!
I'm glad to have the opportunity to see you here.

範例　A: Glad to see you here. 很高興在這裡見到你。
B: Me too. 我也是。

提示　opportunity [ˌɑpəˈtjunətɪ] *n.* 機會；時機

0010　很高興又見到了你。
Good to see you again.

替換　Pleased to see you again.
How nice to see you again.
It is good to see you again.

範例　A: Good to see you again. 很高興又見到了你。
B: It's been a long time. 好久不見了。

0011　很高興你能來。
It's nice to have you here.

替換　Nice having you here!
I'm so glad you could come.
What an unexpected surprise!

範例　A: It's nice to have you here. 很高興你能來。
B: It's my pleasure. 樂意之至。

提示　unexpected [ˌʌnɪkˈspɛktɪd] *adj.* 想不到的；意外的

0012　我正要找你。
You're just the person I was looking for.

替換　I was just looking for you.
You're just the person I wanted to see.

範例　A: You're just the person I was looking for. 我正要找你。
B: What's up? 什麼事？

0013	想不到又見面了！ **Small world, isn't it?**
替換	It's a small world, isn't it?
範例	**A:** What? You again? 啊，又是你？ **B:** Small world, isn't it? 想不到又見面了！

0014	什麼風把你吹來啦？ **What brings you here today?**
範例	**A:** Good day, mate! 夥伴，你好！ **B:** What brings you here today? 什麼風把你吹來啦？
提示	good day【尤澳】你好〔意思同 hello，多用於上午和下午打招呼時〕 mate [met] *n*.【英，澳，非正式】夥伴〔特別常用於男人對男人友好的稱呼〕

0015	我很好。 **I'm fine.**
替換	(Just) fine. Great. Pretty good. Wonderful. I am doing fine.
範例	**A:** How are you doing? 你好嗎？ **B:** I'm fine. 我很好。

0016	還可以。 **OK.**
替換	Alright. Not too bad. No complaints. I can't complain.
範例	**A:** How are you? 你好嗎？ **B:** OK. 還可以。

1.2　詢問姓名 Asking Someone's Name

　　有人說，姓名是一個人最寶貴的財富。在見面時能立刻叫出某人的姓名，便能拉近雙方的距離，奠定雙方的關係。詢問人的姓名也有很多表達方式，中文有「您貴姓？」等禮貌的說法，英語中也有很多禮貌的表達方式，口語中的 "What's your name?" 其實是不禮貌的說法，並不適用於正式場合，因此光懂此句是不足以應付各種會話場合的。

0017　請問，你叫什麼名字？　　　　　　　　　　(003)
Your name, please？

（替換）
What's your full name?
What's your name, please?
May I know/have your name?
Would/Could you give me your name, please?
Who shall I say is calling?〔電話用語〕

（範例）
A: My name is Rip. Your name, please? 我叫瑞普。請問，你叫什麼名字？
B: My name is Betty. 我叫貝蒂。

0018　你是…嗎？
Are you...?

（替換）
Are you called...?
Is your name...?

（範例）
A: Are you Mr. Johnson? 你是詹森先生嗎？
B: Yes, I am. 是的，我就是。

0019　我想你就是…吧？
I believe you're..., aren't you?

（替換）
..., I presume?

（範例）
A: I believe you're Mrs. Johnson, aren't you? 我想你就是詹森夫人吧？
B: Yes, I am. 是的，我就是。

（提示）
presume [prɪˈzum] v. 認為

0020	你姓什麼？ **What's your family name?**
替換	What's your last name?
範例	**A:** What's your family name? 你姓什麼？ **B:** Johnson. 詹森。
提示	"family name" 即 "last name"，指歐美人士放在名字後面的姓氏。

1.3 見面介紹 Making an Introduction

　　介紹是社交場合常見的禮儀活動，透過他人介紹，還是自我介紹，要視情況而定。介紹人的基本規則是：向年長者介紹年輕者，向女士介紹男士，向地位高者介紹地位低者。自我介紹很簡單，一方只要走上前說聲 "Hello!"，告知自己的姓名，並做簡單的自我介紹就可以了，對方聽到後自然就會有反應。當然，介紹時因年齡、地位和介紹場所不同，而有正式和非正式之分，因此使用的語言差別也很大，要特別注意。

　　商業上的介紹與一般的社交慣例不同。在商界，介紹不分性別和年齡。一般是把地位低的人介紹給地位高的人。如果兩人地位相同且有女士在場，則先介紹女士。女士被介紹給地位比她高的男士時，無須起立。

0021	這位是…。 **This is...**	(004)
替換	Here's... Meet...	
範例	**A:** This is Mr. Wang, manager of our company. 　這位是我們公司的王經理。 **B:** It's nice to meet you. 　很高興認識你。	

0022	你們彼此認識嗎？ **Do you know each other?**
替換	Have you two met?

| 範例 | A: Do you know each other? Peter Davis, Joan Brooks.
　　你們彼此認識嗎？這位是彼德・大衛斯，這位是瓊・布魯克絲。
B: Glad to meet you, Ms. Brooks.
　　布魯克絲女士，很高興認識你。 |

0023　我給你介紹過…嗎？
Have I introduced you to...?

| 範例 | A: Joan, have I introduced you to Peter Johnson?
　　瓊，我給你介紹過彼德・詹森嗎？
B: No, you haven't. How do you do, Mr. Johnson?
　　沒有。您好，詹森先生。 |

0024　你認識…嗎？
Do you know...?

| 替換 | Have you met...? |

| 範例 | A: Joan, do you know Peter?
　　瓊，你認識彼德嗎？
B: No, I don't think so. Pleased to see you, Peter.
　　不，不認識。彼德，很高興見到你。 |

0025　我希望你見見…。
I want you to meet...

| 替換 | I'd like you to meet... |

| 範例 | A: I want you to meet Mrs. Jackson. 我希望你見見傑克遜夫人。
B: How do you do? 您好！ |

0026　請允許我介紹…。
May I introduce...?

| 替換 | Allow me to introduce...
Please let me introduce...
May I present...?
Perhaps I could introduce...
I'd like to introduce... |

| 範例 | A: May I introduce Mr. Davis? 請允許我介紹大衛斯先生。
B: How do you do? 您好！ |

0027	很榮幸向各位介紹…。 **I'm honored to present...**
替換	I'm very pleased to present... It's with great pleasure that I introduce you to...
範例	A: I'm honored to present Mr. Davis. 很榮幸向各位介紹大衛斯先生。 B: Good evening, ladies and gentlemen. 各位先生女士們，晚安。

0028	你好！我是…。 **Hi! I'm...**
替換	How do you do? I'm...
範例	A: Hi! I'm Peter Davis. 你好！我是彼德・大衛斯。 B: I'm Linda Smith. Nice to meet you. 我是琳達・史密斯。很高興認識你。

0029	我相信我們沒有見過面。我是…。 **I don't believe we've met. I'm...**
替換	I don't think we've met. My name is...
範例	A: I don't believe we've met. I'm Peter Davis. 我相信我們沒有見過面。我是彼德・大衛斯。 B: I'm Linda Smith. Nice to meet you. 我是琳達・史密斯。很高興認識你。

0030	喂？我是…。 **Hello? This is...**
替換	Hello?...here. Hello? (This is)...speaking.
範例	A: Hello? This is Peter Davis. 喂？我是彼德・大衛斯。 B: Hello? This is Linda Smith. 喂？我是琳達・史密斯。
提示	以上表達法均為電話用語。

0031	請允許我自我介紹：我叫…。 **Allow me to introduce myself...**
替換	May I introduce myself... Please let me introduce myself:...

(範例) **A:** Allow me to introduce myself—I'm Peter Davis.
請允許我自我介紹：我叫彼德‧大衛斯。
B: How do you do, Mr. Davis?
大衛斯先生，您好！

0032 對不起，打攪了。我叫…。
Excuse me, I'm...

(替換) Excuse me, my name's...

(範例) **A:** Excuse me, I'm Peter Davis.
對不起，打攪了，我叫彼德‧大衛斯。
B: I'm Linda Smith. Nice to meet you.
我叫琳達‧史密斯。很高興認識你。

0033 很榮幸認識你。
I'm honored to meet you.

(替換) It's a privilege to know you.

(範例) **A:** I'm Peter Davis. How do you do?
我是彼德‧大衛斯。您好！
B: How do you do, Mr. Davis? I'm honored to meet you.
您好，大衛斯先生。很榮幸認識你。

(提示) privilege ['prɪvl̩ɪdʒ] *n.* 特權；特別待遇

0034 久仰，久仰。
I've heard a lot about you.

(替換) I've heard so much about you.
You have a good reputation.
...often talks about you.

(範例) **A:** How do you do? I'm Peter Davis.
您好，我是彼德‧大衛斯。
B: How do you do, Mr. Davis? I've heard a lot about you.
大衛斯先生，您好。久仰，久仰。

(提示) reputation [ˌrɛpjə'teʃən] *n.* 名譽；名聲

1.4 開始交談 Starting up a Conversation

在會話當中，二人見面如何打破僵局、選擇好的開場白、愉快地交談起來很重要。開始談話時，態度要友善，可以陳述事實，也可以問問題，但話題不要太嚴肅或者太觸及隱私。與西方人見面，我們可以用 "Hi!"、"Hello!" 等寒暄語來開場，我們也可以用下面介紹的禮貌開場語來開始交談。天氣是常見的話題，因爲談天氣不會冒犯到任何人，但回答時要注意不要頂撞對方。開場時，還可以從相關的嗜好、家庭、朋友、工作、學校、體育或旅遊度假等話題開始，但不要涉及收入、女士年齡、宗教、政治等問題。

0035	嗨！你就是…，對吧？ **Hi! You're..., right?** (005)
範例	A: Hi! You're Mr. Davis, right? 嗨！你就是大衛斯先生，對吧？ B: You must be Ms. Smith. 你一定是史密斯女士了。
0036	嘿，我們是不是在什麼地方見過？ **Say, don't I know you from somewhere?**
範例	A: Say, don't I know you from somewhere? 嘿，我們是不是在什麼地方見過？ B: Well, I'm not sure. 哦，我不能肯定。
提示	say [se] *interj.* 喂〔用於表達驚奇或吸引他人的注意力〕
0037	打攪一下，我們是不是在…見過？ **Excuse me, didn't we meet in...?**
範例	A: Excuse me, didn't we meet in Paris? 打攪一下，我們是不是在巴黎見過？ B: Yes. Last year, to be exact. 是的，確切地說，是去年。
提示	to be exact 確切說，用法同於"to be honest（老實說）"、"to be frank（坦誠地說）"。

0038

對不起，我們是不是在哪裡見過面？
Excuse me, haven't we met somewhere before?

（替換）I hope you don't mind my asking, but haven't we met somewhere before?

（範例）A: Excuse me, haven't we met somewhere before?
　　　對不起，我們是不是在哪裡見過面？
B: Yes. In Paris, to be exact.
　　是的，確切地說，是在巴黎。

0039

對不起，我可以⋯嗎？
Sorry, but can I...?

（範例）A: Sorry, but can I have a look at it? 對不起，我可以看一下嗎？
B: Certainly. 當然可以。

0040

對不起，你不就是⋯嗎？
Excuse me, aren't you...?

（替換）Excuse my asking, but are you...?
Pardon me for asking, but aren't you...?

（範例）A: Excuse me, aren't you Peter Davis?
　　　對不起，你不就是彼德・大衛斯嗎？
B: Yes, I am, but I don't think I've met you before.
　　正是，但是我想我沒見過你。

0041

打攪一下，可以請你告訴我現在幾點了嗎？
Excuse me, but could you tell me the time?

（範例）A: Excuse me, but could you tell me the time?
　　　打攪一下，可以請你告訴我現在幾點了嗎？
B: Sure. It's ten-thirty.
　　當然可以，現在是十點半。

（提示）用"Could you...?" 請求對方做某事時，是有禮貌的表達方式。

0042

對不起，你介意我坐在這裡嗎？
Excuse me, do you mind if I sit here?

（範例）A: Excuse me, do you mind if I sit here? 對不起，你介意我坐在這裡嗎？
B: Go ahead. 你請。

0043 對不起，這裡有人坐嗎？
Excuse me, is anyone sitting here?

範例 A: Excuse me, is anyone sitting here? 對不起，這裡有人坐嗎？
B: No. 沒有。

0044 打擾一下，可以借個火嗎？
Excuse me, could you give me a light, please?

替換 Excuse me, do you have a light by chance?

範例 A: Excuse me, could you give me a light, please?
打擾一下，可以借個火嗎？
B: Sure. Here you are.
可以。給你。

0045 對不起，我無意中聽見你提到…？
Sorry, I couldn't help overhearing. Did you mention something about...?

範例 A: Sorry, I couldn't help overhearing. Did you mention something about Professor Peter Davis?
對不起，我無意中聽見你提到彼德·大衛斯教授？
B: Yes. Do you know him?
是的，你認識他嗎？

提示 overhear [ˌovəˈhɪr] v. 無意中聽到；偷聽

0046 對不起，打擾一下。
Excuse me for interrupting.

替換 Sorry to trouble/interrupt you.
I beg your pardon.

範例 A: Excuse me for interrupting, but do you happen to know where our hostess is? 對不起，打擾一下，你知道我們的女主人在哪裡嗎？
B: Yes. She's over there with Mr. Davis. 知道。她和大衛斯先生在那邊。

提示 interrupt [ˌɪntəˈrʌpt] v. 打斷（正在說話的人）；插嘴
happen [ˈhæpən] v. 碰巧；剛好（＋ to）

0047 對不起。
Excuse me.

替換　Pardon me for asking.

範例　A: Excuse me, but do you mind if I close the door?
　　　　對不起，你介意我把門關上嗎？
　　　B: No, go ahead.
　　　　不介意，請吧。

0048　喂，你不就是…？
Say, aren't you...?

範例　A: Say, aren't you Peter Davis? 喂，你不就是彼德・大衛斯嗎？
　　　B: Yes, I am. 正是。

0049　天氣真好／差，不是嗎？
Nice/lousy weather, isn't it?

替換　Nice day, isn't it?

範例　A: Nice weather, isn't it? 天氣真好，不是嗎？
　　　B: It sure is. 就是呀。

提示　lousy ['lauzɪ] adj.【尤口】非常糟糕的

1.5　繼續交談 Keeping a Conversation Going

　　用英語談話時，很注意 "keep the ball rolling"，也就是使交談不要冷場或中斷。有時要有技巧的打斷對方，有時要澄清一些事實，有時要控制談話不離題，有時要爭取交談的控制權。在這些情況下，語言的運用是相當講究技巧的。

006

0050　對不起，插一下話，你是說…？
Sorry to butt in, but did you say...?

替換　Sorry to cut in, but did I hear you say...?
　　　Sorry to interrupt, but did I hear you say...?

範例　A: Sorry to butt in, but did you say there was an explosion downtown
　　　　yesterday? 對不起，插一下話，你是說昨天市中心發生爆炸嗎？
　　　B: Yes, in Main Street. 是的，在梅恩街。

提示　butt/cut in 插話；插嘴
　　　explosion [ɪk'sploʒən] n. 爆炸

0051

真奇怪你會說這個！
Funny you should say that!

(替換) Strange you should bring that up!
It's strange you should say that!

(範例) A: Taipei is very cold this time of year.
台北這個時候非常冷。
B: Funny you should say that! I'm leaving for Taipei tonight.
真奇怪你會說這個！我今晚正要動身去台北。

0052

談到…。
Speaking of...

(替換) About...
Talking of...
On the subject of...

(範例) A: Speaking of love, I think it's very important.
談到愛情，我認為它非常重要。
B: I can't agree more.
我完全同意。

0053

既然你提到…。
Now that you mention...

(替換) While we're on the subject of...

(範例) A: Can you tell me what happened between them?
你能告訴我他們倆怎麼了嗎？
B: Now that you mention it, I have to tell it like it is.
既然你提到了，我就得把實情說出來了。

0054

等一等，我們可以繼續談…的問題嗎？
Hang on. Can we stick to the subject of...?

(範例) A: Hang on. Can we stick to the subject of love?
等一等，我們可以繼續談關於愛情的問題嗎？
B: Of course, for as long as you like.
當然，只要你願意。

0055

真巧！
What a coincidence!

範例

A: I like Mary very much.
我非常喜歡瑪麗。

B: What a coincidence! She says she is very fond of you, too.
眞巧！她說她也很喜歡你。

0056

你這麼說很有意思，因為⋯。
It's interesting you should say so, because...

範例

A: I like Peter. 我喜歡彼德。

B: It's interesting you should say so, because I just met him this morning. 你這麼說很有意思，因爲今天上午我才剛遇見他。

0057

這使我想起了⋯。
This reminds me of...

範例

A: This reminds me of my school days.
這使我想起了我的學生時代。

B: It's always fun to look back on our childhood, isn't it?
回顧小時候總是很有趣，不是嗎？

0058

回到你剛才談到的⋯。
Going back to what you were saying about...

替換

Returning to your point about...

範例

A: Going back to what you were saying about Beijing, it can be unbearable in spring with the sandstorms.
回到你剛才談到的北京，它到了春天就有沙塵暴，天氣讓人無法忍受。

B: I quite agree.
我十分同意。

提示

unbearable [ʌnˈbɛrəbl̩] *adj.* 令人無法忍受的
sandstorm [ˈsændˌstɔrm] *n.* 沙暴；沙塵暴

0059

你剛才提到⋯。
You mentioned...just now.

範例

A: You mentioned sandstorms just now—they are the result of human destruction of the environment.
你剛才提到沙塵暴，那是人類對環境破壞的結果。

B: You can say that again.
你說的眞對。

提示

destruction [dɪˈstrʌkʃən] *n.* 破壞；毀滅

0060	你提出了很重要的一點，因為⋯。 **You brought up an important point, because...**
替換	The problem you raised just now is important, because...
範例	**A:** The environment is getting worse year by year. 環境逐年惡化。 **B:** You brought up an important point, because we should pay more attention to environmental protection. 你提出了很重要的一點，因為我們應該更加關注環境保護。
提示	environmental [ɪnˌvaɪrən'mɛntḷ] *adj.* 周圍的；環境的 protection [prə'tɛkʃən] *n.* 保護
0061	請容許我回到你所談到的一點，⋯。 **If I may go back to the point you made, ...**
替換	If I might refer back to the problem we were discussing, ...
範例	**A:** If I may go back to the point you made, I think they are mistaken. 請容許我回到你所談到的一點，我認為他們弄錯了。 **B:** I'm all ears. 我洗耳恭聽。

1.6 改變話題 Changing the Topic

　　交談中會出現很多情況。有時會出現冷場，有時對方談話離題，有時雙方互搶發言權。這時，改變話題可能是一個非常必要的手段。除了有意識的談論自己的話題外，英美人士接受的大眾話題很多，可以是工作、住所、個人喜好、旅遊度假、電影、電視、天氣、地方或國際大事等。改變話題必定會影響到對方，因此要特別注意說話的方式。

0062	呀，差點忘了。 **Hey, I almost forgot!**	(007)
替換	Oh, it nearly slipped my mind!	
範例	**A:** Hey, I almost forgot! Linda gives you her best regards. 呀，差點忘了，琳達要我代她向你問好。	

B: That's most kind of her! How is she?
她人眞好。她最近怎麼樣？

（提示） slip one's mind 忘記

0063
哦，還有件事要告訴你。
Oh, there's something else I was meaning to tell you.

（替換） Oh, there's something else I want to tell you.

（範例） **A:** Oh, there's something else I was meaning to tell you. The Simpsons moved to our neighborhood.
哦，還有件事要告訴你。辛普森家搬到了我們的社區。
B: That's unbelievable!
眞令人難以置信！

（提示） unbelievable [ˌʌnbɪ'livəbl] *adj.* 難以置信的

0064
哦，趁我還沒有忘記，…。
Oh, before I forget, ...

（替換） Oh, while I'm thinking of it, ...

（範例） **A:** Oh, before I forget, have you visited the Simpsons?
哦，趁我還沒有忘記，你去拜訪辛普森家了嗎？
B: Not yet. Have they called on us yet?
還沒。他們拜訪我們了嗎？

0065
順便一提，… ?
By the way, ...?

（替換） Incidentally, ...?

（範例） **A:** By the way, can I have one of the kittens?
順便一提，我可以要一隻小貓嗎？
B: No problem.
沒問題。

（提示） incidentally [ˌɪnsə'dɛntl̩ɪ] *adv.* 附帶地；順便提及

0066
我們換個話題談點別的。
Let's talk about something different.

（替換） Just to change the subject for a while.
Let's change/drop the subject.

範例
> **A:** Let's talk about something different. Have you seen the film *The Lord of the Rings*? 我們換個話題談點別的，你看了電影《魔戒》嗎？
> **B:** Yes. It's cool, isn't it? 看了。很棒，不是嗎？

0067
我們現在可以接著討論…嗎？
Could we move on now to...?

替換
> I think we can continue on to...

範例
> **A:** Could we move on now to the subject of higher education?
> 我們現在可以接著討論高等教育的主題嗎？
> **B:** Of course. What's your idea?
> 當然。你有什麼看法？

0068
現在我們著手討論議程上的主要議題。
Now we've come to the main item on the agenda.

範例
> **A:** Now we've come to the main item on the agenda.
> 現在我們著手討論議程上的主要議題。
> **B:** Is it about environmental protection?
> 是環境保護的問題嗎？

提示
> agenda [ə'dʒɛndə] *n.* 議程

0069
現在是關於一個完全不同的主題，我們來談談…。
And now onto an entirely different subject, let's talk about...

範例
> **A:** And now onto an entirely different subject, let's talk about higher education. 現在是關於一個完全不同的主題，我們來談談高等教育。
> **B:** Let me voice my opinion on this matter. 我來講一下我這方面的看法。

提示
> voice [vɔɪs] *v.* 宣揚；發表（意見等）

0070
議程上的下一個項目是…。
The next item on the agenda is...

範例
> **A:** The next item on the agenda is writers' responsibility.
> 議程上的下一個項目是作家的責任。
> **B:** Shouldn't we start with current literary trends?
> 我們難道不應該先討論一下當代的文學思潮嗎？

提示
> literary ['lɪtə,rɛrɪ] *adj.* 文學（上）的；文藝的

0071	我們著手討論…問題。 **Let's turn to the problem of...**

範例 A: Let's turn to the problem of pollution. 我們著手討論污染問題。
B: It certainly affects everyone. 這當然和每個人都有關。

1.7 吸引注意 Getting Someone's Attention

　　交談時，吸引他人的注意是非常必要的，也是非常講究技巧的。手勢、表情或一聲乾咳等非語言性的動作都能夠發揮吸引他人注意的功能，但多數情況下，人們還是透過語言來達此目的。吸引注意的語言表達方法和交談的內容、場合密切相關。因此，我們不僅要注意表達的方法，還要注意談話的內容和交談的場合。

(008)

0072	喂！ **Hey!**

替換 Hello there!
Look here!
Hey! You (there)!
I say!

範例 A: Hey! Who's that guy? 喂，那個人是誰？
B: I don't know him. 我不認識。

0073	聽著！ **Listen!**

替換 Listen here.

範例 A: Listen! I was told the chairman is here.
聽著！別人告訴我主席在這裡。
B: Really?
真的嗎？

0074	瞧！ **Look!**

A: Look! Linda is coming this way. 瞧！琳達朝這邊走來了。
B: Isn't she beautiful today? 她今天很漂亮吧？

0075

小心！
Watch out!

替換　Look out!

範例　**A:** Watch out! A car! 小心，車子！
B: Oh! That was close. 哦！好險喔。

0076

對不起，打擾一下。
Excuse me.

替換　Pardon me!
Sorry.
Sorry to bother/trouble you.

範例　**A:** Excuse me, but could you give me a hand?
對不起，打擾一下，請問你能幫我忙嗎？
B: Sure.
當然。

0077

嗯（喲、啊）
Um...

替換　Er...

範例　**A:** Um, could I just suggest we begin our discussion now?
嗯，我能建議我們現在就開始討論嗎？
B: Well, I'd prefer to finish the other items first.
嗯，我傾向先完成其他項目比較好。

0078

請注意了！
Attention, please!

替換　Pay attention, please!
Let me have your attention, please.
May I have your attention, please?

範例　**A:** Attention, please! Allow me to introduce Professor Tompkins.
請注意了！請讓我為大家介紹湯姆金斯教授。
B: How do you do, Professor Tompkins?
您好，湯姆金斯教授。

1.8 談論天氣 Talking about the Weather

天氣是英美人士的大眾話題，它不涉及個人隱私。因此，喜歡和人談論天氣是英美人士交談的一大特點，尤其在英國，天氣是個談不盡、講不煩的話題，人人擅於此道。不過，談天氣時要說一些評論性的意見，不要只是死板地陳述。談天氣還有一條重要的原則：人家評論天氣時，千萬不要反駁。例如，有人說 "Nice day, isn't it?"（天氣很好，不是嗎？），你就要毫不猶豫地回答："Isn't it lovely?"（是啊，真是太好了！）

0079	今天天氣真好！ **Isn't it beautiful today?** 009
替換	Isn't it gorgeous today? What a pleasant/beautiful/wonderful day! What lovely weather we're having! Nice day, isn't it? Wonderful, isn't it? A lovely day, isn't it? Isn't this lovely weather?
範例	**A:** Isn't it beautiful today? 今天天氣真好！ **B:** What a lovely day! 多好的天氣！
提示	gorgeous ['gɔrdʒəs] *adj.* 極好的；漂亮的
0080	早上天氣很好，是吧？ **It's a nice morning, isn't it?**
替換	Nice morning, isn't it? Isn't it a nice morning?
範例	**A:** It's a nice morning, isn't it? 早上天氣很好，是吧？ **B:** It's really beautiful weather! 天氣真不錯！
0081	今天天氣比昨天好。 **It's better today than yesterday.**
範例	**A:** It's better today than yesterday. 今天天氣比昨天好。

B: Yes, it's quite a contrast to yesterday's weather.
是的，與昨天的天氣大不相同。

提示 contrast ['kɑn,træst] *n.* 對比；（對照中的）差異（+ to）

0082 這裡的天氣好極了。
The weather is marvelous here.

範例 **A:** The weather is marvelous here. 這裡的天氣好極了。
B: It sure is. 的確很棒。

提示 marvelous ['mɑrvələs] *adj.* 令人驚異的；不可思議的；非凡的

0083 今天陽光明媚，天氣宜人，對吧？
Nice and sunny today, isn't it?

範例 **A:** Nice and sunny today, isn't it? 今天陽光明媚，天氣宜人，對吧？
B: Yes, it's much better today than yesterday. 是呀，比昨天好多了。

0084 結果是個好天氣。
It turned out to be a nice day.

範例 **A:** I worried about the weather all night. 我整晚都在擔心天氣。
B: It turned out to be a nice day. 結果是個好天氣。

0085 就現在這個時間來說，天氣是相當溫和了。
It's fairly mild for this time of year.

範例 **A:** Isn't it beautiful weather?
天氣不錯吧！
B: It's fairly mild for this time of year.
就現在這個時間來說，天氣是相當溫和了。

0086 這種天氣已持續一週了。
It's been like this for a week.

範例 **A:** Lovely weather, isn't it? 天氣很好，不是嗎？
B: It's been like this for a week. 這種天氣已持續一週了。

0087 但願這種天氣會持續下去。
Let's hope it'll last.

範例 **A:** This is fairly mild for this time of year.
就現在這個時間來說，天氣是相當溫和了。
B: Let's hope it'll last.
但願這種天氣會持續下去。

0088	天氣太糟糕了。 **What dreadful weather!**

替換	What awful weather! Isn't this dreadful weather? Lousy weather we're having. Awful weather, isn't it? Nasty day, isn't it? Nasty weather outside, isn't it? The weather's a drag, isn't it?
範例	**A:** What dreadful weather! 天氣太糟糕了。 **B:** It's really a drag! 真的很惱人！
提示	drag [dræg] *n.* 【非正式】乏味無聊的人、事、物

0089	我看我們難免要遇到一陣乾旱了。 **I think we're in for a dry spell.**

範例	**A:** It hasn't rained for almost two weeks. 快兩個星期沒下雨了。 **B:** I think we're in for a dry spell. 我看我們難免要遇到一陣乾旱了。
提示	be in for 要遇到 spell [spɛl] *n.* 一段時間

0090	我一點也不喜歡這種天氣。 **I don't like it at all.**

範例	**A:** Nasty weather, isn't it? 天氣真糟，不是嗎？ **B:** I don't like it at all. 我一點也不喜歡這種天氣。

0091	想不到…有這種天氣，對吧？ **Strange weather for..., isn't it?**

範例	**A:** Strange weather for August, isn't it? 想不到八月有這種天氣，對吧？ **B:** Isn't it awful? 太糟了，不是嗎？

0092	天氣老是這樣嗎？ **Is the weather always like this?**

範例	**A:** Is the weather always like this? 天氣老是這樣嗎？ **B:** Isn't it pleasant? 難道天氣不宜人嗎？

0093

天氣明顯在變。
Obviously the weather is changing.

範例
A: Obviously the weather is changing. 天氣明顯在變。
B: We're hoping for a change. 我們正希望天氣有變化。

0094

天氣的確變了，是吧？
The weather certainly has changed, hasn't it?

範例
A: The weather certainly has changed, hasn't it? 天氣的確變了，是吧？
B: Let's hope it's sunny tomorrow. 但願明天是晴天。

0095

天氣變化無常，不是嗎？
The weather is certainly unpredictable, isn't it?

範例
A: We're expecting a change in the weather.
　　天氣可能會有變化。
B: The weather is certainly unpredictable, isn't it?
　　天氣變化無常，不是嗎？

提示
unpredictable [ˌʌnprɪˈdɪktəbļ] *adj.* 出乎意料的；不可預料的

0096

天氣看起來不大會好轉。
It doesn't look too promising.

範例
A: There might be a change in the weather. 天氣可能會有變化。
B: It doesn't look too promising. 天氣看起來不大會好轉。

0097

天氣變好了！
It has changed for the better!

範例
A: Today's weather is better than yesterday's. 今天天氣比昨天好很多。
B: It has changed for the better! 天氣變好了！

0098

…的天氣怎麼樣？
What's the weather like in...?

替換
How's the weather in...?
How do you like the weather in...?

範例
A: What's the weather like in winter? 冬天的天氣怎麼樣？
B: It's quite mild. 十分溫和。

0099	…天氣怎麼樣？ **What was the weather like...?**〔用於過去的天氣〕
〔替換〕	What will the weather be like...?〔用於未來的天氣〕
〔範例〕	**A:** What was the weather like yesterday? 昨天的天氣怎麼樣？ **B:** It was quite nice. 不錯。

0100	…的天氣不同嗎？ **Is the weather different in...?**
〔範例〕	**A:** Is the weather different in Taipei? 台北的天氣不同嗎？ **B:** Yes. It's quite hot in Taipei now. 是的，台北現在很熱。

0101	不知…天氣會怎麼樣。 **I wonder what it's going to be like...**〔用於未來的天氣〕
〔替換〕	I wonder what the weather will be like...〔用於未來的天氣〕
〔範例〕	**A:** I wonder what it's going to be like tomorrow. 不知明天天氣會怎麼樣。 **B:** Let's hope for the best. 希望天氣很好。

0102	天氣預報怎麼說的？ **What does the weather forecast say?**
〔替換〕	What's the weather forecast for tomorrow?
〔範例〕	**A:** What does the weather forecast say? 天氣預報怎麼說的？ **B:** It's going to rain tomorrow. 明天會下雨。
〔提示〕	forecast ['for‚kæst] *n.* 預測；預報

0103	今天的天氣和天氣預報不同。 **Today's weather is different from the forecast.**
〔替換〕	The weather is not the same as the weather forecast.
〔範例〕	**A:** It's raining. 下雨了。 **B:** Today's weather is different from the forecast. 今天的天氣和天氣預報不同。

0104	今天的氣溫是多少？ **What's the temperature today?**
〔替換〕	Do you know what the temperature is today?

範例 A: What's the temperature today? 今天的氣溫是多少？
B: 20°C~26°C.攝氏 20 到 26 度。

提示 temperature ['tɛmprətʃɚ] *n.* 溫度
20°C 也可以讀作 20 degrees centigrade。

0105 氣溫已上升到⋯度。
The temperature has climbed to...

替換 The temperature has risen to...

範例 A: It's been so hot recently. 最近天氣很熱。
B: The temperature has climbed to 37°C.氣溫已上升到攝氏 37 度。

0106 氣溫已經降到⋯。
The temperature has dropped to...

範例 A: What's the temperature today?
今天溫度是多少？
B: The temperature has dropped to the freezing point.
氣溫已經降到零度。

0107 今天氣溫已經下降許多。
The temperature has dropped a lot today.

範例 A: It's so cold this morning. 今天早上真冷。
B: The temperature has dropped a lot today. 今天氣溫已經下降許多。

0108 昨天氣溫高達三十多度。
The temperature was in the thirties yesterday.

範例 A: The temperature was in the thirties yesterday.
昨天氣溫高達三十多度。
B: Let's hope this hot weather won't last.
希望這樣炎熱天氣不會持續。

0109 溫度在⋯以上。
It's above...

範例 A: It's not as cold as I expected. 天氣沒我想的那麼冷。
B: It's above freezing. 溫度在零度以上。

0110 溫度在⋯以下。
It's below...

範例
A: It's below zero. 溫度在零度以下。
B: Is it? Well, it doesn't feel that cold. 是嗎？嗯，感覺似乎沒那麼冷。

0111
天氣有點多雲，是不是？
It's a bit cloudy, isn't it?

範例
A: It's a bit cloudy, isn't it? 天氣有點多雲，是不是？
B: Yes, but I like this kind of weather. 是的，但我喜歡這種天氣。

0112
今天下午將轉多雲。
It'll turn cloudy this afternoon.

範例
A: Fine weather, isn't it?
天氣不錯，是吧？
B: Yes, but it'll turn cloudy this afternoon.
是的，但是今天下午將轉多雲。

0113
恐怕天氣要轉陰了。
It's going to cloud over, I'm afraid.

範例
A: It's going to cloud over, I'm afraid.
恐怕天氣要轉陰了。
B: The weather forecast says we can expect rain this afternoon.
天氣預報說今天下午會下雨。

0114
我討厭這雨天！
I hate the rain!

範例
A: I hate the rain! 我討厭這雨天！
B: So do I. How I miss the sunshine! 我也是。我多麼懷念陽光啊！

0115
開始下小雨了。
It's beginning to sprinkle.

範例
A: It's beginning to sprinkle. 開始下小雨了。
B: Hopefully it won't begin to pour. 希望不要變大。

提示
sprinkle ['sprɪŋkl] v. 【美】下小雨

0116
那不過是陣雨。
It's only a shower.

範例
A: You'd better wait until the rain stops. 你最好等到雨停。
B: Don't worry. It's only a shower. 別擔心。那不過是陣雨。

0117

正在下大雨。
It's pouring.

(替換) It's raining heavily/hard/buckets.

(範例) **A:** It's pouring! You should stay here tonight.
正在下大雨。你今晚住在這裡吧。
B: It seems I have no choice.
我似乎也沒有別的選擇了。

0118

看來要下雨了。
It looks like it's going to rain.

(替換) It looks like rain.

(範例) **A:** It looks like it's going to rain. 看來要下雨了。
B: Shall we go now or wait until later? 我們應該現在出發還是等一會兒？

0119

這裡⋯月份經常下雨嗎？
Does it rain very much here in...?

(範例) **A:** Does it rain very much here in May? 這裡五月份經常下雨嗎？
B: Not as far as I know. 據我所知並不常。

0120

不知明天是否會下雨。
I wonder if it's going to rain tomorrow.

(範例) **A:** I wonder if it's going to rain tomorrow.
不知明天是否會下雨。
B: Of course it won't! We're going hiking tomorrow.
我們明天要遠足，當然不會下雨。

0121

我看雨不會下很久。
I don't think the rain will last long.

(範例) **A:** I don't think the rain will last long. 我看雨不會下很久。
B: Hopefully. 但願如此。

0122

我擔心就要下一場大雷雨了。
I fear a thunderstorm's brewing.

(範例) **A:** I fear a thunderstorm's brewing. 我擔心就要下一場大雷雨了。
B: What did the weather forecast say? 天氣預報怎麼說？

提示 | thunderstorm [ˈθʌndɚˌstɔrm] *n.* 大雷雨
brew [bru] *v.* 釀造；醞釀

0123

看起來快下大雷雨了。
It looks like a thunderstorm is coming.

範例 | A: What's the weather like? 天氣怎麼樣？
B: It looks like a thunderstorm is coming. 看起來快下大雷雨了。

0124

看起來像要下雨了，你說是嗎？
It looks like rain, don't you think so?

範例 | A: It looks like rain, don't you think so? 看起來像要下雨了，你說是嗎？
B: I'm afraid so. 恐怕是的。

0125

好像要下一場雷陣雨。
It seems like there'll be a thundershower.

範例 | A: It seems like there'll be a thundershower. 好像要下一場雷陣雨。
B: I agree. 我也這麼想。

提示 | thundershower [ˈθʌndɚˌʃauɚ] *n.* 雷陣雨

0126

今天恐怕會是下雨天。
It'll be a wet day today, I'm afraid.

範例 | A: It'll be a wet day today, I'm afraid. 今天恐怕會是下雨天。
B: Oh, don't you like rain? 哦，你不喜歡雨嗎？

0127

據說明天會下毛毛雨。
It's supposed to start drizzling tomorrow.

範例 | A: Will it be fine tomorrow? 明天好天氣嗎？
B: It's supposed to start drizzling tomorrow. 據說明天會下毛毛雨。

提示 | drizzle [ˈdrɪzl̩] *v.* 下毛毛雨

0128

雨開始小了。
The rain's beginning to let up.

替換 | The rain's letting up a little.

範例 | A: Can I go out now? The rain's beginning to let up.
我現在能出去嗎？雨開始小了。
B: Not until it stops.
雨停了才可以。

0129
開始下雨了。
The rain's setting in.

範例
A: The rain's setting in. We have to put off our outing now.
開始下雨了。我們的出遊得延期了。
B: What a pity!
太遺憾了！

0130
雷陣雨現在逐漸平息。
The thundershower's beginning to subside.

範例
A: The thundershower's beginning to subside. The weather might be fine. 雷陣雨現在逐漸平息。天氣可能會很好。
B: Can we go out then? 那麼我們能出去嗎？

提示
subside [səb'saɪd] *v.* 平息；減退；衰減

0131
氣象員預測今天下午有陣雨。
The weatherman predicted showers for this afternoon.

範例
A: The weatherman predicted showers for this afternoon.
氣象員預測今天下午有陣雨。
B: What about our soccer match?
我們的足球比賽怎麼辦？

0132
我希望雨拖到明天再下。
I hope the rain will hold off till tomorrow.

範例
A: The weather forecast says it's going to rain this evening.
天氣預報說今晚會下雨。
B: I hope the rain will hold off till tomorrow.
我希望雨拖到明天再下。

0133
我們已經好幾個星期都沒遇到這樣的大雷雨了。
We haven't had a thunderstorm like this in weeks.

範例
A: We haven't had a thunderstorm like this in weeks.
我們已經好幾個星期都沒遇到這樣的大雷雨了。
B: I hope it won't cause any damage.
我希望雨不要造成任何損害。

0134
起風了。
The wind's blowing harder.

範例
A: The wind's blowing harder. 起風了。
B: I hope it won't start raining. 希望不會開始下雨。

0135
今天風很大。
It's rather windy today.

替換 There's a lot of wind today.

範例
A: It's rather windy today. 今天風很大。
B: It's a good day to fly kites. 是放風箏的好天氣。

0136
風愈刮愈大了。
The wind is picking up.

替換 The wind is getting stronger.

範例
A: The wind is picking up. 風愈刮愈大了。
B: Is it? 是嗎？

0137
風勢在減弱。
The wind's letting up.

範例
A: The wind's letting up.
　 風勢在減弱。
B: Do you think we'll have fine weather tomorrow?
　 你覺得明天會是好天氣嗎？

0138
今天微風徐徐，天氣宜人。
It's breezy and pleasant today.

範例
A: It's breezy and pleasant today. 今天微風徐徐，天氣宜人。
B: Let's go for a walk. 我們出去散步吧。

0139
幾乎沒什麼風。
There's hardly any breath of wind.

範例
A: It's so hot. 太熱了。
B: Yeah. There's hardly any breath of wind. 是啊，幾乎沒什麼風。

0140
今天的天氣熱得要命。
It's boiling hot today!

範例
A: It's boiling hot today!
　 今天的天氣熱得要命。

B: I just want to stay inside and do nothing.
我只想待在屋裡，什麼也不做。

提示　boiling ['bɔɪlɪŋ] *adj.* 非常熱的；酷熱的

0141　天氣總是這樣熱嗎？
Is it always hot like this?

範例　**A:** Is it always hot like this? 天氣總是這樣熱嗎？
B: No, it's usually cool in November. 不，十一月天氣會涼爽些。

0142　恐怕我們要遇到一股熱浪了。
I'm afraid we're going to have a heat wave.

範例　**A:** It has been so hot recently.
最近很熱。
B: I'm afraid we're going to have a heat wave.
恐怕我們要遇到一股熱浪了。

0143　今天熱得叫人發昏。
It's sweltering today.

範例　**A:** It's sweltering today. 今天熱得叫人發昏。
B: Yeah, it's unbearable. 是呀，真令人難以忍受。

提示　sweltering ['swɛltərɪŋ] *adj.* 悶熱的；中暑的；酷熱的

0144　今天天氣很悶熱。
It's very sultry today.

範例　**A:** It's very sultry today. 今天天氣很悶熱。
B: I hope it'll be cooler soon. 我希望涼爽的天氣很快到來。

提示　sultry ['sʌltrɪ] *adj.* 悶熱的

0145　天氣悶熱黏膩。
It's hot and sticky.

範例　**A:** It's hot and sticky. 天氣悶熱黏膩。
B: Let's hope it won't last. 希望這種天氣不會持久。

提示　sticky ['stɪkɪ] *adj.* 黏的；黏性的

0146　好熱的天氣！
What a scorcher!

35

範例　A: What a scorcher! 好熱的天氣！
　　　B: It's for a vacation. 該去度個假了。

提示　scorcher [ˈskɔrtʃɚ] *n.*【口】大熱天

0147　**天氣放晴了。**
It's clearing up.

範例　A: It's clearing up. 天氣放晴了。
　　　B: Finally. 終於放晴了。

0148　**明天將是晴天。**
It's going to be fine tomorrow.

範例　A: What does the weather forecast say? 天氣預報怎麼說？
　　　B: It's going to be fine tomorrow. 明天將是晴天。

0149　**我希望天氣一直晴朗。**
I hope it stays fine.

範例　A: We're having wonderful weather these days. 最近的天氣一直不錯。
　　　B: I hope it stays fine. 我希望天氣一直晴朗。

0150　**天氣終於又放晴了，不是嗎？**
It turned out to be a nice day again, didn't it?

範例　A: It turned out to be a nice day again, didn't it?
　　　　天氣終於又放晴了，不是嗎？
　　　B: Hopefully this fine weather will last.
　　　　希望好天氣會持續。

0151　**天氣變暖和，是不是？**
It's getting warmer, isn't it?

範例　A: It's getting warmer, isn't it? 天氣變暖和，是不是？
　　　B: It sure is. 當然了。

0152　**看到太陽又出來了，真叫人高興。**
It's good to see the sun again.

範例　A: It's finally clear. 天氣終於放晴了。
　　　B: It's good to see the sun again. 看到太陽又出來了，真叫人高興。

0153
天氣有多冷？
How cold is it?

範例
A: How cold is it? 天氣有多冷？
B: It's below zero. 零度以下。

0154
…很涼快，是吧？
It's pretty cool..., isn't it?

範例
A: It's pretty cool this morning, isn't it? 今天早上很涼快，是吧？
B: Yes. How pleasant! 是呀。真舒服。

0155
這裡…很涼爽。
It's quite cool here in...

範例
A: Is it hot here in summer? 這裡夏天熱嗎？
B: It's quite cool here in July. 這裡七月份很涼爽。

0156
今天天氣冷得厲害。
It's bitterly cold today.

範例
A: It's bitterly cold today. 今天天氣冷得厲害。
B: Yes, it is. 就是呀。

提示
bitterly ['bɪtəlɪ] *adv.* 非常地；厲害地

0157
正在下大雪。
It's snowing hard.

範例
A: It's snowing hard. 正在下大雪。
B: Tomorrow will be a good day for skiing. 明天會是滑雪的好天氣。

0158
我看要下雪了。
I think it's going to snow.

範例
A: The sky has turned cloudy. 天氣轉陰了。
B: I think it's going to snow. 我看要下雪了。

0159
他們說將有一場暴風雪。
They say we're in for a snowstorm.

範例
A: They say we're in for a snowstorm. 他們說將有一場暴風雪。
B: I hope it isn't true. 希望不是真的。

提示
snowstorm ['sno,stɔrm] *n.* 暴風雪

1.9　談論時間 Talking about Time

　　談論時間時，我們可以獲得有關時間的資訊。但有時談論時間卻是一種策略的社交行為，它可以有催促的作用，可以作為結束談話的信號，還可以表示有意與某人進行交談。交談過程中要注意談論時間的真實意圖，並做適當的反應和回答。

010

0160

今天幾月幾號？
What's the date today?

（替換）
What date is it?
What's today's date?

（範例）
A: What's the date today? 今天幾月幾號？
B: July 4th. 七月四號。

0161

…是哪天？
When's...?

（範例）
A: When's your birthday? 你生日是哪天？
B: August 9th. 八月九號。

0162

今天是…月…號。
Today is...

（替換）
It's...

（範例）
A: What is the date today? 今天幾月幾號？
B: Today is July 4th. 今天是七月四號。

0163

在…月…號。
It's on...

（範例）
A: When's the meeting? 會議在哪天？
B: It's on August 9th. 在八月九號。

0164

今天星期幾？
What day is it?

（替換）
What day is today?
What day of the week is it?

| 範例 | A: What day is it? 今天星期幾？
B: It's Monday. 星期一。 |

| 0165 | 現在幾點了 ?
What time is it? |

| 替換 | What's the time/hour?
What time do you have?
What time have you got?
What's the time by your watch?
Could you give/tell me the time?
Can you tell me what time it is?
Do you know what time it is?
Do you happen to know the time? |

| 範例 | A: What time is it? 現在幾點了？
B: It's six. 六點。 |

| 0166 | 現在是…。
It's...now. |

| 替換 | The hour is... |
| 範例 | A: What's the time, please? 請問幾點了？
B: It's 6:30 now. 現在是六點三十分。 |

| 0167 | 我的手錶是…
My watch says... |

| 替換 | My watch has...
I have...
It's...by my watch. |
| 範例 | A: Can you tell me the time, please? 請問幾點了？
B: My watch says six-thirty. 我的手錶是六點三十分。 |

| 0168 | …點整。
It's...o'clock sharp. |

| 範例 | A: Can you tell me the time, please? 請問幾點了？
B: It's three o'clock sharp. 三點整。 |

| 0169 | 大約…點。
It's about...o'clock. |

替換
It's something like...o'clock.

範例
A: Do you have the time? 幾點了？
B: It's about seven o'clock. 大約七點。

0170
接近⋯點了。
It's almost...o'clock.

替換
It's close upon...o'clock.
It's about to strike...

範例
A: It's almost seven o'clock. Let's go. 接近七點了。我們出發吧。
B: There's still time. 還早呢。

0171
剛過⋯點。
It's a little after...

替換
It's shortly past...

範例
A: Do you have the time? 幾點了？
B: It's a little after seven. 剛過七點。

0172
還不到⋯點。
It's not quite...

範例
A: What time is it? 幾點了？
B: It's not quite seven. 還不到七點。

0173
到⋯點還早呢。
It won't be...for awhile yet.

範例
A: It won't be seven for awhile yet. You can sleep in.
　　到七點還早呢。你可以再睡一會兒。
B: I should get up.
　　我應該起來了。

0174
早上⋯點開始。
It starts at...a.m.

範例
A: When does the meeting start? 會議什麼時候開始？
B: It starts at 9:00 a.m. 早上九點開始。

0175
哪一天？
On which day?

A: Linda's birthday's coming! 琳達的生日快到了！
B: On which day? 哪一天？

0176
要多久？
For how long?

 A: I will be on a business trip to New York next month.
我下個月去紐約出差。
B: For how long?
要多久？

0177
持續了多久？
How long did it last?

 A: You weren't at the meeting last Friday.
你沒去參加上禮拜五的會議。
B: I was sick and went home. How long did it last?
我生病回家去了。（會議）持續了多久？

0178
你在這裡已經很久了嗎？
Have you been here long?

 A: Sorry for being late. Have you been here long?
對不起，我遲到了。你在這裡已經很久了嗎？
B: No, just a few minutes.
沒有，只有幾分鐘。

0179
…要花多久時間？
How much time will it take to...?

 A: The theater isn't far.
電影院並不遠。
B: How much time will it take to get there by bus?
坐公車去要花多久時間？

0180
…之前…。
...ago.

 A: When did he get here? 他什麼時候到的？
B: An hour ago. 一個小時之前。

0181
還有…分鐘。
There're still...minutes to go.

替換　There're still...minutes left.

範例　A: Hurry up! 快點！
B: There're still ten minutes to go. Don't worry. 還有十分鐘。別擔心。

0182　…分鐘後…。
...in...minutes.

範例　A: When will David come? 大衛什麼時候來？
B: He will come in twenty minutes. 他二十分鐘後到。

0183　從上午…到下午…。
From...a.m. till...p.m.

範例　A: When is the club open? 俱樂部的營業時間是什麼時候？
B: From 9:00 a.m. till 6:00 p.m. 從上午九點到下午六點。

0184　…年左右。
...years, more or less.

範例　A: How long does it take to get a doctorate? 要花多久拿到博士學位？
B: Two years, more or less. 兩年左右。

提示　doctorate [ˈdɑktərɪt] *n.* 博士學位

0185　…最遲不超過…點鐘。
...by...at the latest.

範例　A: When's David coming? 大衛什麼時候來？
B: He should be here by four at the latest. 他最遲不超過四點鐘。

0186　我花了整整…小時…。
It took me...whole hours to...

範例　A: It took me two whole hours to walk there.
我花了整整兩個小時走到那裡。
B: You must have been exhausted when you got there.
你到那裡時，一定筋疲力盡了。

提示　exhausted [ɪgˈzɔstɪd] *adj.* 耗盡的；疲憊的

0187　…大約需要兩周時間。
It'll take about a fortnight to...

範例 | **A:** How long will this job take?
這項工作要多久？
B: It'll take about a fortnight to finish it.
完成這項工作大約需要兩周時間。

提示 | fortnight ['fɔrt,naɪt] *n.* 兩星期

0188 ⋯隨時都⋯。
...any minute now.

範例 | **A:** Where's Dad? 爸爸在哪裡？
B: He should get here any minute now. 他應該隨時都會到。

0189 每天這個時間⋯。
...at this time of day.

範例 | **A:** Let's go to the supermarket.
我們去超市吧。
B: We'd better wait. It's usually very crowded at this time of day.
我們最好等一等。每天這個時間通常都很擁擠。

0190 每隔一天⋯。
...every other day.

範例 | **A:** When is the swimming pool open? 游泳池什麼時候開放？
B: It's open every other day. 每隔一天開放。

0191 ⋯下星期⋯。
...next...

範例 | **A:** What will you do next Sunday? 你們下星期日做什麼？
B: We'll go swimming next Sunday. 我們下星期日去游泳。

0192 ⋯這個星期⋯。
...this...

範例 | **A:** Are you free this Saturday? 你這個星期六有空嗎？
B: No, I have classes this Saturday. 沒有，我這個星期六有課。

0193 時鐘準嗎？
Is the clock right?

替換 | Does the clock keep good time?
Does the clock tell the right time?

範例
A: Is the clock right? 時鐘準嗎？
B: Yes, it always is. 一向很準。

0194
這時鐘總是停住。
The clock is always stopping.

替換 | The clock keeps stopping.

範例 | **A:** What's wrong with the clock? 時鐘怎麼了？
B: The clock is always stopping. 這時鐘總是停住。

0195
我的手錶停了。
My watch stopped.

替換 | The battery in my watch has run down.

範例 | **A:** Do you have the time? 幾點了？
B: Sorry, my watch stopped. 對不起，我的手錶停了。

0196
我的錶壞了。
My watch is broken.

範例 | **A:** Do you have the time? 幾點了？
B: My watch is broken. 我的錶壞了。

0197
錶慢了。
It's running slow.

替換 | It's lost a little time.
My watch is a bit slow.

範例 | **A:** My watch says six-twenty. 我的錶是六點二十分。
B: It's running slow. 錶慢了。

0198
錶有點快。
It's running fast.

替換 | My watch is a bit fast.
My watch has gained a little time.

範例 | **A:** What time is it now?
幾點了？
B: My watch says six-ten, but it's running fast.
我的錶是六點十分，但是它有點快。

0199	我才剛依照電臺的報時信號調整（手錶）時間。 **I just set my watch to the radio time signal.**

範例	**A:** Your watch is running slow. 你的錶慢了。 **B:** That's impossible. I just set my watch to the radio time signal. 不可能。我才剛依照電臺的報時信號調整（手錶）時間。
提示	impossible [ɪmˈpɑsəbl̩] *adj.* 不可能的

0200	我撥快了…分鐘。 **I set it ahead...minutes.**

替換	I've set the clock...minutes fast. I've moved the hands of the clock forward...minutes.
範例	**A:** Does your watch tell the right time? 你的錶準嗎？ **B:** Not really. I set it ahead 5 minutes. 不準，我撥快了五分鐘。

0201	只是要上發條。 **It just needs to be wound up.**

範例	**A:** What's wrong with my watch? 我的錶怎麼了？ **B:** Nothing. It just needs to be wound up. 沒什麼。只是要上發條。

0202	我把鐘撥慢了。 **I've set the clock back.**

範例	**A:** Your clock doesn't tell the right time. 你的鐘不準。 **B:** Yes. I've set the clock back. 是的，我把鐘撥慢了。

1.10 肯定回答 Affirmative Responses

　　"Yes." 是最簡單的肯定回答，但肯定的回答不一定只用 "Yes."。做肯定回答時，可以使用的表達法很多，有時候避開簡單的肯定回答，反而是比較好的選擇。

011

0203	是的。 **Yes.**

| 替換 | Right.
Correct.
That's it/OK/right. |
| 範例 | A: Are you new here? 你是新來的嗎？
B: Yes. 是的。 |

0204　一點兒也沒錯。
Exactly.

替換	Precisely. Absolutely. Spot on. You're quite/dead right. That's quite right/correct. That's perfectly correct.
範例	A: So you've been here for eight years. 　　這麼說，你已經在這裡待八年了。 B: Exactly. 　　一點兒也沒錯。
提示	absolutely ['æbsə,lutlɪ] *adv.* 完全地；絕對地

0205　沒錯呀。
There's nothing wrong with that.

| 替換 | Nothing wrong with that. |
| 範例 | A: Do you think it's OK that I call him? 你覺得我打電話給他對嗎？
B: There's nothing wrong with that. 沒錯呀。 |

0206　我想你是對的。
I guess you're right.

| 替換 | I think that's right.
I don't think there's anything wrong with that. |
| 範例 | A: What do you think? 你怎麼想？
B: I guess you're right. 我想你是對的。 |

0207　你這麼說是對的。
You're correct in saying that.

範例　**A:** Do you think it's a proper thing to say? 你覺得我這麼說對嗎？
B: Yes, you're correct in saying that. 對的，你這麼說是對的。

提示　proper ['prɑpɚ] *adj.* 適當的；正確的

0208　我沒有發現…有錯。
I didn't find any mistake in...

範例　**A:** Did Tom make any mistakes in spelling?
湯姆的拼字有錯嗎？
B: No, I didn't find any mistake in his spelling.
沒有，我沒發現他的拼字有錯。

0209　差不多。
That's about right.

替換　Kind of looks that way.

範例　**A:** Do you mean he won't come back again? 你是說他不會再回來了嗎？
B: That's about right. 差不多。

0210　我認為…完全正確。
I suppose...is absolutely right.

替換　I should say...is perfectly right.

範例　**A:** What's your opinion? 你的看法是什麼？
B: I suppose what you said is absolutely right. 我認為你說的完全正確。

0211　看來你是對的。
It would seem that you're right.

範例　**A:** What do you think? 你認為呢？
B: It would seem that you're right. 看來你是對的。

0212　我確定…。
I can confirm that...

範例　**A:** Did he say that? 他是那麼說的嗎？
B: Yes, I can confirm that he said it. 是的，我確定他是那麼說的。

提示　confirm [kən'fɝm] *v.* 確定；肯定

1.11　否定回答 Negative Responses

否定性的回答需要一些技巧，否則很容易引起不愉快。否定回答時，記得要表示歉意或者遺憾。此外，爲了避免任何的不愉快，必須要說明原因。

0213　全錯了。
It's all wrong.

（012）

替換
You've got it all wrong.
You're all wet.
That's not at all right.

範例
A: Is this how it should be? 這應該是如此嗎？
B: No, it's all wrong. 不，全錯了。

提示
be all wet【美，非正式】大錯特錯

0214　錯了。
You're wrong.

替換
That's not correct.

範例
A: I believe he was born in the year 1787. 我想他是一七八七年出生的。
B: You're wrong. 錯了。

0215　你把…錯了。
You've...wrong.

範例
A: Excuse me, but you've spelled my name wrong.
　　對不起，你把我的名字拼錯了。
B: Oh, I'm terribly sorry.
　　哦，眞是抱歉。

0216　瞎說。
That's rubbish.

替換
That's nonsense.
That's bullshit. 〔粗魯的表達法〕

範例
A: Susan must be in love with you. 蘇珊一定是愛上你了。
B: That's rubbish. 瞎說。

提示　nonsense [ˈnɑnsɛns] *n.* 胡說；廢話
bullshit [ˈbulˌʃɪt] *n.* 【諱】胡說；亂說

0217
我認為你弄錯了。
I think you're mistaken.

範例　A: I was told they were here yesterday. 有人告訴我他們昨天在這裡。
B: I think you're mistaken. 我認爲你弄錯了。

0218
我必須告訴你…不正確。
I have to tell you that...is not true.

範例　A: What terrible news!
這消息太糟了！
B: I have to tell you that the news is not true.
我必須告訴你這消息並不正確。

0219
我可以這麼說，實際情況並非如此。
If I may say so, that's actually not the case.

範例　A: I'm aware that you've done this without authorization.
我知道你們這麼做並沒有得到授權。
B: If I may say so, that's actually not the case.
我可以這麼說，實際情況並非如此。

提示　authorization [ˌɔθərəˈzeʃən] *n.* 授權；認可

0220
我可以這麼說，…是不正確的。
If I may say so, ...is incorrect.

範例　A: Do you have any doubts about his story?
你對他的話有何懷疑嗎？
B: If I may say so, what he said is incorrect.
我可以這麼說，他說的話是不正確的。

0221
恐怕這有點誤解。
I'm afraid there has been some misunderstanding here.

範例　A: Wasn't he supposed to be here at nine?
他不是九點到這裡嗎？
B: I'm afraid there has been some misunderstanding here.
恐怕這有點誤解。

提示　misunderstanding [ˌmɪsʌndɚˈstændɪŋ] *n.* 誤會；誤解

0222

對不起，但我真的應該指出…是不正確的。
I'm sorry, but I really should point out that...is/are not correct.

範例
A: I'm sorry, but I really should point out that his statistics are not correct. 對不起，但我眞的應該指出他的統計數字是不正確的。
B: Oh, what's wrong with them? 哦，問題出在哪？

提示
statistics [stə'tɪstɪks] *n.* 統計學；統計數字

0223

…似乎是不正確的。
It doesn't seem correct to...

替換
It is perhaps incorrect to...

範例
A: He lied to us again.
他又對我們說謊了。
B: It doesn't seem correct to say that he's honest.
說他誠實似乎是不正確的。

0224

我不這樣認為。
I don't think so.

範例
A: He'll be a success. 他會成功的。
B: I don't think so. 我不這樣認爲。

0225

我認為你這麼想是不對的。
I don't think you're right about that.

替換
I don't think you're correct.

範例
A: I think all of them are chumps. 我想他們全部都是傻瓜。
B: I don't think you're right about that. 我認爲你這麼想是不對的。

提示
chump [tʃʌmp] *n.* 【非正式】易受騙的人；傻瓜

0226

恐怕它是不對的。
I'm afraid it's wrong.

替換
I'm afraid it isn't right.

範例
A: Are you doubtful of this figure? 你懷疑這個數字嗎？
B: I'm afraid it's wrong. 恐怕它是不對的。

1.12 感激道謝 Gratitude

　　致謝是各民族都遵循的禮儀規範，用於表達感激他人幫助的意思。它可以促進人際關係的良好發展。英美人士善於表達感激，我們隨時隨地都能聽到他們的感謝之辭。無論他人給予的幫助多寡（指路、找零錢、回答詢問、饋贈禮物、購買物品、參加宴請、受到稱讚等），對象為何（上下級、同事、陌生人、親戚、朋友、父母、子女等），他們都會適時適地的表達感激之意。但是感謝要適度，否則會讓人感到不自在或者不眞誠；回答感謝要得體，否則也會讓人感到尷尬。

● 表示感激 Expressing Gratitude

0227	謝謝！ **Thanks.**	013

替換	Thank you. I appreciate that.
範例	**A:** Here you are. 給你。 **B:** Thanks. 謝謝。
提示	appreciate [əˈpriʃɪˌet] v. 感謝；感激

0228	多謝。 **Thanks a lot.**

替換	Thanks a million. Thanks very/so much. Many thanks. Much obliged. That's so nice/sweet of you. Thank you very much (indeed). That's very kind of you. I'm much obliged to you. I'm extremely grateful to you. I'm very much indebted to you.

範例 | A: Thanks a lot. 多謝。
B: I'm glad to help. 很高興能幫忙。

提示 | obliged [ə'blaɪdʒd] *adj.* 感激的
indebted [ɪn'dɛtɪd] *adj.* 感恩的；受惠的

0229
非常感謝…。
Thanks a lot for...

替換 | Many thanks for...
Thanks a million for...
Thanks very much for...
Thank you (very/so much) for...
Thank you very much indeed for...
I'm really very grateful to you for...
I'm much obliged to you for...
I do appreciate...

範例 | A: Thanks a lot for your help. 非常感謝你幫忙。
B: You're welcome. 別客氣。

0230
你人真好…
It was very nice of you to...

替換 | It was so sweet of you to...
It was very good of you to...
That was extremely good of you to...

範例 | A: It was very nice of you to drive me home.
你人真好，開車送我回家。
B: Don't mention it.
不客氣。

0231
你真是太好了。
You're very kind.

替換 | You're just wonderful.

範例 | A: You're very kind. 你真是太好了。
B: It's my pleasure. 我很樂意。

0232
我對你感激不盡。
I can never thank you enough.

(替換) I really can't thank you enough.

(範例) A: I can never thank you enough. 我對你感激不盡。
B: It was nothing. 這沒什麼。

0233 **謹表示我的謝意。**
I would like to express my appreciation.

(替換) I would like to express how grateful I am.

(範例) A: I would like to express my appreciation. 謹表示我的謝意。
B: No trouble at all. 沒什麼。

(提示) appreciation [əˌpriʃɪ'eʃən] *n.* 感謝；感激

0234 **對⋯謹表示我的謝意。**
I would like to express my gratitude for...

(替換) I would like to express how grateful I am for...

(範例) A: I would like to express my gratitude for your support.
對你的支持謹表示我的謝意。
B: I'm delighted I could help.
我很高興能幫得上忙。

(提示) gratitude ['grætəˌtjud] *n.* 感謝；感激

0235 **你想得真周到。**
You're very thoughtful.

(替換) It was most thoughtful of you.

(範例) A: This is our schedule for the whole week.
這是我們整個星期的日程安排。
B: You're very thoughtful.
你想得真周到。

(提示) thoughtful ['θɔtfəl] *adj.* 體貼的；周到的

0236 **好極了。**
Great!

(範例) A: I prepared this for you. 我為你準備了這個。
B: Great! 好極了。

● 回應感激 Responses to Gratitude

0237	應該的。 **Sure.**
(替換)	You bet. Sure thing.
(範例)	**A:** Thanks a lot. 多謝。 **B:** Sure. 應該的。

0238	那沒什麼。 **That's all right.**
(替換)	That's OK. It's all right. Not at all. No problem. No bother/trouble at all. You are welcome. Think nothing of it.
(範例)	**A:** I can't thank you enough. 我對你感激不盡。 **B:** That's all right. 那沒什麼。

0239	我很樂意。 **My pleasure.**
(替換)	It's my pleasure. The pleasure was all mine. I'm delighted I could help. I'm delighted to have been of some help. It's a pleasure to have been of some assistance. I'm glad to be of some assistance.
(範例)	**A:** Thank you so much for your timely help. 非常感謝你的及時幫助。 **B:** My pleasure. 我很樂意。
(提示)	assistance [ə'sɪstəns] *n.* 協助；援助 timely ['taɪmlɪ] *adj.* 及時的；適時的

0240
我願意為你效勞。
I'm always at your service.

(替換) I'm glad to have been of some service.

(範例) **A:** I'm indebted to you forever. 我永遠對你感激不盡。
B: I'm always at your service. 我願意為你效勞。

0241
我隨時都可以（幫忙）。
Any time.

(範例) **A:** Thanks a lot. 多謝。
B: Any time. 我隨時都可以（幫忙）。

0242
我很高興你喜歡。
I'm very glad you enjoyed it.

(範例) **A:** Thank you so much for dinner. 非常謝謝你的晚餐。
B: I'm very glad you enjoyed it. 我很高興你喜歡。

0243
該謝謝你才是。
Thank you.

(範例) **A:** Thank you very much for coming. 非常感謝你能來。
B: Thank you. 該謝謝你才是。

(提示) 當你覺得應該是你要好好感謝對方時，you 要讀重音。

0244
這實在微不足道，不過盡力而已。
It was the least I could do.

(範例) **A:** I really can't thank you enough. 我對你真是感激不盡。
B: It was the least I could do. 這實在微不足道，不過盡力而已。

0245
如果你是我，一定也會這麼做的。
You would have done the same for me, I'm sure.

(範例) **A:** I would like to express my gratitude for your kindness.
對於你的好意，我謹表示我的謝意。
B: You would have done the same for me, I'm sure.
如果你是我，一定也會這麼做的。

1.13 道歉賠罪 Apologies

在會話當中，我們有時會冒犯到他人。適時表達歉意是修補人際關係的重要手段。道歉不僅是為了禮貌，更是為了維持人際關係的和諧。在英美等國家，道歉有時很簡單，只需說聲 "I'm sorry."，有時則要表示歉意、說明原因、承擔責任、提出補救方法，並做保證。在聽到別人道歉之後，我們應該有積極友善的反應，給予諒解，有時還要勇於承擔責任。這不僅是有禮貌、有教養的表現，而且還有助於解決問題和改善關係。

● 表示歉意 Making an Apology

0246	**對不起！** **I'm sorry.** (014)
替換	Sorry!
範例	**A:** I've been waiting here for one hour! 我已經在這裡等一個小時了！ **B:** I'm sorry. 對不起！

0247	**對不起，…。** **I'm sorry for...**
替換	Sorry for... Pardon me for...
範例	**A:** I'm sorry for not meeting you. 對不起，沒能和你碰面。 **B:** It's quite all right. 沒關係的。

0248	**我為…感到很抱歉。** **I'm terribly sorry for...**
替換	I really feel bad about... I'm very sorry about... I'm extremely sorry for...
範例	**A:** I'm terribly sorry for the stupid mistake. 　　我為這個愚蠢的錯誤感到很抱歉。 **B:** It's not your fault. 　　這又不是你的錯。

提示	extremely [ɪkˈstrimlɪ] *adv.* 極端地；非常地

0249

請原諒我。
Pardon me.

替換

Excuse me.
Please forgive me.

範例

A: Pardon me. I didn't know you were here. 請原諒我，我不知道你在這。
B: It's all right. 沒關係。

0250

請原諒我…。
Excuse me for...

替換

Please forgive/pardon me for...

範例

A: Excuse me for smoking here. 請原諒我在這裡吸煙。
B: Never mind. 沒關係。

0251

對不起。我不是有意…。
I'm sorry. I didn't mean to...

範例

A: I'm sorry. I didn't mean to hurt your feelings.
　　對不起，我不是有意要傷害你的感情。
B: It's nothing.
　　沒什麼。

0252

都是我的錯。
It's all my fault.

替換

Oh, it's my fault.
I'm wrong.

範例

A: It's all my fault. 都是我的錯。
B: Let's forget it. 忘了它吧。

0253

…是我的錯。
It was wrong of me to...

範例

A: It was wrong of me to lose the telephone number.
　　弄丟了電話號碼是我的錯。
B: Don't worry about it.
　　別擔心了。

0254

我真笨，…。
How silly of me to...!

範例　A: How silly of me to forget that! 我真笨，竟然會忘記這件事！
B: It's OK. It can happen to the best of us. 沒關係，這誰都會發生。

0255

我真是非常抱歉。
I can't tell you how sorry I am.

替換　I'm really/awfully/extremely sorry.

範例　A: I can't tell you how sorry I am. 我真是非常抱歉。
B: It's really no big deal. 這沒什麼大不了的。

0256

請你一定要原諒我。
I do beg your pardon.

範例　A: I do beg your pardon. 請你一定要原諒我。
B: It's really not necessary to apologize. 你真的不必道歉。

提示　apologize [ə'pɑlə,dʒaɪz] v. 道歉；賠不是

0257

我希望你原諒我…。
I hope you will pardon me for...

替換　I hope you will forgive me for...

範例　A: I hope you will pardon me for my carelessness.
我希望你原諒我的粗心大意。
B: No apologies are necessary.
你實在沒有必要道歉。

提示　apology [ə'pɑlədʒɪ] n. 道歉

0258

我必須為…向你道歉。
I owe you an apology for...

替換　I must apologize for...
I must make an apology for...
I've got to apologize for...

範例　A: I owe you an apology for the delay. 我必須為延誤的事情向你道歉。
B: Never mind. Accidents will happen. 沒關係，難免會有意外。

0259	對於…，謹向你表示最深切的歉意。 **I must offer my sincerest apologies for...**
替換	May I offer my profoundest apologies for...?
範例	**A:** I must offer my sincerest apologies for the inconvenience. 對於造成你的不便，謹向你表示最深切的歉意。 **B:** Please don't blame yourself. 別責備自己了。
提示	profound [prəˈfaund] *adj.* 深刻的；意義深遠的

0260	…，真的非常抱歉。 **A thousand pardons for...**
範例	**A:** A thousand pardons for keeping you waiting so long. 讓你等了這麼久，真的非常抱歉。 **B:** No problem. 沒關係。

0261	對於…，請代我向…道歉。 **Please extend my apologies to...for...**
範例	**A:** Please extend my apologies to Susan for my forgetfulness. 對於我的健忘，請代我向蘇珊道歉。 **B:** I will. 我會的。

0262	我真不知該說什麼好。 **I just don't know what to say.**
範例	**A:** I just don't know what to say. 我真不知該說什麼好。 **B:** It's really of no importance. 這真的不要緊。

0263	恐怕我已經給你帶來許多麻煩。 **I'm afraid I've caused you too much trouble.**
範例	**A:** I'm afraid I've caused you too much trouble. 恐怕我已經給你帶來許多麻煩。 **B:** No, I haven't been put out at all. 不，一點都不麻煩。

0264

我真是非常粗心。
It was most careless of me.

範例　A: I should have known better. It was most careless of me.
　　　我早應該知道的。我真是非常粗心。
　　　B: It's not worth mentioning.
　　　這實在不值得一提。

0265

這實在不是有意的。
It was totally unintentional.

範例　A: It was totally unintentional. I hope you will forgive me.
　　　這實在不是有意的。我希望你會原諒我。
　　　B: No problem.
　　　沒問題。

提示　unintentional [ˌʌnɪnˈtɛnʃənl̩] *adj.* 非故意的；無心的

0266

我必須道歉。
I must apologize.

範例　A: I must apologize. 我必須道歉。
　　　B: There is no reason to apologize. 你不必道歉。

0267

我為我剛才說的話向你道歉。
I apologize for what I said just now.

範例　A: I apologize for what I said just now.
　　　我為我剛才說的話向你道歉。
　　　B: There is no reason to apologize for such a trifling thing.
　　　不必為這麼一點微不足道的事道歉。

提示　trifling [ˈtraɪflɪŋ] *adj.* 不重要的

0268

對於…，請接受我的歉意。
Please accept my apologies for...

範例　A: Please accept my apologies for not attending the ceremony.
　　　對於沒能參加典禮，請接受我的歉意。
　　　B: Never mind. It doesn't really matter.
　　　別介意，真的沒關係。

提示　ceremony [ˈsɛrəˌmonɪ] *n.* 典禮；儀式

● 回應歉意 Responses to an Apology

0269	沒有關係。 **That's quite all right.**
(替換)	That's OK. That's all right. Never mind about that. Don't worry about that.
(範例)	**A:** I'm terribly sorry. 眞對不起。 **B:** That's quite all right. 沒有關係。

0270	一點也沒有關係。 **Not at all.**
(替換)	Not a bit. It doesn't matter at all. That's perfectly all right.
(範例)	**A:** I'm so sorry for what I said. 我爲我說的話感到很抱歉。 **B:** Not at all. 一點也沒有關係。

0271	別提它了。 **Forget it.**
(替換)	Let's forget it. Don't think any more of it. Please think nothing of it. Please don't give it a second thought.
(範例)	**A:** Do pardon me for this. 一定要原諒我這件事。 **B:** Forget it. 別提它了。

0272	不用掛在心上。 **Don't let it worry you.**
(替換)	Don't let it distress you. Please don't feel bad about it. Please don't take it too hard.
(範例)	**A:** How stupid I was to make such a mistake! 我怎麼這麼笨，犯了這樣的錯！

B: Don't let it worry you.
不用掛在心上。

提示　distress [dɪsˈtrɛs] *v.* 使苦惱；使悲痛

0273　何必？
What for?

範例　**A:** I'm so sorry. 我很抱歉。
B: What for? 何必？

0274　噢，這事很平常啊。
Well, it's just one of those things.

範例　**A:** I'm sorry for the inconvenience. 很對不起造成你的不便。
B: Well, it's just one of those things. 噢，這事很平常啊。

0275　你完全不必擔心。
There's no need for you to worry in the least.

範例　**A:** Do forgive me for such foolishness. 請一定要原諒我的愚蠢。
B: There's no need for you to worry in the least. 你完全不必擔心。

● 失陪告退 Excusing Oneself when Leaving

0276　對不起，失陪一下。
Excuse me.

替換　'Scuse me.
Will you excuse me, please?

範例　**A:** Excuse me. 對不起，失陪一下。
B: Of course. 當然沒問題。

0277　等一會兒。
Just a minute.

替換　Hang on (a minute/second).

範例　**A:** Just a minute. 等一會兒。
B: OK. 好的。

0278　對不起，我馬上就回來。
Excuse me. I'll be right back.

替換　'Scuse me. I'll be back in a flash.

範例　A: Excuse me. I'll be right back. 對不起，我馬上就回來。
B: No problem. 沒問題。

提示　flash [flæʃ] *n.* 瞬間；立刻

0279
對不起，我一會兒就回來。
Excuse me. I won't be a minute.

替換
'Scuse me. I'll be back in a flash/second.
'Scuse me. I'll be with you in a second.
Excuse me a moment.
Excuse me. I won't be long.
Excuse me. I won't be a moment.
Excuse me. I'll be back in a minute.
Excuse me. I'll be back in a short while.

範例　A: Excuse me. I won't be a minute. 對不起，我一會兒就回來。
B: It's all right. 沒關係。

0280
對不起，可以失陪一下嗎？
Excuse me. Can you give me a minute?

替換
May I be excused for a minute?
Would you excuse me for a short while, please?

範例　A: Excuse me. Can you give me a minute? 對不起，可以失陪一下嗎？
B: Never mind. 沒關係。

0281
恐怕我得暫時離開一會兒。
I'm afraid I'll have to leave you for a while.

替換　I'm afraid you'll have to excuse me for a minute or two.

範例　A: I'm afraid I'll have to leave you for a while.
恐怕我得暫時離開一會兒。
B: That's quite OK.
沒關係。

0282
不知能否恕我暫時告退。
I wonder if I might be excused for a moment.

替換　I wonder if you'd excuse me for a moment.

範例 | **A:** I wonder if I might be excused for a moment. 不知能否恕我暫時告退。
B: That's perfectly all right. 完全沒問題。

1.14 結束談話 Closing a Conversation

結束談話時，要自然得體，不告而別是不禮貌的行為。因故需要終止談話時，首先要表示歉意或遺憾，有時還必須說明不能繼續交談的理由。

0283	我得走了。 **It's time for me to go.**	015

替換 | It's about time to leave.
Well, I must dash.
I must be moving along now.
I guess I have to go now.
I really have to be going.
I really must leave you.
I really should be going.
I really must be off now.

範例 | **A:** It's four o'clock. 現在四點了。
B: It's time for me to go. 我得走了。

提示 | dash [dæʃ] *v.* 奔跑；急衝

0284	對不起，我得走了。 **Excuse me, please. I really ought to be on my way now.**

替換 | Sorry, gotta go.
Sorry, I must fly now.
Sorry, I must be off now.
Sorry, I must be running along.
Sorry, I must be getting on my way.
Sorry, I ought to get going.
Sorry, I've got to dash/run now.
Sorry, I've got to be pushing off now.
Excuse me, I have to take off.
I'm sorry, I must dash now.

範例
A: Excuse me, please. I really ought to be on my way now.
對不起，我得走了。
B: Do stay for dinner.
你一定要留下來吃晚餐。

0285
我很想再談一會兒，可是我該走了。
I'd really like to stay and chat, but I have to be going now.

範例
A: I'd really like to stay and chat, but I have to be going now.
我很想再談一會兒，可是我該走了。
B: See you, then.
那麼再見吧。

0286
時候不早了，我該走了。
It's getting late. I have to leave.

範例
A: It's getting late. I have to leave. 時候不早了，我該走了。
B: It's still quite early. 時間還早呢。

0287
和你談話很有意思，但我真的該走了。
It's been really nice talking to you, but I really should be off now.

範例
A: It's been really nice talking to you, but I really should be off now.
和你談話很有意思，但我真的該走了。
B: Nice to have met you.
很高興認識你。

0288
對不起，我真的該走了。
If you'll excuse me, I really have to go now.

範例
A: If you'll excuse me, I really have to go now. 對不起，我真的該走了。
B: Do stay a little longer. 再待一會兒吧。

0289
恐怕我得走了。
I'm afraid I have to go.

替換
I'm afraid I have to leave.
I'm afraid I have to run along.
I'm afraid I really must be going.
I'm afraid I'll have to be going.
I'm afraid I shouldn't stay any longer.
It's about time I was going, I'm afraid.

範例　A: How time flies! It's six now. 時間過得真快啊！現在六點了。
　　　B: I'm afraid I have to go. 恐怕我得走了。

0290
希望你不要介意，但我真的不能再待了。
I hope you don't mind, but I really mustn't stay any longer.

替換　I hope you don't mind, but I really can't stay any longer.

範例　A: I hope you don't mind, but I really mustn't stay any longer.
　　　　希望你不要介意，但我真的不能再待了。
　　　B: Do come again.
　　　　下次一定要再來喔。

0291
我不能再占用你的時間了。
I won't take any more of your time.

範例　A: I won't take any more of your time. 我不能再占用你的時間了。
　　　B: That's all right. It's been fun talking to you. 沒關係。和你談話很有意思。

0292
恐怕占用你太多時間了。
I'm afraid I've taken up too much of your time.

範例　A: I'm afraid I've taken up too much of your time.
　　　　恐怕占用你太多時間了。
　　　B: I'm glad to help.
　　　　很高興能有幫助。

0293
我要走了。
I'm going now.

替換　I'm off now.
範例　A: I'm going now. 我要走了。
　　　B: So long. 再見。
提示　"so long" 為非正式場合的用法，用於表達「再見」。

0294
哦，我最好還是得走了。
Well, I'd better go.

替換　Well, I'd better be going.
　　　Well, I'd better be moving along.

範例　A: Well, I'd better go. 哦，我最好還是得走了。
　　　B: Let's go together. I'm going shopping. 我們一起走。我要去買東西。

0295
天呀，是不是已經…？
Goodness, is it already...?

範例
A: Goodness, is it already 10 o'clock? 天呀，是不是已經十點了？
B: Yes, it's 10:10 now. 是的，現在是十點十分。

0296
我得掛斷電話了。
I have to hang up now.

替換
I have to ring off now.

範例
A: I have to hang up now. 我得掛斷電話了。
B: OK, see you tomorrow. 好的，明天見。

0297
謝謝你打電話來。
Thanks for calling.

替換
It was nice of you to call.

範例
A: Thanks for calling. Bye-bye. 謝謝你打電話來。再見。
B: Bye-bye. 再見。

0298
好了，該讓你走了。
Well, I'd better let you go.

替換
Well, I'd better not keep you.

範例
A: I must be going. 我得走了。
B: Well, I'd better let you go. 好了，該讓你走了。

0299
對不起，我得…。
I'm sorry, but I've got to...

範例
A: I'm sorry, but I've got to attend a meeting. 對不起，我得參加一個會。
B: That's all right. See you. 沒關係。再見。

0300
很高興和你談話。
It's been nice talking with you.

替換
Nice to have a talk with you.
I've enjoyed talking with you.

範例
A: It's been nice talking with you. 很高興和你談話。
B: I feel the same. 我有同感。

0301	那麼謝謝你⋯。 **Well, thank you for...**

範例 | **A:** Well, thank you for the wonderful time.
那麼謝謝你陪我渡過美好的時光。
B: Thank you.
該謝謝你才是。

0302	好了，我們就到此為止吧。 **Well, let's leave it at that.**

範例 | **A:** Well, let's leave it at that. 好了，我們就到此為止吧。
B: I agree. 我同意。

0303	請你見諒，我得走了。 **You'll have to excuse me.**

範例 | **A:** You'll have to excuse me. 請你見諒，我得走了。
B: See you, then. 那麼再見了。

1.15 道別送行 Leaving and Seeing Off

　　英美等西方國家的人士在告別時，會使用固定的語言表達模式，但還是會視時間、地點、人物和民族文化而略有調整。告別時，若有主客之分時，一般是客人向主人告別；無主客之分時，告別則無特定先後順序。須注意的是，在英美等西方人士的聚會上，客人提出告辭之語後，不應該馬上離去，離去的時間應在十、十五分鐘之後，期間需反複告辭兩三次。主人送客不遠送，只送到大門為止。客人離開時要表達感謝，主人則要表示再次相聚的期望。在語言上，英語中有比較固定的告別用語，我們應該熟記。

0304	再見！ **Bye!**	016

替換 | Good-bye!
Bye-bye!
Ciao!
Cheerio!

So long!
Bye (for) now!
Catch you later!
See you (later/soon/around)!
See you again soon!
I'll be seeing you!
I'd like to say goodbye to you all.

範例 A: Bye! 再見！
B: Bye-bye! 再見！

提示 ciao [tʃaʊ] *interj.*【非正式】再見
cheerio [ˌtʃɪrɪˈo] *interj.*【英，非正式】再見〔分手時的感歎詞〕

0305 保持聯絡！
Stay in touch!

替換 Keep in touch!

範例 A: Stay in touch! 保持聯絡！
B: OK! Bye! 好的！再見！

0306 祝你好運！
All the best!

替換 Good luck (to you)!

範例 A: Good-bye then, and all the best! 那麼再見了，祝你好運！
B: Good luck to your family! 祝你們全家好運！

0307 再見了，謝謝你！
Bye-bye, and thanks for everything.

替換 Good-bye and thank you for all you've done for me.

範例 A: Bye-bye, and thanks for everything. 再見了，謝謝你。
B: Bye-bye. 再見。

0308 代我向…問好！
Give my regards to...!

替換 Give my love to...!
Send...my best!
Mention me to...!
Remember me to...!

Say hello to...!
Please give my best regards to...

範例
A: Give my regards to Susan! 代我向蘇珊問好！
B: Thank you, I will. 謝謝你，我會的。

0309

再見，要保重！
Take care. Bye!

替換
Take care now, you hear?
Take care of yourself! Bye!
Look after yourself. Bye!

範例
A: Take care. Bye! 再見，要保重！
B: Bye-bye! 再見！

0310

別忘記捎封信來！
Be sure to drop me a line.

替換
Remember to drop me a line.
Remember to give me a ring.〔別忘記打電話來！〕
Don't forget to give me a ring.〔別忘記打電話來！〕

範例
A: Be sure to drop me a line. 別忘記捎封信來！
B: I will. 我會的。

提示
a line 指的是「寫信」；a ring 指的是「打電話」。

0311

記得再來看我。
Come and see me.

替換
Remember to look me up.
See you again next time.
Au revoir!
Until we meet again!
I hope we'll get together again soon.
I hope we will meet again at some future date.
I look forward to seeing you again soon.

範例
A: Come and see me. 記得再來看我。
B: Remember to drop me a line. 記得捎封信來！

提示
au revoir [ˌorə'vwɑr] *interj.* 【法】再會；再見

70

| 0312 | 很高興有機會和你在這見面。
I'm glad to have had the opportunity to see you here. |

 A: I'm glad to have had the opportunity to see you here.
很高興有機會和你在這見面。
B: So am I.
我也是。

| 0313 | 我會很想念你的！
I'm really going to miss you. |

 A: I'm really going to miss you. 我會很 想念你的！
B: I'm going to miss you, too. 我也會想你的。

第2章
思想溝通

2.1 能力 Ability

在對話中，有時我們會詢問他人是否具備某些能力，有時也會要表達自身的才能，這時候便可以用 "can"、"able"、"know how to" 及其否定形式來表達能力方面的語意。表達不具備做某事的能力，除了直接了當的表達方法之外，還可以用 "I wish I could..." 等表達意願的間接方式。其實，能根據不同場合和談話內容，使用不同風格的語言，就是展現了某方面的能力。

● 詢問具備的能力 Asking about Ability

0314	你行嗎？ **Are you any good?**

範例 A: Are you any good? 你行嗎？
B: Of course. 當然行。

0315	你會…嗎？ **Can you...?**

替換 Are you able to...?

範例 A: Can you swim? 你會游泳嗎？
B: Of course. 當然會。

0316	你擅長…嗎？ **Are you good at...?**

替換 Are you adept at...?
Are you capable of...?
Are you proficient/well-versed in...?

範例 A: Are you good at English? 你擅長英語嗎？
B: Yes, I'm well-versed in it! 當然，我的英語很熟練的！

提示 adept [ə'dɛpt] *adj.* 善於…的（+ at）
proficient [prə'fɪʃənt] *adj.* 熟練的；精通的（+ in/at）
well-versed [ˌwɛl'vɝst] *adj.* 知道得很多的；很熟悉的（+ in）

017

0317 你認為你能…嗎？
Do you think you can...?

(替換)
Think you can...?
Do you reckon you could...?
Do you feel able to...?
Do you think you have the ability/capability to...?

(範例)
A: Do you think you can win the football match?
你認爲你能贏這場足球賽嗎？
B: Yes, it'll be a piece of cake!
能，小事一樁。

(提示)
reckon ['rɛkən] v. 猜想；估計
capability [ˌkepə'bɪlətɪ] n. 能力；才能

0318 你認為你有能力…？
Do you think you're capable of...?

(範例)
A: Do you think you're capable of doing it on your own?
你認爲你有能力獨立完成它嗎？
B: Yes, it's quite easy!
可以，很簡單。

0319 你知道怎樣…嗎？
Do you have any...know-how?

(範例)
A: Do you have any computer know-how? 你知道怎樣操作電腦嗎？
B: Computer science is my major. 電腦是我的專業。

(提示)
know-how ['noˌhau] n. 技能

0320 你懂…嗎？
Do you know anything about...?

(範例)
A: Do you know anything about gardening?
你懂園藝嗎？
B: Yes, I learned a little from my father.
懂，我從我父親那兒學了一點。

0321 你肯定不會…對吧？
I bet you can't..., can you?

範例　A: I bet you can't play cards, can you? 你肯定不會打牌，對吧？
　　　　B: No. I'm hopeless at games. 是啊。我對遊戲一竅不通。

0322　你…怎麼樣？
What are you like at...?

範例　A: What are you like at writing compositions?
　　　　　你的作文寫得怎麼樣？
　　　　B: I'm hopeless. I don't even know where to begin.
　　　　　一竅不通，我甚至不知道從哪兒下手。

提示　composition [ˌkɑmpəˈzɪʃən] n. 寫作；作文

0323　你有…的天賦。
You have a talent for...

替換　You have a gift for...

範例　A: You have a talent for music. Everyone envies you.
　　　　　你有音樂的天賦，人人都羨慕你。
　　　　B: It's nothing special.
　　　　　沒什麼了不起的。

0324　你擅長…嗎？
Are you proficient at...?

範例　A: Are you proficient at doing interpretation?
　　　　　你擅長口譯嗎？
　　　　B: Well, I consider it within my capacity.
　　　　　哦，我認為這是我能力所及的。

提示　interpretation [ɪnˌtɝprɪˈteʃən] n. 翻譯；口譯

0325　你有經驗嗎？
Do you have any experience?

範例　A: Do you have any experience? 你有經驗嗎？
　　　　B: I think I have the right experience. 我想我正好有這種經驗。

0326　你有…所必需的資歷嗎？
Do you have the necessary qualifications to...?

範例　A: Do you have the necessary qualifications to be a teacher?
　　　　　你有教書所必需的資歷嗎？

B: I've received four years' training at Taiwan Normal University.
我在台灣師大學接受了四年的師範教育。

(提示) qualification [ˌkwɑləfəˈkeʃən] *n.* 資格

0327
你會…，對吧？
You can..., can't you?

(範例) **A:** You can swim, can't you? 你會游泳，對吧？
B: Yes. I'm a very good swimmer. 沒錯，我游得很好。

● 陳述能做某事 Stating One Can Do Something

0328
我想我能…。
I think I can...

(替換) I reckon I can...
I feel able to...
I believe I have the ability/capability to...

(範例) **A:** Shall I do it for you?
我幫你做，好嗎？
B: No thanks. I think I can handle this myself.
不用，謝謝。我想我能自己處理這件事。

0329
我想我有…的能力。
I feel capable of...

(替換) I think I have the competence necessary for...
I think I have the capability of...

(範例) **A:** I feel capable of judging works of art.
我想我有鑑賞藝術品的能力。
B: I don't believe it.
我不相信。

(提示) competence [ˈkɑmpətəns] *n.* 能力

0330
我很擅長…。
I'm pretty good at...

(替換) I'm excellent at...
I'm clever with...
I'd say I am quite proficient at...

範例　A: I'm pretty good at running. 我很擅長跑步。
B: And I'm good at swimming. 我擅長游泳。

0331
我…還不賴。
I'm not too bad at...

替換　...isn't too difficult to me.
...is not too much a problem for me.

範例　A: Are you good at swimming? 你擅長游泳嗎？
B: Well, I'm not too bad at it. 哦，我這方面還不賴。

0332
我知道怎樣…。
I have...know-how.

範例　A: I have dog-training know-how. 我知道怎樣訓練狗。
B: Where'd you learn it? 你哪裡學的呢？

0333
當然能。
Sure.

替換　No problem.

範例　A: Can you give me directions? 你能為我指路嗎？
B: Sure. 當然能。

0334
這很容易。
It's nothing.

替換　It's a cinch.
It's quite easy.
It's a piece of cake!

範例　A: Do you know how to start the machine? 你知道如何啟動這台機器嗎？
B: Yes, it's nothing. 知道，這很容易。

提示　cinch [smtʃ] *n.*【非正式】極容易做的事

0335
我能…。
I can...

替換　I'm able to...

範例　A: Do you know anything about taking shorthand? 你懂速記嗎？
B: I can do it very well. 我能將它做得很好。

| 提示 | shorthand [ˈʃɔrtˌhænd] *n.* 速記 |

| 0336 | 我懂一點兒…。
I know something about... |
| 範例 | **A:** Can anyone tell us? 誰能告訴我們呢？
B: Well, I know something about it. 哦，我懂一點兒這個。 |

| 0337 | 我知道…。
I know... |
| 範例 | **A:** Where is Peter? 彼德在哪兒？
B: I know where to find him. 我知道在哪裡能找到他。 |

| 0338 | 我也許能…。
I might be able to... |
| 範例 | **A:** Do you think you're a match for him? 你覺得你是他的對手嗎？
B: Well, I might be able to defeat him. 哦，我也許能打敗他。 |

● 陳述不能做某事 Stating One Cannot Do Something

0339	我不確定我能…。 **I'm not sure I can...**
替換	I don't reckon I can... I don't think I'm able to... I don't think I have the competence necessary to...
範例	**A:** Do you think you can pass the test? 你認為你能通過考試嗎？ **B:** Well, I'm not sure I can pass it. 哦，我不確定我能通過。

0340	恐怕我不能…。 **I'm afraid I can't...**
替換	I'm not sure I'm able to... I'm not sure I have the capability to...
範例	**A:** Tell me, will you? It'll be just between us. 告訴我一點兒，好嗎？我不會告訴別人的。 **B:** I'm afraid I can't tell you. 恐怕我不能告訴你。

0341

我不確定我知道…。
I'm not sure I know how to...

(替換) I don't reckon I've got the know-how to...

(範例) **A:** Be quick. Time is up.
　　快點，時間到了。
B: I'm not sure I know how to answer this question.
　　我不確定我知道怎麼回答這個問題。

0342

我對…一竅不通。
I'm useless at...

(替換) ...just isn't my line.
I'm no good at...
I'm hopeless at...
I don't know anything about...
...might be beyond my ability.

(範例) **A:** I'm old! I'm useless at numbers! 我老了，我對數字一竅不通！
B: You shouldn't say that. 別這麼說。

0343

我沒辦法…。
There's no way I can...

(替換) I can't...
I can't manage to...
I won't be able to...
I haven't a clue how to...
I haven't the faintest idea how to...
I have no idea how to...
I don't know how I can...
It's impossible for me to...
I think that would prove impossible for me to...

(範例) **A:** He talks with a strong accent. 他講話口音很重。
B: Yes. There's no way I can understand him. 是啊，我沒辦法聽懂。

(提示) accent ['æksənt] *n.* 口音；腔調

0344

我…很差勁。
I'm pretty bad at...

(範例) **A:** Can you translate it? 你可以翻譯一下嗎？
B: I'm pretty bad at translation. 我的翻譯很差勁。

提示 | translation [trænsˈleʃən] *n.* 翻譯

0345

我不知道怎樣才能做好。
I don't know how I can get it done.

範例 | **A:** I don't know how I can get it done. 我不知道怎樣才能做好。
B: Neither do I. 我也不知道。

0346

我不知道該從哪裡著手…。
I don't know where to begin...

範例 | **A:** I don't know where to begin the work.
我不知道該從哪裡著手這件工作。
B: Why not ask John for help?
何不找約翰幫忙呢？

0347

我認為我沒有經驗。
I don't think I have any experience.

範例 | **A:** I don't think I have any experience. 我認爲我沒有經驗。
B: Don't be so modest. 不要過於謙虛。

提示 | modest [ˈmɑdɪst] *adj.* 謙虛的

2.2 勸告 Advice

　　俗語說：「旁觀者清，當局者迷。」在現實生活中，人們對自己存在的弱點往往看不清。勸告正是清醒的「旁觀者」對迷惘的「當局者」的一種規勸和指點。一般情況下，規勸具有疏通、開導、勸誡、撫慰以及激勵作用。當然要想達到規勸的效果，規勸的語言要講究技巧。

　　在勸說時可以考慮以下情況：你所建議的事情的難度和引起他人不快的程度，還有談話時，自身所扮演的角色以及對方的身份。因爲西方人不喜歡涉及他人的「隱私」，別人沒徵求你的意見，或關係不夠親密，最好不要貿然向別人提出關於私事的建議和忠告。

● 尋求忠告 Asking for Advice

0348
你能幫我解決⋯嗎？
Can you help me straighten...out?

(018)

替換
Can you help me get...straightened out?
Help me sort...out, will you?

範例
A: Can you help me straighten this out? 你能幫我解決這件事嗎？
B: Sure. It'll be a piece of cake for me. 當然，對我來說是輕而易舉。

0349
你要是我會怎麼辦呢？
What would you do if you were me?

替換
What would you do if you were in my shoes?
What would you do in my position?

範例
A: It's not an easy decision. You'd better look before you leap.
下這個決心不容易，你最好三思而後行啊。
B: Yes, I know. But what would you do if you were me?
是的，我知道，但是你要是我會怎麼辦呢？

0350
你看我該怎麼辦呢？
What do you reckon I should do?

替換
What do you think I should do?
What do you think I ought to do?
What would you say I should do?
What would you advise/counsel me to do?

範例
A: Have you straightened out that problem? 那件事你解決了嗎？
B: No. What do you reckon I should do? 沒有，你看我該怎麼辦呢？

提示
counsel ['kaʊnsl] v. 勸告；忠告

0351
你認為我該⋯嗎？
Do you think I should...?

替換
Do you reckon I should...?

範例
A: Do you think I should keep to the right?
你認為我該靠右走嗎？
B: Certainly. You're in Taiwan, not Britain.
當然了，你是在台灣，不是在英國。

0352
我該怎麼做呢？
How do I go about it?

（替換）What can/should I do?

（範例）
A: How do I go about it? 我該怎麼做呢？
B: Let's ask Jack for help. 我們找傑克幫忙。

0353
我應該…嗎？
Ought I...?

（替換）Should I...?

（範例）
A: I don't feel well today. Ought I get a check-up?
今天我覺得不太舒服，我應該檢查一下嗎？
B: Yes, I think so.
是的，我想應該。

（提示）check-up ['tʃɛk,ʌp] *n.* 身體檢查

0354
我想請你對…提些忠告。
I'd like your advice about...

（替換）
I'd like to consult you on...
I'd like to have your advice on...

（範例）
A: I'd like your advice about my work.
我想請你對我的工作提些忠告。
B: It's good enough.
已經很不錯了。

0355
你能不能指點一下…？
Could I ask you for some advice about...?

（替換）
Can you give me some advice on...?
Could I ask your opinion on...?
Could I have your advice on...?

（範例）
A: Could I ask you for some advice about my research?
你能不能指點一下我的研究？
B: Sure. It'll be my pleasure.
當然，很榮幸。

（提示）research [rɪ'sɝtʃ] *n.* 研究；調查

0356

如果你能給我指點指點，我會很感激的。
I would appreciate your advice.

（替換）　I would appreciate some advice from you.
　　　　 I would appreciate it if you could give me some advice.

（範例）　A: I think you've done a good job.
　　　　　　我覺得你做得不錯。
　　　　 B: I would appreciate your advice.
　　　　　　如果你能給我指點指點，我會很感激的。

0357

不知你對…有什麼反應？
Could I ask what your reaction would be to...?

（替換）　I was wondering what your reaction would be to...?

（範例）　A: Could I ask what your reaction would be to a reduction in production? 不知你對減產有什麼反應？
　　　　 B: I'd be concerned. 我很擔憂。

0358

請問…是否正確？
I'd like to ask whether it's right to...?

（範例）　A: I'd like to ask whether it's right to evade taxes?
　　　　　　請問逃稅這種作法是否正確？
　　　　 B: How can you ask such a silly question?
　　　　　　你怎能問這種愚蠢的問題？

（提示）　evade [ɪ'ved] *v.* 逃避

● 勸進 Advising Someone to Do Something

0359

如果你明白我的意思，就應該…。
You should..., if you know what I mean.

（替換）　You ought to...if you get my meaning.

（範例）　A: You should quit smoking, if you know what I mean.
　　　　　　如果你明白我的意思，就應該戒煙。
　　　　 B: You know how difficult that is for me.
　　　　　　你知道這對我來說太難了。

（提示）　quit [kwɪt] *v.* 戒除

0360	你為什麼不⋯呢？ **Why not...?**
（替換）	Why don't you...?
（範例）	**A:** I want to tell Lisa I love her. 我想告訴麗莎我愛她。 **B:** Why not go do it now? 你為什麼現在不去做呢？

0361	我看你應該⋯。 **I reckon you should...**
（替換）	The way I see it, you should...
（範例）	**A:** I feel pretty sad after quarrelling with her. 和她吵完架之後，我覺得很難過。 **B:** I reckon you should say sorry to her first. 我看你應該先和她道歉。

0362	你最好⋯。 **You'd better...**
（替換）	You would be wise to... I think you ought to... I think you should... You should..., if you ask me.
（範例）	**A:** You'd better start now. 你最好現在就開始做。 **B:** Don't you think it's too late? 難道你不認為太晚了嗎？

0363	如果我是你的話，我就⋯。 **I'd...if I were in your shoes.**
（替換）	If I were in your position, I would... I would...if I were in your place.
（範例）	**A:** I'd go on a diet if I were in your shoes. 如果我是你的話，我就節食。 **B:** I think I'm quite slim. 我覺得我還挺苗條的。
（提示）	in one's position 相當於 in one's place 和 in one's shoes，意為「身在某人的處境」。

0364	我認為你可以⋯。 **I think you can...**
（替換）	I think you may...

| 範例 | A: I think you can come along with us. 我想你可以和我們一塊去。
B: That's a good idea. 好主意。 |

0365

我勸你…。
I advise you to...

| 替換 | I'd suggest that you should... |

| 範例 | A: I advise you to take it seriously. 我勸你認真對待這件事。
B: I think I'm being serious enough. 我想我已經夠認真了。 |

0366

你…倒也不錯。
It might be a good idea if...

| 範例 | A: Do you think I can do it all by myself?
你覺得我一個人能做成這件事嗎？
B: Sure. It might be a good idea if you do it with your own hands.
當然能，你一個人做倒也不錯。 |

0367

你不妨…。
You might as well...

| 替換 | It might be just as well to... |

| 範例 | A: I don't know what I should do next. 我不知道下一步該怎麼辦。
B: You might as well ask our teacher for advice. 你不妨問問老師的意見。 |

0368

我的意見是…。
My advice would be to...

| 替換 | My idea would be to... |

| 範例 | A: My advice would be to teach him a lesson. 我的意見是給他一個教訓。
B: That's a really good idea. 好主意。 |

0369

如果你聽我的勸告，就不會…。
If you take my advice, you won't...

| 替換 | If you follow my recommendation, you won't... |

| 範例 | A: I'm afraid my boss will fire me.
恐怕我老闆要炒我魷魚了。
B: If you take my advice, you won't lose your job.
如果你聽我的勸告，就不會失去這份工作。 |

| 提示 | recommendation [ˌrɛkəmɛn'deʃən] n. 勸告；建議 |

0370

你要是不…就不明智了。
You'd be ill-advised not to...

(替換) You would be unwise not to...

(範例) **A:** You'd be ill-advised not to ask her for help.
你要是不求助於她，就不明智了。
B: I don't agree.
我可不這麼認為。

● 勸退 Advising Someone Not to Do Something

0371

如果你明白我的意思，就不該…。
You shouldn't...if you see what I mean.

(替換) You can't...if you get what I mean.

(範例) **A:** You shouldn't waste your time if you see what I mean.
如果你明白我的意思，就不該浪費時間。
B: Time is very important to me.
時間對我很重要。

0372

我看…對你沒什麼好處。
I don't think it'll do you any good to...

(替換) I don't reckon it'll do you any good to...

(範例) **A:** I don't think it'll do you any good to exercise more.
我看多做運動對你沒什麼好處。
B: But I want to lose weight.
但是我想減肥。

0373

我認為…並不好。
I don't think it's a good idea to...

(替換) I don't reckon it's a good idea to...

(範例) **A:** We should get here at six o'clock tomorrow morning.
我們應該明天早上六點鐘到。
B: I don't think it's a good idea to get up too early.
我認為太早起並不好。

0374

我認為你不該…。
I don't think you should...

87

替換) I don't reckon you should...

範例) **A:** I don't think you should quit your job now.
我認為你不該現在辭職。

B: But there is so much for me to learn, so I want to go back to school.
但是我有許多東西需要學，所以我想重新回到學校。

0375

如果我是你，我就不會…。
I wouldn't...if I were in your shoes.

替換) If I were you, I wouldn't...
I wouldn't...if I were in your position.

範例) **A:** What I did disappointed my mother.
我的所作所為讓我媽媽很失望。

B: I wouldn't make her angry if I were in your shoes.
如果我是你，我就不會惹她生氣。

0376

我勸你不要…。
I'd advise you not to...

替換) I wouldn't advise you to...
I would recommend you not to...

範例) **A:** I'd advise you not to blame him for it. 我勸你不要為這件事責備他。
B: But it's all his fault. 但這都是他的錯。

0377

如果你聽我的話，就不要…。
If you follow my advice, you won't...

替換) If you follow my recommendation, you won't...

範例) **A:** If you follow my advice, you won't leave your girlfriend now.
如果你聽我的話，就不要在這個時候離開你的女友。

B: But I don't love her any more.
可是我已經不愛她了。

0378

聽我的勸告，不要…。
Take my advice and don't...

範例) **A:** Take my advice and don't put any sugar in it.
聽我的勸告，不要在裡面放糖。

B: But I like sugar.
但是我就喜歡糖。

0379	你不該⋯。 **You mustn't...**
範例	**A:** I don't feel well today. 今天我覺得不太舒服。 **B:** You mustn't eat too much oily food. 你不該吃那麼多油膩的食物。

0380	⋯可能不太好。 **It might not be a good idea to...**
範例	**A:** It might not be a good idea to accept the job. 接受那份工作可能不太好。 **B:** But the salary is appealing. 但是薪水很令人心動。

0381	如果你徵求我的意見，我想⋯是不明智的。 **If you want my advice, I think it would be unwise to...**
範例	**A:** If you want my advice, I think it would be unwise to play chess all day long. 如果你徵求我的意見，我想整天下棋是不明智的。 **B:** Maybe you're right. 也許你是對的。

0382	我的忠告是：不要⋯。 **My advice would be not to...**
範例	**A:** My advice would be not to drink too much. 我的忠告是：不要喝得太多。 **B:** Thank you for telling me that. 謝謝你告訴我。

0383	我的意見是：不要⋯。 **My reaction would be to never...**
範例	**A:** What do you think I should do? 你覺得我該怎麼辦？ **B:** My reaction would be to never trust him. 我的意見是：不要相信他。

2.3　同意 Agreement

　　同意與不同意是對某種主張或想法表達意見。表示同意時，要熱情，但要有分寸；表達不同意時，要講求技巧，同時要表達歉意和遺憾；表示部分同意時，通常在語言上要有保留。

● 詢問是否同意 Asking if Someone Agrees

0384	對嗎？ **Right?**	(019)

替換 | Yeah?

範例 | **A:** It's really beautiful. Right? 它真的很漂亮，對嗎？
B: Of course. 當然了。

0385	…這不是瞎說吧？ **..., or am I speaking through my neck?**

替換 | ..., or is that a heap of garbage?

範例 | **A:** Young people are getting lazy, or am I speaking through my neck?
現在的年輕人愈來愈懶了，這不是瞎說吧？
B: You're right.
你說的沒錯。

0386	好嗎？ **OK?**

替換 | OK by you?
Don't you agree?
All right with you?
Would you agree?

範例 | **A:** Let's go home now, OK? 現在回家，好嗎？
B: OK. 好的。

0387	你同意…嗎？ **Do you go along with...?**

替換 | Do you agree/concur with...?
Would you agree with...?

範例 | **A:** Do you go along with my proposal? 你同意我的提案嗎？
B: Yes. You're always right. 同意，你總是對的。

提示 | concur [kən'kɝ] v. 同意（+ with）

0388	你不這樣認為嗎？ **Don't you think so?**

(替換) Wouldn't you say so?

(範例) A: Boxing is a rough sport. Don't you think so?
拳擊真野蠻！你不這樣認為嗎？
B: Yes. It's just too cruel.
是的。太殘忍了。

0389 你不認為…嗎？
Don't you think...?

(替換) Wouldn't you say...?
Don't you feel...?

(範例) A: Don't you think she's a nice girl? 你不認為她是一個好女孩嗎？
B: She sure is. 她當然是。

0390 請問你是否同意…？
Can I ask if you agree with...?

(替換) I wonder if you would consent to...?
I'd like to ask/know if you agree with...?
May I ask if you agree with...?

(範例) A: The painting exhibition is worth visiting. Can I ask if you agree with me? 這畫展值得一看，請問你是否同意我的看法呢？
B: It sure is. 當然了。

0391 你跟我想的一樣嗎？
Do you think the same as I do?

(範例) A: Children are too spoiled these days. Do you think the same as I do?
現在的孩子被寵壞了。你跟我想的一樣嗎？
B: Yes, I think so too.
是的，我也這麼想。

0392 你認為你會同意…嗎？
Do you think you would consent to...?

(範例) A: Do you think you would consent to his request?
你認為你會同意他的要求嗎？
B: Yes, I would.
是的，我想我會的。

0393

你接受他在…上的觀點嗎？
Do you accept his opinion on...?

範例

A: Do you accept his opinion on this problem?
你接受他在這個問題上的觀點嗎？
B: I'm afraid not.
恐怕不會。

0394

你不會不同意，是嗎？
You don't disagree, do you?

替換　You wouldn't disagree, would you?

範例

A: Modern painting is worthless. You don't disagree, do you?
現代派繪畫毫無價值。你不會不同意，是嗎？
B: No, I don't. It is worthless.
是的，太沒價值了。

0395

你會接受…，不是嗎？
You accept..., don't you?

範例

A: You accept my plan, don't you? 你會接受我的計畫，不是嗎？
B: Yes, I do. 是的，我會的。

● 表示同意 Expressing Agreement

0396

在這點上我同意你的看法。
I'm with you there.

替換　I'd go along with you on that.

範例

A: Cigarettes should be banned. 香煙應該被禁止。
B: I'm with you there. 在這點上我同意你的看法。

0397

的確是這樣。
That's too true.

替換

It sure is!
How true!
True enough.
It certainly is!
How right that is!
They certainly are.

範例 **A:** This city is really convenient to live in. 在這個城市生活很便利。
B: That's too true. 的確是這樣。

0398 **對！**
Yes.

替換 Yeah.
Right.
Righto!
You got/said it!
You are right!
Right you are.
That's right.
That is very true.
Hear! Hear!

範例 **A:** Some of the teachers are too hard on the students.
有些老師對學生太嚴厲了。
B: Yes.
對。

提示 righto ['raɪto] *interj.*【英俚】好；對
Hear! Hear!【尤英】對，對！〔用於較正式場合，用來強烈表示同意剛剛所說的話〕

0399 **我也是這麼想。**
Same with me.

替換 My thoughts exactly.
That goes for me, too.
I think so too.
That makes two of us.
That's my feeling/opinion, too.
That's just what I was thinking.
I'm of exactly the same idea.
I was thinking the same thing.

範例 **A:** I hate hot weather! 我討厭大熱天！
B: Same with me. 我也是這麼想。

0400 **我非常同意。**
I couldn't agree more.

替換　I quite agree with you.

範例　**A:** I think she's a promising writer. 我認為她是個很有前途的作家。
　　　B: I couldn't agree more. 我非常同意。

提示　promising ['prɑmɪsɪŋ] *adj.* 有前途的

0401　　我完全同意你的看法。
I agree with you completely.

替換　I concur absolutely with you.

範例　**A:** We must face reality. 我們必須面對現實。
　　　B: I agree with you completely. 我完全同意你的看法。

提示　absolutely ['æbsə͵lutlɪ] *adv.* 完全地；絕對地

0402　　我認為沒有人會不同意⋯。
I don't think anyone would disagree that...

替換　I don't think anyone would debate/argue that...
　　　I think no one would disagree that...

範例　**A:** Many students like online games. 許多學生喜歡線上遊戲。
　　　B: I don't think anyone would disagree that they spend too much time
　　　　　playing them. 我認為沒有人會不同意他們花了太多時間在那上面。

提示　debate [dɪ'bet] *v.* 反駁；駁斥

0403　　我完全同意你的觀點。
I completely accept your point of view.

替換　I think I entirely agree with you.

範例　**A:** I think smoking should be banned. 我認為應該禁止吸煙。
　　　B: I completely accept your point of view. 我完全同意你的觀點。

提示　completely [͵kəm'plitlɪ] *adv.* 十分；完全地

0404　　我的想法和你完全相同。
I completely share your opinion.

替換　I'm of exactly the opinion as you.

範例　**A:** I think Professor Smith is too hard on us.
　　　　　我認為史密斯教授對我們太苛刻了。
　　　B: I completely share your opinion.
　　　　　我的想法和你完全相同。

0405
我完全同意她關於…的意見。
I totally agree with what she said about...

範例
A: Do you agree with Mrs. Brown?
你同意布朗夫人的意見嗎？
B: I totally agree with what she said about school management.
我完全同意她關於學校管理的意見。

● 表示部分同意 Agreeing with Reservation

0406
對，不過…。
It sure is, but...

替換
OK, but...
Right, but...
Yes, but...
Mmm, but...
You're right, but...
That's quite true, but...
That's right, but...

範例
A: It's a really good plan. 這眞是一個好計畫。
B: It sure is, but it needs some improvement. 對，不過仍需要一些改進。

提示
improvement [ɪmˈpruvmənt] *n.* 改良；改進

0407
可能是這樣，不過…。
Could be, but...

替換
Yes, perhaps, but...
Maybe, but...

範例
A: It looks like Tom is late again.
看樣子湯姆又遲到了。
B: Could be, but I don't think he'll be too late.
可能是這樣，不過我不認爲他會太晚到。

0408
我當然明白這一點，不過…。
I can see that, yes, but...

替換
I certainly see what you mean, but...
I surely understand what you mean, but...

範例 A: I think we should help him.
我想我們應該幫他。
B: I can see that, yes, but it may cause trouble.
我當然明白這一點，不過可能會有些麻煩。

0409 我多半同意，不過…。
I go along with most of that, but...

替換 There's a lot to what you say, but...
I certainly accept most of what you said, but...

範例 A: I think the textbooks should be revised again.
我認為這些教材應該再修訂。
B: I go along with most of that, but we should do some research first.
我多半同意，不過我們應該先做一些研究調查。

0410 我知道你說的有道理，但是…。
I know you have a point there, but...

替換 There's a lot in what you say, but...

範例 A: We should love him as if he were our son.
我們應該像愛兒子那樣愛他。
B: I know you have a point there, but he is quite different from us.
我知道你說的有道理，但是他真的太不像我們了。

0411 我同意你所說的，但是…。
I quite agree with what you said, but...

替換 I think we're very much in agreement on this; however, ...

範例 A: I quite agree with what you said, but the world is changing.
我同意你所說的，但是這個世界正在改變。
B: Don't be so pessimistic.
別這麼悲觀。

提示 pessimistic [ˌpɛsə'mɪstɪk] *adj.* 悲觀的

0412 在某個程度上我同意，但是…。
Yes, to some extent, but...

替換 I agree up to a point, but...
I agree with you to a certain extent, but...
I concur with you in a sense, but...

範例　A: The politician is corrupt.
　　　這位政治人物已經貪污腐化了。
　　　B: Yes, to some extent, but he's still very popular.
　　　在某個程度上我同意，但是他仍然相當受歡迎。

提示　politician [ˌpɑləˈtɪʃən] *n.* 政客；從政者
　　　corrupt [kəˈrʌpt] *adj.* 貪污腐化的

0413

原則上我同意，但是…。
I agree in principle, but...

替換　I endorse your plan in principle, but...

範例　A: I think we should complete the project ahead of time.
　　　我想我們應該提前完成這項工程。
　　　B: I agree in principle, but there are still some difficult problems to solve.
　　　原則上我同意，但是我們還是有些困難要克服。

提示　principle [ˈprɪnsəbl] *n.* 原則
　　　endorse [ɪnˈdɔrs] *v.* 認可；贊同

0414

儘管你這麼說，但是我認為…。
Despite what you said, I think...

替換　In spite of what you said, I think...

範例　A: I think we can stay here another week.
　　　我想我們可以在這裡再待一個禮拜。
　　　B: Despite what you said, I think perhaps we'd better leave now.
　　　儘管你這麼說，但是我認為我們最好現在離開。

0415

這是一種看法，但是…。
That's one way of looking at it, but...

範例　A: Now's a good time to invest in stocks.
　　　現在是投資股票的最佳時機。
　　　B: That's one way of looking at it, but there are other things to consider.
　　　這是一種看法，但是還有很多事情需要考慮。

● 表示不同意 Expressing Disagreement

0416

正好相反，…。
On the contrary, ...

(替換) Quite the opposite, ...

(範例) **A:** Do you think it's too cold today?
你不覺得今天挺冷的嗎？

B: On the contrary, I think it's quite warm.
正好相反，我覺得今天相當暖和。

0417

門都沒有！
Never!

(替換) No way!

(範例) **A:** Do you want to dance with me? 你想和我去跳舞嗎？
B: Never! 門都沒有！

0418

你不是當真的吧！
You can't be serious!

(替換) You can't mean that!

(範例) **A:** I want to quit school. 我想休學了。
B: You can't be serious! 你不是當真的吧！

0419

我不同意你…。
I can't go along with you on...

(替換) I can't agree with you on...

(範例) **A:** I think Jack is a bad guy. 我覺得傑克是個壞傢伙。
B: I can't go along with you on that. 我不同意你的觀點。

0420

我認為這是沒有道理的。
I don't think that's reasonable.

(替換) I think it's unreasonable.

(範例) **A:** The boss said that we would lose our jobs if we were late even once.
老闆說，如果我們遲到一次就會失去這份工作。

B: I don't think that's reasonable.
我認為這是沒有道理的。

0421

我不這麼認為。
I don't think so.

(替換) I wouldn't say that.
That's not how I see it.

範例　A: Mr. Thomson is very cruel. 湯姆遜先生很殘酷。
B: I don't think so. 我不這麼認為。

0422　我不能說我贊同…。
I can't say that I share...

替換　I can't say that I concur with...

範例　A: David is a promising young man. 大衛是個有前途的青年。
B: I can't say that I share your opinion. 我不能說我贊同你的觀點。

0423　恐怕我不能同意…。
I'm afraid I have to disagree with...

替換　I'm afraid I can't agree with...

範例　A: The manager said that you should work in the sales department.
經理說你應該在業務部工作。
B: I'm afraid I have to disagree with him.
恐怕我不能同意他說的。

0424　我根本不相信…。
I'm not at all convinced that...

範例　A: Mr. Brown was murdered by his wife.
布朗先生是被他太太謀殺的。
B: I'm not at all convinced that she's guilty.
我根本不相信她有罪。

提示　convinced [kən'vɪnst] *adj.* 確信的；深信的
murder ['mɝdɚ] *v.* 謀殺；兇殺

0425　你在開玩笑吧？
Are you kidding?

範例　A: I'm getting married next week. 下週我就要結婚了。
B: Are you kidding? 你在開玩笑吧？

0426　不要胡說！
Come off it!

範例　A: Our company is going bankrupt. 我們公司要破產了。
B: Come off it! 不要胡說。

提示　bankrupt ['bæŋkrʌpt] *adj.* 破產的

| 0427 | 我看不出有什麼理由。
I don't see why. |

範例 A: The boss fired that guy. 老闆解雇了那個傢伙。
B: I don't see why. 我看不出有什麼理由。

● 承認有錯 Admitting One Is Wrong

| 0428 | 好吧，算你對。
All right, you win. |

替換 OK, you're the expert.
Oh, yes, how silly of me!

範例 A: See? Even Mom agrees with me! 看吧，連媽媽都同意我的想法。
B: All right, you win. 好吧，算你對。

提示 expert ['ɛkspɚt] n. 專家；行家

| 0429 | 對不起，我弄錯了。
Sorry, my mistake. |

替換 Sorry, I slipped up there.
Sorry, I got it all wrong.

範例 A: These figures are wrong! 這些數字是錯的！
B: Sorry, my mistake. 對不起，我弄錯了。

| 0430 | 在這點上我也許錯了。
Perhaps I'm wrong here. |

範例 A: Perhaps I'm wrong here. 在這點上我也許錯了。
B: No harm done. Next time try harder. 沒關係。下次努力做好就行了。

| 0431 | 也許我錯了。
Maybe I'm wrong. |

範例 A: Maybe I'm wrong. 也許我錯了。
B: It's OK. You're only human. 沒關係，你畢竟也是凡人。

| 0432 | 哦，是的，我本來應該要記得...。
Oh, yes, I should've remembered that... |

範例 A: Oh, yes, I should've remembered that you need that book.
哦，是的，我本來應該要記得你需要那本書。
B: Never mind. I won't need it until tomorrow.
沒關係，我明天才用。

0433 哦，是的，你是對的。
Oh, yes, you're right.

範例 A: The leaf turned yellow just like I said yesterday.
這片葉子就像我昨天說的那樣變黃了。
B: Oh, yes, you're right.
哦，是的，你是對的。

0434 現在想起來，…。
Come to think of it, ...

範例 A: Come to think of it, you were right to leave that place.
現在想起來，你離開那個地方是對的。
B: Of course I was.
當然了。

0435 對不起，我沒想到這點。
Sorry, I didn't think of that.

範例 A: Sorry, I didn't think of that. 對不起，我沒想到這點。
B: Not to worry. 別擔心。

0436 是的，對不起。你非常對。
Yes, sorry. You're quite right.

範例 A: Yes, sorry. You're quite right. 是的，對不起。你非常對。
B: Forget it. It can happen to the best of us. 忘了吧，這種事誰都難免。

0437 …我很可能錯了。
I may have been mistaken about...

範例 A: I may have been mistaken about this problem.
這個問題我很可能錯了。
B: That's OK.
沒關係。

0438 我得承認…。
I must admit that I...

範例 **A:** I must admit that I didn't take all factors into account.
我得承認我沒有把所有因素都考慮在內。
B: It doesn't matter.
沒關係。

0439
我一定是⋯。
I must have...

範例 **A:** I must have mistaken you for Kate. 我一定是把你當成凱特了。
B: Don't worry about it. 沒關係。

0440
我想我忽略了⋯。
I think I overlooked...

替換 I must have failed to consider...

範例 **A:** I think I overlooked that point. 我想我忽略了那一點。
B: Don't think any more about it. 不要再去想它了。

提示 overlook [ˌovɚˈluk] *v.* 看漏；忽略

● 達成共識 Reaching Agreement

0441
就這樣了。
That's that.

替換 So that's that, then.
OK, it's agreed then.
Well, it's settled then.
We all agree then.
We are all agreed, then.

範例 **A:** We've all come to a decision. 我們已經有所決定了。
B: That's that. 就這樣了。

0442
看來我們達成共識了。
It seems we're all in agreement.

替換 We seem to be thinking the same now.

範例 **A:** It seems we're all in agreement. 看來我們達成共識了。
B: Good. 太好了。

0443

看來我們在…上達成共識了。
It looks like we've all agreed on...

(替換)
We appear/seem to agree on...
We seem to be in complete agreement on...
We seem to have come to a complete agreement on...

(範例)
A: I think your plan is feasible.
　　我認為你的計畫可行。
B: It looks like we've all agreed on what to do.
　　看來我們在下一步該做什麼上達成共識了。

(提示) feasible ['fizəbl] *adj.* 可行的

0444

很高興我們終於取得共識。
I'm glad we've come together at last.

(替換) I'm glad that we have finally reached an agreement.

(範例)
A: I'm glad we've come together at last. 很高興我們終於取得共識。
B: I'm glad, too. 我也是。

0445

那麼好吧。
All right, then.

(範例)
A: Let's relax, OK? 讓我們放鬆一下，好嗎？
B: All right, then. We'll meet in the club. 那麼好吧。我們在俱樂部見。

0446

那麼，我們對…都很滿意了，是嗎？
So we're all satisfied with..., aren't we?

(範例)
A: So we're all satisfied with the plan, aren't we?
　　那麼，我們對這個計畫都很滿意了，是嗎？
B: Sure we are.
　　當然了。

0447

我們似乎已經掃除所有障礙並取得共識了。
We seem to have removed every obstacle and reached an agreement.

(範例)
A: We seem to have removed every obstacle and reached an agreement.
　　我們似乎已經掃除所有障礙並取得共識了。
B: Congratulations.
　　恭喜！

103

| 提示 | obstacle [ˈɑbstək!] *n.* 障礙；妨害物 |

0448 那麼，我們基本上意見一致了。
So, we're basically in agreement on that.

範例
A: That's just what I have been thinking about.
　　這也是我一直在考慮的。
B: So, we're basically in agreement on that.
　　那麼，我們基本上意見一致了。

0449 我可以說我們對這個計畫都滿意了嗎？
Can I say that we're all satisfied with the plan?

範例
A: Can I say that we're all satisfied with the plan?
　　我可以說我們對這個計畫都滿意了嗎？
B: Yes.
　　是的。

0450 那麼，我們還爭論什麼呢？
So, what are we arguing about?

範例
A: I also think that your proposal is reasonable.
　　我也認為你的建議是合理的。
B: So, what are we arguing about?
　　那麼，我們還爭論什麼呢？

0451 很好，每個人似乎都滿意這安排。
Good. The arrangement seems to have satisfied everyone.

範例
A: Good. The arrangement seems to have satisfied everyone.
　　很好，每個人似乎都滿意這安排。
B: Let's have a drink.
　　讓我們喝一杯吧。

提示 arrangement [əˈrendʒmənt] *n.* 安排

2.4　約定 Appointments

在現代社會與人來往，見面前先約定好是很重要的。見經理、上司、教授、醫生要先預約，洽公談話要先約定，私人拜訪也要先約好，甚至去理髮店也要預約。根據階層差別、時間早晚、關係遠近，約定的方式有所不同。但是徵得對方的同意，確定見面的時間則是交往中通常要遵守的準則。預先約定見面可以當面進行，也可以通過電話、書信、傳真或電子郵件進行。與重要人物預約要提前，與教授或系主任預約要透過祕書，絕對不可無預約就貿然闖入。特殊場合未預約拜訪，要表示歉意，並說明原因。

由於某些特殊原因而無法如期赴約，應該及時通知對方，讓對方有時間調整自己的計畫。

● 事先約定 Making Appointments

(020)

0452	…你有空嗎？ **Are you free...?**
替換	Are you going to be busy...? Are you doing anything special...?
範例	**A:** Are you free tomorrow? Let's go have a picnic, OK? 明天你有空嗎？我們去野餐怎麼樣？ **B:** Great idea. 好主意。
0453	你…剛好有空嗎？ **Do you happen to be free...?**
替換	Are you doing anything..., by any chance?
範例	**A:** Do you happen to be free this evening? 你今晚剛好有空嗎？ **B:** Not really. 沒有。
0454	…能見我嗎？ **Can...see me...?**
替換	Could...see me...? Will...be able to see me...?
範例	**A:** Can Mr. David see me today? 大衛先生今天能見我嗎？ **B:** Sorry, I'm afraid not. 對不起，恐怕不行。
0455	不知…是否方便見我們？ **I wonder if it would be convenient for...to meet us...?**

範例 A: I wonder if it would be convenient for Mr. Lee to meet us tomorrow? 不知李先生明天是否方便見我們？
B: Will Sunday do? 星期天怎麼樣？

0456

我想找你…。
I thought I'd drop over...

替換 I'd like to meet/see you...
I'd like to call on you...
I'd like to drop by...

範例 A: I thought I'd drop over for a drink. 我想找你喝一杯。
B: Will tomorrow night do? 明晚行嗎？

0457

我想和你約見面。
I'd like to arrange an appointment with you.

替換 I'd like to make an appointment with you.

範例 A: I'd like to arrange an appointment with you. 我想和你約見面。
B: How is five o'clock? 五點鐘怎麼樣？

0458

我們約一個時間…。
Let's make a date to...

範例 A: Let's make a date to see the movie. 我們約一個時間去看電影吧。
B: Good idea. 好主意。

0459

我想…見你，行嗎？
I hope I can meet you...Is that alright?

替換 Can I see you...?

範例 A: I hope I can meet you at my office tomorrow morning. Is that alright? 我想明早在辦公室見你，行嗎？
B: It's OK. 好的。

0460

不知…能否安排一個時間給我？
I wonder if...could fit me in...?

範例 A: I wonder if the dentist could fit me in tomorrow?
不知牙醫明天能否安排一個時間給我？
B: Let's try.
我們試一下吧。

0461	我可以定個時間見面嗎？ **May I make an appointment?**
替換	May I have an appointment with you?
範例	**A:** May I make an appointment? 我可以定個時間見面嗎？ **B:** Sure. 當然了。

0462	不知…能否給我…？ **I wonder if...could spare me...?**
範例	**A:** I wonder if the manager could spare me ten minutes? 不知經理能否給我十分鐘的時間？ **B:** Sorry. He's booked up today. 對不起，他今天沒空。

0463	不知…能否和我商量…？ **I wonder if...could talk with me about...?**
範例	**A:** Is there anything I can help you with? 有什麼可以幫你的嗎？ **B:** I wonder if Mr. Green could talk with me about the meeting tomorrow? 不知格林先生能否和我商量明天會面的事情？

● 改變約定 Changing Appointments

0464	我們延遲一點時間好嗎？ **Can we make it a little later?**
替換	Could we put it off until...? Let's postpone our date for..., if you don't mind.
範例	**A:** Can we make it a little later? 我們延遲一點時間好嗎？ **B:** Fine by me. 可以。
提示	postpone [post'pon] *v.* 使延期；延遲

0465	對不起，我不能來…。 **Sorry, but I can't join you for...**
範例	**A:** Sorry, but I can't join you for the evening party. 對不起，我不能來你的晚宴。 **B:** That's really a pity. 真遺憾。

0466	我得延期…。 **I'll have to take a rain check on...**

範例　A: I'll have to take a rain check on that. 我得延期那件事情。
B: OK. 好的。

0467	我們得把約會往後延一下。 **We'll have to make our appointment a little later.**

範例　A: We'll have to make our appointment a little later.
我們得把約會往後延一下。
B: What a shame!
真遺憾。

0468	很抱歉造成你的不便，但我們不得不將…往後延。 **I'm sorry to inconvenience you, but we have to post-pone...**

範例　A: I'm sorry to inconvenience you, but we have to postpone our meeting. 很抱歉造成你的不便，但我們不得不將我們的會議往後延。
B: I'm sorry to hear that. 很遺憾聽到這消息。

0469	我們可以約別的時間見面嗎？ **Could you make it some other time?**

範例　A: Could you make it some other time? 我們可以約別的時間見面嗎？
B: OK. 好的。

0470	恐怕我們得改變約會的時間。 **I'm afraid we'll have to change our appointment.**

範例　A: I'm afraid we'll have to change our appointment.
恐怕我們得改變約會的時間。
B: Will next week do?
下週行嗎？

0471	我們明天不在…見面，改在…見面怎麼樣？ **Could we meet at...instead of...tomorrow?**

範例　A: Could we meet at eight instead of seven tomorrow?
我們明天不在七點見面，改在八點見面怎麼樣？
B: That's OK.
好的。

0472
我們得另外約時間，可以嗎？
We'll have to make it some other time. Is that all right?

範例
A: We'll have to make it some other time. Is that all right?
我們得另外約時間，可以嗎？
B: Yes. Will tomorrow do?
可以，明天行嗎？

0473
萬一我不能赴約，我…見你。
If by any chance I don't make it, I'll see you...

範例
A: If by any chance I don't make it, I'll see you sometime next month.
萬一我不能赴約，我下個月再找個時間見你。
B: OK.
好的。

0474
我…有急事，約會只能取消。
I have something urgent..., so the appointment will have to be canceled.

範例
A: I have something urgent tomorrow, so the appointment will have to be canceled. 我明天有急事，約會只能取消。
B: It doesn't matter. 沒關係。

0475
對不起，但是出現意外了。
I'm terribly sorry, but something unexpected came up.

範例
A: I'm terribly sorry, but something unexpected came up.
對不起，但是發生意外了。
B: That's alright.
沒關係。

提示
unexpected [ˌʌnɪkˈspɛktɪd] *adj.* 意外的；想不到的

0476
不知我們能否把約會時間改在…？
I wonder if we could change the time of our meeting to...?

範例
A: I wonder if we could change the time of our meeting to next Monday?
不知我們能否把約會時間改在下週一？
B: Good.
好的。

2.5　爭論 Arguing

　　爭論是指雙方對某事情意見不同時，所提出來的疑問或者意見。由於西方國家的個人主義高漲，因此若有爭論發生時，往往也會直接對對方表達心裡所想的話，但是在使用這類語言表達時，要特別小心，因為表達方式可以直接或者婉轉，對於陌生人或者不熟的人，還是要採取婉轉的表達方式才好。

021

0477	你難道不明白…？ **Don't you see that...?**

替換	Don't you think that...?
範例	**A:** Don't you see that the payment should be made with a check? 你難道不明白貨款應以支票支付？ **B:** Yes, I can see that. 好，我能理解。

0478	這毫不相關。 **That's irrelevant.**

替換	That's beside the point. That's off the point.
範例	**A:** We have to deal with the time problem. 我們得解決時間問題。 **B:** That's irrelevant. 這毫不相關。
提示	irrelevant [ɪ'rɛləvənt] *adj.* 不相關的

0479	你說…是什麼意思呢？ **What do you mean by...?**

範例	**A:** What do you mean by your theory of the role of TV education for children? 你說電視扮演教育孩子的角色是什麼意思呢？ **B:** I mean that it teaches children a great many things. 我是說電視可以教給小孩子很多東西。

0480	你似乎忘記…。 **You seem to be forgetting...**

替換　You've missed the whole point...

範例　**A:** Where is Tom at present?
　　　湯姆現在在哪裡？
　　　B: You seem to be forgetting that he went abroad.
　　　你似乎忘記他出國去了。

0481　這沒道理。
That makes no sense.

範例　**A:** Maybe we have to wait another two days. 也許我們得再等上兩天。
　　　B: That makes no sense. 這沒道理。

0482　你到底想表達什麼？
What point are you making?

替換　What (exactly) are you getting at?
　　　What's the point?
　　　What are you driving at?

範例　**A:** What point are you making? 你到底想表達什麼？
　　　B: I wonder if you can explain it more clearly. 你可否再詳細解釋嗎？

0483　我不太理解你的意思。
I can't quite see your point.

替換　I'm completely mixed up.
　　　I'm completely confused/mistaken.

範例　**A:** How do you feel about my explanation? 你對我的解釋有何感想？
　　　B: I can't quite see your point. 我不太理解你的意思。

提示　explanation [ˌɛksplə'neʃən] *n.* 解釋；說明

0484　這太荒謬了。
That's absurd.

替換　That's ridiculous.

範例　**A:** I think George should be the boss. 我認為喬治應該是老闆。
　　　B: That's absurd. 這太荒謬了。

提示　absurd [əb'sɝd] *adj.* 荒謬的；可笑的

2.6 相信 **Beliefs**

聽到某些消息，人們可能會相信，也可能會產生懷疑。表達相信或懷疑可以用不同的句型。例如：

疑問句：Are you kidding me?

否定句：I don't believe a word of it.

肯定句：It's too good to be true.

附加問句：You're not serious, are you?

祈使句：Get out of here.

● 表示相信 Expressing Belief

0485

看來可信。
That sounds true.

022

(替換)
It looks credible.
It seems credible/believable.

(範例)
A: I think John got a job.
　　我認為約翰有工作了。
B: That sounds true. He did graduate last month.
　　看來可信。他的確上個月畢業了。

(提示)
credible ['krɛdəbḷ] *adj.* 可信的；可靠的
believable [bɪ'livəbḷ] *adj.* 可信的

0486

這我相信。
I can believe that.

(替換)
That's what I believe.
That can be believed.
I think it's believable.

(範例)
A: Jack! I heard that Bill made $5 million this year.
　　傑克，據說比爾今年賺了五百萬美元。
B: I can believe that. His business is booming.
　　這我相信。他的生意很好。

(提示)
boom [bum] *v.* 興隆；繁榮

0487	我相信你的話。 **I'll take your word for it.**

替換
I believe what you said.
I don't doubt you.
I think what you said is true.
I have the conviction that he's telling the truth.

範例
A: There's going to be a thunderstorm. 即將有大雷雨。
B: I'll take your word for it. 我相信你的話。

提示
conviction [kən'vɪkʃən] *n*. 深信；確信

0488	我可以相信…。 **I can trust that...**

替換
I'm in the belief that...
It is my belief that...
I have confidence that...
I'm convinced that...

範例
A: Jane said her car can go 200 miles per hour.
珍說她的車一小時能跑 200 公里。
B: I can trust that she's telling the truth.
我可以相信她說的是真的。

提示
convinced [kən'vɪnst] *adj*. 確信的；深信的

0489	我相信…。 **I believe...**

替換
I feel confident of...

範例
A: Tom said that there is also a Wal-Mart in Beijing.
湯姆說北京也有個沃爾瑪。
B: I believe him.
我相信他的話。

0490	我完全相信…。 **I can well believe...**

替換
I have perfect trust in...
I have complete faith in...

範例
A: I never said anything of the sort. 我從來沒有說過這類事情。
B: I can well believe that. 我完全相信。

0491	我相信無疑。 **I can easily believe that.**

範例　A: There's not a student in this school who doesn't study hard.
　　　　這個學校的學生沒有一個不努力學習的。
　　　　B: I can easily believe that.
　　　　我相信無疑。

0492	令人信服。 **It's convincing.**

範例　A: Tom's argument makes total sense, doesn't it?
　　　　湯姆的論據完全有理，對吧？
　　　　B: Yes. It's convincing.
　　　　是的，令人信服。

提示　convincing [kən'vɪnsɪŋ] *adj.* 使信服的

0493	我很相信…。 **I have much belief in...**

範例　A: George says that Marie is busy all the time. 喬治說瑪麗總是很忙。
　　　　B: I have much belief in him. 我很相信他。

0494	我想我完全相信…。 **I think I can give full credit to...**

範例　A: To tell the truth, I never talk about others behind their backs.
　　　　說實話，我從未在別人背後說三道四。
　　　　B: I think I can give full credit to your words.
　　　　我想我完全相信你的話。

0495	我想我相信…。 **I think I will accept...**

範例　A: Kate said that she would go on waiting for her boyfriend.
　　　　凱特說她會繼續等她的男朋友。
　　　　B: I think I will accept what she said.
　　　　我想我相信她的話。

● 表示不相信 Expressing Disbelief

0496
別開玩笑了。
No kidding.

(替換) Don't pull my leg.

(範例) **A:** Scientists say that people will be able to live on the moon in the future. 科學家們說人類將來能夠在月球上居住。
B: No kidding. 別開玩笑了。

(提示) scientist ['saɪəntɪst] *n.* 科學家；科學工作者

0497
別胡扯了！
Come off it.

(替換) Get out of here.
Don't talk trash!
Give me a break.

(範例) **A:** Did you know that Betty struck it rich in real estate?
你知道貝蒂經營房地產發了財嗎？
B: Come off it.
別胡扯了！

(提示) estate [ɪs'tet] *n.* 不動產；財產

0498
你一定是在開玩笑。
You must be joking.

(替換) You can't be serious.

(範例) **A:** I'm told that Professor Smith will continue to teach us next year.
聽說史密斯教授明年會繼續教我們。
B: You must be joking.
你一定是在開玩笑。

0499
我才不信呢！
Don't tell me!

(替換) Tell me another one!
That's what you say.
That story isn't good enough for me.
I don't think so.
I don't believe you.

I don't believe a word of it.
I refuse to believe that.
I know better than that.

範例 A: Richard asked for another chance. 理查要求再一次機會。
B: Don't tell me! 我才不信呢！

0500
別指望我會相信…。
Don't expect me to believe...

替換 You can't expect me to believe...

範例 A: Dr. Thompson said he could cure your daughter's disease.
湯姆森醫生說他能治好你女兒的病。
B: Don't expect me to believe him.
別指望我會相信他。

0501
我認為不太可能。
I think it's unlikely.

替換 I find that hard to believe.
I think it's hard to believe.

範例 A: Do you think he'll be here to help you? 你認為他會來這裡幫你嗎？
B: I think it's unlikely. 我認為不太可能。

0502
你是在開我玩笑吧？
Are you kidding me?

範例 A: I haven't got enough money right now. I'll pay your money back
next Monday. 我現在手頭不夠。我下周一還你錢吧。
B: Are you kidding me? 你是在開我玩笑吧？

0503
別傻了！
Don't be silly.

替換 Don't be ridiculous.

範例 A: I'm going to quit my job and join the circus.
我要辭掉工作加入馬戲團。
B: Don't be silly.
別傻了！

0504
你可別說…。
Don't tell me...

範例　**A:** John said he wanted to ask the dean about it.
　　　約翰說他想問一下系主任。
　　B: Don't tell me he did it.
　　　你可別說他真的這麼做了。

提示　dean [din] *n.* 系主任；教務長

0505　那是做夢。
Dream on.

範例　**A:** I think he will help me. 我想他會幫我的。
　　B: Dream on, Mary. 瑪麗，那是做夢。

0506　我不相信你的鬼話。
I don't buy it.

範例　**A:** Those magazines will be banned on campus.
　　　那些雜誌在學校會被禁止的。
　　B: I don't buy it.
　　　我不相信你的鬼話。

0507　聽你胡說！
Listen to you!

範例　**A:** He will come by for us at about six. 他會在六點左右來接我們。
　　B: Listen to you! 聽你胡說！

0508　你以為我會相信這樣的謊話嗎？
Do you think I'd believe a story like that?

範例　**A:** Do you think I'd believe a story like that?
　　　你以為我會相信這樣的謊話嗎？
　　B: But it's true.
　　　但是這是真的。

0509　那怎麼可能呢？
How is that possible?

範例　**A:** I think he will betray us. 我想他會背叛我們。
　　B: How is that possible? 那怎麼可能呢？

　betray [bɪˈtre] *v.* 出賣；背叛

0510
哪有這麼好的事。
It's too good to be true.

範例
A: Our boss will give us each a camera as a present.
我們老闆要給我們每人一台照相機作為禮物。
B: It's too good to be true.
哪有這麼好的事。

0511
你不是當真的，是嗎？
You're not serious, are you?

範例
A: I want to marry you. 我想和你結婚。
B: You're not serious, are you? 你不是當真的，是嗎？

0512
這不可能是真的。
It can't be true.

範例
A: I'm going to travel around the world. 我要去環遊世界。
B: It can't be true. 這不可能是真的。

0513
編得倒挺像。
That's a good one.

範例
A: I'm as poor as a church mouse now. 我現在一貧如洗。
B: That's a good one. 編得倒挺像。

提示
as poor as a church mouse【俚】一貧如洗；窮光蛋

2.7　確定 Certainty

有人說 "Life is full of uncertainties."。這是說我們的生活中充滿著許多的不確定。交談中，我們有時要確切了解某種資訊或某人的態度，有時要準確表達自己對事物的把握程度。英語中有很多表達確定和不確定的方法。

● 詢問是否確定 Asking if One Is Sure

0514
肯定嗎？
Are you sure?

（023）

(替換)
Really?
For sure?
You're sure?
Definitely?
Are you certain/positive?

(範例)
A: The engine is running nicely, and we can move out now.
引擎運轉得很好，我們可以開車啦。
B: Are you sure?
肯定嗎？

(提示) definitely ['dɛfənɪtlɪ] *adv.* 明確地；乾脆地

0515
你能肯定…嗎？
Are you sure as fate that...?

(替換)
Are you certain/positive/sure that...?
Can you be positive that...?
Can you say with any certainty that...?
Do you know for certain/sure that...?
Do you think you're confident that...?

(範例)
A: He won't leave his wife and son. 他不會離開妻子和兒子的。
B: Are you sure as fate that he won't? 你能肯定他不會這樣做嗎？

(提示) fate [fet] *n.* 結局；結果

0516
你相當確定嗎？
You're quite sure?

(替換) You're absolutely certain?

(範例)
A: He's taking advantage of me. 他正在利用我。
B: You're quite sure? 你相當確定嗎？

0517
你對…真的有把握嗎？
Can you really be certain...?

(替換) Can you really be sure...?

(範例)
A: Can you really be certain who he is? 你對他到底是誰真的有把握嗎？
B: Yes, I can. 是的，我有。

0518
對不起，不過你確定嗎？
Forgive me, but are you really certain?

| 替換 | Pardon me, but are you really certain about it? |

| 範例 | A: He spent $1,000 on this watch.
他花了一千美元買這手錶。
B: Forgive me, but are you really certain?
對不起，不過你確定嗎？ |

0519

對⋯還有疑問嗎？
Is there any room for doubt about...?

| 替換 | Is there any doubt about...? |

| 範例 | A: He's holding something back, isn't he? 他隱瞞了事情，是不是？
B: Is there any room for doubt about that? 對這還有疑問嗎？ |

| 提示 | hold sth. back 隱瞞（消息等） |

0520

對⋯你心中不存疑嗎？
Is there any doubt in your mind about...?

| 範例 | A: Is there any doubt in your mind about what he said?
對他的話，你心中不存疑嗎？
B: None at all.
一點兒也不。 |

0521

肯定沒錯嗎？
Is there no mistake?

| 範例 | A: You said he was taking advantage of me. Is there no mistake?
你是說他正在利用我。肯定沒錯嗎？
B: No.
是的。 |

0522

也許我誤解了，不過你有把握⋯嗎？
Perhaps I misunderstood, but are you quite certain about...?

| 範例 | A: Perhaps I misunderstood, but are you quite certain about what to do?
也許我誤解了，不過你有把握下一步該怎麼辦嗎？
B: Sure, I am.
當然了。 |

0523

我想你對⋯毫不懷疑吧。
I gather you have no doubt about...

A: I haven't seen him for a long time. He must be preparing for TOEFL.
　　我很久沒看到他了。他一定在準備托福考試。
B: I gather you have no doubt about that.
　　我想你對此事毫不懷疑吧。

● 表示確定 Expressing Certainty

0524	我敢斷定…。 **I bet...**

範例 **A:** Is he still in Paris? 他還在巴黎嗎？
B: Yes. But I bet he'll be back soon. 是的，但我敢斷定他很快就會回來。

0525	絕對沒錯。 **I'm absolutely certain.**

替換 I'm absolutely positive.

範例 **A:** Are you certain you put my bag on the rack?
　　你能肯定把我的包包放在行李架上了嗎？
B: I'm absolutely certain.
　　絕對沒錯。

0526	…肯定會…。 **It's a sure bet...**

替換 ...for sure.
It's a cinch...
It's quite certain that...

範例 **A:** Are you sure he will pass the exam? 你肯定他會通過考試嗎？
B: It's a sure bet he will make it. 他肯定會的。

提示 cinch [sɪntʃ] *n.* 有把握之事

0527	毫無疑問…。 **...and there's no mistake.**

替換 There is no mistake about it, ...
It's definite that...
It is a certainty that...

範例 **A:** Do you agree with her?
　　你同意她的意見嗎？

121

B: Sure. She's the boss and there's no mistake.
當然了。毫無疑問，她是老闆。

0528

我完全可以肯定。
I'm a hundred percent certain.

（替換）　I'm absolutely positive.

（範例）　**A:** Are you sure we'll be welcome? 你確定我們會受到歡迎嗎？
　　　　B: I'm a hundred percent certain. 我完全可以肯定。

0529

一定是這樣。
You bet it is.

（替換）　It must be.
　　　　It can't be otherwise.

（範例）　**A:** Is it possible that Tom will be our new monitor?
　　　　湯姆可能會是我們的新班長嗎？
　　　　B: You bet it is.
　　　　一定是這樣。

0530

這是毫無疑問的。
There is no doubt about that.

（替換）　That's for sure.
　　　　There's no question about it.
　　　　There's no room for doubt about it.
　　　　There can't be any doubt about that.
　　　　There's no doubt whatsoever about it.
　　　　There can't be any room for doubt about that.

（範例）　**A:** This is a business secret. Be cautious with it.
　　　　這是個商業機密，對此要謹慎。
　　　　B: There is no doubt about that.
　　　　這是毫無疑問的。

（提示）　cautious ['kɔʃəs] *adj.* 謹慎的；小心的

0531

…是毫無疑問的。
There can't be any doubt about...

（範例）　**A:** There can't be any doubt about our team's winning the upcoming tournament. 我們的隊伍將在之後的錦標賽中獲勝，這是毫無疑問的。
　　　　B: Is that for sure? 肯定嗎？

| 提示 | upcoming [ˈʌpˌkʌmɪŋ] *adj.* 即將來臨的；預定將要
tournament [ˈtɝnəmənt] *n.* 錦標賽；比賽 |

| 0532 | 肯定是。
That's for sure. |
| 範例 | A: He must be there in the dining room. 他一定在餐廳。
B: That's for sure. 肯定是。 |

0533	你可以肯定⋯。 **You can be sure about...**
替換	You may be certain of... You can rest assured of...
範例	A: He didn't turn up at the meeting last night. Maybe he didn't know about it. 昨天晚上他沒來開會。或許他不知道。 B: You can be sure about that. 你可以肯定是這樣。

0534	我認為⋯毫無疑問的。 **I don't think I have any doubt about...**
替換	I don't think there can be any doubt/question of...
範例	A: Are you sure you will win the game? 你確定會贏這場比賽嗎？ B: I don't think I have any doubt about that. 我認為這是毫無疑問的。

| 0535 | 我看沒問題。
I don't see any problem. |
| 範例 | A: Do you think we will finish it on time? 你覺得我們會按時完成嗎？
B: I don't see any problem. 我看沒問題。 |

0536	是的，肯定。 **Yes, really.**
替換	Yes, definitely.
範例	A: The car is beautiful! Do you think so? 這車好漂亮。你也這樣認為嗎？ B: Yes, really. 是的，肯定。

| 0537 | 他一定…。
He must... |

替換　He certainly...

範例　**A:** I can't find him in his office. 我在辦公室找不到他。
B: He must be out of town. 他一定是出城了。

| 0538 | 我肯定。
I'm sure. |

替換　I'm certain.
I'm quite convinced.

範例　**A:** Are you sure he will come back? 你肯定他會回來嗎？
B: I'm sure. 我肯定。

| 0539 | 這是顯而易見的事，不是嗎？
It's obvious, isn't it? |

範例　**A:** He must have read *The Old Man and the Sea*.
他一定讀過《老人與海》。
B: It's obvious, isn't it?
這是顯而易見的事，不是嗎？

提示　obvious ['ɑbvɪəs] *adj.* 明顯的；顯而易見的

| 0540 | 可以肯定…。
..., you bet. |

範例　**A:** He will win a prize for his thesis, you bet.
可以肯定他的論文一定會獲獎的。
B: It's really good news.
這真是個好消息。

提示　thesis ['θisɪs] *n.* 論文；論題

| 0541 | 我可以向你保證。
I give you my word on it. |

範例　**A:** Are you sure you can design the building well?
你肯定會把這座大樓設計好嗎？
B: I give you my word on it.
我可以向你保證。

● 表示不確定 Expressing Uncertainty

0542
這件事我不太有把握。
I'm not too sure of it.

（替換） I wouldn't be too sure about that.

（範例）
A: Is it definite that he will get a master's degree?
他肯定會得到碩士學位嗎？
B: I'm not too sure of it.
這件事我不太有把握。

0543
我不知道…。
I haven't a clue about...

（替換） I've no idea about...

（範例）
A: Do you know about his plan? 你知道他的計畫嗎？
B: I haven't a clue about what he will do. 我不知道他會做什麼。

0544
我沒有把握…。
I can't say for certain...

（替換）
I couldn't say, really, ...
I'm not certain...
I'm not sure...
I can't say with any certainty...

（範例）
A: I can't say for certain whom to invite. 我沒有把握要邀請誰。
B: What about your close friends? 你的好朋友怎麼樣？

0545
我不能肯定。
I'm not sure.

（替換）
I'm not certain.
I can't be sure/certain.
I can't say for certain.

（範例）
A: Is he honest? 他誠實嗎？
B: I'm not sure. 我不能肯定。

0546
我決定不了。
I can't decide.

（替換） I can't make up my mind.

範例
A: Which one do you like best? 你最喜歡哪一個？
B: I can't decide. 我決定不了。

0547
我不能判斷…。
I can't tell...

替換
I can't work out...

範例
A: Who do you want to be the new manager? 你想讓誰當新經理？
B: I can't tell who is more capable. 我不能判斷誰比較有能力。

0548
我覺得很難下結論。
I find it difficult to come to a conclusion.

替換
I find it difficult to draw a conclusion on that.

範例
A: I find it difficult to come to a conclusion. 我覺得很難下結論。
B: So do I. 我也是。

0549
恐怕我不能肯定…。
I'm afraid I can't be certain about...

替換
I'm afraid I can't be positive about...

範例
A: Will Mark be at the party? 馬克會去參加晚會嗎？
B: I'm afraid I can't be certain about that. 恐怕我不能肯定這件事。

0550
我根本無法確信。
I'm not at all convinced.

範例
A: I think environmental awareness is an important hallmark of social progress. 我認為環境意識是社會進步的一個重要象徵。
B: I'm not at all convinced. 我根本無法確信。

提示
hallmark ['hɔl,mɑrk] *n.* 特徵；標誌

0551
我根本不能肯定。
I'm not at all certain.

範例
A: It's an easy job, isn't it? 這個工作很簡單，不是嗎？
B: I'm not at all certain. 我根本不能肯定。

0552
我對…存疑。
I have my doubts about...

替換
There is some doubt in my mind about...

範例　A: I think he's from New York. 我認為他來自紐約。
B: I have my doubts about that. 我對此存疑。

0553　…仍然有些疑問。
There's still some doubt about...

替換　There's still some doubt as to...
There's still some doubt of...
There's still an element of doubt about...

範例　A: Do you think there is something wrong with my computer?
你覺得是不是我的電腦出了什麼問題？
B: There's still some doubt about that.
這仍然有些疑問。

提示　element ['ɛləmənt] *n.* 要素；成分

0554　難說。
It's hard to tell.

範例　A: Do you think he's the murderer?
你覺得他是兇手嗎？
B: It's hard to tell. He could be the man you're looking for.
難說，他可能是你正在找的人。

提示　murderer ['mɝdərɚ] *n.* 殺人犯；兇手

0555　我覺得腦子裡一團糟。
I'm in such a muddle.

範例　A: Are you clear about the result? 你對這樣的結果清楚嗎？
B: I'm in such a muddle. 我覺得腦子裡一團糟。

提示　muddle ['mʌdl] *n.* 頭腦混亂；糊塗

0556　我本來這麼想的。
I thought so.

範例　A: It must be John. He's changed his hairstyle.
一定是約翰，他換了髮型。
B: I thought so. But how come he looks so old?
我本來這麼想的。但是他怎麼看起來年紀這麼大呢？

0557　我們聽天由命吧。
Let's leave it to chance.

127

範例 A: Let's leave it to chance. 我們聽天由命吧。
B: OK. 好吧。

0558 我實在沒法判斷。
I really can't tell.

範例 A: Is that person with long hair a man or woman?
那個長頭髮的人是男還是女？
B: I really can't tell.
我實在沒法判斷。

0559 我想可能是…吧。
I suppose it could be...

範例 A: Who will be our new manager? 誰將會是我們的新經理？
B: I suppose it could be Mary. 我想可能是瑪麗吧。

0560 我想那也許是…之類的。
I think it was...or something like that.

範例 A: What book did Tom buy yesterday?
昨天湯姆買了什麼書？
B: I think it was a bestseller or something like that.
我想也許是暢銷書之類的。

提示 bestseller [ˌbɛst'sɛlɚ] *n.* 暢銷書

0561 我覺得…，不過我可能不對。
I have a feeling that..., but I may be wrong.

範例 A: I have a feeling that he found the right person, but I may be wrong.
我覺得他已經找到了那個人，不過我可能不對。
B: Oh, really?
真的嗎？

2.8 比較 Comparing

　　沒有比較，就不能鑑別。只有以同類事物為參照，我們才能衡量好壞、強弱、大小、新舊等。英語中有同級比較、比較級和最高級之分，三者既有區別，又有相關。即便句法差別很大的句子，有時卻可以表達相同的概念。

024

0562
…比不上…。
...isn't a bit like...

(替換) ...has nothing on...

(範例) **A:** Chicago isn't a bit like New York. 芝加哥比不上紐約。
B: Yeah. 是的。

0563
在…方面，…當然比不上…。
...is no match for...in...

(替換) ...is surely not to be compared to...in...
...can't match...in...

(範例) **A:** Jane is no match for Helen in music.
在音樂方面，珍當然比不上海倫。
B: I think so, too.
我也這麼認為。

(提示) match [mætʃ] *n. v.* 敵得過；比得上

0564
總體來說，…。
On the whole, ...

(替換) By and large, ...

(範例) **A:** Who is cleverer between the two boys? 這兩個男孩誰更聰明一些？
B: On the whole, Jim is brighter. 總體來說，吉姆更聰明一些。

0565
和…相比，…。
Compared to..., ...

(替換) In comparison to..., ...

(範例) **A:** Compared to other students, he's more diligent.
和其他學生相比，他更勤奮一些。
B: How do you know that?
你怎麼知道的？

(提示) comparison [kəmˈpærəsn̩] *n.* 比較
diligent [ˈdɪlɪdʒənt] *adj.* 勤勉的；用功的

0566
我認為…比不上…。
I consider...to be inferior to...

(替換) | I don't think...can equal...

(範例) | A: Do you like desktop computers?
你喜歡桌上型電腦嗎？
B: I consider them to be inferior to notebooks.
我認爲它比不上筆記型電腦。

0567

我認爲…在…上要勝過…。
My assessment is that...has an advantage over...in...

(替換) | My judgment is that...is superior to...in...

(範例) | A: Which piece of cloth do you like better, yours or mine?
我們倆的這兩塊布，你比較喜歡哪一個？
B: My assessment is that my piece of cloth has an advantage over yours in color.
我認爲我的布在顏色上要勝過你的。

(提示) | assessment [ə'sɛsmənt] *n.* 評估

0568

我不明白你怎麼能把…和…相提並論。
I don't see how you can talk about...and...in the same breath.

(範例) | A: I don't like prose or novels. 我不喜歡散文或小說。
B: I don't see how you can talk about prose and novels in the same breath. 我不明白你怎麼能把散文和小說相提並論。

(提示) | prose [proz] *n.* 散文

0569

…比…略勝一籌。
...is one up on...

(範例) | A: Who is better? 誰更好一些？
B: Mary is one up on Helen. 瑪麗比海倫略勝一籌。

0570

…可沒哪一點比…好。
There's no way...is better than...

(範例) | A: Which do you like better, walking or cycling?
散步和騎自行車，你比較喜歡哪一個？
B: There's no way walking is better than cycling.
散步可沒哪一點比騎自行車好。

0571	你壓根沒法把…和…相比。 **You just can't compare...and...**
範例	**A:** Which city do you like better, London or Birmingham? 倫敦和伯明罕，你比較喜歡哪一個？ **B:** You just can't compare London and Birmingham. 你壓根沒法把倫敦和伯明罕相比。

0572	…跟…一樣…。 **...as...as...**
範例	**A:** What are you doing? 你在幹什麼？ **B:** I'm looking out of the window. Look! A man is running as fast as that truck. 我正往窗外看。快看！有個人跑得跟那輛卡車一樣快。

0573	…不再是…了。 **...is no longer the same...**
範例	**A:** Kate is no longer the same girl she was five years ago. 凱特不再是五年前的那個女孩了。 **B:** I think so, too. 我也這麼認為。

0574	…幾乎跟…一樣。 **...is almost equal to...**
範例	**A:** Do you think she dances well? 你覺得她跳得好嗎？ **B:** She is almost equal to May in dancing. 她跳得幾乎跟梅一樣（好）。

0575	…可以和最好的媲美。 **...is comparable to the best.**
範例	**A:** What do you think of her novel? 你認為她的小說怎麼樣？ **B:** It's comparable to the best. 它可以和最好的媲美。
提示	comparable ['kɑmpərəbl] *adj.* 可比較的；比得上的

0576	我一般認為…比…更…。 **I generally find...more...than...**
範例	**A:** I generally find reading more rewarding than watching TV. 我一般認為閱讀比看電視更有用。 **B:** Really? I don't think so. 真的嗎？我可不這麼認為。

0577
如果你拿⋯和⋯相比，後者更⋯。
If you compare...with..., the latter is more...

範例
A: Who is more hardworking, Jane or John?
誰更努力，珍還是約翰？
B: If you compare Jane with John, the latter is more hardworking.
如果你拿珍和約翰相比，後者更努力。

0578
這⋯得多了。
It's much more...

範例
A: Try to be punctual. It's much more important than anything else.
儘量做到守時。這比其他事情重要得多了。
B: OK.
好的。

提示
punctual ['pʌŋktʃuəl] *adj.* 守時的；準時的

0579
和⋯相比，⋯顯得⋯。
...look quite...compared to...

範例
A: You look quite mature compared to your classmates.
和你同學相比，你顯得很成熟。
B: Really?
真的嗎？

提示
mature [mə'tjʊr] *adj.* 成熟的；理智的

0580
實際上，在⋯方面，無人能和⋯相提並論。
Actually no one can beat..in...

範例
A: Her English is quite good.
她的英語不錯。
B: Actually no one can beat her in English.
實際上，在英語方面，無人能和她相提並論。

0581
總體來說，⋯比⋯更⋯。
All in all, ...more...than...

範例
A: Do you think he's better?
你不覺得他更好了嗎？
B: All in all, he's more experienced than he was two months ago.
總體來說，他比兩個月前更有經驗了。

0582	我不認為…有什麼比…更…。 **I don't consider...to be in any way more...than...**
範例	A: I like bowling very much. 我非常喜歡保齡球。 B: I don't consider bowling to be in any way more interesting than reading. 我不認為保齡球有什麼比閱讀更有趣。

0583	…不如…。 **...is less...than...**
範例	A: Mary dances much better than Susan, doesn't she? 瑪麗跳舞跳得比蘇珊好，不是嗎？ B: Yes. But Mary is less diligent than Susan in terms of studying. 是的，但是在學習方面，瑪麗不如蘇珊勤奮。

0584	…遠比…更…。 **...is incomparably more...than...**
範例	A: Your handwriting is incomparably more beautiful than his. 你的字跡遠比他的更漂亮。 B: Thank you. 謝謝你。
提示	incomparably [ɪnˈkɑmpərəblɪ] *adv.* 無比地；無敵地

2.9 理解 Comprehension

　　言語溝通就是要讓人理解所談的內容，因此表達時要注意思路清晰、語言準確。對內容有疑問時，還要注意去確認內容。

● 確認理解內容 Confirming Comprehension

025

0585	如果我沒弄錯的話，…。 **If I see your point right, then...**
替換	If I've got it right, then... If I got the picture, then... If I understand right, ...

If I follow you correctly, then...?
If I perceive your meaning correctly, then...?
If I understand you rightly, ...?
If I take your point rightly, ...?

範例 **A:** If I see your point right, then you don't agree with her.
如果我沒弄錯的話，你不同意她的意見。
B: That's right.
當然了。

提示 perceive [pɚ'siv] *v.* 理解

0586
換句話說…，對嗎？
In other words, ..., right?

範例 **A:** In other words, you don't want to take part in the activity, right?
換句話說，你不想參加這項活動，對嗎？
B: Whatever you say.
隨你怎麼說。

0587
總歸一句…。
So what it boils down to is...

替換 So the basic idea is that...?

範例 **A:** So what it boils down to is you don't believe me.
總歸一句，你不相信我。
B: That's right.
沒錯。

0588
那麼你的意思是…，對嗎？
So what you mean is..., right?

替換 So what you intend to say is that...?
So what you're really saying is... Right?
You mean... Right?
Do you intend to say that...?
Do you mean...?

範例 **A:** So what you mean is you will go instead of me tomorrow, right?
那麼你的意思是，明天你要去，而不是我，對嗎？
B: Yes.
是的。

0589

對不起，我不太明白你的意思。你是說…？
Sorry, I don't quite get you. Do you mean...?

(替換) I'm sorry, I'm not sure I get the gist of what you said. Do you mean...?

(範例) A: Sorry, I don't quite get you. Do you mean your son never comes to see you except to ask for money?
對不起，我不太明白你的意思。你是說，你兒子除了跟你要錢之外，從來沒有來看過你嗎？
B: Yes.
是的。

(提示) gist [dʒɪst] *n.* 要點；主旨

0590

對不起，我不太明白這意思，是不是說…？
Sorry, I don't quite get the point. Does it mean...?

(替換) Sorry, I'm not clear on what you said. Does it mean...?
I'm not certain I've grasped what you meant. Is it that...?

(範例) A: Sorry, I don't quite get the point. Does it mean all the people who live there know him quite well?
對不起，我不太明白這意思，是不是說所有住在那裡的人都很了解他？
B: No. I'm afraid you've misunderstood me.
不是，恐怕你誤解我了。

(提示) grasp [græsp] *v.* 理解；領會

0591

這是說…，對嗎？
That means..., right?

(替換) Does that mean...?
So that means...?

(範例) A: That means nobody is responsible for it, right?
這是說沒人會對此負責，對嗎？
B: Yes. That's right.
是的，沒錯。

0592

…我這麼說對嗎？
Am I to understand that...?

(替換) So am I right in saying...?
Would I be correct in supposing...?
Would I be right in saying...?

A: Am I to understand that nothing happened last night?
昨晚什麼也沒發生，我這麼說對嗎？
B: That's right.
當然了。

0593 如果我說…是不是誤解你？
Would I be mistaken if I say...?

 A: Life here is quite different.
這裡的生活很不同。
B: Would I be mistaken if I say you haven't got used to the life here?
如果我說你還沒習慣這裡的生活，是不是誤解你？

0594 我不清楚我是否聽懂了你的意思。你是不是說…？
I'm not sure if I'm following you. Do you mean that...?

 A: I'm not sure if I'm following you. Do you mean that you have never heard of it?
我不清楚我是否聽懂了你的意思。你是不是說你從來沒有聽過這件事？
B: That's correct.
是的。

0595 請原諒我有點遲鈍，不過我不確定是否理解了，這是不是說…？
I'm sorry if I'm being a little slow, but I'm not sure I understand. Do you mean...?

 A: I'm sorry if I'm being a little slow, but I'm not sure I understand. Do you mean the best he can do is to apologize?
請原諒我有點遲鈍，不過我不確定是否理解了，這是不是說他所能做的只是道歉？
B: Yes, of course.
當然了。

0596 那麼…。
So...

 A: The boss is pushing again.
老闆又在催了。
B: So we'd better finish the job as soon as possible.
那麼我們得儘快完成這項任務了。

| 0597 | 我可以弄清楚一件事嗎？你認為…，是不是這個意思？
Can I get one thing clear? Do you think...? |

範例 **A:** Can I get one thing clear? Do you think I don't know why I was fired?
我可以弄清楚一件事嗎？你認為我還不知道我為什麼被解雇，是不是這個意思？
B: Sorry. You must have misunderstood me.
對不起，你一定是誤解我了。

| 0598 | 我只是想搞清楚剛才說的話：…。
Just to be quite clear about what's just been said, ...? |

範例 **A:** Just to be quite clear about what's just been said, you knew nothing about Japanese before you came here, right?
我只是想搞清楚剛才說的話：你來這裡之前一句日語也不會說，是嗎？
B: No, I didn't.
是的，我不會說。

| 0599 | 這似乎是說…。
The implication seems to be... |

替換 That seems to be tantamount to saying...

範例 **A:** The implication seems to be that neither of the jobs is important.
這似乎是說，這兩份工作都不重要。
B: That's not what I mean.
我不是這個意思。

提示 implication [ˌɪmplɪˈkeʃən] *n.* 含意；暗示
tantamount [ˈtæntəˌmaʊnt] *adj.* 同等的；相當於（+ to）

● 詢問是否明白 Asking if Someone Understands

| 0600 | 明白了嗎？
OK? |

替換 See?
Understand?
Get it?
Got that?
OK so far?

See what I mean?
Get the picture?
Are you with me?
Got the message?
Have you got it right?
Know what I mean?
Know what I'm driving/getting at?
Know what I'm trying to say?
Do you get/follow me?
Do you see my point?
Do you see/get/know what I mean?
Do you get the picture?
Do you understand what I said?
Can you make sense of what I said?
Did you catch my meaning?
Did you grasp the point of what I said?
Is that clear to you?
That's clear, isn't it?
You get it, don't you?

範例 **A:** We need you at the meeting. OK? 我們需要你出席會議，明白了嗎？
B: Sure. I will be there on time. 當然，我會準時到達。

0601
對吧？
Right?

替換 Yeah?

範例 **A:** We're totally different people. Right?
我們是完全不同的兩個人。對吧？
B: You're quite right. I think we have nothing in common.
你說得太對了。我想我們之間毫無共同點。

0602
明白了嗎？
Does that make sense?

範例 **A:** This is how to do it. Does that make sense? 就這樣做。明白了嗎？
B: Oh, yes. 哦，是的。

0603
你不明白嗎？
Don't you get it?

| 範例 | A: It's a trick. Don't you get it? 這是個惡作劇,你不明白嗎? |
| | B: A trick? I feel like such a fool. 惡作劇?我覺得我真像個笨蛋。 |

0604 …如果你明白我的意思。
.., if you see what I mean.

替換	..., if you get my point.
	..., if you catch/get my drift.
	..., if you understand what I mean.
範例	A: That girl's trouble, if you see what I mean.
	那女孩是個麻煩,如果你明白我的意思。
	B: Why?
	爲什麼?

0605 我想我說得很清楚吧!
I hope that's clear.

替換	I hope I've made myself clear.
範例	A: We will meet on the day when I give you the material. I hope that's clear. 我們會在我交給你材料的那天碰面。我想我說得很清楚吧!
	B: Yes, it is. 當然了。

0606 我說得清楚了嗎?
Do I make myself clear?

替換	Have I made myself clear?
	Am I making myself clear?
	Did I make everything clear?
範例	A: I want to buy some CDs! Do I make myself clear?
	我想買一些CD!我說得清楚了嗎?
	B: Yes, you do.
	是,很清楚。

0607 如果你還有什麼不明白的地方,請提出來。
If there's anything you're still not clear on, please say so.

替換	If there's still something you don't understand, please let me know.
範例	A: If there's anything you're still not clear on, please say so.
	如果你還有什麼不明白的地方,請提出來。
	B: I'm OK.
	沒有了。

0608
這麼說你明白我的意思了嗎？
Can I say that you understand what I mean?

範例
A: Go straight down the street, and turn right at the second crossing. Can I say that you understand what I mean?
沿大街一直走，在第二個十字路口向右轉。這麼說你明白我的意思了嗎？
B: Yes, many thanks.
是的，謝謝。

0609
我不知道我是否說清楚了。
I don't know if I'm making myself clear.

範例
A: You still seem lost. I don't know if I'm making myself clear.
你似乎仍然不解。我不知道我是否說清楚了。
B: Sorry, I just don't understand.
對不起，我真的不懂。

0610
我相信你明白我的意思了。
I trust you understand me.

範例
A: You should find a part-time job. I trust you understand me.
你該找份兼職工作，我相信你明白我的意思了。
B: Sure. I understand.
明白了。

0611
差不多清楚了嗎？
Is that reasonably clear?

範例
A: Is that reasonably clear? You look puzzled.
差不多清楚了嗎？你看起來有點迷惑。
B: I really don't understand where you get such ridiculous ideas.
我真不明白你哪裡來這些荒唐的想法。

2.10 正確性 Correctness

　　一般來說，詢問某種觀點或結論是否正確時，語氣要委婉；說明觀點或結論是否正確時，要有技巧，或者有所保留；糾正他人提供的資訊時，更要有禮貌，以避免讓人感到尷尬。

● 詢問是否正確 Asking if Someone Is Right

026

0612 這樣對嗎？
Is it OK?

(替換) Is it correct, please?
Is that right, please?
Is this correct?

(範例) A: Here is my composition. Is it OK? 這是我的作文。這樣對嗎？
B: Yes. The writing is very beautiful. 對，寫得很美。

(提示) composition [ˌkɑmpəˈzɪʃən] *n.* 作文；寫作

0613 對嗎？
Am I right?

(替換) Have I got it right?

(範例) A: There are two hundred people in the hall. Am I right?
大廳裡有二百人。對嗎？
B: Yes, you are.
對了。

0614 這樣說對嗎？
Would it be true to say so?

(範例) A: Those headphones are no good. Would it be true to say so?
那些耳機對健康無益處，這樣說對嗎？
B: You said it. They're bad for our ears.
你說對了。它們對聽覺不好。

0615 …，對嗎？
It's..., isn't it?

(替換) ..., yes?
..., right?

(範例) A: It's the actual figure, isn't it? 這是實際數目，對嗎？
B: Yes, it is. 是的。

0616 我這樣想對嗎？
Am I correct in supposing so?

範例
A: This drug will clear up my problem. Am I correct in supposing so?
這種藥會消除我的病痛，我這樣想對嗎？
B: Yes, you're exactly right.
是的，完全正確。

0617
你覺得⋯正確嗎？
Do you think...is correct?

範例
A: Do you think the decision is correct? 你覺得這個決定正確嗎？
B: Yes, I do. 是的，正確。

0618
這麼做對嗎？
Is this the right thing to do?

範例
A: Jack likes to impose his views on others. Is this the right thing to do?
傑克喜歡把自己的觀點強加於他人。這麼做對嗎？
B: Absolutely not.
當然不對。

提示
impose [ɪm'poz] v. 強加

0619
有錯嗎？
Are there any mistakes?

替換
Is there anything wrong (with it)?

範例
A: Here's the essay. Are there any mistakes? 這是我的文章，有錯嗎？
B: No. 沒有。

0620
我對了，是吧？
I've got it right, haven't I?

範例
A: I've got it right, haven't I? 我對了，是吧？
B: Who said that? 誰說的？

0621
能不能請你告訴我⋯對不對？
Could you please tell me if...is correct?

替換
Could I ask if...is correct?
Would you mind telling me if...is correct?

範例
A: Could you please tell me if my judgment is correct?
能不能請你告訴我，我的判斷對不對？
B: Sorry. It's too early to tell.
對不起，現在說還太早。

0622
我想確認一下我是否把…弄對了。
I'd like to check to see if I got...right.

(替換)
I'd like to find out if I've got...right.
I'd like to make sure that...is correct.

(範例)
A: I'd like to check to see if I got it right.
我想確認一下我是否把它弄對了。
B: It's too soon to tell.
現在說還太快。

0623
我想…。
I assume that...

(範例)
A: I assume that the train had already left when they reached the platform. 我想他們到達車站月臺的時候，火車已經離開了。
B: Oh, really? 哦，真的嗎？

(提示)
assume [ə'sjum] v. 認為；設想

0624
…我這麼想，不知道是否正確。
I wonder if I'm right in supposing that...

(範例)
A: I wonder if I'm right in supposing that you will keep this in mind.
你會記住這件事的，我這麼想，不知道是否正確。
B: You are.
你是正確的。

● 肯定回答 Affirmative Replies

0625
對。
Right.

(替換)
Correct.
That's it.
That's (all) right.

(範例)
A: He's a newcomer here, right? 他是新來的，對嗎？
B: Right. 對。

(提示)
newcomer ['nju͵kʌmɚ] n. 新來者

0626
看來是這樣。
It kind of looks that way.

範例　A: Our boss is angry again. 我們老闆又發火了。
B: It kind of looks that way. 看來是這樣。

0627
完全正確。
You're spot on.

替換　Nothing wrong with it.

範例　A: You're quitting early with full benefits, right?
你會提早退休並享有全部福利，對嗎？
B: You're spot on.
完全正確。

提示　benefit [ˈbɛnəfɪt] *n.* 利益；好處

0628
我覺得沒有任何問題。
I didn't find any problem with it.

替換　I think there's nothing wrong with it.
I don't think there's anything wrong with it.

範例　A: What do you think of the article? 你覺得這篇文章怎麼樣？
B: I didn't find any problem with it. 我覺得沒有任何問題。

0629
差不多。
That's about right.

範例　A: The book is about the war, right? 這本書跟戰爭有關，對嗎？
B: That's about right. 差不多。

0630
你完全正確。
You're dead right.

替換　Exactly.
Precisely.
Absolutely.
You're quite right.
That's quite correct.
That is perfectly correct.

範例　A: I think the man with the glasses is untrustworthy.
我認為那位戴眼鏡的男人不值得信賴。
B: You're dead right.
你完全正確。

提示　precisely [prɪˈsaɪslɪ] *adv.* 正好；明確地

0631

我認為…完全正確。
I suppose...is absolutely true.

範例
A: I suppose what he said is absolutely true. 我認爲他的話完全正確。
B: But I don't think so. 但我可不這麼認爲。

0632

我得說…完全正確。
I should say...is perfectly correct.

範例
A: I should say your decision is perfectly correct.
我得說，你的決定完全正確。
B: Thank you.
謝謝。

0633

我想你是對的。
I guess you're right.

範例
A: I think Ted will be fired. 我想泰德會被解雇。
B: I guess you're right. 我想你是對的。

0634

看來你是對的。
It would seem that you are right.

範例
A: It would seem that you are right. 看來你是對的。
B: Of course I am! 那當然了。

0635

我認為非常正確。
I think that's quite right.

範例
A: I think that's quite right. 我認爲非常正確。
B: Thank you. 謝謝。

0636

是的，你…是對的。
Yes, you're correct in...

範例
A: Don't you think I should do more for my company?
你不覺得我應該爲公司多做點嗎？
B: Yes, you're correct in thinking that way.
是的，你這麼想是對的。

0637

是的，我可以確認…。
Yes, I can confirm that...

範例　A: I guess something must have happened upstairs.
　　　　　我猜樓上一定發生了什麼事。
　　　　B: Yes, I can confirm that the couple had a fight.
　　　　　是的，我可以確認那對夫妻倆打架了。

提示　confirm [kən'fɚm] v. 使確認；進一步證實

● 否定回答 Negative Replies

0638　完全弄錯了。
It's all wrong.

替換　You've got it all wrong.
　　　　You're all wet.
　　　　That's not at all right.

範例　A: How's the project going?
　　　　　這個計畫進行得如何？
　　　　B: It's all wrong. We'll have to start all over.
　　　　　完全弄錯了。我們必須從頭開始。

0639　你錯了。
You're wrong.

範例　A: These shoes are so expensive!
　　　　　這雙鞋好貴！
　　　　B: You're wrong. Look at the price tag. They're only five dollars.
　　　　　你錯了。看標籤，只有五塊美元。

提示　tag [tæg] n. 標籤

0640　你…錯了。
You...wrong.

範例　A: You translated the sentence wrong. 你把這個句子翻錯了。
　　　　B: I'm sorry. 對不起。

提示　translate [træns'let] v. 翻譯

0641　我想你錯了。
I don't think you're right about it.

替換　I think you're mistaken there.

範例	A: I don't think you're right about it. 我想你錯了。 B: Oh, really? 哦！真的嗎？

0642	亂說。 **Rubbish!**

替換	Nonsense. Bullshit!〔粗魯的表達法〕
範例	A: I'm under the impression that your manager is an agitated man. 我對你們經理的印象是：他是個激動的人。 B: Rubbish! 亂說。
提示	agitated [ˈædʒəˌtetɪd] *adj.* 激動的

0643	我不認為…。 **I didn't think...**

替換	I don't think...
範例	A: I didn't think he was the best in the class. 我不認為他是班上最好的。 B: Then who was? 那誰是呢？

0644	…不正確，是嗎？ **...isn't right, is it?**

範例	A: The answer isn't right, is it? 這個答案不正確，是嗎？ B: No. 是的。

0645	我認為不對。 **I don't think it's correct.**

範例	A: I don't think it's correct. 我認為不對。 B: Then what should we do? 那我們該怎麼辦？

0646	恐怕…是錯的。 **I'm afraid...is wrong.**

替換	I'm afraid...is not quite right.
範例	A: Is this answer right? 這個答案對嗎？ B: I'm afraid it's wrong. 恐怕是錯的。

0647	我不能肯定你…是對的。 **I'm not sure you're correct about...**

範例 A: I'm not sure you're correct about that.
　　　我不能肯定你的看法是對的。
　　B: Oh, really?
　　　哦，真的嗎？

0648 對不起，這不正確。
Sorry, it's not correct.

範例 A: What do you think of my answer? 你覺得我的答案怎麼樣？
　　B: Sorry, it's not correct. 對不起，這不正確。

0649 我想我必須告訴你⋯不正確。
I think I must tell you that...is not right.

範例 A: I think I must tell you that your answer is not right.
　　　我想我必須告訴你，你的答案不正確。
　　B: Thank you anyway.
　　　不管怎麼說，還是要謝謝你。

0650 對不起，但是我應該指出⋯並不正確。
I'm sorry, but I really should point out...is not correct.

範例 A: Is my job OK?
　　　我的工作怎麼樣？
　　B: I'm sorry, but I really should point out that your method is not
　　　correct.
　　　對不起，但是我應該指出你的方法並不正確。

0651 如果我可以這麼說的話，實際上情況並非如此。
If I may say so, it's actually not the case.

範例 A: If I may say so, it's actually not the case.
　　　如果我可以這麼說的話，實際上情況並非如此。
　　B: Oh, my goodness!
　　　哦，我的天哪！

0652 如果我可以這麼說的話，⋯是不正確的。
If I may say so, ...is incorrect.

範例 A: What do you think of my choice?
　　　你覺得我的選擇怎麼樣？
　　B: If I may say so, your choice is incorrect.
　　　如果我可以這麼說的話，你的選擇是不正確的。

0653	恐怕這裡面有些誤會。 **I'm afraid there has been some misunderstanding here.**

範例 A: I'm afraid there has been some misunderstanding here.
恐怕這裡面有些誤會。
B: But I don't think so.
但我不這麼認為。

● 糾正錯誤 Correcting Mistakes

0654	等一等。 **Hang on a minute.**

替換 Hold on a minute.
Wait a minute.

範例 A: It's a pity we can't see the movie.
很遺憾我們不能看這場電影了。
B: Hang on a minute. I've got the tickets.
等一等,我已經買票了。

0655	不行,…。 **No, ...**

範例 A: Can we go in? 我們可以進去嗎?
B: No, no one is there. 不行,沒人在。

0656	就我所知,…。 **As far as I know, ...**

範例 A: As far as I know, there are no crocodiles in the river.
就我所知,這條河裡沒有鱷魚。
B: Thank God.
謝天謝地。

0657	可是…。 **But...**

範例 A: I think we can go to the country.
我覺得我們可以去鄉下。
B: But I spent my summer vacation in the country last year.
可是去年暑假我就在鄉下度過。

0658

當然…，不是嗎？
Surely, it's..., isn't it?

範例　**A:** Surely, it's the young man who takes care of the old woman every day, isn't it? 當然就是那個每天照顧老太太的年輕人，不是嗎？
B: Yes. 是的。

0659

哦，實際上…。
Well, actually, ...

替換　Well, as a matter of fact, ...
Well, in fact, ...
Well, the fact is, ...

範例　**A:** Were all the books safe and sound after the fire?
火災後，所有的書都完好無缺嗎？
B: Well, actually, many of the books were damaged by the fire.
哦，實際上許多書都毀於火災。

0660

請允許我糾正你：…。
Allow me to correct one thing you said:...

替換　If I may correct you, ...
I'm afraid I have to correct you there. Actually...

範例　**A:** Allow me to correct one thing you said: he's not our enemy.
請允許我糾正你：他不是我們的敵人。
B: He's not your enemy but mine.
他不是你的敵人，而是我的。

0661

我想這麼說可能更確切：…。
I suppose it might be more correct to say...

替換　I think it might be more accurate to say...

範例　**A:** I suppose it might be more correct to say he feels guilty.
我想這麼說可能更確切：他有罪惡感。
B: Don't be so harsh.
別這麼苛刻。

提示　accurate ['ækjərɪt] *adj.* 確切的；精確的
harsh [hɑrʃ] *adj.* 嚴厲的；苛刻的

2.11　推論 Deducing

推論是指由一個或幾個已知的情況判斷出另一個新的判斷。英語中，推論這一語言功能是由一些特定的表達方法來實現的，有時常用 so、then、can、must 來表達。

0662	我不太確定，但是我想…。 **I'm not sure, but I think...**

替換	I don't know, but I suppose...
範例	**A:** What are you driving at? 　　你在說什麼？ **B:** I'm not sure, but I think I said the proper thing. 　　我不太確定，但是我想我說的是正確的。

0663	假如…。 **Suppose...**

替換	What if...? Imagine...
範例	**A:** Suppose we had no computer, what would life be like? 　　假如沒有電腦，生活會是什麼樣子？ **B:** It's hard to say. 　　很難說。

0664	我想…。 **I think ...**

替換	I suppose/guess...
範例	**A:** What did you get from his speech? 　　從他的演講中，你有何收穫？ **B:** I think he must have read the same book as I. 　　我想他一定和我讀過同一本書。

0665	很顯然…。 **Obviously, ...**

範例 A: Why not go over and talk with Bobby? 為何不過去和鮑比談一談？
B: Obviously, he's unhappy. 很顯然他不高興了。

0666

一定是…。
It seems clear to me that...

替換 It is perfectly obvious that...

範例 A: Why hasn't Mr. Wang come yet? 王先生為什麼還沒來？
B: It seems clear to me that he has forgotten about it. 一定是他忘了。

0667

…肯定是…。
...must...

範例 A: Where is Janet? 珍妮特在哪兒？
B: She must have got up late today. 她今天肯定是睡過頭了。

0668

…不可能…。
...couldn't have...

範例 A: What are you laughing at? 你笑什麼？
B: She couldn't have done that! 她不可能做了那件事。

0669

如果…，就…。
Assuming that...

範例 A: Assuming that we're in the right place, there's no need to keep on looking. 如果我們找對地方，就不用繼續再找了。
B: Let's hope so. 希望如此。

2.12 描述 Describing

　　在日常會話中，我們最常描述的就是人的年紀和身高，或者是描述風景名勝，這類的表達法，我們不可不知。

(028)

0670

她大約三十歲。
She is about 30.

替換 She is in her early/mid/late thirties.

範例 **A:** How old is our math teacher? 我們數學老師多大了？
B: She is about 30. 她大約三十歲。

0671 他身材中等。
He's of average height.

範例 **A:** Is your brother tall? 你弟弟很高嗎？
B: Not really. He's of average height. 不高，他身材中等。

0672 有何特別之處嗎？
What's so special about it?

替換 What's interesting/remarkable about it?

範例 **A:** Have you ever been to Beijing? 你去過北京嗎？
B: Never. What's so special about it? 沒有。有何特別之處嗎？

提示 remarkable [rɪ'mɑrkəbl] *adj.* 不平常的；值得注意的

0673 它以…聞名。
It's famous for...

替換 It's well-known/noted for...

範例 **A:** What city in Taiwan do you recommend going to?
你推薦去台灣哪個城市走走？
B: I'd say Keelung. It's famous for its seafood.
那就基隆吧。它以海鮮聞名。

提示 noted ['notɪd] *adj.* 著名的
recommend [ˌrɛkə'mɛnd] *v.* 推薦；介紹

0674 這個城市有…。
This city's got...

範例 **A:** What are we going to see in this city?
我們要去看這個城市的什麼東西呢？
B: This city's got gardens.
這個城市有花園。

2.13　欲求 Desire

　　人人都有各種希望跟要求，也都希望自己的要求獲得滿足，不管是為了眼前利益，或是為了長遠目標。在交談中，我們有必要根據自己的要求、事物和場合，使用不同的表達方法。

0675	我想要…。 **I'm dying for...**
替換	I'm itching/craving/longing for... I could do with... I very much want... I feel like. I fancy...
範例	**A:** What do you want to eat? 想吃點什麼？ **B:** I'm dying for cake. 我想要蛋糕。
提示	itching [ˈɪtʃɪŋ] *adj.* 渴望的；貪得的
0676	我很想…。 **I'm dying to...**
替換	I am anxious/longing to... I really desire to... I particularly want to... I'd give anything to... I would really love to... I would very much like to...
範例	**A:** I'm dying to hear your news. 　　我很想知道你的消息。 **B:** OK. As soon as I arrive, I will give you a call. 　　好，等我一到，我就打電話給你。
0677	我想要…。 **I'd love...**
替換	I feel like... I want...

029

I need...
I'd like...

範例 A: I'd love you to come along. 我想要你來。
B: But I have no time. 但是我沒時間。

0678
哦，我可不會反對…。
Well, I wouldn't say no to...

替換 Well, I wouldn't object to...

範例 A: Well, I wouldn't say no to a day off. 哦，我可不會反對放一天假。
B: Then it's done. 就這麼定了。

0679
…挺合我的胃口。
...would go down well.

範例 A: What do you want to have?
你想吃點什麼？
B: A nice dish of vegetables would go down well.
一盤好吃的青菜挺合我的胃口。

0680
要是我能…就好了。
If only I could...

範例 A: If only I could have a pen like that. 要是我能有枝那樣的鋼筆就好了。
B: Of course you can have one. 你當然能。

0681
我得…。
I've just got to...

替換 I must...

範例 A: I've just got to have my hair cut. 我得剪頭髮了。
B: Good idea. 好主意。

0682
我要一份。
I'd love one.

範例 A: Do you want a hamburger?
你想要漢堡嗎？
B: I'd love one. I haven't had a thing to eat all day.
我要一份。我整天沒吃東西了。

0683

啊，…正合我意。
Well, ...would suit me just fine.

範例　A: Let's take a few days off. 我們休幾天假吧！
B: Well, a holiday would suit me just fine. 啊，一個假期正合我意。

0684

為什麼我不能…？
Why can't I...?

範例　A: You can't go to college. 你不能上大學。
B: Why can't I go? 為什麼我不能？

0685

…該有多好。
Wouldn't it be nice to...?

範例　A: Wouldn't it be nice to go picnicking? 去野餐該有多好。
B: Yes, it would. 當然了。

0686

…一定很妙。
It would be wonderful to...

範例　A: It would be wonderful to go fishing today. 今天去釣魚一定很妙。
B: I don't think so. 我可不這麼認為。

0687

…倒不錯。
It'd be nice to...

範例　A: It'd be nice to have a break. 休息一下倒不錯。
B: But we can't. 但是我們不能。

0688

我要的是…。
What I need is....

範例　A: What I need is to relax.
我要的是放鬆。
B: But I think you've had enough relaxation.
可是我覺得你已經輕鬆夠了。

提示　relaxation [ˌrilæksˈeʃən] *n.* 放鬆；輕鬆

2.14 概括 Generalizing

由分析一些事物得到共同性，進而推論全類事物也都有這個特性的過程，稱爲概括。英語中，表達這一個語言功能時，要特別注意一些固定的方法。

030

0689
通常…。
Usually, ...

(替換)
Generally, ...
Apparently, ...

(範例)
A: Usually, boys are more adventurous than girls.
通常男孩子比女孩子更富冒險精神。
B: I agree.
我同意。

(提示)
adventurous [əd'vɛntʃərəs] *adj.* 喜歡冒險的；敢做敢為的

0690
經常…。
Again and again, ...

(替換)
Time and again, ...
Most of the time, ...

(範例)
A: Why are you so busy?
你怎麼如此忙？
B: Again and again, I have to work overtime on weekends.
我經常週末也得加班。

0691
根據我的經驗…。
In my experience, ...

(範例)
A: I doubt the kids would like to go out.
我不知道孩子們是否願意出去。
B: In my experience, they like any outdoor activities.
根據我的經驗，什麼戶外活動他們都喜歡。

0692
總而言之…。
As a rule, ...

替換 | On the whole, ...
By and large, ...

範例 | **A:** What's your impression of young people?
你對年輕人有何印象？
B: As a rule, young people are more creative and curious.
總而言之，年輕人更具創造力與好奇心。

0693 | **多數情況下，…。**
In most cases, ...

範例 | **A:** It seems that more and more people like junk food.
人們好像愈來愈喜歡垃圾食物。
B: Maybe. However, in most cases, people prefer fresh food to junk food.
也許吧，但是多數情況下，人們喜歡新鮮的食物勝於垃圾食物。

0694 | **看來…。**
It seems that...

替換 | It appears that...

範例 | **A:** Do you often watch TV serials?
你經常看電視連續劇嗎？
B: Well, it seems that there are too many soap operas on TV.
嗯，看來電視裡的連續劇過於氾濫了。

2.15　舉例 Giving Examples

　　說明問題或闡述觀點時，有時需要舉出實例。英語中不同場合使用的舉例用語不同。本節將對英語舉例用語進行歸納，從中可以發現中英文舉例用語有很多相似之處。

031

0695 | **像…。**
...like...

替換 | Like..., for example.
..., such as...

範例
A: Films like *Titanic* are well-known.
像《鐵達尼號》這樣的電影很有名。
B: Of course.
當然了。

提示
Titanic [taɪˈtænɪk] *n.* 電影鐵達尼號

0696
看看…。
Look at...

範例
A: Look at the Great Wall. It's one of the seven wonders in the world.
看看長城，它是世界七大奇景之一。
B: It's really a wonder.
真是個奇景。

0697
此外，…。
What's more, ...

範例
A: What's more, she's won a silver medal. 此外，她還贏得了一塊銀牌。
B: She is really something. 她真了不起。

0698
舉例來說…。
..., for example, ...

替換
..., for one, ...
..., for instance, ...

範例
A: Cars made in Japan, for example, are world famous.
舉例來說，日本產的轎車世界聞名。
B: They sure are.
的確是如此。

0699
…怎麼樣？
What about...?

範例
A: What about pizza? It's quite delicious. 比薩怎麼樣？很好吃喔。
B: OK. 好的。

0700
不僅如此，…。
Not only that, ...

範例
A: I think she is very stubborn. 我覺得她很頑固。
B: Not only that, her ideas are out-dated. 不僅如此，她思想也很過時。

0701 拿⋯來說，⋯。
Take...for instance; ...

(替換) Take the case of...; ...

(範例) A: Take violence for instance; it has a very bad influence on children.
拿暴力來說，它對孩子有很不好的影響。
B: I agree with you.
我也這樣想。

0702 讓我舉個例子。
Let me give you an example.

(替換) Allow me to cite an example.
Let me provide an example.
Let me cite a few instances.

(範例) A: Let me give you an example. 讓我舉個例子。
B: Alright. 好的。

(提示) cite [saɪt] v. 引用；引證

0703 這是根據這點得出的：⋯。
It follows thus:...

(範例) A: It follows thus: People should not drive when they are drunk.
這是根據這點得出的：人們醉酒時，不該駕車。
B: You're right.
沒錯。

0704 ⋯就是這方面的例證。
...is evidence of that.

(範例) A: The quality is better. 品質提高了。
B: The higher price is evidence of that. 價格較高就是這方面的例證。

(提示) evidence ['ɛvədəns] n. 證據；根據

0705 你只要看看⋯，就⋯。
You need only look at...

(範例) A: It seems that she is an important person.
看起來她像是個重要人物。
B: You need only look at her appearance to see that.
你只要看看她的外表，就知道了。

0706	一個這方面的例子就是：⋯。 **An example of this would be that...**
範例	**A:** It's a big factory. 它是個大工廠。 **B:** An example of this would be that in 1999 the output was 5 million US dollars. 一個這方面的例子就是：1999 年的產值達到五百萬美元。
提示	output ['aʊtˌpʊt] *n.* 產量；輸出量

0707	為舉例說明⋯，我們來⋯。 **To give an example..., let us...**
範例	**A:** To give an example of this theory, let us examine some plants. 為舉例說明這個原理，我們來檢視一些植物。 **B:** Good. 好的。

0708	為了闡明⋯，讓我們以⋯為例。 **To illustrate..., let us consider the case of...**
範例	**A:** To illustrate my point, let us consider the case of Mike. 為了闡明我的觀點，讓我們以麥可為例。 **B:** This has nothing to do with Mike. 這和麥克沒關係。
提示	illustrate ['ɪləstret] *v.* （用圖、實例等）說明；闡明

0709	為了讓你更清楚，讓我們來看看⋯。 **To make it clear to you, let us have a look at...**
範例	**A:** To make it clear to you, let us have a look at the back of the paper. 為了讓你更清楚，讓我們來看看紙的背面。 **B:** Now I see. 現在我懂了。

0710	為了給你這方面的例子，我們以⋯為例。 **To give you an example of this, take...for instance.**
範例	**A:** To give you an example of this, take London for instance. 為了給你這方面的例子，我們以倫敦為例。 **B:** Do you think London is a case in point? 你認為倫敦是個恰當的例子嗎？

2.16　指示 Giving Instructions

　　指示在這裡指的是進行口頭說明。指示語的使用受場合、地位、關係親疏等因素的限制。指導性的語言常使用祈使句。語言要力求簡明、準確。爲了表明時間的順序，我們可以使用 first of all、second、third、finally 等明確的指示性辭彙。

0711	瞧！ 032 **Look!**
範例	**A:** Excuse me, would you please tell me how to get to the museum? 　對不起，請告訴我去博物館的路好嗎？ **B:** OK. Look! You go this way, not that way. 　好的。瞧！從這條路走，別走那條路。
0712	首先… **First of all...**
替換	First... The first thing/step...
範例	**A:** First of all, you should switch it on. 首先要把它打開。 **B:** OK. 好的。
0713	瞧，你只要…。 **Look, all you do is...**
範例	**A:** Look, all you do is press it and wait. 　瞧，你只要按一下它，然後等一會。 **B:** That's easy. 　這很容易。
0714	很簡單。 **It's quite easy.**
範例	**A:** It's quite easy. You lift the lid, and pour some water in it. 　很簡單，你打開蓋子，倒一些水進去。 **B:** OK. 　好的。

0715

之後你⋯。
After you've done that, you...

(替換)
And then, don't forget to...
The next thing you do is to...

(範例)
A: After you've done that, you press the button.
之後你按一下這個按鈕。
B: Is that all?
就這樣嗎？

0716

照這樣做⋯。
You do it like this: ...

(範例)
A: You do it like this: switch it on and then wait for the signal.
照這樣做：開啓然後等待信號。
B: How long should I wait?
我得等多久？

0717

像這樣，首先⋯然後⋯
Let me show you: first you..., and then you...

(替換)
It's like this: first you..., and then...
This is how you do it: you...then...

(範例)
A: Let me show you: first you find the right button, and then you press
it. 像這樣，首先找到正確的按鈕，然後按下去。
B: But which one is the right one? 但是哪個是正確的？

0718

一定要記住⋯。
Make sure you remember to...

(範例)
A: Make sure you remember to correct the mistakes.
一定要記住改掉這些錯誤。
B: Don't worry.
放心吧。

0719

小心不要⋯。
Be careful not to...

(範例)
A: Be careful not to lose it. 小心不要弄丟了。
B: OK. 好的。

| 0720 | 你要採取下列步驟：…。
You should proceed as follows: ... |

替換　The following procedure should be adopted: ...
The job should be done according to the following procedure: ...
This project should be carried out according to the following proce-
　　dure: ...

範例　**A:** You should proceed as follows: insert the plug, switch on the
　　power, and then press START.
　　你要採取下列步驟：插上插頭，打開電源，然後再按「開始鍵」。
B: Like this?
　　這樣就行了嗎？

提示　proceed [prəˈsid] v. 著手；進行
procedure [prəˈsidʒɚ] n. 步驟；手續
adopt [əˈdɑpt] v. 採取
according to 根據

2.17 訊息 Information

　　人們常常透過提問來獲得自己所需的資訊。但是在交談中一定要注意提問的技巧，因為提問的語言技巧會影響到人際關係的成敗。一般來說，與關係不密切的英美人士交往，要避免直接使用疑問句提問，而要使用客氣、委婉的方式提問，這樣可以避免給人留下粗魯的印象。在對方的回答過於籠統或明顯存在誤解時，我們可以進一步提問，但也要注意方式。我們可以明確請求對方提供更多的資訊，也可以以未聽懂為由，間接要求對方進行解釋說明。注意提問時，要儘量避開薪水收入、婚姻狀況、年齡、身高、重量等問題。不得已問及這些個人隱私時，應特別注意委婉、客氣。

　　有人向我們詢問資訊時，我們可以設法給予滿意的回答。但是有時問題難以回答，或者想拒絕回答。此時應該巧妙地找藉口回避，或委婉地表示無可奉告。

● 尋求資訊 Asking for Information

0721

你知道嗎？

Do you have any clue?

(替換) Got any idea?

(範例) A: Do you have any clue? How do I get a tourist visa for the United States? 你知道嗎？我要如何辦理美國的觀光簽證？

B: I'm not sure. 我不清楚。

0722

出什麼事了？

What's up?

(替換) What happened?

What's going on?

(範例) A: What's up? 出什麼事了？

B: An old man fell down on the ground. 一位老人摔倒了。

0723

你知道…嗎？

Any clue about...?

(替換) Got any idea about...?

Do you know...?

(範例) A: Any clue about what's going on? 你知道發生什麼事了嗎？

B: Sorry, I don't know. 對不起，不知道。

0724

你會知道…嗎？

Do you happen to know...?

(替換) Would you by chance know...?

(範例) A: Do you happen to know his address? 你會知道他的地址嗎？

B: No. 不知道。

0725

你能告訴我關於…的一些情況嗎？

Can you tell me something about...?

(替換) Could I inquire about...?

I wonder if you could give me some information about...

(範例) A: Can you tell me something about it?

你能告訴我關於那事情的一些情況嗎？

B: Yes, they got engaged.
可以，他們訂婚了。

0726

你能多告訴我一些關於…的情況嗎？
Could you tell me some more about...?

範例　A: Could you tell me some more about it?
你能多告訴我一些關於那事情的情況嗎？
B: That is all I know about it.
這就是我所知道的。

0727

請問…？
Do you know...?

替換　Could you tell me...?
Can you tell me..., please?
Could I ask...?

範例　A: Do you know who they are? 請問他們是誰？
B: I have no idea. 不知道。

0728

我想多知道一點…。
I'd like to know more about...

替換　I'd like to ask about...
I would be interested to know...

範例　A: I'd like to know more about the plan. 我想多知道一點這計畫。
B: Sorry, it's a secret. 對不起，這是個祕密。

0729

你能否告訴我…？
Would you mind telling me...?

替換　I wonder if I could ask...
I wonder if you could tell me...

範例　A: Would you mind telling me how he failed the exam?
你能否告訴我他是怎麼不及格的嗎？
B: You'd better ask him yourself.
你最好問他本人。

0730

我想和人談談關於…的事。
I'd like to speak to someone about...

範例 A: I'd like to speak to someone about the school.
　　我想和人談談關於學校的事。
　　B: Who do you want to speak to?
　　你想和誰說？

0731 另外我還想知道…。
Something else I'd like to know is...

範例 A: Something else I'd like to know is who was punished this time.
　　另外我還想知道這次誰被罰了。
　　B: It was Tom.
　　湯姆。

0732 誰能告訴我…？
Could anyone tell me...?

範例 A: Could anyone tell me who did it? 誰能告訴我誰做的嗎？
　　B: No one witnessed it. 沒有目擊證人。

提示 witness ['wɪtnɪs] v. 目擊

0733 對不起，老纏著你，但是你能告訴我…？
Sorry to pester you, but could you tell me...?

範例 A: Sorry to pester you, but could you tell me who's in charge?
　　對不起，老纏著你，但是你能告訴我誰負責這件事嗎？
　　B: I really don't know.
　　我真的不知道。

提示 pester ['pɛstɚ] v. 使困擾；煩擾

0734 對不起，打擾你，但是…？
Sorry to trouble you, but...?

範例 A: Sorry to trouble you, but did she accept it?
　　對不起，打擾你，但是她接受了嗎？
　　B: It's hard to say.
　　這很難說。

0735 請問…？
Could I ask...?

範例 A: Could I ask who is responsible for it? 請問這件事誰負責？
　　B: I am. 是我。

0736 如果你不介意我問的話，…嗎？
..., if you don't mind my asking?

範例 **A:** Are you studying English, if you don't mind my asking?
如果你不介意我問的話，你在學英語嗎？
B: Yes, I am.
是的。

0737 我希望你不介意我問這個問題，我想知道…。
I hope you don't mind my asking, but I'd like to know...

範例 **A:** I hope you don't mind my asking, but I'd like to know what you're going to do. 我希望你不介意我問這個問題，我想知道你要做什麼。
B: Why should I tell you? 為什麼我得告訴你？

0738 我不知道你能否幫助我。我想知道…。
I was wondering whether you could help me. I'd like to know...

範例 **A:** I was wondering whether you could help me. I'd like to know what you did last night.
我不知道你能否幫助我。我想知道昨晚你在做什麼。
B: I did nothing.
我什麼也沒做。

0739 這聽起來像個愚蠢的問題，不過我想知道…。
This may sound like a dumb question, but I'd like to know...

範例 **A:** This may sound like a dumb question, but I'd like to know what caused the problem.
這聽起來像個愚蠢的問題，不過我想知道問題的起因。
B: Don't ask me.
別問我。

提示 dumb [dʌm] *adj.*【非正式，尤美】愚蠢的

● 詢問是否知道 Asking if Someone Knows

0740 你知道嗎？
Did you know that?

(替換) | Do you know that?

(範例) | **A:** Richard is settling down in his new house. Did you know that?
理查正在安頓新居。你知道嗎？
B: Really?
真的嗎？

0741 你知道⋯嗎？
Do you know anything about...?

(替換) | Have you got any idea about...?
Do/Did you know (about)...?
Are you aware/conscious of...?

(範例) | **A:** Do you know anything about that man? 你知道這個人嗎？
B: Sorry, I don't know him. 對不起，我不認識他。

(提示) | conscious ['kɑnʃəs] *adj.* 有意識的（+ of）

0742 你聽說⋯了嗎？
Have you heard about...?

(替換) | Did you hear about...?

(範例) | **A:** Have you heard about this movie? 你聽說這部電影了嗎？
B: No. 沒有。

0743 有人告訴你了嗎？
Did someone tell you?

(替換) | Has someone told you?

(範例) | **A:** Jane and Brandy have come back. Did someone tell you?
珍和布蘭迪回來了。有人告訴你了嗎？
B: No. When did they come back?
沒有。他們何時回來？

0744 有人告訴你⋯了嗎？
Did someone tell you...?

(替換) | Has someone told you...?

(範例) | **A:** Did someone tell you the problem? 有人告訴你這個問題了嗎？
B: I'm afraid not. 恐怕沒有。

0745

你知道…，不是嗎？
You know..., don't you?

(替換) You know about..., don't you?

(範例) **A:** You know that, don't you? 你知道那件事，不是嗎？
B: No, I don't. 不，我不知道。

0746

請你告訴我…好嗎？
Can you give me any information about..., please?

(替換) Could you give me any information on...?

(範例) **A:** Can you give me any information about the meeting, please?
請你告訴我有關這次會議的資訊好嗎？
B: Sorry, I know nothing about it.
對不起，我對此一無所知。

0747

你知道…？
Do you realize...?

(範例) **A:** Do you realize he got in trouble? 你知道他有麻煩了嗎？
B: How would I know about it? 我怎麼會知道？

0748

不知你是否知道…。
I wonder if you realize that...

(範例) **A:** I wonder if you realize that he needs our help.
不知你是否知道他需要我們的幫助。
B: Sorry, I don't.
對不起，我不知道。

0749

你不知道…嗎？
Didn't you know...?

(範例) **A:** Didn't you know I'm going to America? 你不知道我要去美國嗎？
B: Really? Congratulations. 真的？恭禧你。

(提示) congratulation [kən͵grætʃəˈleʃən] *n.* 祝賀；恭禧

0750

你碰巧知道…嗎？
Do you happen to know anything about...?

(範例) **A:** Do you happen to know anything about the case?
你碰巧知道這個情況嗎？

B: Yes, I do.
是的。

0751

不知你是否能讓我知道⋯。
I wonder whether you could tell me something about...

範例 **A:** I wonder whether you could tell me something about the project.
不知你是否能讓我知道這個計畫。
B: Sure.
當然了。

● 表達知道某事 Stating One Knows Something

0752

我聽說是這樣的。
That's what I heard.

替換 So I hear.

範例 **A:** Al and Cindy got engaged. 艾爾和辛蒂訂婚了。
B: That's what I heard. 我聽說是這樣的。

0753

已經有人告訴我⋯。
I've been told about...

範例 **A:** I've been told about the plane crash. 已經有人告訴我這次空難了。
B: It's terrible. 太可怕了。

提示 crash [kræʃ] *n.* 墜落；墜毀

0754

有人告訴我⋯。
Someone told me about...

替換 Someone has told me about...

範例 **A:** The meeting has been postponed. 會議延期了。
B: Someone told me about that. 有人告訴我了。

提示 postpone [post'pon] *v.* 延期；延遲

0755

是的，我的確知道⋯。
Yes, I do know about...

替換 Yes, I do realize...

A: Do you know that a car broke down in front of us?
你知道我們前面的車拋錨了嗎？

B: Yes, I do know about that.
是的，我的確知道。

0756

我聽說…。
I hear...

 I'm told...

 A: I hear Mr. Lee is coming. 我聽說李先生要來。
B: Really? 真的嗎？

0757

我猜想是這樣。不過謝謝你告訴我。
So I gather. But thank you for telling me.

 A: Mr. Smith won't come today.
史密斯先生今天不來了。

B: So I gather. But thank you for telling me.
我猜想是這樣。不過謝謝你告訴我。

0758

我知道。不過謝謝你告訴我。
So I understand. But thank you for telling me.

 A: Our boss won't come back today.
我們老闆今天不回來了。

B: So I understand. But thank you for telling me.
我知道。不過謝謝你告訴我。

0759

我聽說是這樣。不過謝謝你告訴我。
So I'm told. But thank you for telling me.

A: It's going to rain this evening.
今晚會下雨。

B: So I'm told. But thank you for telling me.
我聽說是這樣。不過謝謝你告訴我。

0760

你猜怎麼著？
Guess what?

A: Guess what? They fell into a ditch yesterday.
你猜怎麼著？他們昨天掉進水溝了。

B: That was unfortunate.
真不走運。

提示 | ditch [dɪtʃ] *n.* 溝；溝渠
unfortunate [ʌnˈfɔrtʃənɪt] *adj.* 不幸運的

0761
就我所知，…。
For all I know, ...

範例 | A: For all I know, he may have already left for London.
就我所知，他可能已經去倫敦了。
B: That's impossible.
這不可能。

0762
我有充分根據知道…。
I have it on good authority that...

範例 | A: I have it on good authority that he's made a lot of money.
我有充分根據知道他賺了很多錢。
B: Everybody knows that.
大家都知道。

提示 | authority [əˈθɔrətɪ] *n.* 依據；來源

● 表達不知道某事 Stating One Has No Idea about Something

0763
我不知道。
I don't know.

替換 | Don't ask me.
I'm in the dark about it.

範例 | A: Do you know if John's case is finished?
你知道約翰的案子是否完成了嗎？
B: Sorry. I don't know.
對不起，我不知道。

0764
我要是知道就好了。
I wish I knew.

替換 | I wish I know something about it.

範例 | A: Is John studying nuclear techology?
約翰現在在唸核能科技嗎？
B: I wish I knew.
我要是知道就好了。

提示　nuclear ['njuklɪɚ] *adj.* 核子的；原子能的
technology [tɛk'nɑlədʒɪ] *n.* 科技；技術

0765

很抱歉，我一點也不知道…。
I'm sorry, I don't know anything about...

替換　I'm sorry, I know nothing about...

範例　**A:** I'm sorry, I don't know anything about that.
　　　　很抱歉，我一點也不知道那件事。
　　　B: It doesn't matter.
　　　　沒關係。

0766

對不起，我不知道。
Sorry, I have no idea.

替換　Sorry, I don't have a clue.

範例　**A:** Do you know who put this here? 你知道誰把這個放在這裡嗎？
　　　B: Sorry, I have no idea. 對不起，我不知道。

0767

很遺憾，我不太知道…。
I'm sorry, I don't know much about...

替換　I'm sorry to say I don't know very much about...

範例　**A:** Do you know how many people were killed in the accident?
　　　　你知道多少人在這次事故中喪生嗎？
　　　B: I'm sorry, I don't know much about that accident.
　　　　很遺憾，我不太知道那個事故。

0768

我得承認，我對…不太了解。
I have to admit I know very little about...

替換　I have to say...is not something I know very much about.

範例　**A:** I have to admit I know very little about her.
　　　　我得承認，我對她不太了解。
　　　B: But she is your wife.
　　　　可是她是你的妻子啊。

0769

我沒法告訴你。
I couldn't tell you.

替換　Don't ask me.

範例	**A:** Who switched out the light? 誰把燈關了？ **B:** I couldn't tell you. 我沒法告訴你。

0770 我根本不知道。
I haven't the faintest idea.

範例	**A:** Do you know who loves her? 你知道誰愛她嗎？ **B:** I haven't the faintest idea. 我根本不知道。

0771 我沒法告訴你…。
I couldn't tell you...

範例	**A:** I couldn't tell you what caused it. 我沒法告訴你事情的原因。 **B:** Why not? 為什麼？

0772 恐怕我沒法告訴你。
I'm afraid I can't tell you.

範例	**A:** Who is the boy's father? 誰是這個男孩的父親？ **B:** I'm afraid I can't tell you. 恐怕我沒法告訴你。

0773 很遺憾，我一點都不知道…。
I'm sorry, I don't know anything about...

範例	**A:** Please tell me, OK? 　　請告訴我，好嗎？ **B:** I'm sorry, I don't know anything about that. 　　很遺憾，我一點都不知道那件事。

0774 那方面我恐怕無法幫助你。
I'm afraid I can't help you there.

範例	**A:** I'm afraid I can't help you there. 那方面我恐怕無法幫助你。 **B:** OK. That's all right. 好的，沒關係。

2.18　意圖 Intention

　　在會話當中，有時我們需要向別人說明自己的打算，有時要了解別人的意圖。但是，如何根據場合、事件、目的等實際情況，恰如其分地表達卻是不容易的。因此，我們必須注意以下三點：（一）掌握必要的表達方法；（二）表達時要清楚明瞭；（三）了解別人的打算或意圖時，不要過於唐突。

● 詢問意圖 Asking What Someone Is Going to Do

0775	**你打算⋯嗎？** (034) **Are you going to...?**
替換	Do you plan/intend to...? Is it your intention to...?
範例	**A:** Are you going to meet them? 你打算見他們嗎？ **B:** Sure, why not? 當然。為什麼不呢？
提示	intention [ɪn'tɛnʃən] *n.* 目的；意圖
0776	**你打算⋯，是嗎？** **You intend to..., don't you?**
替換	It's your intention to..., isn't it? Your intention is to..., isn't it?
範例	**A:** You intend to go back, don't you? 你打算回去，是嗎？ **B:** Yes. I can't bear this place any more. 是的，我再也受不了這地方。
0777	**你打算怎麼辦？** **What are you going to do?**
替換	What's your intention? What do you intend to do?
範例	**A:** What are you going to do? 你打算怎麼辦？ **B:** I don't know actually. 事實上我根本就不知道。
0778	**⋯你要做什麼？** **What'll you do...?**
替換	What'll you be doing...? What're you doing...?
範例	**A:** What'll you do tonight? 今晚你要做什麼？ **B:** I will go to Kate's party. 我要去凱特的舞會。

0779
你打算做什麼？
What do you intend to do?

(替換) What do you plan to do?
What are you thinking of doing?

(範例) **A:** What do you intend to do? 你打算做什麼？
B: I can't tell you that now. 現在我不能告訴你。

0780
你會…嗎？
Will you...?

(替換) Do you reckon you'll...?

(範例) **A:** Will you be there? 你會在那裡嗎？
B: Sure. 當然。

0781
你要…嗎？
Do you intend to...?

(替換) You'll..., won't you?

(範例) **A:** Do you intend to go to the party? 你要參加那個舞會嗎？
B: Yes, I do. 是的。

0782
你打算…嗎？
Do you have any intention of...?

(替換) Are you thinking of...?

(範例) **A:** Do you have any intention of learning computer science?
你打算學電腦嗎？
B: Of course.
當然了。

0783
…你有什麼打算？
Do you have any plans for...?

(範例) **A:** Do you have any plans for the holiday? 這個假期你有什麼打算？
B: I will go to Paris. 我要去巴黎。

0784
你計畫…嗎？
Are you planning to...?

(範例) **A:** Are you planning to go on a trip? 你計畫去旅行嗎？
B: Certainly not. 當然不。

0785	你決定⋯嗎？ **Have you decided to...?**
範例	**A:** Have you decided to give in? 你決定讓步了嗎？ **B:** Yes. 是的。

● 說明打算 Stating One Is Going to Do Something

0786	我打算⋯。 **I plan to...**
替換	I'm going/planning to... I intend/propose to... My intention is to... It's my intention to... I have every intention to...
範例	**A:** I'm told that a great movie is showing. Have you seen it? 　聽說正在上映一部很棒的電影。你看過了嗎？ **B:** No, but I plan to see it tomorrow. 　沒有，不過我打算明天去看。
提示	propose [prə'poz] *v.* 打算

0787	我要⋯。 **I'm...**
範例	**A:** I'm leaving tomorrow. 明天我要離開了。 **B:** Why don't you stay here longer? 為什麼不多待一段時間？

0788	我正打算⋯。 **I'm thinking of...**
替換	I'm figuring on...
範例	**A:** I'm thinking of visiting you. 我正打算拜訪你。 **B:** You're welcome to. 歡迎你。

0789	我想要⋯。 **I mean to...**
替換	I feel inclined to... I think I'll...

| 範例 | A: I mean to give him a hand. 我想要幫他一把。
B: So do I. 我也是。 |

| 0790 | 我想過要…。
I thought I'd... |

| 範例 | A: I thought I'd change myself. 我想過要改變自己。
B: Did you succeed? 你成功了嗎？ |

| 0791 | 我要盡可能地…。
I'll do all I can... |

| 範例 | A: I'll do all I can to help her. 我要盡可能地幫助她。
B: That's really kind of you. 你真好。 |

| 0792 | 我會找時間…。
I'll get around to... |

| 範例 | A: I'll get around to writing to her. 我會找時間寫信給她。
B: That's very considerate of you. 你真是太體貼了。 |

| 提示 | considerate [kən'sɪdərɪt] adj. 體貼的；考慮周到的 |

| 0793 | 我已經決定…。
I've decided to... |

| 範例 | A: I've decided to support him. 我已經決定支持他。
B: So have I. 我也是。 |

| 0794 | 我預計…。
I expect... |

| 範例 | A: I expect I'll be in my office this afternoon. 我預計下午會在辦公室。
B: Good. 好的。 |

● 表達沒打算做某事 Stating One Is Not Going to Do Something

| 0795 | 我沒打算…。
I'm not planning on... |

| 替換 | I have no intention of... |

| 範例 | A: I'm not planning on attending that marathon meeting.
我沒打算參加那個馬拉松會議。 |

B: Neither am I.
我也是。

(提示) marathon ['mærəˌθɑn] *adj.* 馬拉松式的

0796 我不太想⋯。
I don't really feel inclined to...

(替換) I don't really want to...

(範例) **A:** I don't really feel inclined to live here. 我不太想住在這裡。
B: Then where do you want to live? 那你想住哪裡？

0797 我不打算⋯。
I'm not planning to...

(替換) I don't plan/intend/propose to...

(範例) **A:** Will you stay here long? 你會在這裡待很久嗎？
B: I'm not planning to stay here much longer. 我不打算在這裡多待。

0798 我想我不會⋯。
I don't reckon I'll...

(替換) I don't think I'll...

(範例) **A:** I don't reckon I'll accept his offer. 我想我不會接受他的好意。
B: You're too stubborn. 你太固執了。

0799 我根本就沒這打算。
Nothing could be farther from my mind.

(範例) **A:** Do you want to go to that party? 你想去那個派對嗎？
B: Nothing could be farther from my mind. 我根本就沒這打算。

0800 我根本就沒打算⋯。
Nothing could be farther from my mind than...

(範例) **A:** Do not tell her the news.
別告訴她這個消息。
B: Nothing could be farther from my mind than to tell her the truth.
我根本就沒打算告訴她真相。

0801 我怎麼也不會想⋯。
Nothing will induce me to...

A: Nothing will induce me to betray my country.
我怎麼也不會想背叛我的祖國。
B: That's wonderful.
那很好。

提示　induce [ɪn'djus] *v.* 引起；導致

0802　我已經決定不⋯。
I've decided not to...

 A: I've decided not to tell my parents the news.
我已經決定不告訴我父母這個消息。
B: Why not? It's good news.
為什麼不呢？這是好消息啊。

0803　我從沒想過⋯。
It never entered my head to...

 A: You have some talent for acting.
你有些表演的天賦。
B: It never entered my head to become an actor.
我從沒想過要成為一名演員。

0804　我並非故意要⋯。
It wasn't my intention to...

 A: It wasn't my intention to hurt you. 我並非故意要傷害你。
B: It doesn't matter. 沒關係。

0805　我會要⋯才怪呢。
You won't catch me...

範例　**A:** Do you like golf? 你喜歡高爾夫球嗎？
B: You won't catch me playing golf. 我會要玩高爾夫球才怪呢。

2.19　邀請 Invitations

　　為了維繫良好的人際關係，我們有時要舉辦某些社交活動來邀請人參加。口頭邀請可以透過電話或當面進行，邀請時要注意講明參加活動的時間、地點和內容，並請求對方回覆是否參加。

　　值得注意的是，邀請性語言有時只不過是口頭的應酬，並沒有真正邀請的意思，因此要正確理解說話者的語意，並且客氣應對，一般的處理方式是表示感謝，但不要詢問時間和地點，以免對方感到尷尬。無論是邀請一方還是被邀請的一方，都要注意表達得體，避免出現誤解。一般來說，邀請時，使用陳述的語氣有試探性的作用；使用否定疑問句則希望對方接受邀請，語言的試探性較弱，口氣更加誠懇。

　　接受邀請時不能簡單地用 "Yes." 來回答，一定要感謝對方或對對方的安排表示讚賞。拒絕邀請時不能簡單地用 "No." 來回絕，因為這有可能引起不快，適當的謝絕方法是：感謝邀請人，並表示遺憾不能參與，最後並附上一些體面的理由。

● 邀請他人 Inviting Someone

035

0806 我們去…。
Let's go for...

範例　A: Let's go for Chinese food. 我們去吃中國菜吧。
B: OK. 好。

0807 有空…嗎？
Are you free...?

範例　A: Are you free for our party this evening? 今晚有空參加晚會嗎？
B: Sorry. I'm busy this evening. 對不起，我今晚很忙。

0808 …怎麼樣？
What about...?

範例　A: What about meeting my parents? 見見我的父母怎麼樣？
B: I'm not ready. Let's wait till later. 我沒有心理準備。再等等好嗎？

0809 你願意…嗎？
Would you like to come to...?

範例　A: Would you like to come to my birthday party?
你願意參加我的生日會嗎？
B: Sure.
一定去。

0810

想和我們一起…嗎？
Want to join us for...?

範例
A: Want to join us for the parade? 想和我們一起遊行嗎？
B: Not me. 我可不行。

提示　parade [pə'red] *n.* 遊行

0811

你想一起來嗎？
Do you fancy coming along?

範例
A: Do you fancy coming along? 你想一起來嗎？
B: Yes, I'd like to. 好啊，非常願意。

0812

如果你不忙，就留下來…。
Stay for..., unless you're busy.

範例
A: Stay for dinner, unless you're busy. 如果你不忙，就留下來吃晚餐吧。
B: Sorry. Next time, OK? 對不起，下次好嗎？

0813

如果你沒事，…過來玩玩。
Drop by...if you're not doing anything.

範例
A: Drop by tomorrow if you're not doing anything.
如果你沒事，明天過來玩玩。
B: OK. Thank you.
好的，謝謝。

0814

你一定要和我們一起…。
You must join us for...

範例
A: You must join us for a game of tennis.
你一定要和我們一起打網球。
B: I'm afraid I have no time. Next time, OK?
恐怕我沒有時間，下次好嗎？

0815

你為什麼不和我們一起…？
Why don't you come...with us?

範例
A: Why don't you come to the party with us?
你為什麼不和我們一起參加晚會呢？
B: Sorry, I'm going out of town. How about next time?
對不起，我要去外地，下一次行嗎？

0816	我們…好嗎？ **Shall we...?**
範例	**A:** Shall we have a drink at this bar? 我們去酒吧喝一杯好嗎？ **B:** That's a good idea. 好主意。

0817	我很希望你來參加…。 **I'd very much like you to come to...**
範例	**A:** I'd very much like you to come to our dinner party. 　　我很希望你來參加我們的晚宴。 **B:** That'd be great! I'll go if I'm free. 　　太好了！有空我會去的。

0818	你想…嗎？ **Would you care to...?**
範例	**A:** Would you care to see my photos? 你想看看我的照片嗎？ **B:** Of course. 當然了。

0819	我們冒昧邀請你…。 **We thought you might like to...**
範例	**A:** We thought you might like to attend our meeting. 　　我們冒昧邀請你出席我們的會議。 **B:** With pleasure. 　　非常樂意。

● 接受邀請 Accepting an Invitation

0820	好呀。 **OK.**
替換	All right then. Yes, I would. With pleasure.
範例	**A:** Tomorrow we'll go to the museum. Would you like to come along? 　　我們明天要去博物館，你想一起來嗎？ **B:** OK. 　　好呀。
提示	museum [mju'zɪəm] *n.* 博物館

0821

好呀。
Sounds good.

(替換) Sounds great.

(範例) **A:** Drop by for a chat if you're not busy.
　　　如果你不忙，找時間過來聊聊吧。
　　　B: Sounds good.
　　　好呀。

0822

好極了！
That would be lovely!

(替換) That would be marvellous!

(範例) **A:** What are you going to do this Saturday? Let's see a movie, shall we?
　　　這星期六你打算做什麼？我們去看電影，好嗎？
　　　B: That would be lovely!
　　　好極了！

(提示) marvellous ['mɑrvḷəs] *adj.* 奇妙的

0823

我很樂意！
I'd love to very much!

(範例) **A:** You must be hungry. Would you like to join us for dinner?
　　　你一定餓了，想和我們一起吃晚飯嗎？
　　　B: I'd love to very much!
　　　我很樂意！

0824

我接受這個邀請。
I'll take you up on that.

(範例) **A:** Why don't you come to the party with us?
　　　你何不和我們一起參加晚會呢？
　　　B: I'll take you up on that.
　　　我接受這個邀請。

0825

很高興…。
It would be very nice...

(範例) **A:** Shall we have lunch together? 一塊去吃午餐怎麼樣？
　　　B: It would be very nice to have lunch with you. 很高興和你共進午餐。

0826

…再好不過了。
I'd like nothing better than to...

範例
A: I'm going to go running. Would you like to join me?
我要去跑步。你也要去嗎？
B: I'd like nothing better than to go with you.
跟你去再好不過了。

0827

謝謝你。我很樂意。
Thank you. I'd like to very much.

範例
A: I'd very much like you to come to my place and watch a DVD.
我很希望你來我這裡看 DVD。
B: Thank you. I'd like to very much.
謝謝你。我很樂意。

0828

我晚點到，行嗎？
I'll be a little late. Is that OK?

範例
A: Are you going to the beach with us this afternoon?
今天下午你要和我們一起去海灘嗎？
B: I'll be a little late. Is that OK?
我晚點到，行嗎？

0829

這個主意聽起來不錯。
That sounds like a very good idea.

範例
A: Nice seeing you, Peter. Please look me up since we live so close to each other. 彼德，很高興見到你。我們住得很近，請到我家來玩吧。
B: That sounds like a very good idea. 這個主意聽起來不錯。

0830

我們很高興接受你們的邀請。
We'd be very delighted to accept your invitation.

範例
A: We're going to visit the zoo. Will you go with us?
我們要去參觀動物園，你們要和我們一起去嗎？
B: We'd be very delighted to accept your invitation.
我們很高興接受你們的邀請。

0831

真是令人高興的主意，謝謝。
What a delightful idea! Thank you.

範例 A: Let's get together tomorrow. 我們明天小聚一下吧。
B: What a delightful idea! Thank you. 眞是令人高興的主意，謝謝。

● 謝絕邀請 Declining an Invitation

0832	不要。 **No, I don't.**

替換 No, I wouldn't.
Certainly not.

範例 A: Do you want to go swimming with me? 想和我一起去游泳嗎？
B: No, I don't. 不要。

0833	哦，太可惜！ **Oh, what a shame!**

替換 Oh, what a pity!

範例 A: Would you like to go fishing tomorrow?
明天想去釣魚嗎？
B: Oh, what a shame! I have a date tomorrow.
哦，太可惜！我明天有約會。

0834	我很想去，但…。 **I'd love to, but...**

替換 I wish I could, but...

範例 A: If you could manage it, we'd like you to host the meeting for us.
如果你能安排的話，我們想請你來替我們主持會議。
B: I'd love to, but I'm waiting for Jack.
我很想去，但我在等傑克。

0835	還是不要吧。 **I'd rather not.**

替換 I'd better not.

範例 A: Would you like to go dancing with me? 想和我去跳舞嗎？
B: I'd rather not. 還是不要吧。

0836	真的沒有那個必要。 **That's really not necessary.**

A: We would be delighted if you could have a party with us.
如果你能和我們一起聚會，我們會很高興的。

B: That's really not necessary.
真的沒有那個必要。

0837　我恐怕不行。不過還是要謝謝你。
I'm afraid I can't. But thank you all the same.

 A: May I have the pleasure of seeing the movie with you?
我有榮幸和你一起去看電影嗎？

B: I'm afraid I can't. But thank you all the same.
我恐怕不行。不過還是要謝謝你。

0838　恐怕…我已經沒有空了。不過還是要謝謝你。
I'm afraid I'm already booked up for...But thank you just the same.

 A: We thought you might like to see a play with us on Sunday.
我們冒昧邀你週日和我們去看戲好嗎？

B: I'm afraid I'm already booked up for the weekend. But thank you just the same.
恐怕這週末我已經沒有空了。不過還是要謝謝你。

0839　很抱歉，我想我…來不了了。
I'm terribly sorry, but I don't think I can make it...

 A: I'm terribly sorry, but I don't think I can make it tomorrow.
很抱歉，我想我明天來不了了。

B: It doesn't matter.
沒關係。

0840　不湊巧，我得…。
Unfortunately, I have to...

 A: We're having a reception tomorrow. We would be pleased if you could come.
我們明天有個招待會。如蒙光臨，不勝榮幸。

B: Unfortunately, I have to have my car fixed tomorrow.
不湊巧，我明天得修車。

 unfortunately [ʌn'fɔrtʃənɪtlɪ] *adv.* 遺憾地；可惜地

0841	很遺憾，我不能…。 **Regretfully, I won't be able to...**

範例 A: Regretfully, I won't be able to come to your house on Sunday.
很遺憾，我週日不能來你家了。
B: Next time, OK?
下一次，可以嗎？

提示 regretfully [rɪˈgrɛtflɪ] *adv.* 遺憾地；後悔地

0842	很遺憾，我…。不過，我還是謝謝你想到我。 **I regret to say that I...However, thank you for thinking of me.**

範例 A: I regret to say that I have to go to the hospital and take care of my mother. However, thank you for thinking of me.
很遺憾，我得去醫院照顧我媽。不過，我還是謝謝你想到我。
B: That's all right.
不客氣。

2.20 判斷 Making a Judgment

在日常生活中，有很多時候我們必須對事物下判斷。而可能性的大小、交談的場合將直接影響語言的使用。

036

0843	他們很可能會…。 **They'll very likely...**

替換 There's a good chance that they will...
It's probable that they will...

範例 A: Should we ask them to be responsible for this project?
我們應該要求他們負責這項計畫嗎？
B: That's not a good idea. They'll very likely shirk off their responsibilities.
這不是個好主意。他們很可能會推卸責任。

提示 shirk [ʃɝk] *v.* 迴避；退避

0844	不可能…。 **It's unlikely that...**

(替換)　It seems pretty impossible that...
It seems totally out of the question that...

(範例)　**A:** It's unlikely that he will win. 他不可能贏。
B: That's hard to say. 這很難說。

0845	我覺得…。 **I feel as if...**

(替換)　I feel that...

(範例)　**A:** It's so cloudy. 天氣好陰。
B: I feel as if it is going to rain. 我覺得快要下雨了。

0846	差不多是這樣。 **That's about right.**

(範例)　**A:** Since technology is developing so rapidly, nothing can be called absolutely modern.
因為科技快速發展，所以沒有什麼絕對現代化的東西。
B: That's about right.
差不多是這樣。

0847	也許…。 **Perhaps...**

(範例)　**A:** Tom said that no one cares about this matter anymore.
湯姆說沒人會再關心這件事了。
B: Perhaps he's right.
也許他是對的。

0848	聽起來不錯。 **That sounds all right.**

(替換)　It sounds quite all right.

(範例)　**A:** We should have lunch before the meeting.
我們應該在會議之前用中餐。
B: That sounds all right.
聽起來不錯。

0849

看來還行。
It seems all right.

範例
A: What do you think of my plan? 你覺得我的計畫怎麼樣？
B: It seems all right. 看起來還行。

0850

看來是這樣。
That's how it looks.

替換
It kind of looks that way.

範例
A: The watch might work if we replace the battery.
如果我們換電池，這手錶可能會運轉。
B: That's how it looks.
看來是這樣。

0851

好像…。
It looks like...

替換
It seems...
There seems to be...

範例
A: It looks like a fine day today. 今天好像天氣不錯。
B: It sure does. 當然了。

0852

可能…。
It seems likely that...

替換
It seems probable that...

範例
A: It seems likely that he might encounter some trouble.
他可能會遇到麻煩。
B: Why?
為什麼？

提示
encounter [ɪnˈkaʊntɚ] v. 遭遇；遇到

0853

我斷定…。
..., I say.

替換
I figure...

範例
A: She'll be happy, I say. 我斷定她會很高興。
B: Of course she will. 她當然會。

2.21 記憶 Memory

　　記得或忘記過去的事物是常見的一種心理現象，但表達記憶、遺忘或提醒他人，則有可能是一種社交行為。它可以用來陳述事實，也可以作為一種托辭。英語中表達這些概念有很多方式。

● 詢問是否記得 Asking if Someone Remembers

0854 你不記得了嗎？ (037)
Can't you remember?

(替換)
Can't you recall?
Have you forgot?
Don't you remember?

(範例)
A: That girl is Tom's younger sister. Can't you remember?
那個女孩是湯姆的妹妹。你不記得了嗎？
B: Really?
真的？

0855 你還記得…嗎？
Do you remember...?

(替換)
Can you recall/recollect...?
Can you bring to mind...?

(範例)
A: Do you remember where he went? 你還記得他去什麼地方嗎？
B: Yes. 記得。

(提示)
recollect [ˌrɛkə'lɛkt] v. 回憶；想起

0856 你沒忘記，是吧？
You haven't forgot, have you?

(替換)
You haven't forgot, have you?
You remember, don't you?

(範例)
A: Silence is golden. You haven't forgot, have you?
沉默是金。你沒忘記，是吧？
B: Sorry. I can't control myself.
對不起，我實在管不住自己。

192

0857	你還記得…嗎？ **Do you happen to remember...?**

替換 | Do you have any recollection of...?
Do you by any chance remember...?
Could I ask if you remember...?
Haven't you forgotten...?

範例 | **A:** Do you happen to remember his name? 你還記得他的名字嗎？
B: Sorry, I don't. 對不起，我不記得了。

提示 | recollection [ˌrɛkəˈlɛkʃən] *n.* 回憶

0858	我想知道你是否還記得…。 **I was wondering if you could recall...**

替換 | I was wondering whether you remember...
I'd like to know if you could recall...
Would you mind telling me if you still remember...?
I wonder if you remember...

範例 | **A:** I was wondering if you could recall where you met each other.
我想知道你是否還記得你們兩個在什麼地方見的面。
B: It seems like it was in a pub.
好像是在一家酒吧。

0859	也許你已經忘記…吧？ **Perhaps you've forgotten...?**

範例 | **A:** Perhaps you've forgotten what he said?
也許你已經忘記他說的話吧？
B: How could I?
怎麼可能呢？

● 說明還記得 Stating that One Remembers

0860	我想起來了。 **I can remember it now.**

替換 | Now that I think about it.

範例 | **A:** Do you remember when we met? 你記得我們何時見面的嗎？
B: I can remember it now. 我想起來了。

0861

我記得⋯。
What I remember is...

範例　A: Can you remember the murderer? 你還記得那個兇手嗎？
B: What I remember is that he was here. 我記得他在這裡。

0862

我能記起來的是，⋯。
As far as I can remember, ...

替換　As far as I recall, ...
As far as I can recollect, ...
To the best of my memory, ...

範例　A: As far as I can remember, he was tall and handsome.
我能記起來的是，他長得又高又帥。
B: Yes. I like him a lot.
是的，我很喜歡他。

0863

我記得⋯。
I remember that...

替換　As I remember it, ...
As I recall, ...
It is within my recollection...

範例　A: Did they get on well with each other? 他們過去處得好嗎？
B: I remember that they were very good friends. 我記得他們是好朋友。

0864

我很清楚地記得⋯。
I remember quite clearly...

替換　I distinctly recall...

範例　A: I remember quite clearly what Jack looked like.
我很清楚地記得傑克以前的樣子。
B: But I can't remember.
可是我記不起來了。

提示　distinctly [dɪˈstɪŋktlɪ] *adv.* 清楚地

0865

我漸漸想起來了。
It's coming back to me now.

範例　A: Do you have any impression of it? 你有印象嗎？
B: It's coming back to me now. 我漸漸想起來了。

提示 impression [im'prɛʃən] *n.* 印象；感想

0866 我尤其記得…。
I remember especially...

範例 A: Do you have any impression of the man? 你對那個男的有印象嗎？
B: I remember especially his face. 我尤其記得他的臉。

0867 我還大概記得…。
I have some recollection of...

範例 A: Do you remember Tom's girlfriend? 你還記得湯姆的女朋友嗎？
B: I have some recollection of her. 我還大概記得那個女孩。

0868 我永遠不會忘記…。
I'll always remember...

替換 I'll never forget...
What I shall never forget is...

範例 A: Do you still remember our English teacher?
你還記得我們英語老師嗎？
B: I'll always remember her.
我永遠不會忘記她。

0869 如果我沒記錯的話，…。
If I remember correctly, ...

替換 If I'm not mistaken, ...
If my memory serves correctly, ...

範例 A: What were they talking about at the meeting?
他們在會議上談論了什麼？
B: If I remember correctly, you were at the meeting so you should know.
如果我沒記錯的話，你也參加了會議，所以你應該知道。

● 說明已經忘記 Expressing that One Has Forgotten

0870 我不記得了。
I can't remember.

替換 I don't remember.

195

範例　A: Did you return the book or not? 你還書了嗎？
B: Sorry. I can't remember. 對不起，我不記得了。

0871
我不記得…了。
I can't place...

替換　I just can't call/bring...to mind.
I simply can't call up...
I can't remember/recall...
...just won't come to mind.

範例　A: Do you remember Jack? 還記得傑克嗎？
B: I can't place him. 我不記得他了。

0872
恐怕我已經忘了。
I've forgotten, I'm afraid.

替換　I'm afraid I forget it now.
I'm afraid it escapes me.
I'm afraid I have no recollection of it.

範例　A: Do you still remember meeting my uncle? 你還記得見過我叔叔嗎？
B: I've forgotten, I'm afraid. 恐怕我已經忘了。

0873
我一不留神就忘了。
It slipped my mind.

替換　It just slips my memory.
My mind's gone blank.
I've forgotten all about it.

範例　A: Why did you forget about our date? 你為什麼忘了我們的約會？
B: It slipped my mind. 我一不留神就忘了。

0874
對不起，我把它全忘了。
Sorry, it's gone clean out of my mind.

替換　I'm sorry, I've completely forgotten.
I'm sorry, I have no memory of it.
I'm sorry, I had no recollection at all of it.
I'm sorry, but it has escaped my memory.

範例　A: Sorry, it's gone clean out of my mind. 對不起，我把它全忘了。
B: How bad your memory is! 你的記憶力可真差啊！

0875	我好像已經忘了。 **I seem to have forgotten.**
替換	I can't seem to bring to mind.
範例	**A:** Do you remember what she told me? 你還記得她告訴我的話嗎？ **B:** I seem to have forgotten. 我好像已經忘了。

0876	我得承認我不記得了。 **I must confess I forgot.**
替換	I have to admit I don't remember.
範例	**A:** I was wondering if you remember the password for this computer. 我想或許你記得這台電腦的密碼。 **B:** I must confess I forgot. 我得承認我不記得了。
提示	confess [kən'fɛs] *v.* 承認；坦白

● 提醒某人某事 Reminding Someone of Something

0877	喂，別忘了⋯。 **Hey, ...!**
範例	**A:** Hey, your book! 喂，別忘了你的書。 **B:** Thank you. 謝謝。

0878	你準備⋯，是不是？ **You're going to..., aren't you?**
範例	**A:** You're going to ring Kate, aren't you? 你準備打電話給凱特，是不是？ **B:** Yes. 是的。

0879	⋯怎麼樣了？ **What about...?**
範例	**A:** What about your job? 你的工作怎麼樣了？ **B:** It's OK. 還可以。

0880
我想你剛才說過…。
I think you said...

範例　**A:** I think you said you wanted to see Peter.
　　　我想你剛才說過你想見彼德。
　　　B: But I don't want to see him now.
　　　可是我現在不想。

0881
我想提醒你…。
I'd like to remind you of...

替換　I'd like to remind you about...

範例　**A:** I'd like to remind you of the meeting this afternoon.
　　　我想提醒你今天下午的會議。
　　　B: Thank you.
　　　謝謝。

0882
我可以提醒你…嗎？
Can I remind you...?

範例　**A:** Can I remind you to ring Kate? 我可以提醒你打電話給凱特嗎？
　　　B: Sure. Thank you. 當然了。謝謝你。

0883
我想你已經做了，不過…。
I expect you've already done it, but...

範例　**A:** I expect you've already done it, but Mr. Lee wants you to ring him up.
　　　我想你已經做了，不過李先生要你打電話給他。
　　　B: Thank you for telling me.
　　　謝謝你告訴我。

0884
你還記得這件事，對不對？
You haven't forgotten about it, have you?

替換　You'll remember it, won't you?
　　　You won't forget about it, will you?

範例　**A:** You haven't forgotten about it, have you?
　　　你還記得這件事，對不對？
　　　B: No, I haven't.
　　　是的，我沒忘。

0885	我想應該提醒你⋯。 **I think I should remind you...**
替換	I think I must remind you... I think I ought to remind you...
範例	A: I think I should remind you that Mr. Lee is here. 我想應該提醒你，李先生在這裡。 B: Thank you. 謝謝。

0886	希望你不介意我提醒你⋯。 **I hope you don't mind me reminding you of...**
替換	I hope you won't mind my reminding you of...
範例	A: I hope you don't mind me reminding you of the meeting. 希望你不介意我提醒你開會的事。 B: That's very kind of you. 謝謝，你人真好。

0887	如果你還記得的話，⋯。 **If you recall, ...**
範例	A: If you recall, we met somewhere before. 如果你還記得的話，我們在什麼地方見過。 B: But I don't think we have. 我不這麼認為。

0888	恐怕我得提醒你⋯。 **I'm afraid I have to remind you that...**
範例	A: I'm afraid I have to remind you that your time is up. 恐怕我得提醒你時間到了。 B: Thank you. 謝謝。

0889	請允許我提醒你⋯。 **May I remind you...?**
範例	A: May I remind you that you have to help him with his report? 請允許我提醒你應該指導一下他寫報告。 B: Yes. Thank you. 好的。謝謝。

2.22　義務 Obligation

在會話當中，人們不可避免會遇到權利和義務的問題。如何說明義務，如何詢問別人的義務，如何將自己的責、權、利清楚明白地表達出來，都需要我們根據實際場景、對話雙方的關係等具體的情況來適當表述。人際交往的多樣性賦予語言不同的特徵。表達這些語言功能時，一定要注意得體。

038

0890
你必須…。
You must...

（替換）
You have to...
You've got to...

（範例）
A: Wake up, Tom. You must go to school now.
　　湯姆，起床吧，你必須去上學。
B: All right.
　　好吧。

0891
你得…。
You will be required to...

（替換）
You are expected/required to...

（範例）
A: Boss, are there any requirements for tomorrow's meeting?
　　老闆，明天的會議你有何要求？
B: You will be required to arrive before 9 a.m.
　　你得在早上九點之前到。

（提示）
requirement [rɪˈkwaɪrmənt] *n*. 要求；必要條件

0892
你最好…。
You'd better...

（替換）
You ought to...
You should...

（範例）
A: There's another mistake. You'd better be more careful.
　　又一個錯誤。你最好更加仔細些。
B: I'm sorry, I will.
　　對不起，我會的。

0893	你有義務⋯。 **You're obligated to...**
(替換)	You're (in) duty bound to... It's your duty to... You have a duty to... You have an obligation to...
(範例)	**A:** You're obligated to take care of your elderly parents. 　你有義務照顧年老的父母。 **B:** Yes, sir. I will definitely do it. 　是的，先生，我一定會這樣做。
(提示)	obligated ['ɑblɪgetɪd] *adj.* 有義務的

2.23 提供 Offering

　　日常生活中，我們有時會主動幫助他人，有時需要接受別人的東西或幫助。主動提供幫助時，必須了解對方的態度，以免一頭熱；接受別人的東西或幫助時，一般要表示感謝。哪怕是拒絕別人，也要表示感謝，還要說明理由，否則會引起不快。

● 提供某物 Offering Something

039

0894	給你的⋯。 **Your...**
(替換)	Here's...
(範例)	**A:** Your shirt, Tom. 湯姆，給你的襯衫。 **B:** Yes. Thank you. 好，謝謝。

0895	想要⋯嗎？ **Need...?**
(替換)	Fancy some...? Will you have...? Would you like some...?

Won't you have some...?
Would you care for...?

範例 A: Need a drink? 想要飲料嗎？
B: Yes. Thanks. 要，謝謝。

0896
這是給你的。
This is for you.

替換 That's for you.

範例 A: This is for you. 這是給你的。
B: Really? 真的嗎？

0897
請拿著吧。
Please take it.

替換 Do have it.

範例 A: Please take it. 請拿著吧。
B: How can I thank you enough?! 怎麼謝你才好呢？

0898
…怎麼樣？
How about ...?

替換 What would you say to...?

範例 A: How about ice cream?
冰淇淋怎麼樣？
B: No, it's too cold. A cup of hot coffee would be fine.
不，太冷了。來杯熱咖啡就行了。

0899
怎麼不來點…呢？
Why don't you have some...?

範例 A: Why don't you have some black coffee? 怎麼不來點黑咖啡呢？
B: OK. Thanks. 好吧，謝謝。

0900
給你…好嗎？
Could I offer you...?

替換 May I give you...?

範例 A: Could I offer you something to drink? 給你點飲料好嗎？
B: Sure. Thank you. 當然好，謝謝。

0901	幫你拿點…好嗎？ **Can I get you...?**
替換	Can I offer/give you...? May I fetch you...?
範例	**A:** Can I get you some sugar? 幫你拿點糖好嗎？ **B:** Sure. 當然好。
提示	fetch [fɛtʃ] v. 取來；帶來

0902	這是你要的…。 **Here's...you need.**
替換	This is...you asked for.
範例	**A:** Here's the report you need. 這是你要的報告。 **B:** Thank you. 謝謝。

0903	我要你收下…。 **I want you to take...**
替換	I'd like you to have... I'd like to give you...
範例	**A:** I want you to take this. 我要你收下這個。 **B:** How nice! 太漂亮了。

0904	我很高興頒發…給你。 **It is my pleasure to present you with...**
替換	It is with great pleasure that I present you with...
範例	**A:** It is my pleasure to present you with the award. 我很高興頒發這個獎給你。 **B:** Thank you. 謝謝。

0905	請接受…作為我們的感謝之意。 **Please accept...as a token of our appreciation.**
範例	**A:** Please accept this as a token of our appreciation. 請接受這個作為我們的感謝之意。 **B:** Oh, thank you. 哦，謝謝。
提示	token ['tokən] n. 表徵

| 0906 | 如果你能接受…，我將會非常高興。
I'd be very delighted if you would accept... |

範例 A: I'd be very delighted if you would accept this donation.
如果你能接受這項捐贈，我將會非常高興。
B: Thanks.
謝謝。

提示 donation [do'neʃən] *n.* 捐贈； 捐款

● 接受提供 Accepting Offers

| 0907 | 太棒了！
Great. |

替換 Ooh, terrific!
That's just lovely.
That would be very nice.

範例 A: I'd like you to take this. 我想要你收下這個。
B: Great. 太棒了！

| 0908 | 多謝。
Thank you so much. |

替換 That's very kind of you.
Oh, that was extremely good of you.

範例 A: You can have one. 你可以來一個。
B: Thank you so much. 多謝。

| 0909 | 我想這是再好不過的。
I can think of nothing better. |

替換 That'd be most delightful.

範例 A: Here, have this. 拿走它吧。
B: I can think of nothing better. 我想這是再好不過的。

| 0910 | 我想要一點兒。
I'd love some. |

範例 A: Do you want some coffee? 你想來點咖啡嗎？
B: I'd love some. 我想要一點兒。

0911	我很想。 **I'd like it very much, please.**
範例	**A:** Do you want to have this? 你要這個嗎？ **B:** I'd like it very much, please. 我很想。

0912	哦，美極了！ **Oh, it's beautiful!**
範例	**A:** How do you like the painting? 你覺得這幅畫如何？ **B:** Oh, it's beautiful! 哦，美極了！

0913	這會非常有用的。 **It'll be very useful.**
範例	**A:** I want to give you this book. 我想把這本書給你。 **B:** It'll be very useful. 這會非常有用的。

0914	哦，你真是太好了！ **Oh, you're so wonderful!**
範例	**A:** I want to give you a chance. 我想給你一次機會。 **B:** Oh, you're so wonderful! 哦，你真是太好了！

0915	那正是我需要的。 **That's just what I needed.**
範例	**A:** Do you want this material? 你想要這份資料嗎？ **B:** That's just what I needed. 那正是我需要的。

● 謝絕提供 Refusing an Offer Politely

0916	不，謝謝。 **No, thanks.**
替換	None for me, thanks. Thanks all the same, but no. No, thank you, none for me. No, thank you very much. No, I really can't, thank you. I'd better not, thank you.

範例　A: Would you like some more coffee? 還要再喝一些咖啡嗎？
B: No, thanks. 不，謝謝。

0917

不，謝謝，這次不要了。
Not this time, thanks.

替換　No, thanks, not this time.

範例　A: Shall I help you clean the machine? 我可以幫你洗機器嗎？
B: Not this time, thanks. 不，謝謝，這次不要了。

0918

恐怕我不能，不過還是謝謝你。
I'm afraid I can't, but thank you just the same.

範例　A: Would you like to come?
你會來嗎？
B: I'm afraid I can't, but thank you just the same.
恐怕我不能，不過還是謝謝你。

0919

謝謝，我想還是不要了吧。
That's very kind of you, but I'd rather not.

範例　A: Would you like a cup of tea? 你想要來杯茶嗎？
B: That's very kind of you, but I'd rather not. 謝謝，我想還是不要了吧。

0920

恐怕我不能，謝謝你。
I'm not sure I can, thank you.

範例　A: I'm not sure I can, thank you. 恐怕我不能，謝謝你。
B: That's all right. 沒什麼。

0921

如果你不介意，我想還是不要吧。
I'd prefer not, if you don't mind.

範例　A: I'd prefer not, if you don't mind. 如果你不介意，我想還是不要吧。
B: That's OK. It's up to you. 好的，你說了算。

0922

不必了。
That won't be necessary.

範例　A: Want another one? 想再來一個嗎？
B: That won't be necessary. 不必了。

● 主動幫忙 Offering Help

0923

要幫忙嗎？
Need a hand?

(替換) Want some help?
Would you like any help?

(範例) A: Need a hand? 要幫忙嗎？
B: Sure. Thank you. 是的，謝謝。

0924

如果你想的話，我可以幫你…。
If you like, I could...for you.

(替換) If you want, I could...for you.

(範例) A: If you like, I could arrange a plan for you.
　　　 如果你想的話，我可以幫你安排一個計畫。
B: You're so considerate.
　　 你想得太周到了。

0925

你為什麼不讓我幫忙呢？
Why don't you let me help?

(範例) A: I'm afraid that I can't do this all by myself.
　　　 恐怕我不能一個人完成這件事。
B: Why don't you let me help?
　　 你為什麼不讓我幫忙呢？

0926

看來你需要幫助。
You look like you could use some help.

(範例) A: You look like you could use some help. 看來你需要幫助。
B: Yes, we need a hand. 是的，我們需要人手。

0927

看來你要人幫忙…。
You look like you need some help...

(範例) A: You look like you need some help starting the car.
　　　 看來你要人幫忙來發動這輛車。
B: Yes, I do, thanks.
　　 是的，謝謝。

0928

我會帶給你⋯。
I'll bring you...

範例
A: I'll bring you some homemade cookies.
　　我會帶給你一些自己做的餅乾。
B: You're so kind.
　　你太好了。

0929

我能幫你什麼嗎？
What can I do to help?

範例
A: What can I do to help? 我能幫你什麼嗎？
B: That's alright. Just relax. 沒關係，放輕鬆。

0930

也許我能幫你一點吧。
Perhaps I could assist in some way.

範例
A: Perhaps I could assist in some way. 也許我能幫你一點吧。
B: Sure. 當然了。

提示
assist [ə'sɪst] v. 援助；幫助

● 接受幫助 Accepting Help

0931

你真好，謝謝你。
That's nice of you, thank you.

替換
That's very kind of you, thank you.

範例
A: That's nice of you, thank you. 你真好，謝謝你。
B: You're welcome. 你太客氣了。

0932

如果你能幫助我，我會很高興。
I'd be most delighted if you could help me.

替換
I'd be most delighted to have your help.

範例
A: I'd be most delighted if you could help me.
　　如果你能幫助我，我會很高興。
B: Sure I will.
　　我當然能。

0933

我正需要呢！
That's just what I needed!

範例　A: That's just what I needed! 我正需要呢！
B: Really? 真的嗎？

0934 那真是幫了大忙。多謝。
That'd be a big help. Thanks a lot.

範例　A: That'd be a big help. Thanks a lot. 那真是幫了大忙。多謝。
B: That's all right. 沒什麼。

0935 我非常感謝你的幫助。
I'd be most grateful for your help.

範例　A: I'd be most grateful for your help. 我非常感謝你的幫助。
B: You're welcome. 不客氣。

0936 你想得真周到。
You're most thoughtful.

範例　A: You're most thoughtful. 你想得真周到。
B: Thank you. 謝謝。

0937 你想得真周到，…。
It was extremely good of you to...

範例　A: It was extremely good of you to send them all to me.
你想得真周到，把他們都送給我。
B: You're welcome.
不客氣。

● 謝絕幫助 Declining Help

0938 不用擔心，我能處理。
Don't worry. I can handle it.

替換　No, it's all right. I can manage.

範例　A: Can I give you a hand? 我能幫你忙嗎？
B: Don't worry. I can handle it. 不用擔心，我能處理。

0939 不，沒關係，不用擔心。
No, don't worry.

替換
No, it's OK; don't worry about it.
No, it's all right; don't worry about me.

範例
A: I think I need to spend more time with you.
我正考慮多花點時間陪你。
B: No, don't worry.
不，沒關係，不用擔心。

0940
不，沒關係，謝謝。
No, it's all right. Thanks.

替換
No, it's OK. Thanks.

範例
A: May I help you? 我可以幫你嗎？
B: No, it's all right. Thanks. 不，沒關係，謝謝。

0941
不，不用了，我自己能應付。
No, thanks, I can handle it.

替換
No, thanks a lot, but I'm OK.
No, no, I'm OK. I can do it myself.

範例
A: Is there anything I can do for you? 有什麼需要幫忙的嗎？
B: No, thanks, I can handle it. 不，不用了，我自己能應付。

0942
不用費心了。
Don't worry about it.

替換
Please don't bother about it.
Please don't trouble yourself about it.

範例
A: I want to help you with your English. 我想幫你學習英語。
B: Don't worry about it. 不用費心了。

0943
不，真的，我自己來就行。
No, really, I can do it myself.

範例
A: Do you need my help? 需要幫忙嗎？
B: No, really, I can do it myself. 不，真的，我自己來就行。

0944
不，謝謝。
No, thank you.

範例
A: Do you want me to help you? 要我幫你嗎？
B: No, thank you. 不，謝謝。

2.24 意見 Opinions

　　每個人都希望自己的意見受到重視。當你和他人進行意見交流時,隨時徵求他人的意見,不但使人感覺受到尊重,而且還能達到溝通的目的。徵求意見時,我們通常使用問句形式,但有時陳述句也可以間接達到徵求意見的作用。在表達意見時,我們的態度可以是明確的,但要注意避免給人武斷的印象;需要回避某個問題時,要謹慎、委婉,有時甚至要含糊地表明自己的看法。涉及對他人的評論時,語氣要溫和,以顯示自己的修養。為自己的看法辯護時,應該注意語氣的婉轉,儘量避免使用第一人稱,以免給人留下固執己見的印象。

● 徵求意見 Asking for Opinions

0945	你怎麼看…? **How about...?** (040)
替換	What about...?
範例	**A:** How about his intentions? 你怎麼看他的意圖? **B:** I think he meant well. 我認為他是好意。
0946	如果…可行嗎? **Will it do if...?**
範例	**A:** Will it do if both of them have full-time jobs? 如果他們倆都有全職的工作,可行嗎? **B:** Why not? 怎麼不行?
0947	你怎麼看? **What do you say?**
替換	What do you reckon? What's your view/opinion? What do you think (of it)?
範例	**A:** What do you say? 你怎麼看? **B:** We have similar experiences, so I think we'll see eye to eye on this matter. 我們有類似的經驗,所以我想我們對這件事的看法一致。

211

0948

我想聽聽你對…的看法。
I'd be glad to have your views on...

（替換）　I'd be glad to have your comments on...
I'd like to have your opinion on...

（範例）　**A:** I'd be glad to have your views on this matter.
我想聽聽你對這件事的看法。
B: I agree with you, actually.
實際上我和你的觀點一致。

0949

我覺得…沒多大意思，你呢？
I don't think much of..., do you?

（範例）　**A:** I don't think much of being a shop assistant, do you?
我覺得當個售貨員沒多大意思，你呢？
B: I'm afraid I can't agree with you.
恐怕我和你的觀點不一樣。

0950

你看這不錯吧？
Is that all right with you?

（範例）　**A:** Is that all right with you? 你看這不錯吧？
B: Sure. 當然了。

0951

…很糟，不是嗎？
...is pretty awful, isn't it?

（範例）　**A:** The food there is pretty awful, isn't it?
那裡的食物很糟，不是嗎？
B: It sure is.
當然了。

0952

對…你有什麼特殊見解？
Do you have any particular views on...?

（範例）　**A:** Do you have any particular views on the economic crisis in Asia?
對亞洲經濟危機，你有什麼特殊見解？
B: No, not really.
沒什麼特別的。

● 表達意見 Expressing Opinions

0953	你不認為…嗎？ **Don't you think...?**
範例	**A:** Don't you think it's dangerous to swim in that river? 你不認爲在那條河裡游泳很危險嗎？ **B:** No, I don't think so. 不，我不這麼認爲。
0954	我個人認為…。 **Personally, I think...**
替換	Personally, I feel/believe/consider...
範例	**A:** Personally, I think that's a big problem. 我個人認爲那是個大問題。 **B:** You're right. 你是對的。
0955	我的看法是…。 **My own view of the matter is that...**
替換	My position on this problem is that...
範例	**A:** What's your view? 你有什麼見解嗎？ **B:** My own view of the matter is that nobody can take her place. 我的看法是，沒人能取代她的位置。
0956	如果你問我，我認為…。 **If you ask me, I think....**
範例	**A:** If you ask me, I think it's difficult. 如果你問我，我認爲這件事很難。 **B:** Why? 爲什麼？
0957	你知道我怎麼想的？我想…。 **You know what I think? I think...**
範例	**A:** You know what I think? I think it would be romantic to walk in the rain. 你知道我怎麼想的？我想在雨中散步一定很浪漫。 **B:** You must be crazy. 你一定是瘋了。
0958	我不得不認為…。 **I can't help thinking that...**

範例
A: I can't help thinking that you're not qualified for the job.
我不得不認為，你不具備做這個工作的資格。
B: I don't understand. Would you please give me an explanation?
我不明白。請給我個解釋好嗎？

提示
explanation [ˌɛkspləˈneʃən] *n.* 解釋；說明

0959
噢，我得說…。
Well, I must say...

範例
A: Do you like the story? 你喜歡這個故事嗎？
B: Well, I must say the story is very funny. 噢，我得說這個故事很有趣。

0960
我想指出…。
I'd like to point out that...

範例
A: I'd like to point out that we're in great need of water.
我想指出我們急需要水。
B: We will try our best to help you.
我們會盡全力幫你的。

0961
如果我可以這麼說的話，…。
If I may say so, ...

範例
A: If I may say so, people need to have something to do.
如果我可以這麼說的話，人總得有點事做。
B: Yes! Otherwise life would be meaningless.
是啊！否則生活就會失去意義。

● 說明意見 Stating One's Opinion

0962
這對我無所謂。
It makes no difference to me.

範例
A: What do you think we should do? 你認為我們該做什麼？
B: It makes no difference to me. 這對我無所謂。

0963
我確實沒有什麼意見。
I really don't know what to say.

替換
I really don't have any opinion.
I really don't have anything to say.

214

範例　A: I really don't know what to say. 我確實沒有什麼意見。
　　　B: You're too modest. 你太謙虛了。

0964 恐怕這對我的確無關緊要。
It doesn't really affect me, I'm afraid.

替換　It doesn't really matter to me, I'm afraid.

範例　A: What do you think of the new plan? 你怎麼看這個新計畫？
　　　B: It doesn't really affect me, I'm afraid. 恐怕這對我的確無關緊要。

0965 我對此事沒有特別的看法。
I have no strong feelings about the issue.

替換　I can't say I have any particular views on the issue.
　　　I don't hold any particular position on that issue.

範例　A: Will you say a few words? 你能說幾句話嗎？
　　　B: I have no strong feelings about the issue. 我對此事沒有特別的看法。

0966 我說不上來。
I couldn't say.

範例　A: He's innocent. Do you think so? 他是無辜的，你是這樣想嗎？
　　　B: I couldn't say. 我說不上來。

提示　innocent ['ɪnəsənt] *adj.* 無辜的；清白的（+ of）

0967 這恐怕不是我能理解的。
I'm afraid it's beyond me.

範例　A: Is there life after death?
　　　　人死後有來生嗎？
　　　B: I couldn't say. I'm afraid it's beyond me.
　　　　我說不上來。這恐怕不是我能理解的。

0968 我確實不知道怎麼考慮…。
I really don't know what to think about...

範例　A: I really don't know what to think about his plan.
　　　　我確實不知道怎麼考慮他的計畫。
　　　B: Is it too complicated?
　　　　太複雜嗎？

提示　complicated ['kɑmplə‚ketɪd] *adj.* 複雜的；難解的

0969
我對…沒什麼可說的。
I've nothing to say about...

範例　A: I've nothing to say about the decision. 我對這個決定沒什麼可說的。
B: Neither have I. 我也是。

0970
恐怕這事我考慮得不多。
It's not something I've thought a lot about, I'm afraid.

範例　A: What do you think of our future?
你覺得我們的將來會怎樣？
B: It's not something I've thought a lot about, I'm afraid.
恐怕這事我考慮得不多。

● 避免直接表達 Stating in an Indirect Way

0971
這不是我所能知道的。
It's not my department.

範例　A: Do you know anything about their plan? 你了解他們的計畫嗎？
B: It's not my department. 這不是我所能知道的。

提示　department [dɪ'pɑrtmənt] n.【口】負責的事；職責範圍

0972
噢，我真的不知道。
Well, I don't really know.

範例　A: Where's a good hairstylist around here? 這邊哪裡有好的髮型師？
B: Well, I don't really know. 噢，我真的不知道。

0973
你這樣認為嗎？
Do you think so?

範例　A: It's probably going to rain. 很可能會下雨。
B: Do you think so? 你這樣認為嗎？

0974
我得好好考慮一下。
I'd have to think about it.

範例　A: I'd have to think about it. 我得好好考慮一下。
B: Take your time. 別著急。

0975	恐怕我不能對…加以評論。 **I'm afraid I can't comment on...**
範例	**A:** I'm afraid I can't comment on the attack. 恐怕我不能對這次的攻擊加以評論。 **B:** Why not? 為什麼不呢？

0976	我不是專家，但是…。 **I'm no expert, but...**
範例	**A:** I'm no expert, but I think the new policy is wrong. 我不是專家，但是我認為這項新政策是錯誤的。 **B:** Well, I don't. 噢，我不這樣認為。
提示	expert ['ɛkspɚt] *n.* 專家

● 設法改變他人意見 Trying to Change Someone's Opinion

0977	這麼看吧：…。 **Look at it like this:...**
範例	**A:** I can't forgive myself for making such a silly mistake. 我不能原諒自己犯了如此愚蠢的錯誤。 **B:** Look at it like this: a wise man also makes mistakes. 這麼看吧：明智的人也會犯錯。

0978	嗯，你這樣想吧：…。 **Well, think of it this way:...**
範例	**A:** I really hope I can be rich. But it's impossible. 我真的想變有錢，但是這是不可能的。 **B:** Well, think of it this way: money isn't everything. 嗯，你這樣想吧：錢不是萬能的。

0979	你不認為…嗎？ **Don't you think...?**
範例	**A:** Don't you think he'll return to his old job soon? 你不認為他很快就會去舊工作嗎？ **B:** No, I don't think so. 不，我不這樣認為。

0980	我想某個程度上是對的，但是…。 **I guess that's partly true, but...**

範例　A: I should not have been so cold to him.
　　　　　我真的不該對他這麼冷淡。
　　　　B: I guess that's partly true, but everything has two sides.
　　　　　我想某個程度上是對的，但是凡事都有兩面。

0981	是的，但是你沒有抓住重點，…。 **Yes, but you didn't get the main point:...**

範例　A: Yes, but you didn't get the main point: their design is out of fashion.
　　　　　是的，但是你沒有抓住重點，他們的設計已經過時了。
　　　　B: How can you say that?
　　　　　你怎麼能這麼說？

0982	從另一角度看，人們可以說…。 **Seen from another angle, one might say...**

範例　A: Seen from another angle, one might say that every effort is worth-
　　　　　while. 從另一角度看，人們可以說每一份努力都是值得的。
　　　　B: Don't give me that crap. 別說那些廢話。

提示　worthwhile ['wɝθ'hwaɪl] *adj.* 值得做的
　　　　crap [kræp] *n.*【諱】胡言；廢話

0983	你當然不會認為可以…吧。 **Surely you don't think...**

範例　A: Surely you don't think it's right to look down upon women doctors!
　　　　　你當然不會認為可以輕視女醫生吧。
　　　　B: How could I?
　　　　　我怎麼敢呢？

2.25　許可 Permission

　　在日常生活當中，做事有時需要徵得別人的允許。例如，跟人借東西要得到對方的同意，當著他人的面前吸煙，需要徵得對方的允許。英語中表達准許的方法取決於事情的性質、允許的難度、雙方的身份等因素。需要注意的兩點

是：（一）請求別人允許時要客氣；（二）不允許別人做某事時，要有技巧
——首先要表示歉意，之後再以比較委婉的語言加以拒絕。

● 徵求許可 Asking for Permission

0984	行嗎？ **OK?**	041

（替換）| All right?
Is it OK?
Do I have the go-ahead?
Do I have your permission?

（範例）| **A:** Please play the flute. OK? 請吹這個長笛，行嗎？
B: All right. 可以。

（提示）| permission [pɚˈmɪʃən] *n.* 許可；允許

0985	讓我…，好嗎？ **Let me..., would you?**

（範例）| **A:** Let me have a look, would you? 讓我看一下，好嗎？
B: OK. 可以。

0986	我可以…嗎？ **OK if I...?**

（替換）| OK to...?
All right if I...?
Is it OK if I...?
Can I have the go-ahead to...?
Could/May I...?
Can I..., please?
I can..., can't I?
Will you let me...?
Will you allow me to...?
Would it be all right if I...?
Do you think I could...?
Am I allowed to...?
Do I have your permission to...?
Would I be allowed to...?

範例
A: OK if I sing a song for you?
我可以為你唱首歌嗎？
B: All right. But wait till I stuff my ears with cotton.
可以，但是得先等我用棉花把耳朵搗上。

0987
你不反對…吧？
Would you object to...?

範例
A: Would you object to my having a day off? 你不反對我休一天假吧？
B: Of course not. 當然不。

提示
object [əb'dʒɛkt] v. 反對（+ to）

0988
能不能…？
Any chance of...?

替換
What are our chances of...?

範例
A: Any chance of seeing that guy? 能不能見到那個人？
B: I'm afraid not. He has gone to London. 恐怕不能，他去倫敦了。

0989
如果允許，我想…。
I'll...if I may.

替換
I should like to..., if I may.

範例
A: I'll leave my address if I may. 如果允許，我想留下我的地址。
B: Good. Thank you. 好的，謝謝。

0990
我想要…。
I thought I'd...

範例
A: I thought I'd use this dictionary. 我想要用這個字典。
B: Here you are. 給你。

0991
讓我…，好嗎？
You'll let me..., won't you?

範例
A: You'll let me borrow the book, won't you?
讓我借用一下你的書，好嗎？
B: OK.
可以。

0992
你反對嗎？
Do you have any objections?

範例 A: Do you have any objections? 你反對嗎？
B: No, not at all. 一點都不。

提示 objection [əbˈdʒɛkʃən] *n.* 反對

0993 我希望你不介意，我可以…嗎？
I hope you don't mind, but would it be possible for me to...?

範例 A: I hope you don't mind, but would it be possible for me to type a letter here? 我希望你不介意，我可以在這裡打封信嗎？
B: I'm afraid not. 恐怕不行。

0994 我可以…嗎？
Is it possible for me to...?

範例 A: Is it possible for me to put forward another suggestion?
我可以再提另一個建議嗎？
B: Sure. What is it?
當然。什麼建議？

0995 我們想獲得許可…。
We'd like permission to...

範例 A: May I help you?
有什麼事嗎？
B: We'd like permission to stay here for a few more days.
我們想獲得許可在這裡多待幾天。

● 表示許可 Granting Permission

0996 可以。
Fine.

替換 All right.
OK by me.
That's fine.

範例 A: May I sing a song? 我可以唱首歌嗎？
B: Fine. 可以。

0997 沒有什麼不可以的。
No reason why you can't.

替換 | No reason why you shouldn't.

範例 | **A:** May I smoke here? 我可以在這裡吸煙嗎？
B: No reason why you can't. 沒有什麼不可以的。

0998
請吧。
Go ahead.

替換 | Please do.

範例 | **A:** I thought I'd ramble on. 我想我要開始長篇大論了。
B: Go ahead. 請吧。

提示 | ramble ['ræmbl] *v.* 漫談

0999
當然可以。
Sure.

替換 | Sure can.
For sure.
Of course.
By all means.

範例 | **A:** Could I go home for vacation, please? 我可以回家渡假嗎？
B: Sure. 當然可以。

1000
隨你便。
Feel free.

替換 | Suit yourself.
Anything goes!
Feel free to do what you like.
As you wish.

範例 | **A:** Could I buy a new shirt? It's only 20 dollars.
我可以買件新襯衫嗎？才二十美元。
B: Feel free.
隨你便。

1001
你要是…的話，當然可以。
It's OK if you...

範例 | **A:** Do you mind if I change the channel?
你介意我轉台嗎？
B: It's OK if you watch the movie channel.
你要是看電影頻道的話，當然可以。

1002
有什麼不可以呢？
Why shouldn't you?

範例　A: I don't want to express my opinion. 我不想發表我的意見。
B: Why shouldn't you? 有什麼不可以呢？

1003
如果你願意的話。
If you like.

範例　A: Can we bring our own food? 我們可以自備食物嗎？
B: If you like. 如果你願意的話。

1004
請別客氣…。
Please don't hesitate to...

範例　A: It's been nice seeing you. 很高興看到你。
B: Please don't hesitate to come again. 請別客氣再來。

提示　hesitate ['hɛzə,tet] v. 猶豫；躊躇

1005
是的，你當然可以…。
Yes, indeed you may...

範例　A: I want to join you. Can I? 我想和你們一起，可以嗎？
B: Yes, indeed you may join us. 是的，你當然可以。

1006
如果你想的話，可以…。
You may..., if you like.

範例　A: There is nothing for me to do here. 這裡沒有什麼我可以做的。
B: You may leave, if you like. 如果你想的話，可以離開了。

● 不許可 Refusing to Grant Permission

1007
門都沒有。
No way.

替換　That's out of the question.
Over my dead body.〔粗魯的表達法〕
In your dreams.〔粗魯的表達法〕
Not on your life.〔粗魯的表達法〕

範例　A: May I use your Walkman? 我可以用一下你的隨身聽嗎？
B: No way. 門都沒有。

1008

對不起，不行。
Sorry, it's not permitted.

(替換) I'm sorry, that's not allowed.
I'm sorry, but that's not possible.

(範例) A: Can I smoke here? 我可以在這裡抽煙嗎？
B: Sorry, it's not permitted. 對不起，不行。

1009

恐怕不行。
That's not permitted, I'm afraid.

(替換) That's out of the question, I'm afraid.
I'm afraid that's not possible.

(範例) A: Can I have the book? 我可以用一下這本書嗎？
B: That's not permitted, I'm afraid. 恐怕不行。

1010

對不起，你不能。
I'm sorry, you can't.

(範例) A: May I sit in the front of the auditorium? 我可以坐在禮堂的前面嗎？
B: I'm sorry, you can't. 對不起，你不能。

(提示) auditorium [ˌɔdə'torɪəm] *n.* 禮堂；音樂廳

1011

對不起，你不准⋯。
I'm sorry, you're not allowed to...

(範例) A: I'm sorry, you're not allowed to park your car here.
對不起，你不准在這裡停車。
B: OK.
好的。

1012

恐怕我不能讓你⋯。
I'm afraid I can't let you...

(替換) I'm afraid I can't permit you to...
I'm afraid I can't give you permission to...
I'm afraid you can't have permission to...

(範例) A: Can I help settle their dispute? 我能幫忙解決他們的爭端嗎？
B: I'm afraid I can't let you do that. 恐怕我不能讓你做這件事。

(提示) settle ['sɛtl] *v.* 解決

1013	我實在不能⋯。 **I can't possibly...**
範例	A: I can't possibly lend you the money. 我實在不能借給你那筆錢。 B: That's all right. 沒關係。
1014	我願意，但是⋯。 **I'd like to, but...**
範例	A: Do you want to work for me? 你想替我工作嗎？ B: I'd like to, but my boss won't let me. 我願意，但是老闆不准。
1015	恐怕你不可以⋯。 **I'm afraid it's not possible for you to...**
範例	A: May I have the house after we get our divorce? 離婚後我可以擁有房子嗎？ B: I'm afraid it's not possible for you to have the house. 恐怕你不可以擁有房子。
1016	不可以⋯。 **It's not permitted to...**
範例	A: It's not permitted to litter here. 不可以在這亂丟垃圾。 B: Sorry. I didn't know. 對不起，我不知道。
1017	⋯恐怕是違反規定的。 **I'm afraid it's against the rules to...**
範例	A: Can we start early? 我們可以早點開始嗎？ B: I'm afraid it's against the rules to change the schedule. 改時間表恐怕是違反規定的。
1018	誰也不可以⋯。 **Nobody is allowed to...**
範例	A: May I take the book with me? 我可以帶走這本書嗎？ B: Nobody is allowed to take books out. 誰也不可以把書帶出去。

2.26　勸說 Persuasion

　　勸說人既要講求心理戰術，也要講究語言技巧。在我們的建議或勸告遭到拒絕時，首先要表示理解，之後再進一步說明我們的建議是出於替對方考量，最後再請對方三思。只有恰如其分而又富有說服力的語言，才能使你達到勸服人的目的。

1019

別這樣。
Don't be like that!

(替換)　Don't act like that!

(範例)　A: People are getting worse and worse.
　　　　　人變得愈來愈壞。
　　　　B: You're complaining again. Don't be like that!
　　　　　你又在抱怨了。別這樣！

042

1020

請讓我⋯吧！
Please let me...

(替換)　Won't you let me..., please?

(範例)　A: Please let me show you the way. 請讓我給你帶路吧！
　　　　B: OK. Thank you. 好，謝謝。

1021

你會⋯。
You'll...

(替換)　You'll have to...

(範例)　A: Can I do it myself?
　　　　　我可以一個人做嗎？
　　　　B: You'll have to spend a long time on it.
　　　　　你會在這上面花很多時間。

1022

我認為你最好⋯。
I really think you'd do well to...

(替換)　Surely the most sensible thing would be to...
　　　　Surely the best course of action would be to...

範例
A: I really think you'd do well to go and see her.
我認為你最好去看她。
B: Good idea.
好主意。

提示 sensible ['sɛnsəbl] *adj.* 合情理的；明智的

1023
你那樣（想）對你沒有好處。
That'll get you nowhere.

範例
A: You should be more polite.
你應該要更有禮貌。
B: That'll get you nowhere. It's every man for himself in this world.
你那樣（想）對你沒有好處。這世界上的每個人都是為了自己。

1024
就算為了…！
Just for...!

範例
A: No. I won't go there again. 不，我再也不去那裡了。
B: Let's go. Just for me, OK? 我們去吧。就算為了我，好嗎？

1025
就聽我一次，好不好？
Listen to me just once, will you?

範例
A: I don't feel well today. I won't go. 我今天不舒服，我不去了。
B: Listen to me just once, will you? 就聽我一次，好不好？

1026
這所有的努力值得嗎？
Is this all worth the effort?

範例
A: Is this all worth the effort? 這所有的努力值得嗎？
B: Of course. 當然了。

1027
我不明白，我們為什麼不…呢？
I don't see why we shouldn't...

範例
A: I don't see why we shouldn't give them a hand.
我不明白，我們為什麼不幫他們呢？
B: Why should we?
為什麼要幫他們呢？

1028
我不認為…。
I really don't think...

範例　A: I really don't think that they will be interested in a boxing match.
　　　　我不認為他們會對拳擊比賽感興趣的。
　　　　B: It's pretty savage, isn't it?
　　　　它太野蠻了，不是嗎？

提示　boxing ['bɑksɪŋ] *n.* 拳擊
　　　　savage ['sævɪdʒ] *adj.* 野蠻的

1029　這可能不錯，但是我們必須全盤考慮。
That might be so, but we have to take everything into account.

範例　A: That might be so, but we have to take everything into account.
　　　　這可能不錯，但是我們必須全盤考慮。
　　　　B: You're right.
　　　　你是正確的。

提示　take sth. into account 考慮

1030　我真的不這樣認為，因為…。
I really don't think so because...

範例　A: What do you think of Tom? Is he a good boy?
　　　　你覺得湯姆怎麼樣？他是個好孩子嗎？
　　　　B: I really don't think so because he's always absent from class.
　　　　我真的不這樣認為，因為他總是曠課。

提示　absent ['æbsn̩t] *adj.* 缺席的（+ from）

2.27　原因 Reasons

不理解事情的緣由，或不理解他人的行為時，我們有時需要對方做解釋。詢問理由時，多用疑問句，說明理由時，多用 because、so 等句子。當然，特定語氣的肯定句和否定句也能達到要求對方說明理由的目的。詢問或提供理由的語言表達形式與說話者受教育的程度、交談的場合有很大關係。

● 詢問理由 Asking for Reasons

| 1031 | 為什麼？
Why? | (043) |

範例 | **A:** Why? 為什麼？
B: It's because they're short of experience. 原因在於他們缺乏經驗。

| 1032 | 你知道為什麼…？
Do you have any idea why...? |

替換 | Do you know why...?

範例 | **A:** Do you know the result?
知道結果了嗎？
B: Yes. Do you have any idea why he failed?
是的，你知道為什麼他失敗了嗎？

| 1033 | 你想為什麼…？
Why do you think...? |

範例 | **A:** Why do you think she didn't come?
你想為什麼她沒來？
B: Because of the storm, the road was not finished on schedule.
由於暴風雨，公路沒能按照預定時間完工。

| 1034 | 為什麼…？
Why...? |

替換 | What's the reason...?
How did it happen that...?

範例 | **A:** Why did he come back? 為什麼他回來了？
B: Who knows? 誰知道呢？

| 1035 | 這是…的理由嗎？
Is that why...? |

替換 | Is that the reason...?

範例 | **A:** Is that why you're so upset?
這是你如此生氣的理由嗎？
B: Yes. He's not a child any more but he has no manners.
是的。他已經不是孩子了，但是什麼規矩都不懂。

● 提供理由 Giving Reasons

1036

原因是…
The thing is, ...

(替換) The (basic) reason is that...

(範例) **A:** The thing is, the file wasn't saved. 原因是檔案沒儲存。
B: What a shame! 真遺憾！

(提示) save [sev] *v.* 儲存
shame [ʃem] *n.* 憾事

1037

…的原因是因為…。
The reason for...was that...

(範例) **A:** Why didn't you pass the exam?
你怎麼會不及格？
B: The reason for my failure was that I was ill.
我不及格的原因是因為我生病了。

1038

因為…。
It's because...

(範例) **A:** Why don't you use your pen? 你怎麼不用你的鋼筆？
B: It's because I don't like it. 因為我不喜歡它。

1039

哦，因為…
Well, because...

(範例) **A:** Why can't I marry her? 我為什麼不能和她結婚？
B: Well, because she is too young. 哦，因為她太年輕了。

1040

哦，你明白，…。
Well, you see, ...

(範例) **A:** I really don't see why some people are so selfish.
我真不明白為什麼有些人這麼自私。
B: Well, you see, it's human nature.
哦，你明白，這就是人的本性。

(提示) selfish ['sɛlfɪʃ] *adj.* 自私的

1041

我的解釋是：⋯。
If I could explain:...

(範例)
A: Why did the car break down? 車子怎麼拋錨了？
B: If I could explain: the fuel ran out. 我的解釋是：汽油沒了。

1042

⋯，這就是我要⋯的原因。
..., and that's my reason for...

(範例)
A: My car broke down, and that's my reason for canceling the trip.
我的車子拋錨了，這就是我要取消旅行的原因。
B: Sorry to hear that.
真替你感到遺憾。

1043

我相信⋯是對的，因為：⋯。
I believe...is right for the following reason:...

(範例)
A: I believe Kate is right for the following reason: it's healthier to walk than to drive. 我相信凱特是對的，因為：走路比開車更健康。
B: That's why she prefers walking. 難怪她比較喜歡走路。

1044

⋯有充分的理由說明⋯是對的。
...has ample justification for...

(範例)
A: Mr. Smith has ample justification for what he said.
史密斯先生有充分的理由說明他的話是對的。
B: Do you really think so?
你真的這樣想嗎？

(提示)
ample ['æmpl] *adj.* 充足的；豐富的
justification [ˌdʒʌstəfə'keʃən] *n.* 理由

1045

我認為⋯實際上是有充分理由的。
I think there's actually a good reason for...

(範例)
A: I think there's actually a good reason for his absence.
我認為他缺席實際上是有充分理由的。
B: Yes. His mother is ill.
沒錯。他的母親生病了。

(提示)
absence ['æbsn̩s] *n.* 缺席 （+ from）

2.28　重複 Repeating

交談中，有時需要針對內容進行重新確認，這時需要對方重述講過的話。一般說來，要求別人重述時，要有禮貌。進行重述時，要清楚明白。重述時，要注意表達的正確性。

● 要求重複 Asking for Something to Be Repeated

1046	你說什麼？ **What?**	(044)

替換
(I'm) sorry?
Pardon (me)?
What did you say?
What was that you said?
I beg your pardon?

範例
A: What?
　　你說什麼？
B: She's a well-educated woman. Understand?
　　她是一個受過良好教育的女人。明白嗎？

1047	請再說一遍。 **Come again, please?**

替換
Say that again, please.
What was that again, please?
Please say it once more.
Would you repeat what you said, please?
I wonder if you'd mind repeating that.
Please be good enough to reiterate that.

範例
A: Come again, please?
　　請再說一遍。
B: I said that your irresponsible words hurt him.
　　我說，你不負責任的話傷害了他。

提示
reiterate [ri'ɪtəˌret] v. 重申；反覆講
irresponsible [ˌɪrɪ'spɑnsəbl̩] adj. 不負責的

1048	對不起，你說什麼？ **Sorry, what did you say?**
(替換)	I'm sorry. What did you say?
(範例)	A: Sorry, what did you say? 對不起，你說什麼？ B: Please listen to me carefully. 請仔細聽好。

1049	對不起，我沒聽見。 **Sorry, but I missed that.**
(替換)	Sorry, I didn't get that. I'm sorry. I didn't hear/catch that.
(範例)	A: Sorry, but I missed that. 　　對不起，我沒聽見。 B: You're absent-minded. I've told you many times. 　　你心不在焉。我已經告訴你好多遍了。

1050	可以請你重複一下嗎？ **Could you repeat that, please?**
(範例)	A: Could you repeat that, please? 可以請你重複一下嗎？ B: I said that he's a useless bum. 我說他是個一無是處的廢人。
(提示)	bum [bʌm] n.【非正式】能力差的人

1051	我沒聽到，你可以再說一遍嗎？ **I didn't hear you. Could you come again?**
(範例)	A: I didn't hear you. Could you come again? 　　我沒聽到，你可以再說一遍嗎？ B: All I'm trying to say is that hard work pays off. 　　我想說的不過是，努力工作是會有報酬的。

1052	我恐怕沒聽見…。 **I'm afraid I didn't hear...**
(範例)	A: I'm afraid I didn't hear that. 　　我恐怕沒聽見那句話。 B: What I'm trying to say is video games are real fun. 　　我想說的是，電動讓人很開心。

1053
我恐怕沒聽清楚你說的話。
I didn't quite hear what you said.

（替換） I'm afraid I didn't quite catch what you were saying.

（範例） **A:** I didn't quite hear what you said.
我恐怕沒聽清楚你說的話。
B: All I'm suggesting is that you mind your own business.
我的意思是，管好你自己的事。

1054
對不起，我沒聽清楚你說的是什麼。
I'm sorry, but I didn't quite hear what you said.

（替換） I'm sorry, but I didn't quite catch what you were saying.

（範例） **A:** I'm sorry, but I didn't quite hear what you said.
對不起，我沒聽清楚你說的是什麼。
B: I said you look familiar.
我說你看起來很眼熟。

1055
對不起，我沒聽見你說的話。
I'm sorry. I didn't hear what you said.

（替換） I'm sorry. I couldn't hear what you said.

（範例） **A:** I'm sorry. I didn't hear what you said.
對不起，我沒聽見你說的話。
B: I said, "a faint heart never wins a fair lady."
我要說的是：「不入虎穴，焉得虎子。」

（提示） faint [fent] *adj.* 懦弱的；（行動等）軟弱無力的
fair [fɛr] *adj.* 美麗的

● 重複 Repeating

1056
我剛才是說…。
What I said was...

（替換） I was just remarking/saying...
I was just expressing the view that...
I was just making a suggestion that...
I was merely pointing out that...
I was merely putting forward the opinion that...
I was merely stating the fact that...

範例 A: Pardon? 什麼？
B: What I said was he's all right now. 我剛才是說，他現在好了。

1057 我剛才是問…。
I was just asking...

替換 I was just inquiring...

範例 A: I beg your pardon?
能重複一遍嗎？
B: I was just asking when you would do it.
我剛才是問你什麼時候做那件事。

提示 inquire [ɪnˈkwaɪr] v.【美】詢問（=【英】enquire）

1058 我只是想知道…。
I was just wondering...

替換 I was merely wondering...

範例 A: Please say that again.
請再講一遍。
B: I was just wondering who would be the next President.
我只是想知道下一任總統是誰。

提示 president [ˈprɛzədənt] n. 總統

1059 你聾了嗎？我是說…。
Are you deaf? I said...

範例 A: Pardon me? 對不起，你說什麼？
B: Are you deaf? I said it wouldn't work. 你聾了嗎？我是說它壞了。

1060 我是說…。
I said, ...

範例 A: I'm sorry. What was that? 對不起，你說什麼？
B: I said, could you give him a hand? 我是說，你能幫他一下嗎？

● 請求重複的其他方式 Repeating in Another Way

1061 我的意思不過是…。
All I'm trying to say is...

(替換) All I'm suggesting is...

(範例) **A:** I'm sorry? 你說什麼？
B: All I'm trying to say is he's generous. 我的意思不過是，他很大方。

1062 我的意思是…。
I said...

(範例) **A:** I'm sorry, would you mind saying that again?
對不起，請你再說一遍。
B: I said haste makes waste.
我的意思是，欲速則不達。

1063 我想說的是…。
What I'm trying to say is...

(替換) What I'm getting/driving at is...
What I mean is...
What I'm suggesting is...
The point I'm suggesting is that...

(範例) **A:** What did you say? 你說什麼？
B: What I'm trying to say is I will help. 我想說的是，我會幫忙的。

1064 那就是說，…。
Which is to say...

(替換) That is to say, ...

(範例) **A:** Man, life sucks. 老兄，人生爛透了。
B: Which is to say life is a battle. 那就是說，生活就是一場戰爭。

1065 換句話說，…。
In other words, ...

(替換) Let me put it another way, ...
Or you could say...
To put it another way, ...
If I can rephrase that...

(範例) **A:** He often works on weekends. 他常在週末工作。
B: In other words, he's very hardworking. 換句話說，他很努力。

(提示) rephrase [ri'frez] *v.* 改述；改撰

236

1066	⋯，或許更確切地說，⋯。 **..., or rather...**

替換	...or better, ... Perhaps I could make that clearer by saying... Perhaps it would be clearer to say... Perhaps it would be more to the point if I said... If I could restate my point, I think it would be more accurate to say...
範例	**A:** I beg your pardon? 你說什麼？ **B:** These people, or rather those young people, are promising. 那些人，或許更確切地說，那些年輕人是有前途的。
提示	restate [ri'stet] *v.* 重新敘述；重申 accurate ['ækjərɪt] *adj.* 正確的；精確的

1067	基本上這是一個⋯的問題。 **Basically, it's a question of...**

範例	**A:** I didn't hear you. Could you come again? 我沒聽清楚，你可以再說一遍嗎？ **B:** Basically, it's a question of education. 基本上這是一個教育的問題。

1068	這樣說吧。 **Look at it this way.**

範例	**A:** What was that you said? 你說的是什麼？ **B:** Look at it this way. The more you read, the more benefits you have. 這樣說吧：讀書愈多，對你愈有利。

2.29 請求 Requests

一般來說，請求別人幫忙時，要避免直接命令，而要採取委婉的口氣。但在某些特殊場合，過於客氣可能會使人感到不自在，所以請求時，也要根據對方的身份、講話的場合、事情的輕重緩急等因素，使用不同的方法。答覆別人的請求時，也要講究技巧，特別是在不能答應別人請求的情況下，爲了避免傷害對方，我們有必要表示歉意和遺憾，有時需要說明理由，有時需要找個藉口。值得注意的是，你的藉口一定要能夠自圓其說，否則會給對方留下不好的印象。

● 提出請求 Making a Request

1069	請幫我…。 **Do me the favor of...**	045

替換	Please oblige me by...
範例	**A:** Do me the favor of closing the door. 請幫我把門關上。 **B:** OK. 可以。
提示	oblige [ə'blaɪdʒ] v. 施恩惠於；幫…的忙

1070	請…吧。 **Be kind enough to...**

替換	Please...
範例	**A:** Be kind enough to go camping with us. 　　請跟我們一起去露營吧。 **B:** Sorry, I have to hand in my thesis by the end of this week. 　　對不起，這個星期結束前我得交論文。
提示	thesis ['θisɪs] n. 論文

1071	喂，我要…。 **Hey, I need...**

替換	Hey, I'm short of...
範例	**A:** Hey, I need a pen. 喂，我要一支鋼筆。 **B:** Here you are. 給你。

1072	對不起，打擾你一下，你…。 **Sorry to trouble you, but do you...?**

替換	I'm sorry to trouble you, but could you...?
範例	**A:** Sorry to trouble you, but do you have an eraser? 　　對不起，打擾你一下，你有橡皮擦嗎？

B: I'm afraid not.
恐怕沒有。

1073

你能不能…？
Could you...?

範例 **A:** Could you type it? 你能不能把它打出來？
B: Sorry, I can't. 對不起，我不能。

1074

我想要你去…。
I want you to...

範例 **A:** Can I help you? 可以幫什麼忙嗎？
B: I want you to get me some water, please. 我想要你去拿點水。

1075

麻煩你…好嗎？
May I trouble you to...?

範例 **A:** May I trouble you to type it for me?
麻煩你幫我打出來好嗎？
B: Sorry. I'm busy with something else right now.
對不起，我現在手頭正忙著呢。

1076

可以和你談談嗎？
May I have a word with you?

範例 **A:** May I have a word with you? 可以和你談談嗎？
B: What is it? 談什麼？

1077

你認為可能…嗎？
Do you think it would be possible to...?

替換 Could I possibly...?

範例 **A:** Do you think it would be possible to copy it? 你認為可能複製嗎？
B: OK. 可以。

1078

我真不知怎麼說才好，不過你看能否…？
I'm not quite sure how to put this, but do you think you could possibly...?

範例 **A:** I'm not quite sure how to put this, but do you think you could possibly cancel the game?
我真不知怎麼說才好，不過你看能否取消這次比賽呢？

B: What? You must be joking.
什麼？你一定在開玩笑。

1079

不知你是否介意我…？
Would you mind me...?

 A: Would you mind me playing the guitar?
不知你是否介意我彈吉他？
B: Do as you like.
隨你的意思吧。

● 肯定回答 Replying in the Affirmative

1080

當然。
Sure.

（替換） Sure thing.
By all means.
Certainly.
Of course.

 A: Can you tell him to be here at five o'clock tomorrow afternoon?
你能不能告訴他明天下午五點鐘到這裡？
B: Sure.
當然。

1081

我很樂意。
My pleasure.

（替換） I'd love to.
I'd be glad/delighted to.
With pleasure.

（範例） **A:** Help me dish up, will you please? 幫我上菜好嗎？
B: My pleasure. 我很樂意。

（提示） dish up 上菜；盛菜

1082

可以。
OK.

（替換） Will do.
Yes, all right.
I don't mind.

範例　A: Any chance I could use your telephone?
　　　可以用一下你的電話嗎？
　　　B: OK.
　　　可以。

1083 我看沒問題。
I don't see any problem with that.

替換　I think that would be all right.

範例　A: Get me something to drink, OK? 給我一些飲料好嗎？
　　　B: I don't see any problem with that. 我看沒問題。

1084 請便，別客氣。
Be my guest.

範例　A: May I use your pencil? 我可以用一下你的鉛筆嗎？
　　　B: Be my guest. 請便，別客氣。

1085 放心吧，我會的。
Don't worry. I will.

範例　A: Bring the laundry in for me, OK? 拿給我要送洗的衣服好嗎？
　　　B: Don't worry. I will. 放心吧，我會的。

1086 我盡量。是什麼事？
I'll try. What's the matter?

範例　A: Can you help me with something? 你可以幫我一個忙嗎？
　　　B: I'll try. What's the matter? 我盡量。是什麼事？

1087 當然，請便。
Certainly, help yourself.

範例　A: May I have some more rice? 我可以再添飯嗎？
　　　B: Certainly, help yourself. 當然，請便。

1088 我可以馬上幫你。
I can do it for you right away.

範例　A: I can do it for you right away. 我可以馬上幫你。
　　　B: Thank you. 謝謝。

1089	只要你願意。 **If that's what you'd like.**

範例　A: May I have some coffee? 可以給我一點咖啡嗎？
B: If that's what you'd like. 只要你願意。

1090	一點也不介意。 **Not in the least.**

範例　A: Do you mind if I smoke here? 你介意我在這裡吸煙嗎？
B: Not in the least. 一點也不介意。

1091	好吧，要是那樣的話，可以。 **Well, in that case, all right.**

範例　A: Can I use that when you're finished? I can't finish without it.
你用完後，可以讓我用嗎？沒有它，我無法完成。
B: Well, in that case, all right.
好吧，要是那樣的話，可以。

● 否定回答 Replying in the Negative

1092	當然不行！ **Certainly not.**

替換　Absolutely not.
範例　A: May I have a bite? 我能咬一口嗎？
B: Certainly not. 當然不行！

1093	不行！ **No way.**

替換　Not a chance!
In your dreams.〔粗魯的表達法〕
範例　A: May I sleep here? 我可以睡這裡嗎？
B: No way. 不行！

1094	不行。 **It can't be done.**

替換
It can't be helped.
Nothing doing.
That's out of the question.
I'm sorry, I can't (oblige you).

範例
A: Can I have your photo? 我可以要張你的相片嗎？
B: It can't be done. 不行。

1095 恐怕不行。
I'm afraid I can't.

替換
I'm afraid I can't help you.

範例
A: Can you give me a piece of cake? 可以給我一塊蛋糕嗎？
B: I'm afraid I can't. 恐怕不行。

1096 我為什麼要？
Why should I?

範例
A: Help me finish my homework. 幫我完成作業！
B: Why should I? 我為什麼要？

1097 很對不起，我從來不把它借給別人。
I'm very sorry, but I never lend it to anyone.

範例
A: May I borrow your telephone?
　 我可以借用你的電話嗎？
B: I'm very sorry, but I never lend it to anyone.
　 很對不起，我從來不把它借給別人。

1098 對不起，我正在用。
I'm sorry, but I'm using it right now.

範例
A: May I use your dictionary? 可以用一下你的字典嗎？
B: I'm sorry, but I'm using it right now. 對不起，我正在用。

1099 我很願意，但是我⋯。
I'd like to, but I...

範例
A: Want to dance with me? 想和我跳舞嗎？
B: I'd like to, but I don't have time. 我很願意，但是我沒有時間。

1100 很遺憾，我幫不了你。
I'm sorry that I can't help you.

範例 A: I have great difficulty in learning Spanish. 我學西班牙文真的很困難。
B: I'm sorry that I can't help you. 很遺憾,我幫不了你。

1101
我倒是想答應,不過那辦不到。
I'd like to say yes, but it's just impossible.

範例 A: I'd like to say yes, but it's just impossible.
我倒是想答應,不過那辦不到。
B: OK, forget it.
那算了。

1102
如果你不介意,我倒希望不要。
I'd rather you didn't if you don't mind.

範例 A: May I smoke here?
我可以在這裡吸煙嗎?
B: I'd rather you didn't if you don't mind.
如果你不介意,我倒希望不要。

1103
我真的不知道說什麼好。問題是,我需要…。
I don't quite know what to say. The problem is, I need...

範例 A: May I use your glasses?
我可以用你的眼鏡嗎?
B: I don't quite know what to say. The problem is, I need them.
我真的不知道說什麼好。問題是,我需要它們。

1104
我真的想幫你,不過我幫不了。
I'd really like to help you, but I can't.

範例 A: I wish somebody would help me with Japanese.
我希望有人能幫我學日語。
B: I'd really like to help you, but I can't.
我真的想幫你,不過我幫不了。

2.30　建議 Suggestions

懂得如何向別人提出建議是重要的交際手腕。能否在特定的場合用適當的語氣對人提出建議,象徵著一個人的口語表達能力。一般來說,提出建議要客氣，要儘量避免用命令的口氣。當然，客氣的程度取決於談話雙方的關係。關係愈遠，使用的語言愈委婉。我們在學習提出建議時，一定要仔細體會各種不同句型之間的細微差別。

● 提出建議 Making Suggestions

（046）

1105	為什麼不…呢？ **Why don't you...?**
替換	Why not..., then?
範例	**A:** Why don't you raise their salaries? 為什麼不提高他們的工資呢？ **B:** Don't be silly. 別傻了。

1106	…，（你說）怎麼樣呢？ **What would you say to...?**
替換	What/How about...? How does...strike you? What do you think of...? How would you like...?
範例	**A:** What would you say to a trip into the countryside? 　　去鄉下旅行，（你說）怎麼樣呢？ **B:** Sounds great. Thank you for your suggestion. 　　聽起來很棒。謝謝你的建議。
提示	strike [straɪk] *v.* 造成深刻的印象；突然想到

1107	你想過…嗎？ **Have you ever thought of...?**
範例	**A:** Have you ever thought of going to France for a vacation? 　　你想過去法國渡假嗎？ **B:** Not yet. 　　還沒有。

1108	你不妨…。 **You might as well...**
替換	You may as well...

範例　A: You might as well finish the work tomorrow. 你不妨明天把工作結束。
B: Good idea. 好主意。

1109　我建議…。
I would like to make a suggestion: ...

替換　I'd like to suggest that...
I propose...
May I suggest...?
If I may make a suggestion:...

範例　A: I would like to make a suggestion: let's appoint him chairman.
　　　我建議任命他爲主席。
B: I agree.
　　　我同意。

提示　appoint [ə'pɔɪnt] v. 任命；委任

1110　讓我們…吧。
Let's...

替換　Suppose we...

範例　A: Let's take the train to Washington. 讓我們坐火車去華盛頓吧。
B: All right. 好的。

1111　我知道我們應該怎麼做——我們…吧！
I know what we can do—let's...

範例　A: I know what we can do—let's make a nest for the bird.
　　　我知道我們應該怎麼做——我們幫這小鳥做個鳥巢吧！
B: I don't want to waste my time.
　　　我可不想浪費時間。

1112　那麼…吧。
..., then.

範例　A: Take some aspirin, then. 那麼吃點阿斯匹靈吧。
B: OK. 好的。

提示　aspirin ['æspərɪn] n. 阿斯匹靈；解熱鎮痛藥

1113　你總可以…。
You could always...

範例　A: You could always go there another time. 你總可以改天去那裡。
B: But I want to go now! 但是我想現在去。

1114
你應該⋯。
You should...

範例　A: I'm giving up. 我要放棄了。
B: No. You should finish what you start. 不行，你應該堅持到底。

1115
⋯也許是個好主意。
It might be a good idea to...

範例　A: It might be a good idea to read this book.
看看這本書，也許是個好主意。
B: I don't think so.
我可不這麼認為。

1116
⋯不是更好嗎？
Wouldn't it be a good idea to...?

範例　A: Wouldn't it be a good idea to book a ticket first?
先訂張票不是更好嗎？
B: OK. I will do it.
好的，我去辦。

● 肯定回答 Saying Yes

1117
我會這麼辦的。
I believe I will.

範例　A: Why don't you insure your car? 為什麼不幫你的車保險呢？
B: I believe I will. 我會這麼辦的。

提示　insure [ɪnˈʃʊr] v. 給⋯保險

1118
夠好的了。
It's good enough.

範例　A: How about that jacket? 那件夾克如何？
B: It's good enough. 夠好的了。

1119

你這麼說正合我意。
Now you're talking.

範例　A: How about scrambled eggs? 吃炒蛋怎麼樣？
B: Now you're talking. 你這麼說正合我意。

提示　scramble ['skræmbḷ] v. 炒（蛋）

1120

可以。隨你要什麼都行。
OK. Anything you want.

範例　A: Let's put the issue to the committee for decision.
讓我們將這個議題交給委員會決定。
B: OK. Anything you want.
可以。隨你要什麼都行。

1121

你就這麼辦吧。
You just do that.

範例　A: Liz suggests that I try the shop on Maple Road.
麗姿建議我應該試試楓樹路上的商店。
B: You just do that.
你就這麼辦吧。

1122

我很樂意。
I'd love to.

範例　A: Since you have to wait, you might as well sit down and watch TV
with us. 既然你必須等，不妨坐下來和我們一起看電視。
B: I'd love to. 我很樂意。

1123

我無所謂。
I don't mind.

範例　A: Jack proposes we go to the station to meet our guests.
傑克建議我們去車站見客人。
B: I don't mind.
我無所謂。

1124

這大概正是我要做的。
Maybe that's what I'll do.

範例　A: I think you should appoint a new monitor.
我認為你應該任命一位新班長。

B: Maybe that's what I'll do.
這大概正是我要做的。

monitor ['mɑnɪtɚ] *n.* （學校的）班長

1125
我想這是個好主意。
I think that's a lovely idea.

範例
A: Plenty of new projects are on your desk, but wouldn't it be a good idea to finish up the ones you've already started?
你桌上有那麼多新的案子，但是先完成你已經開始的案子不是更好嗎？
B: I think that's a lovely idea.
我想這是個好主意。

1126
這個主意不錯。
That's not a bad idea.

範例
A: May I suggest you put some money into your current account?
我可以建議你在活期戶頭內存入一些錢嗎？
B: That's not a bad idea.
這個主意不錯。

1127
這是個很棒的建議。
I think that's an excellent suggestion.

範例
A: Would it be an idea to make a call and explain to him?
打電話向他解釋一下怎麼樣？
B: Yes, I think that's an excellent suggestion.
對，這是個很棒的建議。

1128
我認為你的建議是可以接受的。
I think your proposal is acceptable.

範例
A: I'd like to suggest you see the dentist.
我建議你去看牙醫。
B: Yes, I think your proposal is acceptable.
對，我認為你的建議是可以接受的。

提示 acceptable [ək'sɛptəbl] *adj.* 可接受的；合意的

1129
我認為這是應該採取的正確步驟。
I think that's the proper course to take.

249

範例 | A: Should we ask our boss first?
我們是否應該先問問我們老闆?
B: Yes, I think that's the proper course to take.
對,我認為這是應該採取的正確步驟。

提示 | course [kors] *n.* 習慣的程序

● 否定回答 Saying No

1130	不行。 **No.**

替換 | No way.
That's impossible.
It can't be done.

範例 | A: I suggest that we wait a while before we make any final decisions.
我建議我們做最後決定之前,再等一下。
B: No.
不行。

1131	絕對不行。 **Absolutely not.**

範例 | A: Let's boycott the meeting. 我們抵制那個會議吧。
B: Absolutely not. 絕對不行。

提示 | boycott ['bɔɪ͵kɑt] *v.* 抵制

1132	我不想再聽到這話了。 **I won't hear of it.**

範例 | A: Let me tell you something. 讓我告訴你一件事情。
B: No. I won't hear of it. 不,我不想再聽到這話了。

1133	我倒希望你不要這樣。 **I'd rather you wouldn't.**

範例 | A: Can I make one suggestion about how we may do this?
我可以建議我們如何做這件事情嗎?
B: I'd rather you wouldn't.
我倒希望你不要這樣。

1134	我倒是希望那樣，但是…。 **I'd like that, but...**
範例	**A:** Might I suggest a white wine with your salmon, sir? 先生，我可以建議你點杯白酒來搭配你的鮭魚嗎？ **B:** I'd like that, but I can't drink tonight. 我倒希望那樣，但是我今晚不能喝酒。
1135	實際上我不太感興趣。 **I'm not too keen on that, actually.**
範例	**A:** Have you considered prospering overseas? 你是否想過向國外發展呢？ **B:** I'm not too keen on that, actually. 實際上我不太感興趣。
提示	prosper ['prɑspɚ] *v.* 成功
1136	我想這倒是個好主意，但是…。 **That's a good idea, I suppose, but...**
範例	**A:** To keep healthy, you can swim in winter. 想要健康，你可以冬泳。 **B:** That's a good idea, I suppose, but it may be very difficult. 我想這倒是個好主意，但是或許很困難。
1137	不用麻煩了。 **Don't bother.**
範例	**A:** Mary proposes dealing directly with the suppliers. 瑪莉建議直接找供應商。 **B:** Don't bother. 不用麻煩了。
1138	不，我們換…吧。 **No, let's...for a change.**
範例	**A:** Wouldn't it be a good idea to have dinner at home? 在家吃晚餐不是更好嗎？ **B:** No, let's eat out for a change. 不，我們換換口味，出去吃吧。

1139	很遺憾我不能接受你的建議。 **I regret to say I can't accept your suggestion.**

範例　A: I think you'd better tolerate your boss.
　　　　　我想你最好容忍一下你的老闆。
　　　　B: I regret to say I can't accept your suggestion.
　　　　　很遺憾我不能接受你的建議。

提示　tolerate ['tɑləret] *v.* 容忍；忍受

1140	你的建議我恐怕無法接受。 **I'm afraid your proposal is not acceptable.**

範例　A: I should like to put forward a suggestion: let's wear uniforms.
　　　　　我想提個建議：我們可以穿制服。
　　　　B: I'm afraid your proposal is not acceptable.
　　　　　你的建議我恐怕無法接受。

1141	那大概會很棒，不過我可能沒有…。 **That would be very nice, but I may not...**

範例　A: Okinawa is boring. We might as well spend our holiday in Tokyo.
　　　　　沖繩很無聊。我們倒不如去東京渡假。
　　　　B: That would be very nice, but I may not have enough money.
　　　　　那大概會很棒，不過我可能沒有足夠的錢。

2.31　催促 Urging

　　英文和中文的催促語有共同之處。表示催促的語言多為祈使句，句型簡短有力。如果使用 "Perhaps..."、"You'd better..."、"I'm afraid..."、"Don't you think..." 等表達方式，其語氣多為比較委婉。

		047
1142	快點兒！ **Quick!**	

替換　Hustle!
　　　　Go/Come on!
　　　　Move it!
　　　　Hurry (up)!

Get moving!
Look sharp!
Step on it!
Come on quick!
Get a move on!
Get on with it!
Be quick about it!

範例 A: Quick! 快點兒！
B: Don't worry. 別著急。

提示 hustle ['hʌs]] v. 催促；趕緊做（某事）

1143 我們快點吧！
Let's hurry!

替換 Let's be quick!
Let's speed up!
We'd better hurry!
We'd better step on it!

範例 A: Let's hurry! 我們快點吧！
B: But I don't want to see him. 可是我不想見他。

1144 你快點！
Pick up the pace!

替換 You'd better hurry up!
You'd better get a move on.
I think you'd better get going!

範例 A: Pick up the pace! 你快點！
B: I'm coming. 我來了！

1145 快點下來！
Get down here, now!

範例 A: Get down here, now! 快點下來！
B: Take it easy. 放輕鬆點。

1146 快進來！
Get in here!

範例 A: It's so cold out. 外面可真冷。
B: Get in here! 快進來！

1147

快來！
Get over here!

範例　A: Get over here! 快來！
B: Wait a minute. 等一下。

1148

再快一點好嗎？
Try to be a little faster, will you?

範例　A: Try to be a little faster, will you? 再快一點好嗎？
B: OK. 好的。

1149

請快一點！
Please be quick!

範例　A: Please be quick! 請快一點！
B: Don't you think I'm quick enough? 你不覺得我已經很快了嗎？

1150

也許現在你應該出發了。
Perhaps you should start now!

範例　A: Perhaps you should start now! 也許現在你應該出發了。
B: OK. See you. 好的，再見。

1151

我們最好快點！
We'd better make haste.

範例　A: Can we catch the bus? 我們能趕上公車嗎？
B: We'd better make haste. 我們最好快點！

1152

恐怕你得快點了！
I'm afraid you need to hurry.

範例　A: I'm afraid you need to hurry. 恐怕你得快點了！
B: Don't worry. 別擔心。

1153

你不認為我們現在應該出發去…嗎？
Don't you think we should leave for...now?

範例　A: Don't you think we should leave for the party now?
你不認為我們現在應該出發去參加晚會嗎？
B: It's too early.
還早呢。

第 3 章
正面表達

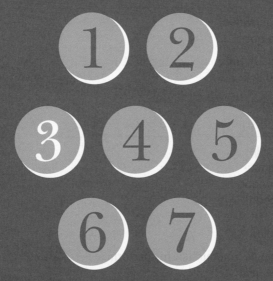

欣賞就是用喜悅的心情領略美好的事物。在會話當中，西方人特別注意用語言充分表達對別人所作所爲的欣賞。這不僅可以取悅對方，而且還能拉近談話雙方的距離。值得注意的是，在表達欣賞時，語氣要眞誠，應答時，則要表示感謝。

1154	真美！ **It's beautiful!**
替換	Very fine!〔常在賞畫時用〕
範例	A: Look at that lake. It's beautiful! 看那湖水，眞美！ B: Yeah, it's really beautiful! 是的，的確很美。
1155	做得好！ **Well done!**
替換	Good show/job! Way to go!
範例	A: I finally finished it. 我終於做完了。 B: Well done! 做得好。
1156	好極了！ **Excellent!**
替換	Admirable! Marvelous! It's very good! Jolly good! Fine! Splendid!
範例	A: What do you think of his performance? 你認爲他的表現怎麼樣？ B: Excellent! 好極了！
提示	jolly good【口】很好〔用來表示對某人剛剛所說的話感到滿意〕

1157	真好吃。 **It's delicious.**

範例 A: How do you like the cake? 這蛋糕怎麼樣？
B: It's delicious. 真好吃。

1158	它給我的印象非常好。 **It's most impressive.**

範例 A: Do you like the city? 你喜歡這個城市嗎？
B: It's most impressive. 它給我的印象非常好。

提示 impressive [ɪmˈprɛsɪv] *adj.* 給人深刻印象的；令人欽佩的

1159	它很可愛。 **It's delightful.**

範例 A: It's delightful. 它很可愛。
B: It sure is! 是的。

1160	我非常欣賞⋯。 **I have a great appreciation for...**

範例 A: What is your favorite piece?
你最喜歡哪首曲子？
B: I have a great appreciation for Beethoven's Fifth Symphony.
我非常欣賞貝多芬的第五號交響曲。

提示 symphony [ˈsɪmfənɪ] *n.* 交響樂；交響曲

3.2 贊成 Approval

　　贊成是指同意別人的主張或行為，或對別人的行為表示肯定或支持。在會話中，我們有時希望得到別人的贊成；有時要表達贊成或不贊成。表達贊成時，應該使人感到愉悅；有所保留地贊成或表達不贊成時，語言要委婉。

● 詢問態度 Asking about Attitude

	你贊成⋯嗎？	049
1161	**Are you in favor of...?**	

替換	Are you for...? Will you support...? Would you favor... Do you favor...? Do you approve of...? Can I take it that...has your support? Can I assume that...meets with your approval?
範例	**A:** Are you in favor of my plan? 你贊成我的計畫嗎？ **B:** Yes, of course. 當然。
提示	approval [ə'pruvl] *n.* 贊成；同意

1162	⋯可以嗎？ **Is it all right to...?**

替換	Is it OK to...? Do you think it is OK to...? Do you reckon it is fine to...? Do you think it's all right to...? Do you think it's a good idea to...?
範例	**A:** Is it all right to meet you at five? 五點鐘來見你，可以嗎？ **B:** That will suit me fine. 正合我意。

1163	你覺得合理嗎？ **Do you think it makes sense?**

替換	Do you think it's a sensible idea? Is it sensible, don't you think? Do you think it's reasonable?
範例	**A:** Do you think it makes sense? 你覺得合理嗎？ **B:** Yes. It sounds very sensible to me. 是的，聽起來非常合理。
提示	sensible ['sɛnsəbl] *adj.* 合情理的；合理的

1164	你贊成⋯，不是嗎？ **You're in favor of..., aren't you?**

替換　You would be in favor of..., wouldn't you?
...has your approval, doesn't it?
I suppose that...has your backing.

範例　A: You're in favor of the plan, aren't you?
你贊成這計畫的，不是嗎？
B: Yes. I would like to do everything to help you.
是的，我會盡全力幫助你。

提示　backing ['bækɪŋ] *n.* 支持

1165　請問你對…有什麼看法？
May I ask your opinion on...?

替換　Could I ask about your feelings concerning...?
Could I ask if you support...?
What was your reaction to...?

範例　A: May I ask your opinion on the issue?
請問你對這議題有什麼看法？
B: Something should be done to solve the problem.
應該採取措施來解決這個問題。

● 表示贊成 Expressing Approval

1166　好！
OK!

替換　Fine!

範例　A: Let's go for a walk there. 我們去那裡散步吧！
B: OK! 好！

1167　好極了！
Great!

替換　Swell!
Terrific!
Excellent!
Fantastic!
Smashing!
Wonderful!
How terrific!

範例　A: Let's go to the concert! 我們去聽音樂會吧！
　　　B: Great! 好極了！

提示　swell [swɛl] *adj.*【美，舊式】極好的；一流的
　　　smashing ['smæʃɪŋ] *adj.*【英，舊式】非常好的；極好的

1168
做得好！
Well done!

替換　Nice going!
　　　Good job!

範例　A: My paper is finished. 我的論文完成了。
　　　B: Well done! 做得好！

1169
正應該這樣！
That's the way it should be.

替換　It was the correct thing to do.
　　　I'll say!
　　　That's it!
　　　You got it!
　　　That's the point!
　　　That's more like it!
　　　That's the way I like it.

範例　A: Do you think it's right to take strict measures against corruption?
　　　你認為採取嚴厲的措施來懲治腐敗對嗎？
　　　B: That's the way it should be.
　　　正應該這樣！

提示　corruption [kə'rʌpʃən] *n.* 腐敗；貪污

1170
好主意！
That's an excellent idea.

替換　The idea's very good!
　　　What an excellent idea!
　　　Good idea!
　　　That's a great idea.
　　　That's good.
　　　It's jolly good.

範例　A: How about a walk? 散步好嗎？
　　　B: That's an excellent idea. 好主意！

1171	非常有道理。 **It makes a lot of sense.**

（替換） It sounds very sensible to me.

（範例） **A:** Do you think it's a sensible idea? 你認為這個主意有道理嗎？
B: Yes, it makes a lot of sense. 是的，非常有道理。

1172	我完全同意…。 **I entirely agree with...**

（替換） I'm all for...
I entirely approve of...
...has my full approval.
I cannot agree more with...

（範例） **A:** It was a wonderful speech. 這是很棒的演講。
B: I entirely agree with you. 我完全同意你的觀點。

1173	你說得有點道理。 **You've got something there.**

（替換） There is something to what you said.

（範例） **A:** What do you think of my proposal? 你認為我的提議怎麼樣？
B: You've got something there. 你說得有點道理。

1174	我同意。 **I would agree with that.**

（替換） I would accept that.
I would go along with that.

（範例） **A:** They're really suited for each other. 他們倆個真的很配。
B: I would agree with that. 我同意。

1175	我就是那個意思。 **That's just what I mean.**

（替換） That's just what I was thinking.
That's just how I see it.
That's just what I had in mind.
That's just what I'm getting at.

A: Tammy always arrives late. She should be fired.
譚美總是遲到。她眞該被炒魷魚。
B: That's just what I mean.
我就是那個意思。

● 表示不贊成 Expressing Disapproval

1176	**真傻！** **How silly!**

 That's silly!

 A: I lost my keys.
我把鑰匙弄丟了。
B: How silly! You must have left them at home.
眞傻！你一定放在家裡了。

1177	**…有什麼用呢？** **What's the use of...?**

(替換) What's the point of...?

(範例) **A:** What's the use of quarreling?
吵架有什麼用呢？
B: I agree with you. We should do something about it.
我贊成你的看法，我們應該做點什麼。

1178	**我絕不贊成…。** **I'm dead set against...**

(替換) I really don't approve of...
I'm definitely opposed to...

(範例) **A:** Shall we help him? 我們要幫他嗎？
B: I'm dead set against helping that guy. 我絕不贊成幫助這個人。

1179	**我不贊成…。** **I don't agree with...**

(替換) I'm certainly not in favor of...
I would find it difficult to approve of...
I certainly cannot give my support to...
I'm not very happy about...

I don't hold with the idea of...
I'm really displeased about...

範例 A: I don't agree with any form of terrorism.
我不贊成任何形式的恐怖主義。
B: Neither do I.
我也是

提示 displease [dɪsˈpliz] v. 使不快；使（人）生氣
terrorism [ˈtɛrəˌrɪzəm] n. 恐怖主義

1180 真的有必要⋯嗎？
Is it really necessary to...?

範例 A: Is it really necessary to lose your temper? 真的有必要發脾氣嗎？
B: No, it isn't. 不，沒必要。

1181 ⋯是不對的。
It isn't right to...

替換 It's not a correct thing to...
It's wrong to...

範例 A: It isn't right to tell lies. 說謊是不對的。
B: I agree with you. 我同意。

1182 我不贊成⋯。
I don't favor...

替換 I don't support...
I can't approve...

範例 A: What do you think of my plan? 你認為我的計畫怎麼樣？
B: I don't favor it. It's not practical. 我不贊成，太不實際了。

1183 ⋯沒有用的。
It's no good...

範例 A: It's no good complaining.
抱怨是沒有用的。
B: Yes, I agree with you. We should do something.
是的。我同意你的看法。我們應該做點什麼。

1184 我恐怕很難贊成⋯。
I'm afraid I can't favor...

替換 | I would find it difficult to approve of...
I would like to say how much I disapprove of...
I really must voice my disapproval of...
I don't think I can give my backing to...

範例 | **A:** Are you in favor of my plan? 你贊成我的計畫嗎？
B: I'm afraid I can't favor your proposal. 我恐怕很難贊成你的建議。

3.3　恭維 Compliments

　　稱讚或恭維是一種社交手段。表面上是對一個人的作爲、個性或物品表示贊許或褒獎，實際上是爲了創造、維繫和促進良好的人際關係。有時還可以用來打招呼、鼓勵、祝賀、緩和批評的語氣、開始交談或致謝等。稱讚的內容多集中在人的才智、技能、表現、業績、儀表、衣飾、住房、家具以及個人其他的收藏品等等。

　　由於美國人較傾向個人主義，使得他們更常從自我的角度出發來表達個人見解和觀點。中國人較具團體意識，因此期望人們在交談中，儘量縮小自我。所以兩種文化對第一人稱的恭維語使用頻率不同。

　　但是我們表達讚美時，要儘量做到自然、眞誠、得體。面對讚美的反應也要自然，因爲英美人士聽到稱讚多表示接受，並感謝，而中國人則是不正面承認，還要謙虛一番。

● 表示恭維 Expressing Compliments

| *1185* | 你真幸運！
How lucky you are! | 050 |

替換 | You're a lucky man!
Lucky you!
Lucky old you!
Aren't you the lucky one?

範例 | **A:** How lucky you are! 你眞幸運！
B: Thank you! 謝謝！

1186	你看起來真棒！ **You look great!**

替換
You really look sharp!
You're looking good!
You're so beautiful!
You look very smart.
You're looking extremely dapper.
You're looking rather glamorous!

範例
A: You look great! 你看起來真棒！
B: Oh, really? 哦，是嗎？

提示
dapper ['dæpɚ] *adj.* 衣冠楚楚的
glamorous ['glæmərəs] *adj.* 富有魅力的；迷人的

1187	太美了！ **It's so beautiful!**

替換
It's breathtaking!
It's so brilliantly beautiful!

範例
A: Look at the lake. It's so beautiful! 看那湖水！太美了！
B: It's breathtaking! 美呆了！

提示
breathtaking ['brɛθˌtekɪŋ] *adj.* 令人驚嘆的；使人興奮的
brilliantly ['brɪljəntlɪ] *adv.* 出色地；亮眼地

1188	太棒了！ **Wonderful!**

替換
That's absolutely super!
You were wonderful.

範例
A: Wonderful! 太棒了！
B: Oh, I'm flattered. 哦，過獎了！

1189	你的…很好！ **Good...!**

替換
Your...is smashing!
What a terrific...you have!
Your...is excellent!
What a nice...you have!
Your...looks very smart!

| 範例 | A: Good pronunciation! 你的發音很好！
B: Thank you! 謝謝！ |

1190	我喜歡…。 **I love...**
替換	I like... I say, I adore...
範例	A: I love your shoes. 我喜歡你的鞋。 B: Oh, thanks. 哦，謝謝！

1191	我很欽佩…。 **I do admire...**
替換	I admire...very much. I've always admired...very much. I must express my admiration for... I should say my admiration for...is great.
範例	A: I do admire your courage. 我很欽佩你的勇氣。 B: Thanks. 謝謝。

1192	…和…真的很配。 **...goes really well with...**
替換	...suits...very well. I should say...matches...fabulously.
範例	A: Your new hairstyle goes really well with your outfit. 　你的新髮型和服裝真的很配。 B: Thank you. I'm so glad. 　謝謝，我很高興。
提示	fabulously ['fæbjələslɪ] *adv.* 難以置信地；驚人地

1193	你穿（戴）…好看極了。 **You look great with/in...**
替換	You look cool/sharp in... You look fantastic with... ...is absolutely made for you. You look really wonderful in...
範例	A: You look great with that hat. 你戴上那頂帽子好看極了。 B: Oh, thank you. 哦，謝謝！

1194	做得好！ **Well done!**
替換	You really did a good job! Nice going!
範例	**A:** Well done! 做得好！ **B:** Thank you very much. 謝謝你！

1195	你對…很有鑑賞力。 **You have good taste...**
範例	**A:** You have good taste in music. 你對音樂很有鑑賞力。 **B:** Thank you. 謝謝！

1196	太可愛了！ **It's lovely!**
替換	How nice! Isn't that lovely? It sure is nice!
範例	**A:** I love your cat. It's lovely! 我喜歡你的貓。太可愛了！ **B:** Oh, thank you. 哦，謝謝。

1197	恭喜你。 **My compliments to you.**
範例	**A:** You're quite successful. My compliments to you. 你的確很成功，恭喜你。 **B:** Thank you. I'm just lucky. 謝謝，我只是幸運罷了。
提示	my compliments...【正式】致意；道賀〔用複數形〕

1198	我從來沒有見過這麼…。 **I have never seen such...**
範例	**A:** I have never seen such a pretty girl. 我從沒有見過這麼美麗的女孩。 **B:** She is really pretty. 她的確很美麗。

1199	恕我直言，…太好吃了！ **If I may say so, ...is absolutely delicious.**

範例　A: If I may say so, the fish is absolutely delicious.
　　　　恕我直言，這魚真的太好吃了。
　　　　B: Really? My father cooked it.
　　　　真的嗎？這是我爸爸煮的。

1200　…簡直不可思議。
　　　　...is absolutely unbelievable.

範例　A: The view is absolutely unbelievable. 這裡的景色簡直不可思議。
　　　　B: Yes, it is very beautiful. 是的，太美了。

提示　unbelievable [ˌʌnbɪˈlivəbl] adj. 難以置信的

1201　我沒法不注意你的…，真是太美了！
　　　　I couldn't help noticing your...It's beautiful.

範例　A: I couldn't help noticing your ring. It's beautiful.
　　　　我沒法不注意你的戒指，真是太美了
　　　　B: That's very kind of you to say so.
　　　　謝謝你這麼說。

1202　我認為你應該得到最高的讚揚。
　　　　I think you deserve the highest praise.

範例　A: I think you deserve the highest praise. 我認為你應該得到最高的讚揚。
　　　　B: Oh, I'm flattered. 哦，過獎了。

1203　我認為…很迷人。
　　　　I do think...is so charming!

替換　If you don't mind my saying so, ...is quite enchanting.
　　　　May I say how charming your...is?

範例　A: I do think your voice is so charming! 我認為你的嗓音很迷人。
　　　　B: How kind of you to say so. 謝謝你這麼說。

提示　enchanting [ɪnˈtʃæntɪŋ] adj. 迷人的；嫵媚的

1204　你的…進步很多。
　　　　Your...has improved greatly.

替換　You have made great progress on...

範例　A: Your pronunciation has improved greatly. 你的發音進步很多。
　　　　B: Thank you. 謝謝。

1205	我要是能像你那樣…就好了。 **I wish I could be as...as you.**

範例 | A: I wish I could be as beautiful as you. 我要是能像你那樣美麗就好了。
B: Actually, you're very pretty, too. 事實上，你也很漂亮。

● 回應恭維 Answering Compliments

1206	謝謝。 **Thank you.**

替換 | Thanks.
範例 | A: You look wonderful! 你看起來氣色不錯。
B: Thank you. 謝謝。

1207	哦，過獎了。 **Oh, I'm flattered.**

替換 | Oh, you flatter me.
Oh, you're exaggerating.
範例 | A: Wow! What a terrific hat you have! 哇，你的帽子真漂亮。
B: Oh, I'm flattered. 哦，過獎了。
提示 | exaggerate [ɪgˈzædʒəˌret] v. 誇張；誇大

1208	哦，那其實真的沒什麼。 **Oh, there was nothing to it, really.**

替換 | Oh, it was nothing really, nothing at all.
範例 | A: You did a good job! 做得好！
B: Oh, there was nothing to it, really. 哦，那其實真的沒什麼。

1209	謝謝你這麼說。 **Thank you very much for saying so.**

替換 | It's nice of you to say so.
It's very good of you to say so.
I appreciate your remarks.
How very kind of you to say so.
範例 | A: You look very nice with that new dress. 你穿這件新衣服很漂亮。
B: Thank you very much for saying so. 謝謝你這麼說。

1210	別瞎說了。 **Don't be ridiculous!**
範例	**A:** You look cool with those sunglasses! 你戴那副太陽鏡帥極了。 **B:** Don't be ridiculous! 別瞎說了！

1211	諂媚是行不通的。 **Flattery will get you nowhere.**
範例	**A:** You look great with that necklace. 你的項鏈很漂亮。 **B:** Flattery will get you nowhere. 諂媚是行不通的。

1212	哈，謝謝。真叫我高興。 **Gee, thanks. You made my day.**
範例	**A:** Nice going! 做得好！ **B:** Gee, thanks. You made my day. 哈，謝謝。眞叫我高興。

1213	哦，不會吧。 **Oh, not really.**
範例	**A:** You look good today! 今天你氣色不錯。 **B:** Oh, not really. 哦，不會吧。

1214	哦，真的嗎？ **Oh, really?**
替換	Do you really think so?
範例	**A:** The new dress suits you very well! 這件新衣服和你很配。 **B:** Oh, really? 哦，眞的嗎？

1215	我只是很幸運罷了。 **I'm just very lucky.**
範例	**A:** Wonderful! My compliments to you. 太棒了，恭喜你。 **B:** Thank you. I'm just very lucky. 謝謝，我只是很幸運罷了。

1216	哦，我和這件事情沒有什麼關係。 **Well, I had very little to do with it.**
範例	**A:** Good job! 做得好！ **B:** Well, I had very little to do with it. 哦，我和這件事情沒有什麼關係。

1217	我還有許多要學的。 **I still have a lot to learn.**

範例 A: You did a good job. 做得很好！
B: I still have a lot to learn. 我還有許多要學的。

1218	哦，真的沒什麼特別的。 **Oh, it's really nothing special.**

範例 A: I love your dress. 我喜歡你的洋裝。
B: Oh, it's really nothing special. 哦，真的沒什麼特別的。

1219	事實上，你自己也很漂亮。 **As a matter of fact, you look pretty good yourself.**

範例 A: I wish I could be as pretty as you are.
　　我要是能和你一樣漂亮就好了。
B: As a matter of fact, you look pretty good yourself.
　　事實上，你自己也很漂亮。

1220	你人真好，不過其實任何人都辦得到的。 **You're very kind, but anyone could have done it.**

範例 A: Well done!
　　做得好！
B: You're very kind, but anyone could have done it.
　　你人真好，不過其實任何人都辦得到的。

1221	你人真好，不過我覺得這應該歸功於⋯。 **That's very kind of you, but all the credit should go to...**

替換 That's very kind of you, but I feel I owe it all to...

範例 A: You're quite successful! My compliments to you.
　　你這麼成功，我要向你致意。
B: That's very kind of you, but all the credit should go to my supervisor.
　　你人真好，不過我覺得這應該歸功於我的主管。

提示 supervisor [ˌsupɚˈvaɪzɚ] *n.* 主管；上司

271

3.4　祝賀 Congratulations

　　生活中有了喜事，人們總希望與親朋好友一起分享快樂。一般來說，升學、畢業、喬遷、店鋪開張、職務升遷、事業有成、獲得獎勵、慶祝佳節時，人們免不了要祝賀一番。恭賀用語在實際生活中用得相當廣泛，因此有必要確切掌握。值得注意的是，對慶賀用語的應答和對恭維語的應答有很多相似之處，讀者可以仔細比較一下。

● 表示祝賀 Expressing Congratulations

1222	好極了！ **Fantastic!** 051
替換	Super!
範例	**A:** Fantastic! 好極了！ **B:** Oh, thanks. 哦，謝謝。

1223	很高興聽說…。 **It was great to hear about...**
替換	It's great to know about...
範例	**A:** It was great to hear about your promotion. 很高興聽說你升遷了。 **B:** Thanks. 多謝。

1224	恭禧你…。 **Congratulations on...**
替換	Many congratulations on... Let me congratulate you on... Allow me to express my heartiest congratulations on... May I offer my congratulations on...
範例	**A:** Congratulations on your success! 　　恭禧你成功了！ **B:** You're very kind, but anyone else could have done it. 　　謝謝，但其實誰都可以做到。

1225
請允許我向你表達祝賀。
May I congratulate you?

(替換) Let me congratulate you.

(範例)
A: This is really a good paper. May I congratulate you?
這的確是一篇很好的論文。請允許我向你表達祝賀。
B: How very kind of you to say so.
謝謝你這樣說。

1226
好樣的…!
Good old...!

(範例)
A: Good old David! 大衛，好樣的。
B: Thanks. 謝謝。

1227
好球，…!
Nice shot, ...!

(替換) What a nice shot, ...!

(範例)
A: Nice shot, Joe! 好球，喬。
B: Thank you. 謝謝。

1228
做得好！
Well done!

(替換)
Good job!
Nice going.

(範例)
A: Well done, Bob! 做得好，鮑伯！
B: Thank you. 謝謝。

1229
恭喜你！
Congratulations.

(範例)
A: Well done, Joe! Congratulations. 做得好，喬！恭喜你。
B: Thank you. 謝謝。

1230
請代表我向…表示祝賀。
Please give...my congratulations.

(範例)
A: I'm told that your brother won first prize. Please give him my congratulations. 聽說你的弟弟獲得第一名，請代表我向他表示祝賀。
B: I will. Thank you. 我會的。謝謝。

1231	我一定得祝賀你…。 **I must congratulate you on...**

範例 | A: I must congratulate you on your success. 我一定得祝賀你的成功。
B: I appreciate your compliment. 謝謝你的恭維。

1232	我想第一個向你表示祝賀。 **I'd like to be the first to congratulate you.**

範例 | A: I'd like to be the first to congratulate you. 我想第一個向你表示祝賀。
B: Thank you. 謝謝。

1233	請接受我最衷心的祝賀。 **Please accept my sincere congratulations.**

替換 | Please accept my warmest congratulations.

範例 | A: Please accept my sincere congratulations. 請接受我最衷心的祝賀。
B: Thank you. 謝謝。

● 回應祝賀 Answering Congratulations

1234	謝謝。 **Thank you.**

替換 | Thanks.

範例 | A: You look wonderful! 你看起來氣色不錯。
B: Thank you. 謝謝。

1235	哦，過獎了。 **Oh, I'm flattered.**

替換 | Oh, you flatter me.
Oh, you're exaggerating.

範例 | A: Wow! You're really wonderful! 哇，你真不錯！
B: Oh, I'm flattered. 哦，過獎了。

1236	哦，那真的沒什麼。 **Oh, there is nothing to it, really.**

替換 | Oh, it was nothing really, nothing at all.

範例 A: You did a good job! Congratulations. 做得好！恭喜你！
B: Oh, there is nothing to it, really. 哦，那真的沒什麼。

1237 謝謝你這麼說。
Thank you very much for saying so.

替換 It's nice of you to say so.
I appreciate your compliments.
It's very good of you to say so.
How very kind of you to say so.

範例 A: I'd like to be the first to congratulate you. 我想第一個向你表示祝賀。
B: Thank you very much for saying so. 謝謝你這麼說。

1238 哦，實際上沒什麼特別的。
Oh, it's nothing special, actually.

範例 A: I must congratulate you on your success. 我一定要恭禧你成功了。
B: Oh, it's nothing special, actually. 哦，實際上沒什麼特別的。

1239 事實上，你看起來也很好。
You look very good yourself, as a matter of fact.

範例 A: I wish I could be as pretty as you are.
我要是能和你一樣漂亮就好了。
B: You look very good yourself, as a matter of fact.
事實上，你看起來也很好。

1240 謝謝你，不過誰都能辦得到的。
You're very kind, but anyone else could have done it.

範例 A: Well done! Many, many congratulations.
做得好！恭喜你。
B: You're very kind, but anyone else could have done it.
謝謝你，不過誰都能辦得到的。

3.5 好奇 Curiosity

人們往往對於新鮮的事物有好奇心，其實，好奇是人的天性。英語中，表達好奇的語言是非常豐富的。應該注意的是，在會話中，不要對他人的私事表現得過分好奇，否則會引起反感。詢問時，也應當注意禮貌。

1241　我很想知道…。
I'd love to know about...

052

（替換）
I'd really like to know about...
I'd particularly like to know about...
I'd be most interested to know...
I'm most curious about...
I'm very keen to find out...
I wonder...
What I'd really like to find out is...

（範例）
A: I'd love to know about the secret of his success.
　　我想知道他成功的祕密。
B: Just ask him. I think he will tell you.
　　儘管問他，我想他會告訴你的。

（提示）
particularly [pɚˈtɪkjələˌlɪ] *adv.* 特別；尤其
keen [kin] *adj.*【尤英】熱衷的；渴望的（+ on）

1242　我倒想知道…。
I wouldn't mind knowing...

（範例）
A: I wouldn't mind knowing who did it. 我倒想知道是誰做的。
B: Maybe Joe did. 可能是喬。

1243　我要是知道…就好了。
If only I knew...

（替換）
I wish I knew...
I wish someone would tell me...

（範例）
A: If only I knew his name! 我要是知道他的名字就好了！
B: He's David. 他叫大衛。

1244　有人能告訴我…？
Can someone tell me about...?

（替換）
Does anyone know...?

（範例）
A: What's going on here? Can someone tell me about it?
　　這裡發生什麼事了？ 有人能告訴我嗎？
B: Oh, a woman was murdered in that building.
　　喔！那棟建築物裡有個女人被謀殺了。

1245	嗨，這裡怎麼了？ **Hey, what's going on here?**
範例	**A:** Hey, what's going on here? 嗨，這裡怎麼了？ **B:** Two women are quarreling. 兩個女人正在吵架。

1246	你在想些什麼呢？ **What's on your mind?**
範例	**A:** What's on your mind? 你在想些什麼呢？ **B:** I'm wondering why he was so angry. 我在想他為什麼這麼生氣？

1247	你能告訴我⋯？ **Could you tell me...?**
替換	I wonder if you could tell me...
範例	**A:** Could you tell me when the train from London will arrive? 你能告訴我從倫敦來的火車幾點到嗎？ **B:** At 2 p.m. 下午兩點。

1248	⋯發生了什麼事？ **What happened...?**
範例	**A:** What happened then? 後來發生了什麼事？ **B:** They got married. 他們結婚了。

1249	你剛好知道⋯嗎？ **Do you happen to know...?**
範例	**A:** Do you happen to know what his problem is? 你剛好知道他的問題嗎？ **B:** Sorry, I have no idea. 對不起，我一無所知。

1250	⋯一定⋯，不是嗎？ **It must..., mustn't it?**
範例	**A:** It must be wonderful being married, mustn't it? 結婚的感覺一定很好，不是嗎？ **B:** Yes, it is. 是的，很好。

| 1251 | 我想⋯吧？
...I suppose? |

範例　A: He's not here, I suppose? 我想他不在這裡吧？
B: You're right. 你說對了。

| 1252 | 你還沒告訴我⋯呢。
You still haven't told me about... |

範例　A: You still haven't told me about your plan. 你還沒告訴我你的計畫呢。
B: I haven't decided on it yet. 計畫還沒有確定下來。

| 1253 | 對不起，我並不想顯得多管閒事，不過⋯？
Excuse me, I don't want to seem inquisitive, but... |

替換　Excuse me, I hope you don't think I'm being inquisitive, but...

範例　A: Excuse me, I don't want to seem inquisitive, but could you tell me where you're from?
對不起，我並不想顯得多管閒事，不過你能告訴我你從哪裡來的嗎？
B: I'm from New York.
我從紐約來的。

提示　inquisitive [ɪnˈkwɪzətɪv] *adj.* 愛打聽的；過分好奇的

| 1254 | 我希望你不介意我問，不過⋯嗎？
I hope you don't mind my asking, but... |

範例　A: I hope you don't mind my asking, but are they your brothers?
我希望你不介意我問，不過他們是你的兄弟嗎？
B: Yes, they are my elder brothers.
是的，他們是我的哥哥。

| 1255 | 有可能獲得⋯的消息嗎？
Is it possible to obtain any information about... |

範例　A: Is it possible to obtain any information about him?
有可能獲得關於他的消息嗎？
B: Sorry, I have no idea about him.
對不起，我不知道。

3.6 欣喜 Delight

問題得以順利解決時，我們會感到寬慰；好消息傳來時，我們會感到心情愉快。寬慰、欣喜是我們經常要表達的心情，因此，英語中表達這些心情的語言也非常豐富。

1256

我太高興了。
I'm on top of the world.

(053)

替換
I'm on cloud nine.
I feel like a million dollars.
I'm tickled pink.

範例
A: We all passed the examination. 我們考試都過了。
B: I'm on top of the world. 我太高興了。

提示
on top of the world【非正式】幸福到了極點；心滿意足
cloud nine【非正式】極樂心境；狂喜狀態
be tickled pink【俚】非常開心；覺得非常有趣的

1257

好極了！
Great!

替換
Super!
Swell!
Terrific!
Fantastic!
Smashing!
That's cool!
Hey, that's terrific!
Oh, how nice/marvelous/wonderful!
Oh, that's marvelous/wonderful!

範例
A: Look! I cleaned the bedroom for you! 你看！我幫你打掃房間！
B: Great! 好極了！

1258

我非常高興。
I'm very pleased.

替換
I'm really delighted.

279

範例　A: Look! I washed the dishes for you! 你看！我幫你洗碗！
B: I'm very pleased. 我非常高興。

1259　我非常高興…。
I'm very pleased to...

替換　I'm mighty glad to...
I'm really delighted to...
It gives me great pleasure to...

範例　A: I'm very pleased to hear your good news.
我非常高興聽到你的好消息。
B: Oh, thank you.
哦，謝謝。

1260　這是我這麼久以來聽到的最好消息。
That's the best news I've heard for a long time.

替換　That's the best thing I've heard in years.

範例　A: David and Fiona got married last month.
大衛和菲歐娜上個月結婚了。
B: That's the best news I've heard for a long time.
這是我這麼久以來聽到的最好消息。

1261　…我說不出有多高興。
I can't say how delightful it is to...

替換　I can't say how pleased/delighted I am to...

範例　A: I can't say how delightful it is to know about your success.
得知你成功了，我說不出有多高興。
B: How nice of you to say so.
謝謝你這麼說。

1262　很高興聽到…。
I'm most delighted to hear about...

替換　I'm really overjoyed to hear about...

範例　A: I'm most delighted to hear about your promotion.
很高興聽到你升遷了。
B: It's very kind of you to say so.
多謝你這麼說。

1263	那是好消息。 **That's good news.**
替換	What delightful news! That's splendid news.
範例	**A:** Tom finally passed the exam. 湯姆最後通過考試了。 **B:** That's good news. 那是好消息。

3.7　容易 Ease

　　事情的難與易是我們日常生活中經常要表達的內容。英文口語中，這方面的表達方法非常豐富，有的還非常有趣。

054

1264	沒問題。 **No problem.**
替換	No sweat.
範例	**A:** Can you do it? 你行嗎？ **B:** No problem. 沒問題。
提示	no sweat【口】一點也不難；毫不費力

1265	小事一椿。 **It's a piece of cake.**
替換	It's nothing.
範例	**A:** Can you open this bottle without an opener? 你能不用開瓶器打開這個瓶子嗎？ **B:** It's a piece of cake. 小事一椿。
提示	be a piece of cake【口】很容易做到的事；輕鬆愉快的事

1266	很簡單。 **It's quite easy.**
範例	**A:** How are you coming along with geography? 你的地理學得怎麼樣？ **B:** It's quite easy. 很簡單。

1267	當然。 **Sure.**

範例	**A:** Can you swim? 你會游泳嗎？ **B:** Sure. 當然。

1268	我很擅長⋯。 **I'm good at...**

替換	I'm brilliant/great at...
範例	**A:** I bet you cannot dance, can you? 你肯定不會跳舞吧，對吧？ **B:** I'm good at it. 我很擅長的。

1269	正巧我會⋯。 **There is a chance I can...**

範例	**A:** My Walkman does not work. 我的隨身聽壞了。 **B:** There is a chance I can fix it. 正巧我會修。

1270	它對我來說並不難。 **It isn't too difficult for me.**

替換	It's not too much a problem for me. I don't think it would be too difficult.
範例	**A:** Don't you think English is hard? 你不認為英文很難嗎？ **B:** It isn't too difficult for me. 它對我來說並不難。

1271	這事我閉著眼睛都能做到。 **I can do it blindfolded.**

範例	**A:** Can you ride a bike? 你會騎自行車嗎？ **B:** I can do it blindfolded. 這事我閉著眼睛都能做到。
提示	blindfolded ['blaɪndˌfoldɪd] *adj.* 閉著眼睛的；盲目的

3.8　鼓勵 Encouragement

　　鼓勵是一種勸人努力上進的期望語。中文中的鼓勵常以成語方式出現，有特殊的語意表達。在英語中，鼓勵人們的話一般是直接提出自己的希望。

1272 振作起來。
Cheer up!

(替換) Buck up!

(範例) A: I failed in the driving test.
我考駕照沒有通過。
B: Cheer up! Lots of people fail their driving test the first time.
振作起來,很多人第一次都沒有通過。

(提示) buck up!【口】振作些!別發愁!

1273 堅持下去!
Go on!

(替換) Keep at it!
Stick to it!

(範例) A: I don't think I can finish it. 我不認為我能完成。
B: Go on! You can do it. 堅持下去,你一定能成功。

1274 拿出點勇氣來。
Come on!

(替換) Be a man!
Don't be a wimp!
Be a good sport and have a try!

(範例) A: I can't do it. 我不行。
B: Come on! Don't give up! 拿出點勇氣來,不要放棄。

(提示) wimp [wɪmp] *n.* 軟弱者;無能者

1275 別灰心!
(Keep your) chin up!

(替換) Don't give up (now)!
Don't give up hope.
Don't let this get you down.

(範例) A: Do you think I can win? 你認為我能贏嗎?
B: (Keep your) chin up. 別灰心。

1276 好極了!
Great!

(替換) │ That's fine/wonderful!
Well done!
You're doing fine.
You're doing very well.

(範例) **A:** What did you think of my performance? 你覺得我的表現怎麼樣？
B: Great! 好極了。

1277
根本沒有理由氣餒。
There's no reason to feel discouraged at all.

(替換) │ There's no reason to lose confidence in yourself.
There's nothing to feel discouraged about.

(範例) **A:** I don't think I can do it well.
我覺得自己做不好。
B: Why? There's no reason to feel discouraged at all. You're the best.
為什麼？根本沒有理由氣餒。你是最好的。

1278
我們絕對支持你。
We're right behind you.

(替換) │ You have our full backing/support.

(範例) **A:** We're right behind you. 我們絕對支持你。
B: Thank you very much. 非常感謝你們。

1279
我們絕對支持你…。
You have our whole-hearted support with...

(替換) │ You have our full backing with...

(範例) **A:** You have our whole-hearted support with this proposal.
我們絕對支持你的提議。。
B: That's very kind of you to say so.
謝謝你這麼說。

1280
再試一次！
Try again!

(範例) **A:** I can't find the answer to this question. 我找不出這個問題的答案。
B: Don't lose hope. Try again! 別灰心，再試一次！

1281
你能辦到的！
You can do it!

範例 | A: Keep at it. You can do it! 堅持下去，你能辦到的！
B: Thank you for saying so. 謝謝你這麼說。

1282 別擔心，我敢肯定這次你會做得更好。
Don't worry. I'm sure you'll do better this time.

範例 | A: I did so poorly on the last exam.
我上次考試考得好爛喔。
B: Don't worry. I'm sure you'll do better this time.
別擔心，我敢肯定這次你會做得更好。

1283 儘量從好的方面看吧。
Try to look on the bright side of things.

範例 | A: The Taiwan football team lost again. They'll never win!
台灣足球隊又輸了。他們從來不會贏！
B: Try to look on the bright side of things.
儘量從好的方面看吧。

1284 我認為你不應該甘於失敗。
I don't think you should give in to defeat.

範例 | A: I will never take part in any speech contest.
我再也不會參加任何演講比賽了。
B: I don't think you should give in to defeat.
我認為你不應該甘於失敗。

1285 我認為你應該鼓起勇氣。
I think you should pluck up your courage.

範例 | A: I get nervous just at the thought of the interview.
我一想到面試就緊張。
B: I think you should pluck up your courage.
我認為你應該鼓起勇氣。

3.9　興奮 Excitement

　　激動是人受到刺激時，所產生的感情衝動。英語中表達激動的心情常用 "Great!"、"Fantastic!"、"Super!"、"Terrific!"、"What a great idea!"、"How exciting!"、"How marvelous!"、"How wonderful!"、"It's so exciting."、"I'm so excited."、"Really!" 等表達方式。不過，使用這些表達方式時，要視程度、場合、事物而定。

1286 好極了！
Great! (056)

(替換)
Super!
Terrific!
Smashing!
Fantastic!
Hey, that's great!
How marvelous/wonderful!

(範例)
A: He won first prize. 他得了第一名！
B: Great! 好極了！

1287 太令人興奮了！
That's very exciting.

(替換)
It's breathtaking.
It's heart stopping.

(範例)
A: The Taiwanese team won the championship! 台灣隊得了冠軍。
B: That's very exciting. 太令人興奮了！

(提示)
championship ['tʃæmpɪənˌʃɪp] n. 冠軍

1288 ⋯非常令人興奮。
...is really exhilarating.

(替換)
...is most fascinating.

(範例)
A: Going abroad is really exhilarating. 出國真是非常令人興奮。
B: Yes, I can't wait. 是的，我已經等不及了。

(提示)
exhilarating [ɪgˈzɪləˌretɪŋ] adj. 令人振奮的；使人高興的

1289 我非常興奮！
I'm so excited!

(替換)
I'm thrilled.
I'm in a good mood.

範例 **A:** I'm so excited. 我非常興奮！
B: So am I. 我也是。

提示 thrilled [θrɪld] *adj.* 非常興奮的；極為激動的

1290
…真是好極了！
How wonderful to...

替換 It is really amazing to...

範例 **A:** How wonderful to see you here. 看見你在這裡，真是好極了。
B: I'm here on business. 我出差到這裡。

提示 amazing [əˈmezɪŋ] *adj.* 驚人的

1291
…的確令我非常興奮。
I'm really very excited about/by...

替換 I'm extremely fascinated by...

範例 **A:** I'm really very excited about the good news.
這好消息的確令我非常興奮。
B: Yes, it is really very exciting.
是呀！的確很令人興奮。

1292
你知道嗎？
Guess what?

範例 **A:** Guess what? He won first prize! 你知道嗎？他得了頭獎。
B: Really? 真的嗎？

1293
我真不敢相信！
I can't believe it!

範例 **A:** I can't believe it! He got a full score on the exam!
我真不敢相信！他考試得了滿分。
B: Really?
是嗎？

1294
聽到…我的確無法控制我的興奮之情。
I can't control my enthusiasm about...

範例 **A:** A Taiwanese player won the championship.
一位台灣選手得了冠軍。

B: I can't control my enthusiasm about the news.
聽到這個消息，我的確無法控制我的興奮之情。

提示　enthusiasm [ɪn'θjuzɪ,æzəm] *n.* 狂熱；熱心

1295　哇！太棒了！
Whoopee!

替換　Hooray!

範例　**A:** Let's go out for dinner tonight. 我們今天晚上出去吃吧！
B: Whoopee! 哇！太棒了！

1296　我等不及了！
I can't wait!

替換　I can hardly wait.

範例　**A:** Let's go camping next weekend. 我們下週末去露營吧！
B: Great. I can't wait! 太好了！我等不及了！

1297　這完全出乎我的意料之外！
It was totally unexpected.

範例　**A:** I heard you won the lottery prize of one million dollars.
我聽說你中了一百萬的彩券。
B: Yeah, it was totally unexpected.
是呀！這完全出乎我的意料之外！

1298　我不敢相信我的耳朵！
I can hardly believe my ears.

範例　**A:** You passed the exam.
你通過考試了。
B: Really? I can hardly believe my ears.
真的嗎？我不敢相信我的耳朵！

1299　美夢成真了！
It's a dream come true.

範例　**A:** It's a dream come true. 美夢成真了！
B: Wow, it's unbelievable. 哇，真令人不敢相信。

1300　沒有什麼比這更好的了！
Nothing could be more wonderful.

範例 A: Our basketball team won. 我們的籃球隊贏了！
B: Nothing could be more wonderful. 沒有什麼比這更好的了！

1301 我覺得再好不過了！
I couldn't feel better.

範例 A: You look good today. 你今天看起來很好！
B: I couldn't feel better. 我覺得再好不過了！

1302 我覺得像在天堂！
I'm in heaven right now.

替換 I'm walking on air.

範例 A: I'm in heaven right now. 我覺得像在天堂！
B: What for? 為什麼呢？

1303 我簡直樂透了。
I jumped for joy.

範例 A: I heard you've won the scholarship.
我聽說你拿到獎學金了。
B: Yes. I jumped for joy when I heard the news.
是呀。我聽到消息時，簡直樂透了。

3.10 祝福 Good Wishes

能使他人快樂的人，自己也能享受到快樂。他人外出旅行、參加考試，或從事一項新的活動時，我們不要忘記送上一句吉祥話，表達最誠摯的祝福。這是基本禮儀。

● 表示祝福 Expressing Good Wishes

1304 祝你成功！
Break a leg!

(057)

範例 A: Break a leg! 祝你成功！
B: Thanks. 謝謝。

1305	祝你好運！ **Good luck!**

(替換)	Good luck to you. (The very) best of luck to you.
(範例)	**A:** Good luck! 祝你好運！ **B:** Thank you. 謝謝。

1306	祝你玩得愉快。 **Enjoy yourself!**

(替換)	Have fun. Have a good time. I hope you have a good time.
(範例)	**A:** Enjoy yourself! 祝你玩得愉快！ **B:** Thanks. 謝謝。

1307	祝你…快樂。 **Happy...**

(替換)	Enjoy your... Have a nice... I hope you have a good... I hope you enjoy your... I hope you'll have a nice...
(範例)	**A:** Happy anniversary! 祝你週年紀念快樂！ **B:** Thank you! 謝謝。
(提示)	anniversary [ˌænəˈvɝsərɪ] *n.* 週年紀念

1308	祝你萬事如意。 **Hope everything goes all right for you.**

(替換)	All the (very) best! I wish you every success! I hope everything goes well. May everything go your way! I'd like to wish you every success.
(範例)	**A:** Hope everything goes all right for you. 祝你萬事如意。 **B:** Same to you. 你也是。

1309	祝你…順利。 **Every success with...**

(替換) | All the best with your...
I hope everything goes well with your...
May I wish you every success with your...
I'd like to wish you every success with your...

(範例) | **A:** Every success with your business! 祝你生意順利！
B: Thank you. 謝謝。

1310	請代我向…問好。 **Please give my regards to...**

(替換) | Say hello to...
Give my love to...
Please remember me to...
Please give...my best wishes.
Please give my best wishes to...
Please send my regards to...
Please give...my best regards.
Would you give...my best wishes?
Please convey my best wishes to...

(範例) | **A:** Please give my regards to your family. 請代我向你家人問好。
B: Thank you. 謝謝。

(提示) | convey [kən've] *v.* 傳達

1311	我希望你能很快康復。 **I hope you'll get well soon.**

(替換) | I hope you'll feel better soon.
I hope you'll get over it soon.

(範例) | **A:** I hope you'll get well soon. 我希望你能很快康復。
B: Thank you very much. 多謝。

1312	祝你…成功。 **I wish you success with...**

(替換) | May you succeed in...!

範例 | **A:** I wish you success with your business! 祝你生意成功！
B: Thank you. 謝謝。

● 回應祝福 Answering Good Wishes

1313 | 謝謝。
Thanks.

替換 | Thank you.
(Very) many thanks.
Thank you very much.

範例 | **A:** I hope you have a good time! 我希望你玩得愉快！
B: Thanks. 謝謝。

1314 | 你也一樣。
You too.

替換 | The same to you.
I wish you the same.

範例 | **A:** Every success to you! 祝你成功。
B: You too. 你也一樣。

● 特別場合的祝福 Good Wishes on a Special Occasion

1315 | 生日快樂。
Happy birthday!

替換 | Many happy returns!
Have a happy birthday!
I'd like to wish you a happy birthday.
I'd like to wish you many happy returns!

範例 | **A:** Happy birthday! 生日快樂。
B: Thank you! 謝謝。

1316 | …快樂！
Happy...!

替換 | A happy/merry...to you!
Have a happy/good...!
May I wish you a happy...?

A: Happy Halloween! 萬聖節快樂。
B: You too. 你也是。

● 舉杯敬酒 Toasts

1317 乾杯！
Cheers!

（替換）
Salud!
Drink/Bottoms up!
Down the hatch!〔俚語說法〕
Here's a toast!
Here's looking at you, kid!
Here's mud in your eye!〔舊式說法〕

（範例）
A: Cheers! 乾杯！
B: Cheers! 乾杯！

（提示）
salud! [sɑ'luð] *interj*. 【西】乾杯

1318 祝你健康。
To your health!

（替換）
Here's to your health.
Here's wishing you good health.

（範例）
A: To your health! 祝你健康。
B: Thank you. 謝謝。

1319 我為…乾杯，願…。
I'd like to drink to...May...

（替換）
I raise my glass to..., wishing...

（範例）
A: I'd like to drink to the bride and the bridegroom. May they have a happy life together.
我為新娘和新郎乾杯，願他們生活幸福美滿。
B: Thank you.
謝謝。

（提示）
bride [braɪd] *n*. 新娘
bridegroom ['braɪd,grum] *n*. 新郎

1320	讓我們為…乾杯。 **Let's drink to...**

(替換) Shall we propose a toast to...?

(範例) A: Let's drink to our new colleague. 讓我們爲我們的新同事乾杯。
B: Cheers. 乾杯。

(提示) colleague ['kɑlig] *n.* 同事；同僚

1321	我請你們和我一起為…乾杯。 **I'd like you to join me in a toast to...**

(替換) I'd ask you to raise your glasses and join me in a toast to...
With great pleasure I'd like you to toast...
It is with great pleasure that I invite you to raise your glasses to...

(範例) A: I'd like you to join me in a toast to the health of our friends.
我請你們和我一起爲朋友們的健康乾杯。
B: Cheers.
乾杯。

1322	敬你一杯。 **Here is to you.**

(範例) A: Here is to you. 敬你一杯。
B: Thank you. 謝謝。

1323	現在，我想提議為…乾杯。 **At this point, I would like to propose a toast to...**

(替換) Let me propose a toast to...

(範例) A: At this point, I would like to propose a toast to our friendship.
現在，我想提議爲我們的友誼乾杯。
B: Cheers!
乾杯。

3.11 愉快期待 Happy Anticipation

期待是對未來的事物或者某人的前途有所期望和等待。英語中有不少表達愉快期待的語言，不過表達期待時，要注意談話的場合和交談的對象。

(058)

1324
我真想立刻…。
I can't wait to...

(替換) I can hardly wait to...

(範例) **A:** I can't wait to see my mom. 我真想立刻見到我媽媽。
B: She will arrive soon. 她很快就到了。

1325
…一定很愉快。
It'll be good to...

(替換) It'll be nice/fun/interesting to...
It'll be really great to...
It would be really marvelous to...
It is going to be wonderful to...

(範例) **A:** Will you go swimming tomorrow? 明天你要去游泳嗎？
B: It'll be good to swim in that lake. 在湖裡游泳一定很愉快。

1326
我盼望…。
I'm looking forward to...

(替換) I'm really looking forward to...
I'm anticipating...
I wait for...with great anticipation.

(範例) **A:** I'm looking forward to seeing our old classmates.
我盼望見到我們的老同學。
B: Me, too.
我也是。

(提示) anticipate [æn'tɪsə,pet] v. 預期；期望
anticipation [æn'tɪsə,peʃən] n. 預期；期望

1327
我渴望…。
I'm longing to...

(範例) **A:** I'm longing to find a boyfriend. 我渴望找到一個男朋友。
B: I'm sure you will find one. 你肯定能找到。

1328
那絕對是值得盼望的事。
That is certainly something to look forward to.

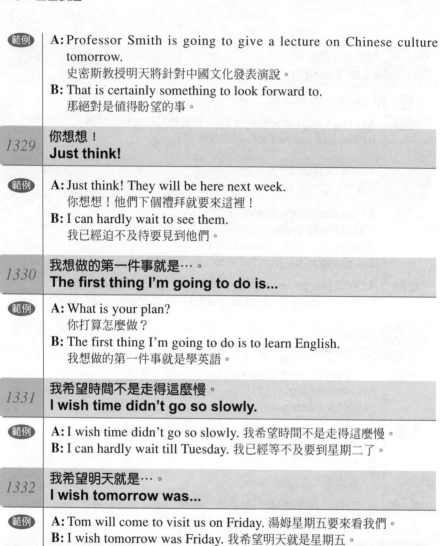

範例　A: Professor Smith is going to give a lecture on Chinese culture tomorrow.
史密斯教授明天將針對中國文化發表演說。
B: That is certainly something to look forward to.
那絕對是值得盼望的事。

1329　你想想！
Just think!

範例　A: Just think! They will be here next week.
你想想！他們下個禮拜就要來這裡！
B: I can hardly wait to see them.
我已經迫不及待要見到他們。

1330　我想做的第一件事就是…。
The first thing I'm going to do is...

範例　A: What is your plan?
你打算怎麼做？
B: The first thing I'm going to do is to learn English.
我想做的第一件事就是學英語。

1331　我希望時間不是走得這麼慢。
I wish time didn't go so slowly.

範例　A: I wish time didn't go so slowly. 我希望時間不是走得這麼慢。
B: I can hardly wait till Tuesday. 我已經等不及要到星期二了。

1332　我希望明天就是…。
I wish tomorrow was...

範例　A: Tom will come to visit us on Friday. 湯姆星期五要來看我們。
B: I wish tomorrow was Friday. 我希望明天就是星期五。

1333　…有多好啊！?
Wouldn't it be nice to...?

範例　A: Wouldn't it be nice to have some new friends?
結識一些新朋友有多好啊！?
B: Yes. I'm so sick of the old ones.
是啊，我厭倦老朋友了。

3.12 希望 Hope

　生活中，我們總想滿足自己的願望。我們既想獲得眼前的利益，也想達到長遠的目標。英語中表達希望的辭彙和語句非常豐富。我們要學會如何表明自己的意圖，學會根據場合，恰當地表達自己的希望。

059

1334　希望…。
Let's hope...

替換
Here's hoping that...
Hopefully, ...

範例
A: Let's hope he comes back soon. 希望他能很快回來。
B: But he doesn't want to come back. 但是他並不想回來。

1335　我希望…。
I hope...

替換
I wish...
My hope is that...
..., I hope.
I'd hope that...

範例
A: I hope I will be a millionaire. 我希望自己成為百萬富翁。
B: Then you have to work very hard. 那你必須非常努力地工作。

1336　讓我們祈禱…。
Let's pray to God...

替換
Let's keep our fingers crossed that...

範例
A: Let's pray to God he will come back safe and sound.
　　讓我們祈禱他能平安回來。
B: He will.
　　他會的。

提示
keep one's fingers crossed（將食指和中指交叉）祈求（好運）

1337　我真誠希望…。
It's my sincere hope that...

297

> **範例**
>
> **A:** It's my sincere hope that you can come to my party.
> 我真誠希望你能來參加我的舞會。
> **B:** Thank you very much for inviting me.
> 謝謝你邀請我。

1338	要是⋯該多好。 **If only...**

> **範例**
>
> **A:** We had some trouble doing it. 我們遇到了一些困難。
> **B:** If only he were here. 要是他在這裡該多好。

3.13 興趣 Interest

人的興趣愛好不盡相同，而表達興趣、說明是否感興趣、說明喜歡什麼、不喜歡什麼的表達方法也是豐富多樣。在日常生活中，熟練掌握相關的表達方法，將有助於提高會話能力，進而促進人際之間的交流。

● 詢問興趣 Asking about Interest

1339	你對⋯有興趣嗎？ **Are you interested in...?**

> **替換**
>
> Are you keen on...?
> Do you go for...?
> Do you have/share any interest in...?

> **範例**
>
> **A:** Are you interested in sports? 你對運動有興趣嗎？
> **B:** Yes, I like them very much. 有，非常喜歡。

1340	你覺得⋯有趣嗎？ **Do you think...is interesting?**

> **替換**
>
> Do you find...attractive?
> I wonder if you find...fascinating?

> **範例**
>
> **A:** Do you think the film is interesting? 你覺得這部電影有趣嗎？
> **B:** Yes, it's very exciting. 是的，非常精彩。

1341	…你感興趣嗎？ **Does...interest you?**
替換	Does...grab/intrigue you? Does...appeal to you? I wonder if...has any attraction for you?
範例	**A:** Does the novel interest you? 這部小說你感興趣嗎？ **B:** Yes, I like it. 是的，我很喜歡。
提示	grab [græb] v.【口】將…吸引住；影響 intrigue [ɪn'trig] v. 激起…的興趣

1342	你是…迷嗎？ **Are you a...fan?**
範例	**A:** Are you a basketball fan? 你是籃球迷嗎？ **B:** No. I like volleyball. 不，我喜歡排球。

1343	你的興趣是什麼？ **What are your interests?**
替換	What are you interested in?
範例	**A:** What are your interests? 你的興趣是什麼？ **B:** I like reading and listening to music. 我喜歡看書，聽音樂。

● 表示有興趣 Expressing Interest

1344	…使我很感興趣。 **...interests me a great deal.**
替換	...is what grabs my attention a lot. ...really turns me on. ...is what switches me on a lot. ...has always interested me. ...intrigues me a lot. ...really appeals to me. ...has great attraction for me.
範例	**A:** Science interests me a great deal. 科學使我很感興趣。 **B:** Me, too. 我也是。
提示	switch/turn sb. on【非正式】使某人感到快樂或興奮

1345

我發現…很有趣。
I find...quite interesting.

(替換) I find...very attractive.
I find...extremely fascinating.

(範例) **A:** I find fishing quite interesting.
我發現釣魚很有趣。
B: Really? Let's go fishing tomorrow, then.
是嗎？那我們明天去釣魚吧。

1346

我的興趣是…。
My interest is...

(替換) My hobby is...

(範例) **A:** My interest is drawing. How about you?
我的興趣是畫畫，你呢？
B: My hobby is collecting stamps.
我的興趣是集郵。

1347

我很喜歡…。
I like...very much.

(替換) I love...
I am keen on...
I go for...in a big way.

(範例) **A:** I like football very much. 我很喜歡足球。
B: I'm also a football fan. 我也是足球迷。

● 表示不感興趣 Expressing Indifference

1348

我對…不感興趣。
I'm not very interested in...

(替換) I don't have any interest in...
I don't take a great interest in...
...isn't all that interesting as far as I'm concerned.
...isn't for me.
...has no attraction for me.

(範例) **A:** How do you like the book? 你覺得這本書如何？
B: I'm not very interested in it. 我對它不感興趣。

1349	我覺得…很無趣。 **I find...rather uninteresting.**
(替換)	I don't find...very interesting/attractive. I don't think...appeals to me very much.
(範例)	**A:** I find cooking rather uninteresting. 我覺得做飯很無趣。 **B:** I don't think it is. 我不這樣認為。

1350	恐怕我對…不感興趣。 **I'm afraid...isn't my cup of tea.**
(替換)	I'm afraid...leaves me cold. I'm afraid I don't give a damn about...
(範例)	**A:** Does boxing interest you? 你對拳擊有興趣嗎？ **B:** I'm afraid it isn't my cup of tea. 恐怕我對它不感興趣。
(提示)	leave sb. cold 未打動某人；未引起…的興趣 not give a damn【口】毫不在乎

1351	事實上，最引不起我興趣的莫過於…。 **Nothing interests me less than..., as a matter of fact.**
(範例)	**A:** Nothing interests me less than listening to lectures, as a matter of fact. 事實上，最引不起我興趣的莫過於聽講座。 **B:** I feel the same way. 我也是。

3.14 喜好 Likes

　　喜歡是指對人或事物有好感或感興趣，這是人們經常要表達的態度，這種語言功能涉及的範圍很廣，衣、食、住、行無所不包。英語中表達喜歡的語言是非常豐富的。

● 詢問是否喜歡 Asking whether One Likes Something or Not

1352	你喜歡…嗎？ **Do you fancy...?**	061

(替換) Do you care/go for...?
Do you like/enjoy...?
Do you feel an attachment to...?
Do you find any pleasure in...?
Are you keen on...?
Are you fond of...?
I wonder if you enjoy...
May I ask if you're fond of...
May I ask if you have a liking for...?
Could you tell me if you have a fondness for...?

(範例) **A:** Do you fancy jazz? 你喜歡爵士樂嗎？
B: Yes, I like it very much. 是的，我非常喜歡。

(提示) attachment [ə'tætʃmənt] *n.* 依戀

1353　你不喜歡…嗎？
Don't you just love...?

(替換) Don't you like...?

(範例) **A:** Don't you just love that painting? 你不喜歡那幅油畫嗎？
B: Yes, I love it. 不，我很喜歡。

1354　…很討人喜歡，不是嗎？
...is nice, isn't...?

(範例) **A:** That girl is nice, isn't she? 那個女孩很討人喜歡，不是嗎？
B: Yes, she's sweet. 是的，她很貼心。

1355　你不覺得…很令人興奮嗎？
Don't you find...very exciting?

(範例) **A:** Don't you find skating very exciting? 你不覺得溜冰很令人興奮嗎？
B: No, I don't. 不，我並不覺得。

1356　你對…的感覺如何？
How do you feel about...?

(範例) **A:** How do you feel about him? 你對他的感覺如何？
B: He's very kind. 他是個很好的人。

● 表示喜歡 Expressing Likes

1357	我喜歡… **I love...**
替換	I adore/like/fancy... I have a fancy for...
範例	A: I love reading. 我喜歡看書。 B: Me, too. 我也是。

1358	我真的很喜歡…。 **I really enjoy...**
替換	I really go for... I do like... I'm really sold on... I'm really fond of...
範例	A: I really enjoy having pets. 我真的很喜歡養寵物。 B: Well, I don't like pets. 嗯，我不喜歡寵物。

1359	我對…非常著迷。 **I'm crazy about...**
替換	I'm nuts/mad about... I'm head over heels about...
範例	A: What do you like? 你喜歡什麼？ B: I'm crazy about pop music. 我對流行音樂非常著迷。
提示	head over heels about 深深愛著…

1360	我特別喜歡…。 **I especially like...**
替換	I'm keen on... I have a special liking for... I have a particular fondness for... I find great pleasure in... I must admit I'm very fond of... I can't find words to express how much I like...
範例	A: I especially like outdoor sports. 我特別喜歡戶外運動。 B: Really? I do, too. 是嗎？我也很喜歡。

1361

…是一種愉快的消遣方式。
...is a great way to pass the time.

(替換) ...is a wonderful way of spending time off.

(範例) **A:** Reading is a great way to pass the time.
看書是一種愉快的消遣方式。
B: Yes, it's very enjoyable.
是的，非常令人愉悅。

1362

…真是好極了。
...is really great.

(範例) **A:** Your painting is really great. 你的畫真是好極了。
B: Thank you for saying so. 謝謝你的誇獎。

1363

我想沒有更喜歡的了！
I don't think I like anything better.

(範例) **A:** Do you like jogging? 你喜歡慢跑嗎？
B: I don't think I like anything better. 我想沒有更喜歡的了！

1364

我一向喜歡…。
I've always liked...

(範例) **A:** What do you do in your spare time? 你空閒時做什麼？
B: I've always liked listening to music. 我一向喜歡聽音樂。

1365

我喜歡上…了。
I've taken a fancy to...

(範例) **A:** I've taken a fancy to dancing. 我喜歡上跳舞了。
B: Well, dancing is very interesting. 哦，跳舞十分有趣。

1366

…是我最喜歡的消遣之一。
...is one of my favorite pastimes.

(範例) **A:** Drawing is one of my favorite pastimes. How about you?
繪畫是我最喜歡的消遣之一。你呢？
B: I find reading the most interesting.
我覺得看書最有趣。

1367

我最喜歡的是…。
What I enjoy most is...

替換 | There is nothing I enjoy more than...

範例 | **A:** What do you like most? 你最喜歡什麼？
B: What I enjoy most is going to movies. 我最喜歡的是電影。

3.15 樂觀 Optimism

擁有樂觀的人生態度，才有幸福的人生。無論在什麼情況下，我們都要學會以一種樂觀向上的積極心態來面對和處理生活中的問題。樂觀的情緒和言談不僅展示個人的魅力，而且還能對他人產生積極的影響。樂觀的態度對中國人和英美人士是同等重要的。但是，在語言的表達形式上，英語有自己的特色。

| *1368* | …肯定…。
There is no doubt... | |

範例 | **A:** How is he now?
他現在怎麼樣？
B: Don't worry. There is no doubt he will be all right.
不用擔心，他肯定會好的。

| *1369* | 我確信…。
..., I'm sure. |

替換 | I'm sure/certain that.
I have no doubt that...
I feel quite sure/certain that...
I am confident that...
I have every confidence that...

範例 | **A:** She will succeed, I'm sure. 我確信，她會成功的。
B: I agree with you. 我同意你的看法。

| *1370* | 你會…。
You'll... |

替換 | You're going/bound to...

範例 | **A:** You'll be a good teacher. 你會成為一位好老師的。
B: Thank you. 謝謝。

1371	一切會沒事的。 **Everything will be OK.**

替換	It's all going to be fine. It'll all turn out fine. Things will work out OK. Things will turn out all right.
範例	**A:** I'm worried about him. 我很擔心他。 **B:** Everything will be OK. 一切會沒事的。

1372	我對…很樂觀。 **I'm very optimistic about...**

範例	**A:** What do you think the result will be? 你認為結果會怎麼樣？ **B:** I'm very optimistic about it. 我對此很樂觀。
提示	optimistic [ˌɑptəˈmɪstɪk] *adj.* 樂觀的；樂天的

1373	我預料…會成功。 **I anticipate success for...**

替換	My expectation is that...will have great success.
範例	**A:** I anticipate success for you. 我預料你會成功。 **B:** It's very kind of you to say so. 謝謝你這麼說。

3.16 偏好 Preference

　　了解他人偏好有利於找到交談的話題；交談中，「投其所好」有利於成功的對話。欲了解他人的偏好時，常用的句型是 wh-疑問句；說明自己的偏好常用陳述句。

● 詢問偏好 Asking for Preference

1374	我們可以…或者…，你說什麼好？ **We can...or...What's it going to be?**

063

替換	We can...or...What do you say?

範例　**A:** We can watch TV or play chess. What's it going to be?
我們可以看電視或者下棋，你說什麼好？
B: I'd prefer to play chess.
我比較喜歡下棋。

1375　你更喜歡…嗎？
Do you like...better?

替換　Do/Would you prefer...?
Like...better?

範例　**A:** Do you like tea better? 你更喜歡喝茶嗎？
B: Yes. I like tea more than coffee. 是的，我喜歡茶勝過咖啡。

1376　你比較喜歡哪一個？
Which would you prefer?

替換　Which would you like better?

範例　**A:** Which would you prefer? 你比較喜歡哪一個？
B: The small one. 小的那個。

1377　和…相比，你更喜歡…？
Do you like...more than...?

範例　**A:** Do you like pop music more than folk songs?
和民謠相比，你更喜歡流行音樂嗎？
B: Yes.
是的。

1378　你比較喜歡…還是…？
Do you prefer...or...?

替換　Would you prefer...or...?
Do you favor...or...?
Which would you prefer; ...or...?
Which attracts you more; ...or...?
Which appeals to you more; ...or...?
Do you find...or...more to your taste?
Which is your preference; ...or...?

範例　**A:** Do you prefer football or basketball? 你比較喜歡足球還是籃球？
B: I prefer basketball. 我比較喜歡籃球。

1379
你最喜歡的…是誰？
Who is your favorite...?

範例
A: Who is your favorite singer? 你最喜歡的歌手是誰？
B: Michael Jackson. 麥克・傑克森。

1380
你覺得哪個更有趣？
Which is more interesting to you?

替換
Which seems better as far as you're concerned?

範例
A: Which is more interesting to you? 你覺得哪個更有趣？
B: The one about Chinese movies. 關於中國電影的那個。

1381
我們可以確定你在…上的選擇嗎？
May we establish your preference on...?

範例
A: May we establish your preference on the question of the agenda?
我們可以確定你在日程安排上的選擇嗎？
B: Yes, I'd like to go to the seashore first.
是的，我想先去海邊。

提示
seashore ['si,ʃɔr] n. 海邊

1382
在你看來，…和…相比如何？
How do...and...compare in your opinion?

範例
A: How do Jack and Peter compare in your opinion?
在你看來，傑克和彼德相比如何？
B: Jack works harder.
傑克更努力一些。

提示
compare [kəm'pɛr] v. 相比；比較

1383
由你選擇，是…還是…？
The choice is yours: ...or...?

替換
...or...: I leave it to you to decide.

範例
A: The choice is yours: today or tomorrow.
由你選擇，是今天還是明天？
B: Tomorrow is better.
最好是明天。

● 表示偏好 Expressing Preference

1384	我總偏愛⋯。 **I'd go for...**
(替換)	I'd choose...any time. My choice would always be...
(範例)	**A:** Which city would you rather live in? 你比較喜歡住在哪個城市？ **B:** I'd go for New York. 我總偏愛紐約。
1385	我比較喜歡⋯。 **I like...better.**
(替換)	I like...more. ...is better for me. I favor...over all the others. I enjoy...more than any others. I'd prefer to..., if possible. I would take...if I had the choice.
(範例)	**A:** Do you like love stories or adventure stories better? 　　你比較喜歡愛情故事還是冒險故事？ **B:** I like love stories better. 　　我比較喜歡愛情故事。
1386	最好是⋯。 **The best is...**
(替換)	The best thing would be... For me, the best thing would be... ...is always my favorite. As far as I'm concerned, ...always seems better. From my point of view, the best choice is...
(範例)	**A:** The best is to stay here. 最好是留在這裡。 **B:** I agree with you. 我同意。
1387	就我來說，⋯比⋯更⋯。 **As far as I'm concerned, ...is more...than...**

範例
A: Where do you want to live?
你想住在哪裡？
B: As far as I'm concerned, living in the city is more exciting than living in the countryside.
就我來說，住在城裡比住在鄉村更令人興奮。

1388
我得說我對⋯有強烈的偏愛。
I must say I have a strong preference for...

替換
I must say...generally attracts me more.
I really find...more to my taste.

範例
A: What do you like?
你喜歡什麼？
B: I must say I have a strong preference for skiing.
我得說我對滑雪有強烈的偏愛。

1389
我會選⋯，其次才是⋯。
I would choose...in preference to...

範例
A: What do you want to do in the future?
你將來想做什麼？
B: I would choose teaching in preference to being a doctor.
我會選教書，其次才是當醫生。

1390
總體說來，⋯比⋯更吸引我。
On the whole, I find...more enjoyable than...

替換
All things considered, ...appeals to me more than...

範例
A: On the whole, I find your performance more enjoyable than the others'. 總體說來，你的表演比其他人的更吸引我。
B: Thank you. 謝謝。

1391
與其⋯，我寧可⋯。
Rather than..., I'd prefer to...

範例
A: I want to study in the room.
我想留在房間念書。
B: Rather than study in the dorm, I'd prefer to study in the library.
與其在宿舍念書，我寧可去圖書館。

3.17 安慰 Reassurance

人生順逆起落，雖說主要取決於自己，但是別人的安慰、鼓勵、幫助，也有著不可忽視的作用。安慰不僅是平復他人心靈創傷的良藥，也是促進他人積極行動，使人走向新生活和新目標的巨大動力。安慰是一門藝術。安慰技巧是要透過人與人之間的相互往來、互相關心逐步獲得的。安慰之中，應給予更多的鼓勵和更多的熱情，而這一切都離不開適當的表達語言。

1392 冷靜些。
Calm down.

(替換)
Calm yourself.
Keep cool.
Pull yourself together.

(範例)
A: Why did I fail again? 為什麼我又失敗了呢？
B: Calm down. You're just unlucky. 冷靜些，你只是不太幸運罷了。

1393 振作起來！
Cheer up!

(替換)
Lighten up!

(範例)
A: Just think. All our work was in vain.
   想想吧，所有的工作都白費了。
B: Cheer up, Jack! You still have a chance.
   振作起來，傑克！你還有機會。

1394 這沒什麼。
It's OK.

(替換)
That's all right.
It's nothing at all.
It's perfectly all right.
It really isn't worth mentioning.

(範例)
A: I was fired.
   我被解雇了。
B: It's OK. You will find another job soon.
   這沒什麼，你很快會再找到另一份工作的。

| 1395 | 別再去想它了。
Take it easy. |

(替換) Snap out of it!
Think no more of it!
Don't take it to heart.
Don't give it a second thought.

(範例) **A:** I was turned down again by Susan. 我又被蘇珊拒絕了。
B: Take it easy. 別再去想它了。

| 1396 | 別讓這事折磨你。
Don't let it get to you. |

(替換) Don't let it bother you.
Don't let that worry you.
Don't take it too hard.

(範例) **A:** I didn't pass the exam. 我考試沒過。
B: Don't let it get to you. 別讓這事折磨你。

| 1397 | 不用擔心。
Don't worry. |

(替換) Don't worry about a thing.
Please don't worry.
You don't have to worry about that.
You really needn't worry about that.
There's nothing to worry about.
There's no point in worrying about it.
There's no need for you to worry in the least.
There is no need to get so worked up.
There's really no reason to be worried (about it).
I believe that your fears are unnecessary.

(範例) **A:** I'm afraid he can't do it by himself.
　　 恐怕他一個人沒法完成這項工作。
B: Don't worry. He will succeed.
　　 不用擔心，他會成功的。

| 1398 | 不用怕！
Never fear! |

替換 Have no fear!
You need have no fear (about that).

範例 **A:** I'm afraid the test will be very difficult. 恐怕這次的考試會非常困難。
B: Never fear! You're the best. 不用怕！你是最好的。

1399 我可以向你保證…。
I give you my word that...

替換 You can take it from me that...
I assure you that...
Let me reassure you that...

範例 **A:** I give you my word that you will succeed.
我可以向你保證，你會成功的。
B: Thank you.
謝謝。

提示 reassure [ˌriəˈʃʊr] v. 使…安心；打消…的疑慮

1400 一切會好起來的。
It'll be all right in the end.

替換 Everything will be all right.
Everything will be OK.
All will turn out fine.
I'm sure it'll be all right.
I'm sure things will turn out all right.
I'm sure things will turn out fine in the end.

範例 **A:** I am having much difficulty doing this.
做這件事時，我遇到了很多困難。
B: It'll be all right in the end.
一切會好起來的。

1401 儘量朝好的方面看吧。
Try and look on the bright side.

替換 Try to look on the bright side of things.

範例 **A:** I still don't know why I was fired. 我還是不知道為什麼我被解僱了。
B: Try and look on the bright side. 儘量朝好的方面看吧。

1402 …還不是那麼糟。
...is not that bad.

313

範例 A: My mother is ill.
我母親病了。
B: Don't worry. Your mother's situation is not that bad.
不用擔心，妳母親的情形還不是那麼糟。

1403

這種事情總是會發生的。
It happens to us all.

替換　It could happen to anybody.

範例 A: My grandfather passed away last night. 我的祖父昨晚過世了。
B: It happens to us all. 這種事情總是會發生的。

提示　pass away 逝世〔委婉語〕

1404

如果我是你，我也會這樣做的。
I would have done the same in your place.

替換　I would have done the same, if I were you.

範例 A: I regret not giving him a helping hand.
我後悔沒有幫助他。
B: Don't be upset. I would have done the same in your place.
別難過了。如果我是你，我也會這樣做的。

1405

用不著感到不安。
You mustn't upset yourself.

替換　There's no need to upset yourself.
There's no need to get upset about it.

範例 A: I'm worried about his safety. 我很擔心他的安全。
B: You mustn't upset yourself. 用不著感到不安。

1406

不要憂傷過度。
Don't eat your heart out.

範例 A: Susan said good-bye to me. 蘇珊和我分手了。
B: Don't eat your heart out. 不要憂傷過度。

提示　eat your heart out【英】沮喪

1407

下次運氣會好一點吧。
Better luck next time.

範例 A: I failed this time. 這一次我失敗了。
B: Better luck next time. 下次運氣會好一點吧。

1408 要有信心！
Have faith!

範例 A: Have faith! You will succeed. 要有信心！你一定會成功的。
B: Thank you. 謝謝。

1409 就隨它去吧。
Take things as they come.

範例 A: I can't understand why he beat me in the competition.
我不明白為什麼我比賽中輸給他。
B: Take things as they come.
就隨它去吧。

1410 這不是什麼大不了的事。
It's not the end of the world.

範例 A: What should I do? I lost my keys.
怎麼辦呢？我把鑰匙弄丟了。
B: Don't worry about it. It's not the end of the world.
別擔心，這不是什麼大不了的事。

1411 你只是運氣不好。
You were just unlucky.

範例 A: I didn't pass the exam. 我考試沒有及格。
B: Don't worry. You were just unlucky. 不用擔心，你只是運氣不好。

1412 現在已經都過去了。
It's all over now.

範例 A: It's been like a nightmare. 這就像是場噩夢。
B: It's all over now. 現在已經都過去了。

1413 別難過。這是難免的事。
Don't feel bad. It's just one of those things.

範例 A: My dog died. 我的狗死了。
B: Don't feel bad. It's just one of those things. 別難過。這是難免的事。

3.18 寬慰 Relief

當問題迎刃而解、心理壓力消除的時候，如釋重負的感受就會透過語言自然流露出來。中文如此，英語也不例外。

1414	謝天謝地。 **Thank goodness!**	065

替換 Thank heavens!

範例 A: Thank goodness! We finally found you! 謝天謝地。終於找到你了。
B: What happened? 發生了什麼事？

1415	謝天謝地…。 **Thank God...**

替換 Thank goodness/heavens...

範例 A: I'm back. 我回來了。
B: Thank God you returned. 謝天謝地，你總算回來了。

1416	我很高興都結束了。 **I'm glad that's over.**

替換 I'm glad that's over with.

範例 A: The exam this morning was difficult. 今天早上的考試很難。
B: I'm glad that's over. 我很高興都結束了。

1417	很高興…。 **I am glad about...**

替換 I'm extremely glad to hear about...

範例 A: I'm glad about your success. 很高興你成功了。
B: Thank you. 謝謝。

1418	幸好…。 **It's a godsend...**

替換 It's fortunate...
It's lucky...

範例 **A:** It's a godsend that you are home. I want to borrow your dictionary.
幸好你在家。我想借你的字典用用。
B: Here you are.
給你。

提示 godsend ['gɑd͵sɛnd] *n.* 天賜之物

1419 真叫人欣慰。
What a relief!

替換 What a relief that all is well.
That's a (great) relief!

範例 **A:** He finally found a job as a salesman.
他終於找到了售貨員的工作。
B: What a relief!
真叫人欣慰。

1420 當…時，我很欣慰。
I was quite relieved when...

替換 It really put me at ease when...
It was a great relief that...
It was quite a relief when...
To my great relief, ...
It's a good thing...
You can imagine my relief when...

範例 **A:** I was quite relieved when I knew that you were not there.
當知道你不在那裡時，我很欣慰。
B: Oh, what happened?
哦，究竟發生了什麼事？

提示 anxiety [æŋ'zaɪətɪ] *n.* 憂慮；焦急

1421 心中一塊大石頭總算落下了。
That's a weight off my mind.

範例 **A:** He was saved. 他獲救了。
B: That's a weight off my mind. 心中一塊大石頭總算落下了。

1422 總算好了。
At last!

| 範例 | **A:** Mr. Black is finally recovered from his illness.
布萊克先生最後終於痊癒了。
B: At last!
總算好了。 |

| 提示 | recover [rɪˋkʌvɚ] *v.* 恢復 |

| *1423* | 那就好了。
That's fine, then. |

| 範例 | **A:** All the problems have been solved. 所有的問題都解決了。
B: That's fine, then. 那就好了。 |

3.19　滿意 Satisfaction

　　滿意是一種心理上的愉悅感覺，當你所得的東西或者所做的事情，達到你所預期的效果，甚至是超過標準時，你就會透過表情、動作、語言來表達這樣的喜悅。

066

| *1424* | 很好。
Fine! |

| 替換 | Very/Jolly good!
Splendid!
Wonderful!
Excellent!
Not bad!
That's just right! |

| 範例 | **A:** How about this leather wallet? 這個皮夾怎麼樣？
B: Fine! I'll take it. 很好，我買下。 |

| *1425* | 這正是我想要的。
It's just what I had in mind. |

| 替換 | It's just what I was looking for.
It is just what I needed. |

| 範例 | **A:** What about this one? 這個怎麼樣？
B: It's just what I had in mind. 這正是我想要的。 |

1426 還算滿意。
I can't complain.

(替換) I can't grumble.

(範例) A: What do you think of the service in this hotel?
這家飯店的服務，你覺得怎麼樣？
B: I can't complain.
還算滿意。

(提示) can't complain【口】（總體上）還算滿意
grumble ['grʌmbl] v. 抱怨；發牢騷

1427 很適合我。
It's perfect for me.

(替換) It's made for me.

(範例) A: How do you like your job? 你的工作怎麼樣？
B: It's perfect for me. 很適合我。

1428 我對⋯很滿意。
I am quite pleased with...

(替換) I am very happy with...
I am completely satisfied with...

(範例) A: What do you say? 你怎麼說？
B: I am quite pleased with your arrangement. 我對你的安排很滿意。

(提示) arrangement [ə'rendʒmənt] n. 安排

1429 我認為我從未⋯這麼棒的東西。
I don't think I've ever...anything so good.

(範例) A: Was the food satisfactory?
對食物還滿意嗎？
B I don't think I've ever eaten anything so good.
我認為我從未吃過這麼棒的東西。

1430 再好不過了。
It couldn't be better.

(範例) A: How's your job? 你的工作如何呢？
B: It couldn't be better. 再好不過了。

3.20　驚訝 Surprise

　　表達驚訝時，可以透過表情、動作等非語言方式來溝通，但更多時候，我們是用言語來直接表達。表達驚訝時，常用感嘆句。在不同會話場合，由於交談內容、論及事物、說話情緒等因素的差異，英文會有不同的表達方式，我們必須仔細體會其中的微妙。

1431	**啊呀。**　（067） **Oh my!**
替換	Gee! Wow! Goodness! I say!
範例	A: He won first prize! 他得了第一名。 B: Oh my! 啊呀！
提示	gee [dʒi] *interj.*【口】哇；咦；啊〔表示驚訝、讚賞等〕
1432	**不會吧。** **No!**
替換	Never! Oh, no!
範例	A: Did you hear about that plane crash? No one survived. 　你聽說那次的空難嗎？無人生還。 B: No! 　不會吧！
提示	survive [sɚˈvaɪv] *v.* 生還；倖存
1433	**你在開玩笑吧！** **You're kidding!**
替換	You can't be serious!
範例	A: You got a perfect score on the exam! 你考了滿分。 B: You're kidding! 你在開玩笑吧！

| 1434 | 簡直難以相信！
Incredible! |

(替換) | I can't believe my eyes.
I can hardly believe my eyes.

(範例) | **A:** He can run 400 meters inside one minute.
他能在一分鐘內跑完 400 公尺。
B: Incredible!
簡直難以相信！

(提示) | incredible [ɪnˈkrɛdəbl̩] *adj.* 難以置信的

| 1435 | 真想不到！
How about that! |

(替換) | Fancy that!
Well, I never!
Well, I'm sure!
Well, I declare!
Imagine that!
What a surprise!
This is really a surprise.
This is most unexpected.
Can you believe that?

(範例) | **A:** Do you know that we will get a day off?
你知道嗎？我們要放一天假。
B: How about that!
真想不到！

(提示) | unexpected [ˌʌnɪkˈspɛktɪd] *adj.* 想不到的；意外的

| 1436 | 我想不到⋯。
I had no idea that... |

(替換) | I was surprised to hear that...
I never would have guessed that...
It really surprises me that...

(範例) | **A:** He just returned to Japan. 他剛回日本了。
B: I had no idea that he's Japanese. 我想不到他是日本人。

| 1437 | 真想不到⋯。
Fancy...! |

範例　**A:** Fancy meeting you here! 眞想不到你在這裡！
B: I came here to attend a lecture. 我來這裡聽演講的。

1438　太驚人了！
How amazing!

替換　How astonishing!
That's amazing!
That's very surprising.
You certainly surprise me.

範例　**A:** Some people say there is life on Mars. 有些人說火星上有生命。
B: How amazing! 太驚人了！

提示　astonishing [ə'stɑnɪʃɪŋ] *adj.* 令人驚訝的；驚人的
Mars [mɑrz] *n.* 火星

1439　我得說…完全出乎我的意料。
I must say...was a great surprise to me.

替換　I should say...took me completely by surprise.

範例　**A:** He successfully finished his work.
　　他圓滿完成了工作。
B: I must say his ability was a great surprise to me.
　　我得說他的能力完全出乎我的意料。

1440　天哪。
Well, bless my soul!

替換　God almighty!
Good gracious/heavens/grief/God/Lord!
(My) goodness!
Goodness gracious (me)!

範例　**A:** Bill Gates became a millionaire in his twenties.
　　比爾・蓋茨在二十幾歲時，就成爲百萬富翁了。
B: Well, bless my soul!
　　天哪！

提示　bless my soul【口，舊式】我的天呀〔表示吃驚〕

1441　真的嗎？
Are you serious?

| 替換 | Really?
Indeed?
You don't say!
Are/Did/Have you really? 〔可用於各種場合，注意助動詞的使用〕 |
| 範例 | **A:** I want to move to London. 我想搬去倫敦。
B: Are you serious? 真的嗎？ |

1442 真怪！
That's strange!

替換	How extraordinary! That's weird! That's really extraordinary! It seems a bit odd, doesn't it?
範例	**A:** No one has arrived yet. 還沒有人到。 **B:** That's strange! 真怪！
提示	extraordinary [ɪkˈstrɔrdn̩ˌɛrɪ] *adj.* 特別的

1443 誰會想到…。
Who would have thought...?

| 範例 | **A:** They got married last month.
他們上個月結婚了。
B: Who would have thought she would marry such an old man!
誰會想到她會嫁給這麼老的一個人。 |

1444 什麼？…。
What, ...?

| 範例 | **A:** What, swimming in the winter? 什麼？冬泳？
B: Don't you think it's a good idea? 你覺得這個主意不好嗎？ |

3.21 同情 Sympathy

同情是人際交往的感情基礎。人與人之間如果失去同情，就不能建立良好的關係。同情，是一種高尚的道德情感，它既能給於人希望和溫暖，也能使自己的精神境界得到昇華。

　　與英美人士交往，聽到他人不幸的遭遇時，首先要表示同情。一般情況下，可以用特定的語言來表達，但情況嚴重時，一般不會提及不幸的事情。

1445　真糟糕。
That's terrible.

(068)

(替換)
That's too bad.
How awful/upsetting!
Oh! What a dreadful thing to happen!
What a dreadful situation!

(範例)
A: To tell the truth, I'm broke. 說實話，我破產了。
B: That's terrible. 真糟糕。

(提示)
upsetting [ʌpˈsɛtɪŋ] *adj.* 令人心煩意亂的；令人苦惱的

1446　真可惜。
What a pity!

(替換)
How unfortunate!
That's a pity/shame.
It's really a pity.

(範例)
A: All my photos were burned. 我所有的照片都被燒了。
B: What a pity! 真可惜。

1447　我真的很難過。
I'm so sorry.

(替換)
I feel so sorry.
I'm dreadfully sorry.

(範例)
A: I crashed my car. 我撞車了。
B: Oh, I'm so sorry. 哦！我真的很難過。

1448　真不幸！
Tough luck!

(替換)
What hard luck!
Oh, that's really rough.
What a sad thing.

(範例)
A: I lost my wallet. 我的錢包丟了。
B: Tough luck! 真不幸！

1449	真可憐！ **Poor man!**
替換	Poor thing!
範例	**A:** Jack lost his job. 傑克失業了。 **B:** Poor man! He must be very sad. 真可憐！他一定很傷心。

1450	哦，真不走運。 **Oh, what bad luck.**
替換	Oh, what a piece of bad luck! Wow, that's tough luck.
範例	**A:** He was fined $1500 for speeding! 他因為超速被罰款 1500 元。 **B:** Oh, what bad luck. 哦，真不走運。

1451	你一定覺得…吧。 **You must be feeling...**
替換	You must be...
範例	**A:** My proposal was turned down. 我的建議被拒絕了。 **B:** You must be feeling very sad. 你一定覺得很難過吧。

1452	我聽到…很難過。 **I'm terribly sorry to hear...**
替換	I'm very sorry to hear (about)... I'm awfully sorry about... I am most upset to hear... I am deeply sorry to know... I was saddened to learn about... I was so sorry to hear... I was most distressed to learn...
範例	**A:** His uncle passed away last night. 他的叔叔昨晚去世了。 **B:** I'm terribly sorry to hear that. 我聽到這消息很難過。
提示	distressed [dɪ'strɛst] *adj.* 哀傷的

1453	我知道那是什麼感受。 **I know how it feels.**
替換	I know just how it is.

範例　**A:** I had a sore throat today. I did not feel very well.
我今天喉嚨痛，感覺不太舒服。
B: I know how it feels.
我知道那是什麼感受。

1454	我對你深表同情。 **You have my deepest sympathy.**

替換　Let me convey my deepest sympathy to you.
You have my sincere condolences at this time.
Please accept my deepest sympathies.
Please accept my heartfelt condolences.

範例　**A:** My uncle has an incurable disease. 我的叔叔患了不治之症。
B: You have my deepest sympathy. 我對你深表同情。

提示　condolence [kən'doləns] *n.* 哀悼；弔唁
heartfelt ['hɑrt,fɛlt] *adj.* 衷心的；真心真意的
incurable [ɪn'kjurəbl̩] *adj.* 不能治癒的

3.22　意願 Willingness

　　在會話當中，我們有時需要表達自己的意願，有時要了解他人的意願。表達意願時，要注意語言的選擇。不同的表達方式能反映出一個人對待事情的態度和觀點。是願意？是拒絕？還是要為做某事提出一定的條件？這些都要根據說話者的意圖和交談的具體場景而定。此外，了解他人意願時，要有禮貌；表達願意時，要乾脆；不完全同意時，表達要有所保留；表達不情願時，則要講究技巧了。

● 表示願意 Expressing Willingness

1455	當然。 **Sure.**	069

替換　You bet.
Surely.
Certainly.

Yes, of course.
Naturally.
By all means.

範例 **A:** Will you go with me? 你要和我一起去嗎？
B: Sure. 當然。

1456
我一定會的。
I sure will.

替換 You bet I will.
Surely/Certainly I will.

範例 **A:** Take care of yourself. 保重。
B: I sure will. 我一定會的。

1457
好的。
OK.

替換 Uh-hum.
Yeah.
Right (you are).
No problem.

範例 **A:** Well, give him the message, OK? 嗯，留言給他，好嗎？
B: OK. 好的。

1458
好的，我會…的。
Yes, I'll...

範例 **A:** Make sure to lock all the doors when you leave.
你離開時，要確定將所有門都鎖好。
B: Yes, I'll remember to do that.
好的，我會記得去做的。

1459
我很樂意…。
I'd be happy to...

替換 I'm quite prepared to...
I'm perfectly willing to...
I would be most happy to...
I should be much pleased to...

範例 **A:** Shall we go to the concert together? 我們一起去聽音樂會好嗎？
B: I'd be happy to go with you. 我很樂意和你一起去。

1460	幹嘛不 ?! **Why not?**

範例	**A:** Will you go to the party tonight? 你今晚會去參加晚會嗎？ **B:** Why not? 幹嘛不 ?!

1461	有何不可呢。 **I don't see why not.**

替換	I see no reason why not. I see no objection whatsoever.
範例	**A:** Can we have pizza for dinner? 我們晚餐可以吃比薩嗎？ **B:** I don't see why not. 有何不可呢。
提示	objection [əbˈdʒɛkʃən] *n.* 反對；異議 whatsoever [ˌhwɑtsoˈɛvɚ] *pron.* 無論什麼（= whatever）

1462	不，我不介意…。 **No, I don't mind...**

替換	I see no objection whatsoever to... No, I don't mind...in the least.
範例	**A:** Do you mind going there on foot? 你介意我們步行到那嗎？ **B:** No, I don't mind walking. 不，我不介意走路。

● 表示不願意 Expressing Unwillingness

1463	我其實不喜歡…。 **I really don't fancy...**

替換	I'm not really keen on...
範例	**A:** Will you go with Jim? 你和吉姆一起去嗎？ **B:** I really don't fancy going with him. 我其實不喜歡和他一起去。

1464	我倒是想這樣，但是…。 **I'd like to, but...**

替換	I wish I could, but... I'd like to be able to, but...

範例 | **A:** Will you go to the park with us?
你要和我們一起去公園嗎？
B: I'd like to, but I have an exam tomorrow.
我倒是想這樣，但是我明天要考試。

1465
我不想…。
I don't want to...

替換 | I won't...
I'm not willing/inclined to...
I'm unwilling/disinclined to...

範例 | **A:** Will you stay here? 你會留在這裡嗎？
B: I don't want to leave now. 我現在不想走。

提示 | inclined [ɪn'klaɪnd] *adj.* 願意的

1466
恐怕我不能…。
I'm afraid I can't...

替換 | I'm not sure that we could find it in ourselves to...

範例 | **A:** How could he talk like that? 他怎麼能這樣說？
B: I'm afraid I can't tolerate his rudeness. 恐怕我不能忍受他的無禮。

提示 | tolerate ['tɑlə‚ret] *v.* 忍受；容忍

1467
我才不願意呢！
Like hell I will!

範例 | **A:** Will you come with him? 你和他一起來嗎？
B: Like hell I will! 我才不願意呢！

提示 | like hell【口】哪有這種事情；絕不會

1468
我其實不想…。
I didn't really want to...

範例 | **A:** You lied. 你說謊。
B: I didn't really want to lie to you. 我其實不想對你撒謊。

1469
恐怕我不能。
I'm afraid I can't.

範例 | **A:** Can you give me the key? 你能把鑰匙給我嗎？
B: I'm afraid I can't. 恐怕我不能。

1470	實際上，我沒把握會不會…。 **I'm not sure I can..., actually.**

範例　A: Do come to our party! 一定要來參加晚會喔！
B: I'm not sure I can go, actually. 實際上，我沒把握會不會去。

1471	實際上，我寧願不要這樣。 **I'd rather not, actually.**

範例　A: Could you wait for a while? 你能再等一下嗎？
B: I'd rather not, actually. 實際上，我寧願不要這樣。

1472	…實在有點困難。 **It'd be a bit difficult to...**

範例　A: Will you help him?
　　　　你會去幫他嗎？
B: It'd be a bit difficult to make such a decision.
　　做這個決定實在有點困難。

1473	我其實不願…。 **I'm not really willing to...**

替換　I don't think I'm willing to...
I must admit I'm rather unwilling to...
I'm afraid I'm not inclined to...
To be honest, I'd rather not...

範例　A: Shall we go now? 我們現在走嗎？
B: I'm not really willing to go shopping now. 我其實不願去逛街。

1474	我對…有些保留。 **I have certain reservations about...**

範例　A: Will you sign the contract?
　　　　你會簽這個合約嗎？
B: Yes, but I have certain reservations about it.
　　會，但我對此有些保留。

提示　reservation [ˌrɛzɚ'veʃən] n. 保留

1475	我才不呢。 **Certainly not!**

| 替換 | No, I sure won't! |
| 範例 | **A:** Will you marry him? 你會嫁給他嗎？
B: Certainly not! 我才不呢！ |

1476 不行！
No way!

| 替換 | That's out of the question!
Not in a million years!
Not a chance!
Not on your life!〔粗魯的表達法〕
In your dreams!〔粗魯的表達法〕 |
| 範例 | **A:** Could you tell me your address? 能告訴我你的地址嗎？
B: No way! 不行！ |

1477 很抱歉，不可以…。
I'm sorry. ...is not permitted.

替換	I regret to say...is not allowed.
範例	**A:** Can we go in? 　我們能進去嗎？ **B:** I'm sorry. Entering without permission is not permitted. 　很抱歉，未經許可不可以進入。
提示	permission [pɚˈmɪʃən] *n.* 許可；允許

1478 …恐怕不大可能。
I'm afraid...will be quite impossible.

| 替換 | I'm afraid...is quite out of the question.
I'm afraid there can be no question about...
...is quite impossible, I'm afraid. |
| 範例 | **A:** Do you think we will get his support?
　你認為我們會得到他的支持嗎？
B: I'm afraid getting his support will be quite impossible.
　想要得到他的幫助，恐怕不大可能。 |

1479 我已經再三考慮過這件事，但是我們不能…。
I've given this matter a good deal of thought but we cannot...

範例　**A:** I've given this matter a good deal of thought but we cannot do business with you.
我已經再三考慮過這件事，但是我們不能和你做生意。
B: That's really a pity.
那確實很遺憾。

1480　但願我可以，但是…。
I wish I could, but...

範例　**A:** Please come to our party! 請來參加我們的晚會！
B: I wish I could, but I'm too busy. 但願我可以，但是我太忙了。

1481　如果可以，我是願意的，但是…。
I would if I could, but...

範例　**A:** Could you lend me your car?
能借給我你的車嗎？
B: I would if I could, but my car is broken down.
如果可以，我是願意的，但是我的車拋錨了。

提示　break down（車）拋錨

第4章
消極流露

① ②

③ ④ ⑤

⑥ ⑦

不喜歡是指對人或事物沒有好感或不感興趣，這是人們經常要表達的態度，這類表達涉及的範圍很廣，衣、食、住、行無所不包。在表達不喜歡時，要注意說話的場合和交談的內容，要學會使用委婉語句。

1482	我不喜歡…。 **I don't like...**	(070)

替換
I don't fancy...
I don't go/care for...

範例
A: I don't like the color red. 我不喜歡紅色。
B: Why? It's a pleasant color. 為什麼？紅色很令人愉悅啊！

1483	我不能容忍… **I can't stand...**

替換
I can't put up with...
I can't bear...

範例
A: I can't stand her. 我不能容忍她。
B: Yes, she is too noisy. 是的，她太吵了。

1484	哦，糟糕！ **Oh, no!**

替換
Oh, hell!
Oh, (my) God!
Oh, how awful!

範例
A: We will have a test tomorrow. 我們明天要考試。
B: Oh, no! I'm not prepared yet. 哦，糟糕！我還沒有準備好。

1485	我最不喜歡的莫過於此了。 **There's nothing I like less.**

替換
There's nothing I like less than that.
I don't think I've seen anything I dislike more.

範例
A: Do you like hamburgers? 你喜歡漢堡嗎？
B: There's nothing I like less. 我最不喜歡的莫過於此了。

1486
我不太喜歡…。
I'm not very fond of...

替換
I'm not very keen on...
I'm not crazy about...
I can't say...appeals to me very much.
I can't say...is very pleasant.
I have to admit I rather dislike...
I must admit I have no liking for...
I have to say that I'm not fond of...

範例
A: How about going to the seashore? 去海邊怎麼樣？
B: I'm not very fond of sightseeing. 我不太喜歡觀光。

1487
我特別不喜歡…。
I especially dislike...

替換
I have a particular aversion to...
I have a particular dislike of...

範例
A: I especially dislike fish. 我特別不喜歡吃魚。
B: Why? That's strange! 爲什麼？太奇怪了！

提示
aversion [ə'vɝʃən] *n.* 厭惡

1488
…真叫我討厭。
...is a real pain in the neck.

替換
...is really awful.

範例
A: That chain-smoker is a real pain in the neck.
那個老煙槍眞叫我討厭。
B: Yes, his breath smells like an ash-tray.
是啊，他的氣味聞起來像煙灰缸。

提示
a pain in the neck【口】令人極其討厭的人事物〔不禮貌的說法〕
chain-smoker [ˌtʃen'smokɚ] *n.* 老煙槍

1489
我真的討厭…。
I really hate...

範例
A: I really hate people gossiping. 我眞的討厭人說閒話。
B: Oh! What did they say? 哦，他們說了些什麼？

提示
gossip ['gɑsəp] *v.* 說閒話；傳播流言

1490	恐怕我從來都不喜歡…。 **I've never liked..., I'm afraid.**
範例	**A:** Have some fish. It's delicious. 吃點魚，很好吃的。 **B:** I've never liked it, I'm afraid. 恐怕我從來都不喜歡吃魚。

1491	…不是我喜歡的…之一。 **...is not one of my favorite...**
範例	**A:** Basketball is not one of my favorite sports. 籃球不是我喜歡的運動之一。 **B:** What is your favorite, then? 那麼，你喜歡什麼運動？

1492	我不覺得…有什麼樂趣。 **I don't find any pleasure in...**
替換	I don't think...is particularly enjoyable. I find...distinctly unattractive.
範例	**A:** He's an interesting man. 他是個有趣的人。 **B:** Well, I don't find any pleasure in talking with him. 哦，我不覺得和他談話有什麼樂趣。
提示	unattractive [ˌʌnə'træktɪv] *adj.* 不吸引人的

4.2　沮喪 Dismay

　　努力但沒有結果，奮鬥但目標落空。這時，人們常常會感到沮喪。沮喪是一種強烈的心理感受，因此表達沮喪的語言往往也帶有強烈的感情色彩。

1493	我覺得沮喪。 **I'm depressed.**	(071)
替換	I feel very miserable.	
範例	**A:** What's wrong with you? 你怎麼了？ **B:** Oh, I'm depressed. 哦，我覺得沮喪。	
提示	miserable ['mɪzərəb]] *adj.* 痛苦的；悲慘的	

1494	花了那麼大力氣卻什麼也沒有。 **All that work was for nothing.**
替換	To think that I went to all that trouble for nothing.
範例	**A:** All that work was for nothing. 花了那麼大力氣卻什麼也沒有。 **B:** Well, you tried your best. 嗯，你盡力了。

1495	我真傻居然⋯！ **What a fool I was to...!**
替換	I feel like such an idiot to...!
範例	**A:** What a fool I was to tell him the truth! 我真傻，居然告訴他事情的真相。 **B:** Don't worry. He won't tell anyone else. 別擔心，他不會告訴別人的。

1496	這有什麼用呢？ **What good will it do?**
範例	**A:** Why are you quarreling? What good will it do? 你們為什麼吵架？這有什麼用呢？ **B:** We're just arguing. 我們只是在辯論。

1497	⋯有什麼用？ **What's the point of...?**
替換	What's the purpose/use of...?
範例	**A:** Maybe we should talk to him. 也許我們該和他談談。 **B:** What's the point of doing that? 做那事有什麼用？

1498	我只是有點厭煩，就這麼回事。 **I'm just a little fed up, that's all.**
範例	**A:** What's up? 怎麼了？ **B:** I'm just a little fed up, that's all. 我只是有點厭煩，就這麼回事。
提示	be fed up 厭煩（+ with）

1499	我只是有點消沉，就這麼回事。 **I'm just feeling a bit low, that's all.**

範例　A: What's wrong with you? 你怎麼了？
B: I'm just feeling a bit low, that's all. 我只是有點消沉，就這麼回事。

1500

我真的恨死我自己了。
I could kick myself!

範例　A: I could kick myself! 我真的恨死我自己了！
B: Don't worry! Everybody makes mistakes. 別擔心！每個人都會犯錯。

1501

真是倒楣的日子。
It's just been one of those days.

範例　A: He broke his leg today. 他今天摔斷腿了。
B: It's just been one of those days. 真是倒楣的日子。

1502

什麼事都一團糟。
Everything's a mess.

範例　A: How is your new project? 你的新計畫進行的如何？
B: Everything's a mess. 什麼事都一團糟。

1503

事情老出錯。
Something always goes wrong.

範例　A: I don't know what to do. Something always goes wrong.
我真不知道怎樣才好，事情老出錯。
B: Don't worry. It will be fine.
別擔心，會沒事的。

1504

今天我真是什麼事都不順心。
Today just isn't my day.

範例　A: What's wrong? You made so many mistakes today.
你怎麼了？今天你犯了很多錯誤。
B: Today just isn't my day.
今天我真是什麼事都不順心。

1505

做了一件多笨的事啊！
What a stupid thing to do!

範例　A: What a stupid thing to do! I told my boss off!
（我）做了一件多笨的事啊！我把老闆罵了一頓。

B: And then?
然後呢?

A: I got fired.
我被炒魷魚了。

提示　tell off 責備;責罵

1506　**真倒楣!**
What luck!

範例　**A:** What luck! I failed again.
真倒楣!又沒有及格。
B: Don't lose heart. You will pass if you work hard.
別灰心。只要你加把勁,就會通過的。

1507　**我真不知道該怎麼辦。**
I just don't know what to do.

範例　**A:** I just don't know what to do.
我真不知道該怎麼辦。
B: Maybe you can start over from the beginning.
或許你可以從頭開始。

1508　**哦,不!我怎麼會遇到這種事啊?**
Oh, no! How could this happen to me?

範例　**A:** Oh, no! How could this happen to me?
哦,不!我怎麼會遇到這種事啊?
B: You must be very annoyed.
你一定很心煩。

1509　**情況使我有點沮喪。**
Things are getting me down a bit.

範例　**A:** How has your work been recently? 你最近的工作怎麼樣?
B: Things are getting me down a bit. 情況使我有點沮喪。

1510　**我只是覺得無法高興起來。**
I just can't seem to get happy.

範例　**A:** What's up? 怎麼了?
B: I just can't seem to get happy. 我只是覺得無法高興起來。

4.3　不滿 Dissatisfaction

　　不滿是當你所得的東西或者所做的事情，達不到你所預期的標準時，你就會透過表情、動作、語言來表達出這樣的負面情緒。與東方人不同，西方人士通常勇於表達自己的想法和意見，所以如果對事情不滿時，便會直接表達，不會有所保留。

1511　糟透了。
It's awful!

〔072〕

（替換）It's dreadful/rotten!

（範例）A: How do you like this food? 你認為食物如何？
B: It's awful! 糟透了。

（提示）rotten ['rɑtṇ] *adj.*【非正式】極差的；令人討厭的

1512　真丟臉！
What a disgrace!

（範例）A: Bob had a disgusting way of eating his soup at the party.
在宴會上，鮑勃喝湯的舉動令人討厭極了。
B: What a disgrace!
真丟臉。

（提示）disgrace [dɪs'gres] *n.* 可恥；不名譽
disgusting [dɪs'gʌstɪŋ] *adj.* 令人厭惡的

1513　不怎麼樣。
It's nothing special.

（範例）A: What do you think of his performance? 你認為他的表現怎麼樣？
B: It's nothing special. 不怎麼樣。

1514　一無是處。
It's no good at all.

（範例）A: What do you think of the new plan? 你認為這個新計畫怎麼樣？
B: It's no good at all. 一無是處。

1515	我不太喜歡…。 **I don't like...very much.**
替換	I don't like...at all. I don't think much of...
範例	**A:** How do you like the novel? 你喜歡這部小說嗎？ **B:** I don't like it very much. 我不太喜歡。

1516	我對…不太滿意。 **I am not satisfied with...**
替換	I am not happy about... I am dissatisfied with... ...is not satisfactory. I cannot say I feel happy about... I cannot say I was satisfied with...
範例	**A:** Are you satisfied with our service? 你對我們的服務滿意嗎？ **B:** No, I'm not satisfied with it. 不，我對此並不太滿意。

1517	…不夠好。 **...is not good enough.**
範例	**A:** What do you think of the book? 你覺得這本書怎麼樣？ **B:** It's interesting, but it's not good enough. 很有趣，但是還不夠好。

4.4 八卦 Gossip

　　說長道短，對他人的弱點非善意地品頭論足是缺乏教養的表現，但這種做法往往有一定的目的，說長道短也往往有一些隱含的意義，了解這些意義有助於採取進一步的應對措施。

1518	你知道嗎？ **Do you know something?**	073
替換	You know something? Do you know that?	

範例
A: Do you know something? Tom got divorced.
你知道嗎？湯姆離婚了。
B: Really? I can't believe it.
是嗎？我真是不敢相信。

1519
你聽說了嗎？
Have you heard?

替換
Did you hear that?

範例
A: Have you heard? Jack is dating another girl.
你聽說了嗎？傑克正在和另一個女孩子約會。
B: Oh, no!
哦，不會吧！

1520
你猜怎麼著？
Guess what?

範例
A: Guess what? She got fired. 你猜怎麼著？她被炒魷魚了。
B: When? 什麼時候？

1521
我最後聽到的消息說⋯。
The last I heard, ...

範例
A: The last I heard, they got married.
我最後聽到的消息說，他們結婚了。
B: Is it true?
這是真的嗎？

1522
嗯，那是他們說的，不過其實⋯。
Well, that's what they say, but...

範例
A: Well, that's what they say, but she was the one who got dumped.
嗯，那是他們說的，不過其實她是被拋棄的那個。
B: Oh, is that right?
哦，是嗎？

提示
dump [dʌmp] v.【非正式】拋棄

1523
你不會相信我看到的事情！
You'll never believe what I saw!

範例
A: You'll never believe what I saw! 你不會相信我看到的事情！
B: Tell me. What was it? 告訴我，是什麼事？

1524
這事情你一個字也別洩露出去，…。
Don't breathe a word of this, but...

範例
A: Don't breathe a word of this, but she used to take drugs.
這事情你一個字也別洩露出去，她過去吸過毒。
B: That's terrible!
太可怕了。

提示
not breathe a word 不透露風聲

1525
這可是最高機密，所以你自己知道就好了。
It's top secret, so keep it under your hat.

範例
A: It's top secret, so keep it under your hat.
這可是最高機密，所以你自己知道就好了。
B: OK, I won't tell anyone.
好吧，我不會告訴任何人。

1526
好吧，我告訴你這祕密，不過不能對任何人洩漏一個字。
All right, I'll tell you the secret, but don't say a word to anyone.

範例
A: All right, I'll tell you the secret, but don't say a word to anyone.
好吧，我告訴你這祕密，不過不能對任何人洩漏一個字。
B: I promise I won't.
我保證不會說的。

1527
你不能把這件事傳出去，…。
Don't pass this on, but...

範例
A: Don't pass this on, but they are not friends any longer.
你不能把這件事傳出去，他們鬧翻了。
B: Really?
是嗎？

1528
嗨，你知道嗎？
Well, what do you know?

範例
A: Well, what do you know? Ann went abroad.
嗨，你知道嗎？安妮出國了。
B: Really? But I saw her yesterday.
是嗎？但是我昨天還看見過她。

| 1529 | 你知道我剛聽說的事嗎？
Do you know what I just heard? |

範例 A: Do you know what I just heard? 你知道我剛聽說的事嗎？
B: What is it? 什麼事？

| 1530 | 你想聽一些有趣的事嗎？
Do you want to hear something interesting? |

範例 A: Do you want to hear something interesting?
你想聽一些有趣的事嗎？
B: Sorry, I'm not interested.
對不起，我不感興趣。

| 1531 | 當然，事情未必正確，但是…。
Of course this may not be true, but... |

範例 A: Of course this may not be true, but she really looks bossy.
當然，事情未必正確，但是她看起來的確跋扈。
B: You're right.
你說得很對。

提示 bossy ['bɑsɪ] *adj.* 跋扈的；頤指氣使的

| 1532 | 我告訴你我所知的，但這事情只有我們倆知道。
Let me tell you what I know, but it's only between you and me. |

替換 I can tell you about that, but you have to keep it to yourself.
I'll tell you, but don't pass it on to anybody else.
I've got something to tell you, but you have to keep it from others.

範例 A: Let me tell you what I know, but it's only between you and me.
Someone was killed in that house.
我告訴你我所知的，但是這事情只有我們倆知道。在那棟房子裡有人被殺了。
B: Has the killer been found?
兇手找到了嗎？

| 1533 | 我不想在背後議論別人，不過…。
I don't want to talk behind someone else's back, but... |

A: I don't want to talk behind someone else's back, but she's not happy with her husband.
我不想在背後議論別人,不過她和她丈夫相處得不太好。
B: Is that true?
是真的嗎?

1534 這不是人身攻擊,不過他們說…。
This isn't a personal attack, but they say...

 A: This isn't a personal attack, but they say she's not very honest.
這不是人身攻擊,不過他們說她不誠實。
B: Who told you that?
誰告訴你的?

1535 當然我不想說三道四,不過你知道嗎?…
Now I don't want to gossip of course, but did you know...?

 Now I don't want to say anything bad about anyone of course, but have you noticed...?

 A: Now I don't want to gossip of course, but did you know he was just set free from prison?
當然我不想說三道四,不過你知道嗎?他剛從監獄出來。
B: Really? But he looks very kind.
是嗎?但是他看起來很和善。

4.5 猶豫 Hesitation

思維與語言密不可分,人在拿不定主意的時候,語言會發生相應的連鎖反應。因此,交談時免不了要停頓,給自己一些時間組織思路以便找出合適的表達方法。但是要記住,關鍵時刻,千萬不要中斷講話而沉默,沉默可能會使你窘迫不堪,有時還會喪失談話的主導權。掌握一些填補沉默的填充語,學會使自己的談話持續下去,這是談話的一個基本技巧。

074

1536 …嗯,
..., um, ...

...er, ...

範例 A: How long does it take to get to London by train?
坐火車去倫敦要多久？

B: It takes about, um, ten hours.
大概要，嗯，十小時。

1537 嗯，這個嘛，…。
Well, let's see now, ...

替換 Well, er, ...

範例 A: When should we come here tomorrow? 我們明天該幾點來？
B: Well, let's see now, eight in the morning. 嗯，這個嘛，早上八點。

1538 這個，我不確定。我得好好想想。
Well, I'm not sure. I'll have to think it over.

範例 A: Would you like to come on a camping trip with me?
你要不要和我一起去露營呢？

B: Well, I'm not sure. I'll have to think it over.
這個，我不確定。我得好好想想。

1539 …我是說…。
..., I mean, ...

範例 A: Will you come tomorrow? 你明天來嗎？
B: Yes, I mean, I will. 是的，我是說，我會來。

1540 你知道的？
You see?

替換 You know?

範例 A: You're a bit late. You see? Six o'clock.
你有點晚了。你知道的？都六點了。

B: Sorry.
對不起。

1541 …實際上…。
..., as a matter of fact, ...

範例 A: Is she a student? 她是學生嗎？
B: She is, as a matter of fact, a teacher. 她實際上是老師。

1542	⋯，記起來了，⋯。 **..., I've got it, it's...**

(範例) A: Where is she from?
她從哪裡來的？
B: She is from, I've got it, it's Australia.
她從，記起來了，她從澳洲來的。

1543	⋯等一會兒，對了，⋯。 **..., hang on a sec. Yes, ...**

(替換) ..., just a moment. Oh yes, ...

(範例) A: What's his telephone number?
他的電話號碼是多少？
B: His number is, hang on a sec. Yes, it's 2343499.
他的電話，等一會兒，對了，2343499。

1544	嗯，問題是⋯。 **Um, the trouble is, ...**

(替換) Well, the thing is, ...

(範例) A: Can we start now? 我們能開始了嗎？
B: Um, the trouble is, he's not here. 嗯，問題是，他不在這兒。

1545	你明白，嗯，⋯。 **You see, um, ...**

(範例) A: What can I do for you? 我能為你做些什麼？
B: You see, um, I have been here for three days, and I'm looking for a job. 你明白，嗯，我來這裡已經三天了，我在找工作。

1546	嗯，讓我想想看⋯。 **Um, let me see, ...**

(替換) Just let me think about it, ...
Er, let me think, ...
I'll have to think about it...
May I think about it?...

(範例) A: How many classes do you have on Monday? 你星期一有幾堂課？
B: Um, let me see, four. 嗯，讓我想想看，四堂課。

1547	…，叫什麼來著？ **..., now, what's the word?**
範例	**A:** He's a, now, what's the word? A sadist. 　　他就是，叫什麼來著？虐待狂。 **B:** Oh, that's terrible. 　　哦，太可怕了。
提示	sadist ['sædɪst] *n.* 虐待狂
1548	…，嗯，叫什麼來著？ **...um, what's she called?**
替換	..., er, what's her name? ..., what's she called?
範例	**A:** Alice, um, what's she called? Alice Green? 　　愛麗絲，嗯，叫什麼來著？愛麗絲・格林？ **B:** No. Alice Smith. 　　不，愛麗絲・史密斯。
1549	我該怎麼說呢？ **How should I put this?**
替換	Now, how can I best say this? Now, how should I phrase this?
範例	**A:** How was his performance last night? 他昨晚的演出怎麼樣？ **B:** How should I put this? A big success? 我該怎麼說呢？很成功吧？
1550	…，讓我弄清楚，…。 **..., just let me get this right, ...**
範例	**A:** You are, just let me get this right, Mr. Black? 　　你是，讓我弄清楚，布萊克先生？ **B:** You're right. 　　正是。
1551	…，嗯，我要說的是，…。 **..., well, what I'm trying to say is, ...**
範例	**A:** What did you think of his lecture? 　　你覺得他的講座怎麼樣？ **B:** It was, well, what I'm trying to say is, a little difficult for me. 　　他的講座，嗯，我要說的是，對我有點難。

1552	…，嗯，請原諒我的猶豫，…。 **..., well, excuse my hesitation, ...**

範例 A: Shall we go bungee jumping!
　　　我們去高空彈跳吧！
　　　B: It's, well, excuse my hesitation, too dangerous.
　　　這，嗯，請原諒我的猶豫，但是這太危險了。

提示 hesitation [ˌhɛzə'teʃən] *n.* 猶豫；躊躇

1553	…，哦，它就在我的嘴邊（但就是記不起來）。 **..., oh, it's on the tip of my tongue.**

範例 A: Who is that movie star?
　　　那個電影明星是誰？
　　　B: His name, oh, it's on the tip of my tongue. Yes, Tom Hanks.
　　　他的名字，哦，它就在我的嘴邊（但就是記不起來），是的，湯姆 ·漢克斯。

提示 on the tip of my tongue 就在嘴邊（但是記不起來）

1554	…嗯，也就是說…。 **...Well, that is to say,...**

範例 A: We will go. Well, that is to say, we will go with you.
　　　我們會去的，嗯，也就是說，和你們一起去。
　　　B: Great!
　　　太好了！

4.6 冷漠 Indifference

　　當有人遭遇不幸時，不同的人會做出不同的反應。有人深表同情，有人則會無動於衷，且態度漠然。學會從別人的話語之中猜測並把握對方的態度，學會適當地表達自己的態度，對於人際溝通都會有很大幫助。

1555	有什麼好擔心的！ **What should I worry!**	075

替換
I don't give a damn.
I won't give a shit (about that)! 〔粗魯的表達法〕
I couldn't care less.
I don't really care.

範例
A: Do you know that he was dismissed? 你知道嗎？他被開除了。
B: What should I worry! 有什麼好擔心的！

提示
not give a damn【口】毫不在乎
not give a shit【諱】毫不在乎；毫不關心

1556
這不關我的事。
It's not my concern.

替換
It's not my business.
It's none of my business.
It has nothing to do with me.
It's no concern of mine.

範例
A: Kent got a job with Microsoft. 肯特在微軟找到了一份工作。
B: It's not my concern. 這不關我的事。

1557
這只能怪你自己。
It's your own fault.

替換
You've only yourself to blame.

範例
A: My girlfriend left me. 我的女朋友離開我了。
B: It's your own fault. 這只能怪你自己。

1558
我不知道！
Search me!

替換
Beats me!
I haven't a clue.
How should I know?
I don't know.
Your guess is as good as mine.
You've got me stumped.

範例
A: Who did it? 誰幹的？
B: Search me! 我不知道！

提示
Search me!【口】我不知道！

1559	對不起，我不是很有興趣。 **I'm afraid I'm not really interested.**

(替換) Sorry, but that doesn't really interest me.

(範例) **A:** Who won the match? 誰贏了這場比賽？
B: I'm afraid I'm not really interested. 對不起，我不是很有興趣。

1560	管它呢！ **Who cares?**

(範例) **A:** Whose book is this? 這是誰的書？
B: Who cares? 管它呢！

1561	別問我。 **Don't ask me.**

(範例) **A:** Is he the man who won the speech contest?
他就是那個在演講比賽中獲勝的人嗎？
B: Don't ask me.
別問我。

1562	那又怎麼樣呢？ **So what?**

(範例) **A:** Tom got promoted. 湯姆升職了。
B: So what? 那又怎麼樣呢？

1563	他活該！ **Serves him right.**

(範例) **A:** Tom failed the exam again. 湯姆考試又沒有及格。
B: Serves him right. 他活該！

1564	這就算不錯了。 **It could be worse.**

(範例) **A:** He was saved, but he lost one of his arms.
他獲救了，但是卻失去了一條手臂。
B: It could be worse.
這就算不錯了。

1565 對不起，此事我無能為力。
I'm afraid there's nothing I can do about it.

範例 **A:** My Walkman doesn't work.
我的隨身聽壞了。
B: I'm afraid there's nothing I can do about it.
對不起，此事我無能為力。

1566 這無關緊要。
That's beside the point.

替換 That's neither here nor there.

範例 **A:** I didn't spell the word right. 這個字我沒有拼對。
B: That's beside the point. 這無關緊要。

1567 我不認為…有多重要。
I don't think...is so important.

替換 I don't think...is of any significance.
...doesn't mean anything to me.

範例 **A:** I don't think what he said is so important.
我不認為他說的話有多重要。
B: I agree with you.
我同意你的看法。

提示 significance [sɪɡ'nɪfəkəns] *n.*（事件、行動等的）意義；重要性

1568 有什麼了不起呢？
What of it?

範例 **A:** He got the highest mark on the exam. 他在考試中得了最高分。
B: What of it? 有什麼了不起呢？

1569 …和我沒關係。
It doesn't matter to me...

替換 It doesn't weigh much with me...

範例 **A:** Don't you want him to come?
你不是希望他來嗎？
B: It doesn't matter to me whether he comes or not.
他來不來和我沒關係。

提示 weigh with sb.【正式】（對結局或決定）有影響

1570	我真的不明白這事有什麼重大關係。 **I really can't see what relevance it has.**

範例	**A:** The income tax has been increased to 30%. 個人收入所得稅提高到 30% 了。 **B:** I really can't see what relevance it has. 我真的不明白這事有什麼重大關係。
提示	relevance ['rɛləvəns] *n.* 關係；相關性

1571	這件事無足輕重。 **It's of no great consequence.**

範例	**A:** The President made a new speech about national security. 總統就國家安全發表了一篇新的演說。 **B:** It's of no great consequence. 這件事無足輕重。
提示	consequence ['kɑnsəˌkwɛns] *n.* 結果；因果關係

4.7 悲觀 Pessimism

　　在遇到困難的時候，人容易喪失信心並產生悲觀的情緒。英文中表達悲觀情緒的語言大多比較消極。

1572	不可能！ **No way!**	(076)

替換	There is no way.
範例	**A:** I want to finish my work within two hours. 我想在兩小時內完成工作。 **B:** No way! 不可能。

1573	我不大相信⋯。 **I don't really believe...**

替換	I don't really think...
範例	**A:** I don't really believe she is so successful. 我不大相信她會那樣成功。 **B:** Why not? 為什麼不相信？

353

| 1574 | 我很懷疑……。
I rather doubt that... |

| 替換 | I highly doubt that...
I'm rather doubtful/skeptical that... |

| 範例 | **A:** Do you think that they will come to the party?
　　你認為他們會來參加晚會嗎？
B: I rather doubt that they will come.
　　我很懷疑他們會來。 |

| 提示 | skeptical [ˈskɛptɪk l] *adj.* 懷疑性的；好懷疑的 |

| 1575 | 我對……沒把握。
I'm not so sure that... |

| 替換 | I'm not at all certain that... |

| 範例 | **A:** Do you think he will succeed? 你認為他會成功嗎？
B: I'm not so sure that he will. 我對這事沒把握。 |

| 1576 | ……肯定會失敗。
...is bound to lose. |

| 替換 | ...is doomed to fail. |

| 範例 | **A:** I'm bound to lose. 我肯定會失敗。
B: Don't be so pessimistic. 不要這麼悲觀。 |

| 提示 | doom [dum] *v.* 註定
pessimistic [ˌpɛsəˈmɪstɪk] *adj.* 悲觀的；厭世的 |

| 1577 | 說實話，我對……一點都不樂觀。
To tell you the truth, I'm rather pessimistic about... |

| 替換 | To be honest, I'm not all that optimistic about... |

| 範例 | **A:** To tell you the truth, I'm rather pessimistic about the result.
　　說實話，我對結果一點都不樂觀。
B: Don't lose heart. You will succeed.
　　不要灰心，你會成功的。 |

| 提示 | optimistic [ˌɑptəˈmɪstɪk] *adj.* 樂觀的 |

| 1578 | 做不到的。
It can't be done. |

| 範例 | **A:** She wants to finish the book within one hour.
她想在一個小時內讀完這本書。
B: It can't be done.
做不到的。 |

| 1579 | 不大可能。
Fat chance. |

| 範例 | **A:** Do you think we will find him here? 你覺得我們能在這裡找到他嗎？
B: Fat chance. 不大可能。 |
| 提示 | fat chance【非正式】可能性極小 |

| 1580 | 別抱太大希望。
Don't get your hopes up too high. |

| 範例 | **A:** I think he will be able to persuade Jane. 我想他會說服珍的。
B: Don't get your hopes up too high. 別抱太大希望。 |
| 提示 | persuade [pɚˋswed] v. 說服；勸說 |

| 1581 | 沒那樣好運。
There's no such good luck. |

| 範例 | **A:** I believe you will pass. 我相信你會通過的。
B: There's no such good luck. 沒那樣好運。 |

| 1582 | 我對…不抱太大希望。
I don't hold out much hope for... |

| 範例 | **A:** I don't hold out much hope for his support.
我對能否得到他的支持不抱太大希望。
B: I know what kind of person he is. He will certainly help you.
我知道他的為人，他一定會幫助你的。 |

| 1583 | 我不想說得過於悲觀，不過恐怕…。
I don't want to sound too pessimistic, but I'm afraid... |

| 範例 | **A:** Do you think he will pass?
你覺得他會通過嗎？
B: I don't want to sound too pessimistic, but I'm afraid he won't.
我不想說得過於悲觀，不過恐怕他不行。 |

1584	我得說我相當悲觀。 **I have to say I'm rather pessimistic.**

範例　A: Do you think we will win? 你認爲我們會贏嗎？
B: I have to say I'm rather pessimistic. 我得說我相當悲觀。

4.8　爭吵 Quarrelling

　　中國是禮儀之邦，因此與人爭吵是我們的禁忌，但爭吵在生活中是在所難免的。在會話當中，了解一些爭吵時常用的語言不是一件壞事，它可以幫助我們更準確的把握他人的態度，使人際關係更爲良好。這裡提供的句子不全然都是粗魯無禮的語言，較正式的表達法能幫你不失禮地表達自己的憤怒。

(077)

1585	我受夠了！ **That's enough!**

替換　I've just about had it.
I've had enough of that!
I've just about had enough.

範例　A: I don't want to speak to you again. That's enough!
我不想再和你說話，我受夠了。
B: OK! I'll leave.
好吧，那我走。

1586	住口！ **Stop it!**

替換　Shut up!
Cut it out!

範例　A: Stop it! How could you speak like that! 住口！你怎麼能那麼說！
B: It's none of your business. 這不關你的事。

1587	滾吧！我不想再見到你了！ **Get lost! I don't want to see you anymore!**

替換　Drop dead! I don't want to see you anymore!
Please leave here immediately!

範例
A: That's enough!
夠了！
B: Get lost! I don't want to see you anymore!
滾吧！我不想再見到你了！

提示
Get lost!【非正式】滾吧！〔用於氣憤地叫人走開〕
Drop dead!【俚】去你的！〔用於氣憤地叫某人保持安靜、別再打擾〕

1588 管它呢！
What the hell?

替換
How do you like that?

範例
A: Hey! Look what happened! 嘿！看看發生什麼事情了！
B: What the hell? 管它呢！

1589 你竟有臉⋯。
You've got some nerve to...

替換
You got the gall to...

範例
A: You've got some nerve to ask for money. 你竟有臉向人家要錢。
B: It's none of your business. 這不關你的事。

提示
gall [gɔl] *n.* 厚臉皮

1590 我再也受不了了！
I can't stand it anymore!

替換
I've run out of patience.

範例
A: I can't stand it anymore! 我再也受不了了！
B: Me, neither. 我也是。

1591 太過分了！
That's really too much!

替換
That's going a bit too far!
I think you've gone much too far.

範例
A: That's really too much! 太過分了！
B: I can't stand you anymore! 我再也受不了了。

1592 多麼無禮的話！
Well, of all the nerve!

替換
How rude!

範例 A: Well, of all the nerve! 多麼無禮的話！
B: Who do you think you are? 你以爲你是誰？

1593

你以爲你是誰？
Who do you think you are?

替換 What do you think you are?

範例 A: Who do you think you are? 你以爲你是誰？
B: Shut up! 閉嘴！

1594

你到底在說什麼？
What on earth are you talking about?

替換 I haven't the faintest idea what you're talking about.

範例 A: What on earth are you talking about? 你到底在說什麼？
B: I'm telling you to shut up. 我叫你閉嘴。

1595

你沒有權利…。
You've got no right to...

替換 You have absolutely no right to...

範例 A: You've got no right to ask that girl to drop out of school.
你沒有權利讓那個女孩輟學。
B: It's none of your business.
這不關你的事。

1596

我跟你已經沒什麼話可說了。
I'm through with you.

範例 A: I'm through with you. 我跟你已經沒什麼話可說了。
B: Then why don't you leave? 那你爲什麼還不走？

1597

你竟敢…。
How dare you...?

範例 A: How dare you say that to me? 你竟敢這樣跟我說話？
B: Who do you think you are? 你以爲你是誰？

1598

我不是小孩子了。
I wasn't born yesterday.

範例 | **A:** Shut up! 住嘴！
B: I wasn't born yesterday. 我不是小孩子了。

1599 | 胡說！
Nonsense!

範例 | **A:** He's a freak. 他是個怪人。
B: Nonsense! 胡說！

1600 | 你真不要臉！
How shameful!

範例 | **A:** How shameful! 你真不要臉！
B: What nerve! 你才厚臉皮！

1601 | 你這個傻瓜。
You dumbbell.

替換 | You silly fool.
You dummy.

範例 | **A:** You can't live without me. 你沒有我活不下去。
B: You dumbbell. 你這個傻瓜。

提示 | dumbbell [ˈdʌmˌbɛl] n. 【非正式，尤美】笨蛋；傻瓜（= dummy）

1602 | 你想把我當傻瓜嗎？
Are you trying to make a fool of me?

範例 | **A:** Are you trying to make a fool of me? 你想把我當傻瓜嗎？
B: Who do you think you are?! 你以為你是誰？

1603 | 你為什麼跟在我後面？
Why are you tagging along with me?

範例 | **A:** Why are you tagging along with me? 你為什麼跟在我後面？
B: I'm going my own way. 我只是走我自己的路。

提示 | tag along 【非正式】（在對方不情願的情況下）跟著

1604 | 我要和你評評理。
I have a bone to pick with you.

替換 | I want a word with you!

範例　A: Why are you here? 爲什麼你會在這裡？
B: I have a bone to pick with you. 我要和你評評理。

1605　你玩笑開得太過分了！
You're carrying that joke too far!

範例　A: Why not call her? 爲什麼不打電話給她？
B: You're carrying that joke too far! 你玩笑開得太過分了！

1606　別忘了你的規矩。
Remember your manners.

範例　A: Don't tell me what to do. 不用你來告訴我該做什麼。
B: Remember your manners. 別忘了你的規矩。

1607　真是厚顏無恥！
What impudence!

範例　A: You have absolutely no right to do that. 你絕對沒有權利這麼做。
B: What impudence! 眞是厚顏無恥！

提示　impudence ['ɪmpjədn̩s] *n.* 厚顏無恥

4.9　責備 Reproach

　　責備的語言和其他任何主題一樣，分爲非正式、一般場合和正式場合三種。在非正式場合的責備語言大都比較粗魯，只能用於家庭成員之間，長輩對晚輩或親密朋友之間。這裡介紹的通用語可用於非正式的場合，而較正式的語言則用於婉轉地批評。

(078)

1608　不害臊！
For shame!

替換　Shame on you!
What a shame for you!

範例　A: For shame! 不害臊！
B: How could you say that? 你怎麼能這麼說？

1609
你本來至少可以⋯。
You could at least have...

(替換) Well, you might at least have...

(範例) **A:** Well, you could at least have avoided doing that.
嗯，你本來至少可以避免這樣做。
B: I'm really sorry for what I have done.
我為我的所作所為感到抱歉。

1610
你瘋了嗎？
Are you mad?

(範例) **A:** Are you mad? How can you be so rude?
你瘋了嗎？你怎麼能這麼無禮？
B: I'm too angry to control myself.
我太生氣了，控制不住自己。

1611
你就不能認真一次嗎？
Can't you be serious for once?

(範例) **A:** Can't you be serious for once? 你就不能認真一次嗎？
B: Sorry. 對不起。

1612
別傻了！
Don't be silly!

(範例) **A:** Don't be silly! He's not Mr. Right. 別傻了！他不是白馬王子。
B: But I love him. 但是我愛他。

1613
我為你感到羞恥。
I felt so ashamed of you.

(範例) **A:** I felt so ashamed of you. 我為你感到羞恥。
B: What did I do to make you so angry? 我做了什麼讓你這麼生氣？

1614
你應該為自己感到恥辱。
You ought to be ashamed of yourself!

(範例) **A:** I'm wrong. 我錯了。
B: You ought to be ashamed of yourself! 你應該為自己感到恥辱。

1615
這不關你的事！
It's none of your business.

361

範例 A: Mom, where are they going? 媽媽，他們要去哪裡？
B: It's none of your business. 這不關你的事。

1616
瞧你做的好事呀！
Now look what you've done!

範例 A: Now look what you've done! 瞧你做的好事呀！
B: I didn't do it on purpose. 我不是故意的。

1617
你看看！我沒告訴你嗎？
There! Didn't I tell you?

範例 A: There! Didn't I tell you? 你看看！我沒告訴你嗎？
B: Did you? 你告訴我了嗎？

1618
你這個調皮鬼！
You naughty boy!

範例 A: Mom, I broke the vase. 媽媽，我把花瓶打破了。
B: You naughty boy! 你這個調皮鬼！

1619
你不為…感到羞恥嗎？
Aren't you ashamed of...?

範例 A: Aren't you ashamed of your rudeness? 你不為你的無禮感到羞恥嗎？
B: I didn't do anything. 我什麼都沒有做啊。

1620
你怎麼可以…呢？
How can you...?

範例 A: How can you do that to an old man like him?
你怎麼可以如此對待像他這樣的老人呢？
B: Sorry, I know I was wrong.
對不起，我錯了。

1621
你…可不好。
It's not nice to...

範例 A: I was late because my mother is ill. 我遲到是因為我媽媽病了。
B: It's not nice to tell lies. 你撒謊可不好。

1622
做的什麼好事啊！
What a thing to do!

範例 A: What a thing to do! 做的什麼好事啊！
B: Did I do something wrong? 我做錯了什麼嗎？

1623 …算什麼意思？
What do you mean by...?

範例 A: What do you mean by keeping silent? 你這樣不說話算什麼意思？
B: I just want to think about it. 我只是想考慮一下。

1624 你知道自己在做什麼嗎？
What do you think you're doing?

範例 A: What do you think you're doing? 你知道自己在做什麼嗎？
B: It's none of your business.不關你的事。

1625 你不能想怎麼樣就怎麼樣。
You can't just do whatever you like.

範例 A: You can't just do whatever you like. 你不能想怎麼樣就怎麼樣。
B: You have no right to teach me. 你沒有權利教訓我。

1626 你不能就這麼…。
You can't just...

範例 A: I'm going. 我要走了。
B: You can't just leave me alone. 你不能就這麼扔下我一個人。

1627 你不應該…。
You shouldn't...

範例 A: You shouldn't be so particular about your appearance.
你不應該對自己的外貌過分講究。
B: That's none of your business.
這不關你的事。

提示 appearance [ə'pɪrəns] *n.* 外貌；外表

1628 …你真是夠傻的了。
You were fool enough to...

範例 A: You were fool enough to tell him the truth.
把真相告訴他，你真是夠傻的了。
B: Yeah, I'm really a fool.
是啊，我真是傻！

1629

恐怕你沒有權利…。
I'm afraid you have no right to...

範例 | **A:** I'm afraid you have no right to come into my room without permission. 恐怕你沒有權利未經許可進入我的房間。
B: I'm really sorry. 真是很抱歉。

提示 | permission [pɚˈmɪʃən] *n.* 許可；允許

4.10 無奈 Resignation

我們都有過這樣的經歷：面對問題無計可施。但是，無可奈何的感受在各種場合中的表達方式是不盡相同的。

1630

真不走運！
What bad luck!

(079)

替換 | Just my luck!

範例 | **A:** I missed the bus! 我沒有趕上公車。
B: What bad luck! 真不走運。

1631

沒辦法！
No dice!

替換 | I give up.
I can't help it.
I can do nothing about it.
I just can't do anything about it.
What else could I do?
There is no way!
There is nothing I can do.

範例 | **A:** Maybe you should have a talk with him. 也許你該和他談談。
B: No dice. 沒辦法！

提示 | no dice【口，尤美】沒辦法；門都沒有

1632

沒希望了。
It's hopeless.

替換 | It's beyond hope now.
It will have to do.

範例 | A: Why not try again? 為什麼不再試試呢？
B: It's hopeless. 沒希望了。

1633 | 命中註定，有什麼辦法。
That's the way it goes.

替換 | That's the way the ball bounces.
That's how the cookie crumbles.

範例 | A: Jerry got fired again. 傑瑞又被解雇了。
B: That's the way it goes. 命中註定，有什麼辦法。

提示 | bounce [baʊns] v.（指球等）彈回

1634 | 已經無法挽回了。
Well, the die is cast.

替換 | Well, we've had it.

範例 | A: Well, the die is cast. 哎，已經無法挽回了。
B: Don't lose heart. You still have a chance. 不要灰心，你還有機會。

1635 | 我只好接受…。
I have to accept...

替換 | I have to resign myself to...
I'm prepared to submit to...
I've become reconciled to...

範例 | A: What will you do? 你打算怎麼辦？
B: I have to accept their decision. 我只好接受他們的決定。

提示 | reconcile ['rɛkənsaɪl] v. 使順從；使甘心於

1636 | 聽天由命吧。
I'm resigned to my fate.

替換 | I suppose there's nothing we can do about it.

範例 | A: What are you going to do next? 你下一步怎麼辦？
B: I'm resigned to my fate. 聽天由命吧。

1637 | 算了，人生就是這樣！
Well, that's life!

範例 A: I can't believe that he could be successful. 我真不敢相信他會成功。
B: Well, that's life! 算了，人生就是這樣！

1638 我沒辦法，只能…了。
I can't help but...

範例 A: What will you do? 你怎麼辦？
B: I can't help but wait. 我沒辦法，只能等了。

1639 我只好隨它去了。
I have to leave it as it is.

範例 A: The situation is a mess. 情況一團糟。
B: I have to leave it as it is. 我只好隨它去了。

1640 我只好將就著…了。
I'll have to make do with...

範例 A: Sorry, we don't have a new pen.
對不起，我們沒有新的筆。
B: Well, I'll have to make do with the old one.
那我只好將就著用舊的了。

提示 make do with（在目前有的情況下）設法應付

1641 這是沒辦法避免的。
There is no avoiding that.

範例 A: Do you know that he was put in prison? 你知道嗎？他被關進監獄了。
B: There is no avoiding that. 這是沒辦法避免的。

1642 恐怕只能如此了。
I'm afraid it will have to do.

範例 A: Is this all we have? 這就是全部嗎？
B: I'm afraid it will have to do. 恐怕只能如此了。

1643 …希望很渺小。
There's little hope of...

範例 A: Do you think he will allow us to go?
你認為他會讓我們去嗎？
B: There's little hope of getting his permission now.
現在要在得到他的允許希望很渺小。

4.11 威脅 Threat

在日常交際中，使用威脅語言的場合不多，但關鍵時刻卻是不可或缺的。一般來說，威脅的語言都不太禮貌。威脅語言的表達方式要根據不同的場合和不同的事物而定。在正式場合使用粗俗的威脅語言有失身份，而在普通的場合使用文縐縐的威脅語言，又難以發揮威脅的作用。

080

1644
你敢！
You just try!

替換
Just you dare!
Don't you dare!

範例
A: If you do it again, I will give you a sound beating.
如果你再這麼做，我就狠狠打你一頓。
B: You just try.
你敢！

1645
你敢…！
Don't you dare...!

範例
A: Don't you dare do that again! 你敢再這麼做！
B: Why not? 有何不？

1646
我遲早會找你算帳。
I'll sort you out sooner or later.

替換
One of these days I'm going to fix you.

範例
A: I'll sort you out sooner or later. 我遲早會找你算帳。
B: I'll be waiting. 我會等著。

提示
sort out【英】收拾（某人）；整治（某人）

1647
我待會找你算帳！
I'll deal with you later.

替換
I'll get you for that.
I'll be back for you.

範例
A: You fool! 你這個傻瓜！
B: I'll deal with you later. 我待會找你算帳！

1648

你要是再犯，我就…！
Just you do that again, and I'll...

(替換) Do that again and I'll...

(範例) A: Just you do that again, and I'll kill you. 你要是再犯，我就殺了你！
B: You wouldn't dare! 你敢！

1649

如果你…，就…！
If you..., ...

(範例) A: If you don't be quiet, you'll be punished.
如果你不安靜下來，就會受到懲罰！
B: I promise I will be quiet.
我保證我會安靜下來。

1650

如果…，我只好…。
If..., I will have to...

(替換) If..., I will be compelled/obliged to...
If..., I will have no choice/alternative but to...

(範例) A: If the plan cannot be carried out, I will have to cancel it.
如果這個計畫不能執行的話，我只好取消它。
B: It would be a pity if you cancelled it.
要是取消就太可惜了。

(提示) alternative [ɔl'tɜ˞nətɪv] *n.* 其他選擇；可供選擇的辦法

1651

不要逼我，否則我就…！
Don't push me too far, or I'll...

(範例) A: Don't push me too far, or I'll run away.
不要逼我，否則我就會逃跑！
B: Take it easy. We will not force you to do what you don't want to.
放輕鬆，我們不會強迫你做不喜歡的事情。

1652

…，否則我就不客氣了。
..., before I do you some damage.

(範例) A: Back off, before I do you some damage. 後退，否則我就不客氣了。
B: OK, I'm leaving. 好，我走。

1653
當心你的小命！
Heaven have mercy on your soul!

範例
A: Heaven have mercy on your soul. 當心你的小命！
B: I'm not scared! 我不怕！

1654
走著瞧！
Just you wait!

範例
A: Just you wait! I will fix you later. 走著瞧！我會找你算帳的。
B: You wouldn't dare! 你不敢！

1655
要是讓我抓到你再犯，我饒不了你。
If I catch you doing that again, I won't forgive you.

範例
A: I promise I will never do that again.
　我發誓不會再犯。
B: If I catch you doing that again, I won't forgive you.
　要是讓我抓到你再犯，我饒不了你。

1656
你最好道歉，不然就讓你知道我的厲害！
You better apologize if you know what's good for you.

範例
A: You better apologize if you know what's good for you.
　你最好道歉，不然就讓你知道我的厲害！
B: Well, I apologize.
　好吧，我道歉。

提示
apologize [əˈpɑləˌdʒaɪz] v. 道歉

1657
你會為此付出代價！
You're going to pay for that.

範例
A: Now you know who you're talking to. 你現在知道我的厲害了吧！
B: You're going to pay for that. 你會為此付出代價！

1658
你會為此後悔的！
You'll be sorry for that!

範例
A: No matter what you say, I'm going to do it this way.
　不管你怎麼說，我都會這樣做。
B: You'll be sorry for that!
　你會為此後悔的！

1659	除非…，否則恐怕我只能…。 **Unless..., I'm afraid I will be forced to...**

(範例) **A:** Unless you finish your work on time, I'm afraid I will be forced to let you go. 除非你按時完成工作，否則恐怕我只能讓你走了。
B: I will do my best. 我會盡力的。

1660	你最好不要…。 **You'd be well advised not to...**

(替換) You'd better not...

(範例) **A:** You'd be well advised not to lie to me. 你最好不要對我撒謊。
B: I won't. 我不會的。

4.12　疲勞 Tiredness

　　疲勞是體力或腦力過度消耗時產生的感覺。表達疲勞的概念時，不同職業、身份、年齡或教育程度的人會根據不同場合，做適當的表達。在以下各種表達中，可以很清楚地發現這一點。因此，我們在表達疲勞的概念時，有必要注意說話的場合、交談的內容等社會因素的差異。

081

1661	我累壞了。 **I'm beat.**

(替換) I'm pooped/bushed/exhausted/drained.
I'm wiped/tuckered out.
I'm worn/tired (out).
I'm (dead) tired.
I feel completely exhausted.
I'm done in/for.

(範例) **A:** What's wrong with you? 你怎麼了？
B: I'm beat. 我累壞了。

(提示) pooped [pupt] *adj.*【美，非正式】筋疲力盡的
bushed [buʃt] *adj.*【非正式】筋疲力盡的
tucker sb. out【美，非正式】使非常疲乏

1662	真累人！ **What a day!**
替換	What a pain! What a bad day I had!
範例	**A:** What a day! 真累人！ **B:** Have a bath first. 先洗個澡吧。

1663	…使我筋疲力盡。 **I'm shagged out because of...**
替換	...has already wiped me out. ...wears me out. I'm worn out by... ...has tired me out. I feel completely wasted because of...
範例	**A:** I'm shagged out because of the work. 這工作使我筋疲力盡。 **B:** Let's have a rest. 我們休息一會兒吧。
提示	shagged [ˈʃægɪd] *adj.* 疲憊不堪的；筋疲力盡的（= shagged out）

1664	我累得不能動了。 **I feel like a beached whale.**
範例	**A:** What's the matter? 怎麼了？ **B:** I feel like a beached whale. 我累得不能動了。

1665	我快累倒了。 **I'm about to collapse from exhaustion.**
範例	**A:** I'm about to collapse from exhaustion. 我快累倒了。 **B:** So am I. 我也是。

1666	…把我累垮了。 **...lays me flat.**
範例	**A:** This work lays me flat. 這工作把我累垮了。 **B:** Have a rest. 休息一會兒吧。

1667	我很久沒有這麼累了。 **I haven't felt so wiped-out in ages.**

範例　A: How are you recently? 你最近怎麼樣？
　　　B: I haven't felt so wiped-out in ages. 我很久沒有這麼累了。

1668　我一定是過於疲勞了。
I must have worn myself out.

範例　A: You don't look well. 你看起來氣色不太好。
　　　B: I must have worn myself out. 我一定是過於疲勞了。

1669　生活對我而言真是太沉重了。
Life is really too much for me.

範例　A: Why are you so upset? 為什麼你這麼沮喪？
　　　B: Life is really too much for me. 生活對我而言真是太沉重了。

4.13　不確定 Uncertainty

有人說："Life is full of uncertainties."。這說明我們的生活中有許多不確定的因素。交談中，我們有時要確切了解某種資訊或某人的態度，有時要準確表達自己對事物的把握程度。英語中有很多表達確定和不確定的方法。

082

1670　這件事我不太確定。
I'm not too sure of it.

替換　I wouldn't be too sure about that.
範例　A: Do you know when he will come? 你知道他什麼時候回來？
　　　B: I'm not too sure of it. 這件事我不太確定。

1671　我一點也不知道…。
I haven't a clue about...

替換　I've no idea about...
範例　A: Why is he so unhappy? 他為什麼不高興？
　　　B: I haven't a clue about it. 我一點也不知道。

1672　我沒有把握…。
I can't say for certain...

替換   I couldn't say, really, ...
I'm not certain/sure...
I can't say with any certainty...

範例   **A:** I can't say for certain who will come. 我沒有把握誰會來。
B: OK, I will ask Jim. He'll know. 好吧,我去問吉姆,他一定知道。

1673   我不能肯定。
I'm not sure.

替換   I'm not certain.
I can't be certain/sure.
I can't say for certain.

範例   **A:** Will he be happy about that? 他會為此高興嗎?
B: I'm not sure. 我不能肯定。

1674   我決定不了⋯。
I can't decide...

替換   I'm confused about...
I can't make up my mind about...

範例   **A:** I can't decide who to turn to.
我決定不了要向誰求救。
B: If I were you, I would go to Mary for help.
如果我是你,我就去找瑪麗幫忙。

1675   我說不準⋯。
I can't tell...

替換   I can't determine...

範例   **A:** I can't tell who is more capable. 我說不準誰更有能力。
B: Neither can I. 我也說不準。

提示   determine [dɪ'tɜ·mɪn] *v.* 確定

1676   我覺得很難下結論。
I find it difficult to come to a conclusion.

替換   I find it difficult to draw a conclusion on that.

範例   **A:** Do you think they will win? 你認為他們會贏嗎?
B: I find it difficult to come to a conclusion. 我覺得很難下結論。

1677

恐怕我不能肯定…。
I'm afraid I can't be certain about...

(替換) I'm afraid I can't be positive about...

(範例) **A:** Who should be responsible for that? 誰應當對此負責呢？
B: I'm afraid I can't be certain about that. 恐怕我不能肯定那事情。

1678

我根本無法確信…。
I'm not at all convinced that...

(範例) **A:** I'm not at all convinced that he's innocent.
我根本無法確信他是無辜的。
B: But everyone said he wasn't guilty.
但是人人都說他是無罪的。

1679

我對…心存疑慮。
I have my doubts about...

(替換) There is some doubt in my mind about...
There are some doubts in my mind about...

(範例) **A:** Do you believe it? 你相信嗎？
B: I have my doubts about what he said. 我對他所說的話心存疑慮。

1680

還不能確定…。
It's questionable...

(替換) I would consider it open to question...

(範例) **A:** It's questionable whether he's the suitable person for this job.
還不能確定他適不適合這一份工作。
B: Why do you say that?
你為什麼這樣說？

1681

很難說，…有可能。
It's hard to tell. It could...

(替換) It's hard/difficult to say.

(範例) **A:** Who did it? 誰幹的？
B: It's hard to tell. It could have been anyone. 很難說，任何人都有可能。

1682

聽天由命吧。
Let's leave it to chance.

範例	A: What shall we do? 我們該怎麼辦？ B: Let's leave it to chance. 聽天由命吧。

1683	我真的沒法斷定。 **I really couldn't say.**

範例	A: Is it true? 是真的嗎？ B: I really couldn't say. 我真的沒法斷定。

1684	我想可能是…吧。 **I suppose it could be...**

範例	A: I suppose it could be his book. 我想可能是他的書吧。 B: I don't think so. 我不覺得。

1685	看情況。 **It depends.**

範例	A: Will he be successful? 他會成功嗎？ B: It depends. 看情況。

4.14 警告 Warning

在會話當中，有時有必要向人提出警告。當然，警告有時是含蓄的，有時則是直截了當的。警告人時，多用祈使句，而且語言簡潔有力。值得注意的是，警告有時相當於威脅。

聖經說：「適時一句勝萬言。」但是，不適當的語言也會產生副作用。因此，我們要特別注意把握語氣和措辭。

1686	規矩點兒！ **Behave yourself!**

替換	Don't be funny! Don't get fresh!

範例	A: Behave yourself! 規矩點兒！ B: OK! 好！

| 1687 | 別管閒事！
Mind your own business! |

替換 | Mind your own potatoes!
Don't get too nosy!

範例 | **A:** I can help you with that. 我可以幫你。
B: Mind your own business! 別管閒事！

提示 | nosy ['nozɪ] *adj.* 好管閒事的；愛打聽別人事情的（= nosey）

| 1688 | 小心！
Watch out! |

替換 | Watch it/yourself!
Look out!
Take care!
Be careful!

範例 | **A:** Watch out! 小心！
B: Thanks. 謝謝。

| 1689 | 當心…！
Mind...! |

替換 | Watch...!
Be ready for...!
Watch out for...!
Be aware/careful of...!
Beware of...
Be on guard against...!

範例 | **A:** Mind your head! 當心你的頭！
B: Thank you. 謝謝。

| 1690 | 別得意忘形了！
Don't lose your head! |

替換 | Don't get carried away!

範例 | **A:** I'm overjoyed. 我太高興了。
B: Don't lose your head! 別得意忘形了！

提示 | overjoyed [ˌovə'dʒɔɪd] *adj.* 狂喜的；極度高興的

1691	如果我是你，我會對…特別小心。 **If I were you, I would be extremely careful of...!**
範例	**A:** If I were you, I would be extremely careful of that! 如果我是你，我會對此特別小心。 **B:** But how can you be so careful? 可是你怎能那樣小心呢？
1692	著火了！ **Fire!**
範例	**A:** Fire! 著火了！ **B:** I'll call 911. 我去打 911。
1693	我警告你！ **I warn you!**
範例	**A:** I warn you! Don't lie to me. 我警告你！不要對我撒謊。 **B:** I will never. 我永遠不會的。
1694	不要耍花招！ **Don't try any tricks!**
範例	**A:** I warn you! Don't try any tricks! 我警告你。不要耍花招！ **B:** I wouldn't dare. 我不敢。
1695	小心開車！ **Drive carefully!**
範例	**A:** Drive carefully! 小心開車！ **B:** Thank you. 謝謝。
1696	你別插手！ **You stay out of this!**
範例	**A:** I want to have a talk with him. 我想跟他談談。 **B:** You stay out of this! 你別插手！
1697	別惹…！ **Leave...alone.**
範例	**A:** Leave the dog alone. 別惹那條狗！ **B:** But it's very cute. 可是牠很可愛。

1698	千萬…！ **Make sure...!**

範例 A: Make sure you close all the windows before you leave!
　　 出門前千萬要關好窗！
　　 B: I'll remember.
　　 我會記住的。

4.15 憂懼 Worry and Fear

　　擔憂與恐懼是人處於困境或遭遇危難時，所產生的強烈心理反應，同時在行爲和語言上也會有所表現。表示擔憂害怕的語言受場合、說話人的性別、年齡、地位及情況嚴重程度等因素影響。

084

1699	我嚇得要死。 **I'm shaking like a leaf.**

替換 I was scared out of my wits.
　　 I'm about to jump out of my skin.
　　 I was scared stiff.

範例 A: I'm shaking like a leaf. 我嚇得要死。
　　 B: Come on, it's just a cat. 得了，只不過是一隻貓。

1700	我怕…。 **I'm scared of...**

替換 I'm all wound up about...
　　 I'm afraid/frightened/terrified of...
　　 I fear...

範例 A: I'm scared of snakes. 我怕蛇。
　　 B: Why are you so afraid of them? 爲什麼你怕蛇？

1701	我很擔心…。 **I'm worried sick about...**

替換 I really care about...
　　 I'm worrying about...
　　 I'm extremely nervous about...

I'm rather apprehensive about...
...gives cause for concern.

範例 A: I'm worried sick about his illness. 我很擔心他的病。
B: Don't worry. He will be fine. 別擔心，他會好的。

提示 apprehensive [ˌæprɪ'hɛnsɪv] *adj.* 憂慮的；擔心的

1702
你把我嚇死了！
You scared me out of my mind!

範例 A: Hi! 嗨！
B: You scared me out of my mind! 你把我嚇死了！

1703
…讓我毛骨悚然。
...gives me the creeps.

範例 A: That guy gives me the creeps. 這傢伙讓我毛骨悚然。
B: Me, too. 我也是。

提示 creep [krip] *n.* （由於厭惡、恐懼等）起雞皮疙瘩；汗毛直豎

1704
對於…我真的緊張極了。
I'm really in a flap about...

範例 A: I'm really in a flap about the performance. 對於表演我真的緊張極了。
B: Take it easy! You will have no problems. 放輕鬆，你不會有問題的。

1705
我對…感到緊張不安。
I feel nervous about...

替換 I must say...upset me a great deal.
I must admit I was rather disturbed about...

範例 A: I feel nervous about the results. 我對結果感到緊張不安。
B: You should have confidence in yourself. 你應該對自己有信心。

1706
我覺得…很令人擔憂。
I find...very worrying.

範例 A: I find his illness very worrying. 我覺得他的病情很令人擔憂。
B: Don't worry. He will be fine. 別擔心，他會好的。

1707
如果…，我真不知如何是好。
I just don't know what I'll do if...

A: I just don't know what I'll do if I don't pass the exam.
如果我不及格，我真不知如何是好。

B: Come on. It's not the end of the world.
算了，又不是世界末日。

1708

我真的嚇得要死…。
I was scared to death that...

 A: I was scared to death that I would be fired.
我真的嚇得要死，以為會被解雇。

B: That's impossible.
那是不可能的。

1709

…我簡直嚇呆了。
I was terrified out of my mind...

 A: I was terrified out of my mind when I saw the car accident.
我看見那起車禍的時候，我簡直嚇呆了。

B: How terrible it was!
真是太可怕了。

1710

我擔心…。
I'm afraid that...

（替換） I fear that...
I feel great concern that...
I have serious misgivings that...
I'm very concerned/anxious that...

 A: I'm afraid that we may not finish the work on time.
我擔心我們不能按時完成工作。

B: Let's try our best.
我們盡力吧。

（提示） misgiving [mɪsˈgɪvɪŋ] *n.* 疑慮；害怕

1711

一想到…我就不寒而慄。
I shiver to think that...

 A: I shiver to think that I'm going to be alone in that big house.
一想到我要一個人住在那棟大房子裡，我就不寒而慄。

B: Do you want me to accompany you there?
你希望我去陪你嗎？

提示 | shiver [ˈʃɪvɚ] *v.* 顫抖
accompany [əˈkʌmpənɪ] *v.* 陪伴

1712 | …令我非常不安。
I'm extremely upset about...

替換 | ...upsets me very much.

範例 | **A:** I'm extremely upset about his dropping out.
他的輟學令我非常不安。
B: Yeah, he's too young to start working.
是的，他太小了，還不能出去工作。

第 2 部分
會話場景篇

第5章
特別時刻

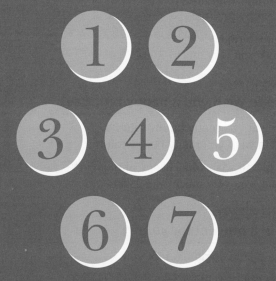

在英美等西方人士看來，生日是一件大事。生日那天一般都有慶祝活動，慶祝活動包括舉行家庭宴會或邀請親朋好友來聚會。參加聚會的人應該要送生日禮物。生日禮物可以是生日蛋糕，也可以是別的東西。送的禮品可以根據過生日人的年齡、性別、愛好、社會地位以及與壽星關係的遠近而定。壽星收到禮物時，一般要在慶祝會上當著送禮人的面前打開。如果客人較少，每接到一份禮品都可以把包裝打開。如果聚會規模較大，客人較多，則可以先把禮品放在一邊，另外再找時間打開，以供客人們欣賞。主人要邊打開，邊感謝送禮人。參加生日宴會一定不要忘記要向壽星祝福。

1713	生日快樂！ **Happy birthday!**
替換	Have a happy birthday! Many happy returns!
範例	A: Happy birthday! 生日快樂！ B: Thank you very much! 非常謝謝你！
1714	謹祝你生日快樂！ **I'd like to wish you a happy birthday!**
替換	May I wish you many happy returns. I'd like to wish you many happy returns.
範例	A: I'd like to wish you a happy birthday! 謹祝你生日快樂！ B: Thank you very much! 非常感謝你！
1715	這是給你的禮物。 **Here is a present for you.**
替換	Here is a little something for you.
範例	A: Here is a present for you. 這是給你的禮物。 B: That's very kind of you. 你太好了。
1716	我想把…送給你。 **I'd like to present...to you.**

085

範例 A: I'd like to present this book to you. 我想把這本書送給你。
B: Thank you so much. 非常感謝。

1717 **我買給你⋯。**
I bought...for you.

替換 I've got...for you.

範例 A: I bought a photo album for you. 我買給你一本相本。
B: Thanks a lot. 多謝。

1718 **我真不知道該如何謝謝你的禮物。**
I don't know how to thank you for the gift.

範例 A: I don't know how to thank you for the gift.
我真不知道該如何謝謝你的禮物。
B: I'm glad you like it.
很高興你喜歡。

1719 **你真好！**
That's very kind of you.

替換 How sweet of you!

範例 A: This is a present for you. 這是給你的禮物。
B: That's very kind of you. 你真好。

5.2 舞會上 At a Dance

　　舞會是重要的社交場合。舞會的服裝雖然有愈來愈隨便的趨勢，但正式舞會對男女的服裝還是有一定的要求。參加舞會時的行為和語言，也必須適當得體。在舞會上，不要翹著二郎腿，懶洋洋地靠在椅子上，不要在舞廳吸煙，女士尤其要注意。舞會上，男士要主動邀請女士，即使事先與女士已經約定好也不例外。男士請女士跳舞，要走上前鞠躬，並有禮貌地邀請。接受邀請時，有特定的表達方法；拒絕邀請時，也要注意說話技巧。女士一旦拒絕某位男士，在該曲目結束之前，就不要和其他人跳舞（男士有冒犯女士言行的情況除外）。有節目單的正式舞會上，女士可以告訴男士要和他跳哪一首曲目。沒有節目單的正式舞會，女士可以接受邀請，也可以找藉口拒絕。正在跳舞的女士不能中途更換舞伴。

一般情況下，男士被女士拒絕後，不能再邀該女士跳舞。跳完一曲之後，男士要表示感謝，女士也要說聲 "Thank you."，男士還必須陪女士一起回到座位。如果男士想另找舞伴，要表示歉意。每一位男士至少要和女主人跳一次。如果有人把男士介紹給女士，男士有必要請該女士跳舞。陪女士去跳舞時，要先帶女士向女主人問候再去跳舞，休息時間要照料女士用點心和飲料。如果舞會在宴會後進行，男士要和女主人或坐在自己旁邊的女士跳舞。離開舞場前，要向女主人表示感謝。

1720
086

你跳舞嗎？
Can you dance?

範例
A: Can you dance? 你跳舞嗎？
B: Certainly. 當然。

1721

你願意和我跳支舞嗎？
Would you like to dance?

替換
Will you accept my arm?
Will you honor me with a dance?
Will you grant me the favor of a dance?

範例
A: Would you like to dance? 你願意和我跳支舞嗎？
B: I'd be delighted. 我很樂意。

1722

願意賞個光和我跳支舞嗎？
May I have the honor of engaging you in a dance?

替換
May I have the honor of a dance?
May I have the pleasure of engaging you for a dance?
May I have the pleasure of the dance?

範例
A: May I have the honor of engaging you in a dance?
願意賞個光和我跳支舞嗎？
B: I would be most willing.
我很樂意。

1723

再跳一隻舞怎麼樣？
How about another dance?

替換 | Why don't we have one more dance?
範例 | A: How about another dance? 再跳一隻舞怎麼樣？
B: Sure. 當然。

1724
好的，跳吧！
Yes, let's do that.

範例 | A: Shall we dance? 我們跳舞好嗎？
B: Yes, let's do that. 好的，跳吧！

1725
對不起，我不會跳。
I'm sorry, I can't dance.

範例 | A: How about a dance? 跳一支舞怎麼樣？
B: I'm sorry, I can't dance. 對不起，我不會跳。

1726
對不起，我跳得不好。
I'm sorry, I'm a poor dancer.

範例 | A: I'm sorry, I'm a poor dancer. 對不起，我跳得不好。
B: So am I. Anyway, let's dance. 我也一樣。不管怎麼說，我們跳吧。

1727
對不起，已經有人約我跳這支舞了。
I'm sorry I'm taken for this dance.

範例 | A: May I have the honor of this dance?
能賞光和我跳這支舞嗎？
B: I'm sorry I'm taken for this dance.
對不起，已經有人約我跳這支舞了。

1728
不，謝謝。我不想…。
No, thanks. I don't care for...

替換 | No, thanks. I won't dance...
No, thanks. I think I'll sit out...
範例 | A: May I dance the tango with you? 能賞光和我跳這支探戈嗎？
B: No, thanks. I don't care for the tango. 不，謝謝。我不想跳探戈。
提示 | sit out 坐在一旁不參加（跳舞等）；一直等到…過去

1729
不，謝謝。我想休息一會兒。
No, thanks. I want to have a rest.

389

（替換） No, thanks. I'm sitting out for a few minutes.

（範例） **A:** Shall we dance? 我們跳舞好嗎？
B: No, thanks. I want to have a rest. 不，謝謝。我想休息一會兒。

5.3　宴會上 At a Dinner

　　西方人的宴會有正式和非正式之分，大致有： Seated　Dinners（有席位宴會）、 Buffet Dinners（自助餐）、 Luncheons（正式午餐）、 Receptions（招待會）、 Cocktail Parties（雞尾酒會）、 BYOB and BYOF（聚餐會）、 Picnics（野餐）、 Tea Parties（茶會）八種形式。西方人對請客的人數沒有特定的限制，主要取決於宴會的性質、場所及經濟條件。請客的時間也沒有特定的限制。當然，不同的宴會有一些不同的要求，準備或參加宴會都有必要對不同的宴會有所了解，熟悉宴會的基本規範（如應邀作客時，不要提前到達，一般要晚於約定的時間 10-15 分鐘，免得主人準備不及而感到尷尬），以免失禮。

1730	乾杯！ **Cheers!**
（替換）	A toast! Drink/Bottoms up! Down the hatch!〔俚語說法〕 Here's mud in your eyes!〔舊式說法〕
（範例）	**A:** Cheers! 乾杯！ **B:** Cheers! 乾杯！
1731	我要為…乾杯！ **To...**
（替換）	Here's to... Let's drink to...! I raise my glass to...! Here's wishing...!
（範例）	**A:** To your health! 我要為你的健康乾杯！ **B:** Thanks. 謝謝。

1732	祝你好運。 **Good luck to you!**
範例	**A:** Good luck to you! 祝你好運！ **B:** Thank you. 謝謝。

1733	祝你們永遠幸福！ **May you both have happiness always!**
範例	**A:** May you both have happiness always! 祝你們永遠幸福！ **B:** You too. 你也是。

1734	敬你一杯！ **Here's to you!**
範例	**A:** Here's to you! 敬你一杯！ **B:** Thanks a lot. 多謝。

1735	我們提議為…乾杯好嗎？ **Shall we propose a toast to...?**
範例	**A:** Shall we propose a toast to our friendship? 我們提議為我們的友誼乾杯好嗎？ **B:** Yes. Cheers! 好的。乾杯！

1736	請允許我為…乾杯。 **Let me propose a toast to...**
範例	**A:** Let me propose a toast to your success. 請允許我為你的成功乾杯。 **B:** Thank you very much. 非常謝謝。

1737	我請大家舉杯，和我一起為…乾杯！ **I'd like you all to raise your glasses and join me in a toast to...**
範例	**A:** I'd like you all to raise your glasses and join me in a toast to Mr. Johnson's health. 我請大家舉杯，和我一起為詹森先生的健康乾杯！ **B:** Thank you so much. 非常感謝。

1738	我非常高興的請各位為…乾杯！ **It's with the greatest pleasure that I invite you to raise your glasses to...**

| 替換 | With great pleasure I ask you to toast... |
| 範例 | A: It's with the greatest pleasure that I invite you to raise your glasses to the president's health. 我非常高興的請各位為總裁的健康乾杯！
B: Cheers! 乾杯！ |

1739	現在，我想提議為…乾杯！ **At this point, I would like to propose a toast to...**
範例	A: At this point, I would like to propose a toast to our honorable guest. 現在，我想提議為我們的貴賓乾杯！ B: Salud! 乾杯！
提示	honorable [ˈɑnərəbl] *adj.* 可尊敬的；光榮的

| *1740* | 我想請你們原諒，並舉杯為…乾杯。
I'd like to ask you for your understanding, and raise your glasses to... |
| 範例 | A: I'd like to ask you for your understanding, and raise your glasses to Professor Smith. 我想請你們原諒，並舉杯為史密斯教授乾杯。
B: To our friendship! 為我們的友誼乾杯！ |

5.4　復活節 Easter

　　復活節（每年春分月圓後的第一個星期日）是基督教紀念耶穌復活的重大節日。復活節的前一天，教徒們要舉行夜間祈禱。當天，很多地方要舉行迎日出的宗教儀式，信奉英國國教的人要到教堂去做禮拜領「聖餐」。復活節還有不少傳統的慶祝活動。彩蛋是復活節最典型的象徵，人們互贈彩蛋，也從事許多和蛋有關的遊戲。復活節這天，人們還要穿上新衣服參加遊行，而父母會給孩子買巧克力雞蛋或小兔糖果，已婚子女則利用復活節假期和父母團聚。

| *1741* | 復活節快樂！
Happy Easter! |
| 替換 | Have a happy Easter! |

範例 | A: Happy Easter! 復活節快樂！
B: Thank you. And a happy Easter to you! 謝謝。你也是！

1742 | **謝謝，你也是！**
Thanks. And you too!

替換 | Thanks. The same to you.
Thanks, and that goes double for you!
Thanks a lot. Same to you!
Thank you. You too!
Thank you. And the same to you!
Thank you. And I wish you the same!

範例 | A: Have a happy Easter! 祝你復活節快樂！
B: Thanks. And you too! 謝謝，你也是！

5.5　耶誕節 Christmas

　　12 月 25 日的耶誕節是英美等基督教國家的盛大節日，是紀念耶穌誕生的日子。如今耶誕節已經成為既有宗教色彩又有民俗風格的傳統節日。一般人從 11 月底開始準備節慶事宜。每個家庭都用彩燈和耶誕樹把室內裝飾得美輪美奐。商店等公共場所也呈現節日的氣象。節日期間，人們到教堂做禮拜，家庭成員或朋友之間互贈耶誕賀卡和禮品以示祝賀。除了象徵「流芳百世」和「長壽」的耶誕樹、兒童喜歡的耶誕老人、表達親情友情的耶誕賀卡、象徵團圓的耶誕大餐和傳報「佳音」的耶誕頌歌之外，耶誕節期間還有特定的慶賀語言。

1743 | **耶誕快樂！**
Merry Christmas!

（089）

替換 | Happy Christmas!
Have a good Christmas!
A merry Christmas to you!

範例 | A: Merry Christmas! 耶誕快樂！
B: Thanks. And you too! 謝謝，你也是！

1744	祝你耶誕快樂，新年快樂！ **Have a merry Christmas and a happy New Year!**

範例
A: Have a merry Christmas and a happy New Year!
　　祝你耶誕快樂，新年快樂！
B: Thank you. The same to you!
　　謝謝，你也是！

1745	請代我向…表達我的耶誕祝賀！ **Please send my Christmas greetings to...**

範例
A: Please send my Christmas greetings to Susan.
　　請代我向蘇珊表達我的耶誕祝賀！
B: Thank you. I will.
　　謝謝你。我會的。

1746	謝謝，你也是！ **Thanks. And you too!**

替換
Thanks. The same to you.
Thanks, and that goes double for you!
Thanks a lot. Same to you!
Thank you. You too!
Thank you. And the same to you!
Thank you. And I wish you the same!

範例
A: A merry Christmas to you! 祝你耶誕快樂！
B: Thanks. And you too! 謝謝，你也是！

5.6 新年元旦 New Year's Day

　　新年即元旦和元旦以後的一段時期，是很多國家都慶祝的節日。但是各國的慶祝方式不盡相同。在英格蘭，有槲寄生驅邪的傳說，有舉杯互祝健康的新年慶祝活動，有化裝舞會表演的遊行，有特拉法加廣場的狂歡和傾聽「大笨鐘」鐘聲後的歡呼；在蘇格蘭，他們具有除夕守歲、新年贈送禮物、聚會、拜訪親友等傳統，過得比耶誕節更具氣氛；在美國，人們以聚會、祈禱、唱詩、傾聽教堂鐘聲和汽笛長鳴、狂歡並參加豐富多彩的地方活動來慶祝新年；在加拿大，還有堆雪築牆，阻止妖魔鬼怪侵襲的風俗。當然，我們每年的此時此刻，也不要忘記對朋友、同事的新年問候！

(090)

1747	新年快樂！ **Happy New Year!**
替換	A happy New Year to you! May I wish you a happy New Year!
範例	A: Happy New Year! 新年快樂！ B: Thank you. The same to you! 謝謝，你也是！

1748	代我祝福…新年快樂！ **Happy New Year to...!**
替換	Give...my best wishes for the New Year!
範例	A: Happy New Year to your family! 代我祝福你們全家新年快樂！ B: Thank you. 謝謝。

1749	謝謝，你也是！ **Thanks. And you too!**
替換	Thanks. The same to you. Thanks, and that goes double for you! Thanks a lot. Same to you! Thank you. You too! Thank you. And the same to you! Thank you. And I wish you the same!
範例	A: A happy New Year to you! 新年快樂！ B: Thanks. And you too! 謝謝，你也是！

5.7 其他重要節日 Other Important Days

除了前面提到的節日外，英語系國家還流行其他重要的節日，以下分別做介紹：

十月三十一日為「萬聖節」，是美國非正式的節日。這一天孩子們都穿起奇裝異服，夜晚打著以南瓜做成的鬼臉燈，集合起來，挨家挨戶要禮物和糖果，不給就惡作劇。一般人們都要準備許多小禮物送給孩子們。

　　美國十一月的最後一個星期四是「感恩節」，是為了紀念當年逃避英國政府迫害而逃到新大陸創業的人所設立的節日，為了慶祝節日，人們舉行各式各樣的慶祝活動，傳統的節日食物有火雞和南瓜餡餅。

　　二月十四日為英美等國的情人節，這天大多數人會寄賀卡給情人，有的也會送給父母師友。

　　五月的第二個星期日為「母親節」，這天兒女會贈送賀卡或禮物給母親，以表達對母親的感恩。

● 情人節 Valentine's Day

1750	情人節快樂！ **Happy Valentine's Day!** (091)
範例	A: Happy Valentine's Day! 情人節快樂！ B: You're so sweet! 你人真體貼！
1751	做我的情人吧！ **Be my Valentine.**
範例	A: Be my Valentine. 做我的情人吧！ B: I'd love to. 我很樂意。

● 母親節 Mother's Day

1752	母親節快樂！ **Happy Mother's Day!**
範例	A: Happy Mother's Day! 母親節快樂！ B: Thank you. 謝謝。
1753	你真是我的好媽媽。 **Thanks for being such a good mom.**
範例	A: Thanks for being such a good mom. 你真是我的好媽媽。 B: How nice! 你真體貼。

● 萬聖節 Halloween

1754	不給糖就搗蛋！ **Trick or treat!**

範例 A: Trick or treat! 不給糖就搗蛋！
B: Oh, you little rascal! 哦，你這個小搗蛋！

提示 rascal ['ræskl] *n.*【幽默】淘氣鬼；小搗蛋

● 感恩節 Thanksgiving

1755	感恩節快樂！ **Happy Thanksgiving!**

範例 A: Happy Thanksgiving! 感恩節快樂！
B: The same to you! 你也是！

1756	我們吃南瓜派吧。 **Let's have pumpkin pie.**

範例 A: Let's have pumpkin pie. 我們吃南瓜派吧。
B: Wonderful! That's my favorite. 太棒了！我最喜歡吃了。

● 結婚紀念 Wedding Anniversaries

1757	結婚紀念日快樂！ **Happy anniversary!**

範例 A: Happy anniversary! 結婚紀念日快樂！
B: It's our twentieth anniversary. 這是我們二十周年紀念。

提示 anniversary [ˌænə'vɝsərɪ] *n.* 周年紀念

1758	謝謝你陪我共度人生。 **Thanks for sharing my life.**

範例 A: Thanks for sharing my life. 謝謝你陪我共度人生。
B: Thank you for twenty wonderful years. 謝謝你給了我美好的二十年。

第6章
商務溝通

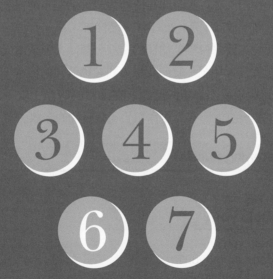

　　接待是商務工作的一部分，因而了解一些接待禮儀和接待技巧是十分重要的。比如：如果有幾位客人同時來訪，這時不能逐位詢問他們的名字，你只能先自我介紹，例如："I'm Susan Lee, Mr. Taylor's secretary." 客人們就會跟你一樣進行自我介紹。如果來訪者直接進入你的辦公室，在他出現的那一刻，你就應該立即招呼他，繼續忙你的事情是失禮的。即使你在打電話，也要點頭示意，或者用手勢來招呼來客。

　　從事商務接待工作，應該了解對待沒有預約來訪客人的處理原則。對於沒有預約，但又很熟悉的外來客人，應問明對方來訪的目的，然後再進行處理，或向上司稟報。對於有預約的陌生者來訪，你應該事先了解一下來訪者的情況，至少要記住名字。如果你和來訪者打招呼時說出對方的名字，會讓來訪者感到有種受重視的感覺。不應該讓有預約的客人久等，讓客人久等是十分失禮的。如果出現讓有預約的客人長時間等待的情況，切記不能慌亂，要以平靜的態度解釋耽擱的原因，並放下手中的工作來陪伴客人。

　　與客人在一起時，要保持輕鬆愉快的交談，談談天氣或當天的新聞等。只要有趣輕鬆的話題就行。切記不要涉及私人問題和公司的機密，還要注意不談及可能讓客人感到尷尬或不舒服的話題。在適當的時候，就一定要和客人聊天，這比起沉默不語，更能使客人對你和公司有良好的印象。

● 接待客人 Receiving Guests

1759	我能幫你嗎？ **Can I help you?**	092

替換	May I help you? What can I do for you? How may I help you?
範例	**A:** Can I help you? 我能幫你嗎？ **B:** I'm here to see Mr. Black. 我來這裡找布萊克先生。

1760	你貴姓？ **May I have your name?**

(替換) May I ask your name?
Your name, please?

(範例) **A:** I have an appointment with Mr. Black. 我和布萊克先生有約。
B: May I have your name? 你貴姓？

1761	你們有約嗎？ **Do you have an appointment?**

(替換) Did you make an appointment?

(範例) **A:** I'd like to see Mr. Brown. 我想見見布朗先生。
B: Do you have an appointment? 你們有約嗎？

1762	請問你找他有什麼事情？ **May I ask what you want to see him about?**

(替換) What do you want to see him about?
Could I ask what you want to see him about?

(範例) **A:** I'm here to see the manager.
　　 我來這裡見經理。
B: May I ask what you want to see him about?
　　 請問你找他有什麼事情？

1763	我來看看。 **Let me check.**

(替換) Let me look into it.
Let me find out.

(範例) **A:** Do you know where it is? 你知道它在哪裡嗎？
B: Let me check. 我來看看。

1764	我看看他在不在。 **Let me see if he's here.**

(替換) Let me check to see if he's available.
Let me see if he's in.

(範例) **A:** Is Mr. Black here? 布萊克先生在嗎？
B: Let me see if he's here. 我看看他在不在。

1765

這裡沒有姓…的人。
There's no Mr...here.

(替換) There's nobody here with that name.
There's nobody here with the name Mr...here.

(範例) **A:** There's no Mr. Wang here. 這裡沒有姓王的人。
B: Could you double-check? 請你再查一查好嗎？

1766

…先生準備見你。
Mr...is ready to see you.

(替換) Mr...will see you now.
Mr...is able to see you now.

(範例) **A:** Mr. Wang is ready to see you. 王先生準備見你。
B: Thank you very much. 非常謝謝。

1767

他一會兒就見你。
He'll be with you in a minute.

(替換) He'll be right with you.
He will see you soon.

(範例) **A:** I'm here to see Mr. Brown. 我來見布朗先生。
B: He'll be with you in a minute. 他一會兒就見你。

1768

我帶你看一看吧。
Let me show you around.

(替換) I'll give you a tour.
I'll show you where everything is.
Shall I show you around?

(範例) **A:** I'm new here. 我對這裡不熟悉。
B: Let me show you around. 我帶你看一看吧。

1769

乘…的電梯。
Take the elevator...

(替換) Get on the...elevator.
The elevator...will take you there.

(範例) **A:** How do I get there? 我怎樣才能到那裡呢？
B: Take the elevator there. 乘坐那裡的電梯。

1770	在…樓。 **It's on the...floor.**
(替換)	It's located/situated on the...floor.
(範例)	**A:** Where is his office? 他的辦公室在那裡？ **B:** It's on the fourth floor. 在四樓。

1771	下電梯，向右轉的第…個門。 **When you get off the elevator, it's the...door on the right.**
(替換)	Turn right when you get off the elevator. It's the...door.
(範例)	**A:** Where is his office? 他的辦公室在那裡？ **B:** When you get off the elevator, it's the third door on the right. 下電梯，向右轉的第三個門。

1772	有人要見你。 **Someone is here to see you.**
(替換)	You have a visitor. There's someone to see you. There's someone who wants to see you.
(範例)	**A:** Someone is here to see you. 有人要見你。 **B:** Please show him in. 請讓他進來。

1773	好了之後我們會告訴你的。 **We'll tell you when it's ready.**
(替換)	We'll let you know when it's time. We'll inform you when it's time.
(範例)	**A:** We'll tell you when it's ready. 好了之後我們會告訴你的。 **B:** Thank you very much. 非常感謝。

1774	請再給我幾分鐘好嗎？ **Could I have a few more minutes?**
(替換)	May I have more time? I need to ask for a few more minutes. Would you mind waiting a few minutes longer?

範例　A: Could I have a few more minutes? 請再給我幾分鐘好嗎？
B: I'll give you five more minutes. 我再給你五分鐘。

1775
我不確定。
I'm not sure.

替換　I'm not certain/positive.

範例　A: What time will he be back?他幾點回來？
B: I'm not sure. 我不確定。

1776
我會告訴他你到了。
I'll tell him that you're here.

替換　I'll let him know you're here.
I'll inform him that you've arrived.

範例　A: We have an appointment. 我們有約。
B: I'll tell him that you're here. 我會告訴他你到了。

● 說明某人不在 Stating that Someone Is Not In

1777
恐怕他不在辦公室。
I'm afraid he isn't in his office.

替換　I'm afraid he's out of the office now.

範例　A: Could I speak to Mr. Wang? 請王先生接電話好嗎？
B: I'm afraid he isn't in his office. 恐怕他不在辦公室。

1778
恐怕他今天不回來了。
I'm afraid he won't be back today.

替換　I'm afraid he's no longer available today.
I'm afraid he won't be in for the rest of the day.

範例　A: When will he be back? 他什麼時候回來？
B: I'm afraid he won't be back today. 恐怕他今天不回來了。

1779
他到…才能回來。
He won't be back till...

替換　He won't return until...
He will be back at...

範例 A: When will he be back? 他什麼時候回來？
B: He won't be back till 4:00. 他到四點才能回來。

1780 你換個時間再來好嗎？
Could you come back some other time?

替換 Could you return some other time?
Would you come back another time?

範例 A: Could you come back some other time? 你換個時間再來好嗎？
B: OK. 好吧。

1781 他現在很忙。
He's busy now.

替換 He isn't available now.
He's occupied.

範例 A: I'd like to see the person in charge. 我想見主管。
B: He's busy now. 他現在很忙。

提示 occupied ['ɑkjʊpaɪd] *adj.* 無空閒的

1782 他這週外出度假了。
He's on vacation this week.

替換 He's on holiday this week.
He's vacationing this week.

範例 A: I'd like to see Mr. Black, please. 我想見布萊克先生。
B: He's on vacation this week. 他這週外出度假了。

1783 聽說你可以提供細節情況。
I've been told that you could give me the details.

替換 You're the one to ask for details, I'm told.

範例 A: I've been told that you could give me the details.
聽說你可以提供細節情況。
B: I'd be happy to give them to you.
我很高興向你提供情況。

1784 讓別人來幫你可以嗎？
Can someone else help you?

範例 | **A:** I'd like to see the manager, please. 我想見經理。
B: Can someone else help you? 讓別人來幫你可以嗎？

● 與顧客應對 Dealing with Customers

1785
你是…公司的…先生嗎？
Are you Mr...of [*Company*]?

替換 | Are you the Mr...who works at...[*Company*]?
Are you...[*Company's*] Mr...?

範例 | **A:** Are you Mr. Black of Microsoft? 你是微軟公司的布萊克先生嗎？
B: That's right. 是的。

1786
我一直在等你。
I've been expecting you.

替換 | I've been waiting for you.
I've been looking forward to meeting you.

範例 | **A:** I'm Peter Brown of Microsoft. 我是微軟公司的彼得‧布朗。
B: I've been expecting you. 我一直在等你。

1787
讓你久等了。
Thank you for waiting.

替換 | I'm sorry to have kept you waiting.

範例 | **A:** Thank you for waiting. 讓你久等了。
B: Thank you for seeing me. 謝謝你見我。

1788
你久等了吧？
Have I kept you waiting long?

替換 | Have you been waiting long?
I hope you haven't been waiting too long.

範例 | **A:** Have I kept you waiting long? 你久等了吧？
B: No, I just got here. 不，我剛到。

1789
這邊走。
This way, please.

替換 | Right this way.
Come with me.

範例
A: Where's the meeting room? 會議室在那裡？
B: This way, please. 這邊走。

1790
請坐。
Please take a seat.

替換
Please have a seat.
Please sit down.
Please be seated.
Have a seat, please.

範例
A: Please take a seat. 請坐。
B: Thanks. 謝謝。

1791
請隨便。
Please make yourself at home.

替換
Please make yourself comfortable.
Please relax.

範例
A: Please make yourself at home. 請隨便。
B: Thank you. I'll have a seat. 謝謝。我會找個座位。

1792
這是最忙的季節。
This is our busiest season.

替換
We're busiest at this time of year.
This is our busiest time of the year.

範例
A: Everyone seems so busy. 每個人似乎都很忙。
B: Yes, this is our busiest season. 是呀，這是最忙的季節。

1793
你有名片嗎？
Do you have a business card?

替換
May I have your business card?
I'd like your business card, please.

範例
A: Do you have a business card? 你有名片嗎？
B: Sure, here you are. 有，給你。

1794
你為…公司效力嗎？
Are you working for...Company?

替換 So, you work for...Company?
Do you work at...Company?

範例 **A:** Are you working for Star Company? 你為明星公司效力嗎？
B: Yes, I'm in accounting. 是的，我在會計部。

提示 accounting [ə'kaʊntɪŋ] *n.* 會計學

1795
我很熟悉貴公司。
I'm familiar with your company.

替換 I've heard about your company.
Your company sounds familiar.

範例 **A:** I'm familiar with your company. 我很熟悉貴公司。
B: I'm happy to hear that. 很高興聽到你這樣說。

1796
我從⋯先生那裡聽到很多關於你的事。
I've heard about you from Mr...

替換 Mr...has told me about you.
I've heard from Mr...about you.
I've heard a lot about you from Mr. ...

範例 **A:** I've heard about you from Mr. Black.
　　我從布萊克先生那裡聽到很多關於你的事。
B: How so?
　　怎麼會呢？

1797
久仰大名。
I've heard your name many times.

替換 I've heard your name mentioned often.
Your name has been mentioned often.

範例 **A:** I've heard your name many times. 久仰大名。
B: I've heard of you, too. 我也久仰你的大名。

提示 mention ['mɛnʃən] *v.* 提及

1798
請你告訴我怎麼一回事好嗎？
Could you tell me what it's about?

替換 Could you let me know what it's about?
Could you give me some idea of what it's about?

範例 **A:** Could you tell me what it's about? 請你告訴我怎麼一回事好嗎？
B: Not now. 待會兒吧。

1799 以前我們見過，對不對？
We've met before, haven't we?

替換 Have we met before?
Do I know you?
Have we ever met?
Don't I know you from somewhere?

範例 **A:** We've met before, haven't we? 以前我們見過，對不對？
B: I'm not sure. What's your name? 我不確定。你尊姓大名？

1800 謝謝你遠道而來。
Thank you for coming all the way over here.

替換 Thank you for coming all this way.
Thank you for coming over.

範例 **A:** Thank you for coming all the way over here. 謝謝你遠道而來。
B: Not at all. 不客氣。

1801 我幫你叫輛計程車。
I'll call a taxi for you.

替換 Let me call you a cab.
I'll call a cab for you.

範例 **A:** I really should be getting back. 我真的要回去了。
B: I'll call a taxi for you. 我幫你叫輛計程車。

1802 我最好幫他叫輛計程車。
I'd better call him a taxi.

替換 Let me call him a taxi.
I'd better get him a cab.

範例 **A:** He needs a ride home. 他要坐車回家。
B: I'd better call him a taxi. 我最好幫他叫輛計程車。

1803 讓我開車送你。
Let me give you a ride.

替換 I'll take you there.
Let me drive you there.

範例 | A: I'm going to walk back to my hotel now. 我要步行回飯店了。
B: Let me give you a ride. 讓我開車送你。

1803　謝謝你來這裡。
Thank you for coming.

替換 | Thank you for coming today.
Thank you for being here today.

範例 | A: Thank you for coming. 謝謝你來這裡。
B: Thank you for having me. 感謝你的招待。

1805　代我問候…先生。
Say hello to Mr...

替換 | Say hello to Mr...for me.
Tell Mr...I said hello.
Give my regards to Mr...

範例 | A: Say hello to Mr. Black. 代我問候布萊克先生。
B: I will. 好的。

1806　請留下你的名片和型錄。
Please leave your card and brochures.

替換 | I'd like you to have your card and brochures.
May I have your card and brochures?

範例 | A: Are you interested in our products? 你對我們的產品有興趣嗎？
B: Please leave your card and brochures. 請留下你的名片和型錄。

提示 | brochure [broˈʃʊr] *n.* 型錄

● 其他應對 Other Ways of Dealing with Guests

1807　你要些茶嗎？
Would you like some tea?

替換 | Can I get you some tea?
Would you care for some tea?
How about some tea?
Would you like to have some tea?

範例 | A: Would you like some tea? 你要些茶嗎？
B: I'd prefer some coffee. 我比較想要咖啡。

1808

你要什麼口味的咖啡？
How would you like your coffee?

（替換）How do you take/want your coffee?

（範例）**A:** How would you like your coffee? 你要什麼口味的咖啡？
B: I take it black. 我要黑咖啡。

1809

需要加奶精或糖嗎？
Do you take cream or sugar?

（替換）Cream or sugar?
Would you like cream or sugar with your coffee?

（範例）**A:** Do you take cream or sugar? 需要加奶精或糖嗎？
B: One teaspoon of sugar, please. 請加一茶匙糖吧。

1810

請自便。
Help yourself.

（替換）Go ahead and take one.
You can help yourself.

（範例）**A:** Help yourself. 請自便。
B: Thanks a lot. 謝謝。

1811

這裡很冷，是不是？
It's cold in here, isn't it?

（替換）Do you find it cold in here?
It's chilly in here, isn't it?
Isn't it cold in here?

（範例）**A:** It's cold in here, isn't it? 這裡很冷，是不是？
B: Yes, it is. 是的。

（提示）chilly ['tʃɪlɪ] *adj.* 寒冷的

1812

等候的時候，請過目。
Please take a look at it while you're waiting.

（替換）Please look at it while you're waiting.
Please glance it over while you're waiting.

（範例）**A:** Is this the proposal?
這是提案嗎？

B: Yes. Please take a look at it while you're waiting.
　是的，等候的時候請過目。

提示　glance [glæns] *v.* 掃視；匆匆一看

1813　我想帶你參觀我們公司。
I'd like to show you around our company.

替換　Let me show you our company.
　I'd like to give you a tour of our company.

範例　**A:** I'd like to show you around our company. 我想帶你參觀我們公司。
　B: Please do. 麻煩你。

1814　能請你參觀我們的展覽室嗎？
Can I show you our showroom?

替換　Would you like to see our showroom?
　I'd like to show you our showroom.

範例　**A:** Can I show you our showroom? 能請你參觀我們的展覽室嗎？
　B: Thanks. 謝謝。

提示　showroom ['ʃoˌrum] *n.* （樣品的）陳列室；展覽室

1815　我會帶你去的。
I'll show you where it is.

替換　Let me show you where it is.

範例　**A:** Can I have a look at your showroom? 能看一下你的展覽室嗎？
　B: I'll show you where it is. 我會帶你去的。

1816　何不試試…？
Why don't you try...?

替換　How/What about trying...?

範例　**A:** I can't figure out where to stay. 我想不出要住哪裡。
　B: Why don't you try the Red Rose? 何不試試紅玫瑰飯店呢？

1817　對…你覺得如何？
What do you think of...?

替換　How do you feel about...?
　What's your opinion of...?

範例 | **A:** What do you think of our company? 對我們公司你覺得如何？
B: It's very impressive. 印象很好。

提示 | impressive [ɪmˈprɛsɪv] *adj.* 給人深刻印象的；令人欽佩的

1818 **目前你怎麼想？**
What do you think so far?

替換 | What's your opinion so far?

範例 | **A:** What do you think so far? 目前你怎麼想？
B: I've never seen anything like it. 我從未遇過類似的事情。

1819 **我與…先生只有一面之緣。**
I know Mr...only by sight.

替換 | I don't know much about Mr...
I hardly know Mr...

範例 | **A:** I know Mr. Black only by sight. 我與布萊克先生只有一面之緣。
B: I don't know much about him, either. 我對他也不太熟悉。

1820 **我聽過他的大名。**
I've heard of him by name.

替換 | I know him by name only.
I'm familiar with his name.

範例 | **A:** Do you know Mr. Wang? 你認識王先生嗎？
B: I've heard of him by name. 我聽過他的大名。

6.2 商務洽談 Business Discussion

　　商務工作中，自然會涉及到與外商進行談判，因此，我們有必要掌握用英語進行商務談判的知識和技能，學習一些商務談判的規則和禮儀。從事這項工作，應該了解商品的價格構成，知道公司的價格策略。接到客戶詢問價格後，要儘快報價。在回覆報價時，要特別注意其法律效力。在針對價格進行談判時，要把握好尺度；言語要友善，不能因為對方要價太高或還價太低，就挖苦對方。說明價格時，要說得慢些，一是為了讓對方聽清楚，避免不必要的誤解；二是為了避免說錯，造成不必要的麻煩。

　　包裝是商品銷售中不可缺少的一部分。應該具備一定的包裝知識，了解不同國家對商品包裝的要求，既要儘量滿足客戶對包裝的要求，又要儘量降低包裝費用。包裝大體上分為銷售包裝和運輸包裝；在對運輸包裝進行談判時，還應注意商品使用的運輸標誌。在勸說對方改變包裝時，應提出充分的理由，還應考慮包裝因素對價格的影響，要隨著包裝的改變適當地調整價格。

　　交貨的時間和方式對貿易的成敗有直接的影響，許多貿易糾紛也是由此而引發的。交貨的時間、地點、方式、費用等一定要具體、準確，像「送貨上門」之類的表達方式是不夠具體的；對外貿易應採用國際法規和慣例；談判時，應注意 shipment 和 delivery 的含義；出口時，應儘量爭取以 CIF（包括運費、保險費在內的到岸價格）成交；進口時，應儘量爭取以 FOB（船上交貨價格）成交。這樣，有利於降低成本。

　　當一筆貿易的全部細節都達成協定時，就需要雙方共同簽訂合約，這是商務談判中的最後也是最關鍵的一步。為了避免將來進行貿易的雙方發生誤會或爭議，凡是有關的細節內容，包括買賣條件、各種狀況條件等，都必須盡可能明確指出。

● 預算評估 About Budgets and Estimates

1821	你的預算是多少？ **What's your budget?**	093

(替換)	What price range do you have in mind? How big is your budget? What's the size of your budget? What price range are we talking about?
(範例)	**A:** What's your budget? 你的預算是多少？ **B:** It's pretty small. 很少。

1822	大約是多少錢？ **About how much will it cost?**

(替換)	Can you give me a ballpark figure? Do you know about how much?

範例　**A:** About how much will it cost? 大約是多少錢？
　　　B: $1,000, more or less. 大約一千美元。

提示　a ballpark figure【俚】大約正確的數字

1823　我手頭上有…美元。
　　　I have $...to work with.

替換　My budget is $...
　　　I can't go over $...

範例　**A:** I have $1,000 to work with. 我手頭上有一千美元。
　　　B: That's great! 太好了！

1824　最多…美元。
　　　No more than $...

替換　$...maximum.
　　　$...or less.

範例　**A:** How much would it be? 要價多少？
　　　B: No more than $5,000. 最多五千美元。

提示　maximum ['mæksəməm] *n.* 最大；最多

1825　我需要估價。
　　　I'd like to have an estimate.

替換　I need a ballpark figure on it.
　　　Could I have an estimate?
　　　Just give me an estimated figure.
　　　I just need an idea of how much.

範例　**A:** I'd like to have an estimate.
　　　　我需要估價。
　　　B: Please give me a few minutes to calculate it.
　　　　請給我幾分鐘計算。

提示　estimate ['ɛstə,met] *n. v.* 估價；估計
　　　calculate ['kælkjə,let] *v.* 計算

1826　我馬上好。
　　　I'll have it ready soon.

替換　I'll finish it soon.
　　　I'll be done soon.

範例 | A: When will the budget be ready? 預算何時完成？
B: I'll have it ready soon. 我馬上好。

1827

你要求單價⋯美元嗎？
Are you asking $...per unit?

替換 | Is your asking price $...per unit?
Does your proposal state $...per unit?

範例 | A: Are you asking $200 per unit? 你要求單價兩百美元嗎？
B: That's what it's worth. 它就值這個價。

1828

我們給單價⋯美元。
We can give you $...per unit.

替換 | We're willing to pay $...per unit.
We can go to $...per unit.

範例 | A: Is that price acceptable? 價格可以接受嗎？
B: Well, we can give you $100 per unit. 哦，我們給單價一百美元。

提示 | acceptable [ək'sɛptəbl] *adj.* 可接受的

1829

你的預算要求不太合理。
Your budget request is way out of line.

替換 | Your budget request is ridiculous.
You're asking for an unreasonable amount of money.

範例 | A: Your budget request is way out of line. 你的預算要求不太合理。
B: Not at all, sir. 先生，一點也不會不合理。

提示 | be out of line【美】不可以接受的
unreasonable [ʌn'riznəbl] *adj.* 不合理的；不切實際的

1830

這個價錢太誇張了。
I find this estimate hard to believe.

替換 | This estimate seems unreal to me.
This estimate doesn't seem feasible.

範例 | A: I find this estimate hard to believe. 這個價錢太誇張了。
B: I thought it was too high, too. 我也覺得這個價格太高了。

提示 | feasible ['fizəbl] *adj.* 可行的；切實可行的

● 商討價格 About Price

1831 價格是多少？
What does it cost?

(替換) How much does it cost?
Could you tell me how much it is?
How much (money) is it?

(範例) **A:** It's on sale this week. 這星期大減價。
B: What does it cost? 價格是多少？

1832 租金是多少？
How much is the rent?

(替換) What's the rent?
How much does it rent for?

(範例) **A:** How much is the rent? 租金是多少？
B: $500 a month. 每月五百美元。

1833 這個多少錢？
How much is this?

(替換) How much are you asking for this?
What is your asking price for this?

(範例) **A:** How much is this? 這個多少錢？
B: Thirty dollars. 三十美元。

1834 這個價格含稅嗎？
Does that price include tax?

(替換) Is tax included?
Is tax already included in the price?

(範例) **A:** Does that price include tax? 這個價格含稅嗎？
B: Yes, 5%. 是的，含百分之五的稅。

1835 批發價是多少？
What does it cost you wholesale?

(替換) What's the wholesale price?
How much do you pay wholesale?

範例 A: What does it cost you wholesale? 批發價是多少？
B: $500. 五百美元。

提示 wholesale ['hol͵sel] *adj.* 批發的 *adv.* 批發地

1836
零售價是多少？
What's the retail price?

替換 What does it go for retail?
How much does it sell for retail?

範例 A: That is the wholesale price. 這是批發價。
B: What's the retail price? 零售價是多少？

提示 retail ['ritel] *n.* 零售 *adj.* 零售的

1837
請出價。
Let's hear your offer.

替換 Make us an offer.
What's it worth to you?

範例 A: We're very interested. 我們非常有興趣。
B: Let's hear your offer. 請出價。

1838
得看價錢成本。
It depends on the cost.

替換 That depends on the price.

範例 A: Are you interested? 有興趣嗎？
B: It depends on the cost. 得看價錢成本。

1839
你開價…美元，是嗎？
You're asking $..., right?

替換 Your offering price is..., right?
You are offering it to us at..., right?
The price you're offering it at is..., right?
The price you're requesting is..., right?

範例 A: You're asking $5,000, right? 你開價五千美元，是嗎？
B: Yes, but that's not including tax. 是的，是未稅價。

1840
大約…美元。
Around $...

418

替換 $..., give or take.
Close to $...
In the neighborhood of $...

範例 **A:** What's the bottom line? 底價是多少？
B: Around $500. 大約五百美元。

1841 我們以每個…美元出售。
We'll sell them for...dollars each.

替換 We'll sell them for...dollars apiece.
You can have them for...dollars apiece.

範例 **A:** We'll sell them for ten dollars each. 我們以每個十美元出售。
B: Would you take eight dollars? 八塊美元你接受嗎？

1842 每件…美元怎麼樣？
How about $...apiece?

替換 I'm offering them to you at $...apiece.
You can have them for $...apiece.

範例 **A:** How much are they? 多少錢？
B: How about $10 apiece? 每件十美元怎麼樣？

1843 含稅價為…美元。
That'll be $...including tax.

替換 It comes to...dollars and...cents, including tax.
The total is $...with tax included.

範例 **A:** That'll be $10 including tax. 含稅價為十美元。
B: That's really a good price. 價格真的不錯。

1844 價格有高有低。
There's quite a range of prices.

替換 There's a wide range of prices.
The prices vary greatly.

範例 **A:** There's quite a range of prices. 價格有高有低。
B: What is the lowest price? 最底價是多少？

1845 標價為…美元。
The price tag shows $...

替換　The sticker price is $...
　　　The sticker indicates $...

範例　A: How much is it? 價格爲多少？
　　　B: The price tag shows $100. 標價爲一百美元。

1846

按時價，這…價值…美元。
At its current price, this...is worth...dollars.

替換　This...costs...dollars today/currently.
　　　This...is valued at...dollars today.

範例　A: At its current price, this piece of jewelery is worth ten thousand dollars. 按時價，這珠寶價值一萬美元。
　　　B: That's really expensive. 眞貴。

1847

零售價為…美元。
The retail price is $...

替換　The consumer price is $...
　　　The price for the consumer is $...

範例　A: The retail price is $100. 零售價爲一百美元。
　　　B: It's much higher than the wholesale price. 比批發價高很多呀。

提示　consumer [kən'sjumɚ] n. 消費者

1848

今天全部打折。
Everything is on sale today.

替換　Everything is marked down today.
　　　For today, everything is on sale.

範例　A: These prices are fairly low. 這些價錢很低。
　　　B: Yes, everything is on sale today. 是的，今天全部打折。

1849

這商品今日特價。
This is on sale today.

替換　This is our special for today.
　　　This is currently on sale.

範例　A: This is on sale today. 這商品今日特價。
　　　B: I'll take it. 我買了。

1850	我們的價格無人可比。 **Nobody can beat our price.**

替換	You won't find better prices. Our prices can't be matched. Our price is unbeatable. Our price is the lowest out there.
範例	A: Nobody can beat our price. 我們的價格無人可比。 B: That's good for you. 那很好。
提示	unbeatable [ʌnˈbitəbḷ] *adj.* 無敵的；打不垮的

1851	價格非常好。 **What a great price!**

替換	What a bargain/deal! What a great buy!
範例	A: What a great price! 價格非常好。 B: Why not order more? 要不多買一些？

1852	很划算。 **This is a real bargain.**

替換	This is a good buy/deal.
範例	A: This is a real bargain. 很划算。 B: The price is reasonable. 價格很合理。

1853	價格很好。 **The prices are great.**

替換	The prices are really attractive. We're impressed with the prices. The prices are very appealing.
範例	A: We thought you'd like them. 我們認為你會喜歡。 B: Well, the prices are great. 嗯，價格很好。

1854	我覺得價格很公道。 **I think the price is reasonable.**

替換	The price is right. This product is reasonably priced.

I think the price is in the ballpark.
This product is priced within reason.
This product has a reasonable price.

範例 A: It's not expensive, is it? 價格不高，是吧？
B: Well, I think the price is reasonable. 嗯，我覺得價格很公道。

1855
價格很公道。
It's very reasonable.

替換 It's inexpensive.
It doesn't cost much.
It isn't very costly.

範例 A: Is it expensive? 貴嗎？
B: No. It's very reasonable. 不貴，價格很公道。

1856
太貴了。
That's expensive.

替換 That's a lot of money.
That's too/pretty high.

範例 A: It's $100. 一百美元。
B: That's expensive. 太貴了。

1857
那太昂貴了。
That's much too expensive.

替換 That's way out of line.
That's way too much money.
That seems somewhat high.

範例 A: 100 dollars apiece. 每件一百美元。
B: That's much too expensive. 那太昂貴了。

1858
這是行情價。
That's the market price.

替換 That's what the going rate is.
That's the going rate here.
That's the way it is.

範例 A: It seems a little high to me. 對我而言價格有點兒太高。
B: That's the market price. 這是行情價。

1859
這是受到匯率影響。
It's because of the exchange rate.

(替換) It was caused by the exchange rate.
The exchange rate caused it.

(範例) A: The price has changed a lot. 價格波動很大。
B: It's because of the exchange rate. 這是受到匯率影響。

● 討價還價 Bargaining

1860
我們可以打九折。
We can give you 10% off.

(替換) We give a 10% discount.
It's discounted 10%.
We sell it at 10% off.
We'd like to offer you a 10% discount.
We can offer you a 10% discount.

(範例) A: We can give you 10% off. 我們可以打九折。
B: I want a 15% discount. 我希望是八五折。

1861
你的價錢可以低一點嗎？
Would you lower the price?

(替換) Would you give me a discount?
Would you make it cheaper?
Would you give me a better price?
Could I have a discount?

(範例) A: Would you lower the price? 你的價錢可以低一點嗎？
B: I'll see what I can do. 讓我想一下。

1862
我希望你能打個折扣。
I was planning to ask you for a reduction.

(替換) I wanted to ask you for a reduction.
I meant to ask you for a discount.

(範例) A: I was planning to ask you for a reduction. 我希望你能打個折扣。
B: How much did you have in mind? 你希望折扣是多少？

(提示) reduction [rɪ'dʌkʃən] *n.* 降低

1863

付現有折扣嗎？
Can you give me a discount if I pay cash?

(替換) Can you make it cheaper if I pay cash?
Will you give me a better price if I pay cash?

(範例) **A:** Can you give me a discount if I pay cash? 付現有折扣嗎？
B: No problem. 沒問題。

1864

大量訂購有折扣嗎？
Can you give us a volume discount?

(替換) Would you consider a volume discount?
Do we get a discount for buying large quantities?

(範例) **A:** Can you give us a volume discount? 大量訂購有折扣嗎？
B: I'm sorry. The price is the same. 對不起，價格一樣。

(提示) quantity ['kwɑntətɪ] *n.* 數量

1865

這產品定價過高。
The price is too high for this product.

(替換) This product is priced too high.
The product is overpriced.

(範例) **A:** The price is too high for this product. 這產品定價過高。
B: We can't go much lower. 我們無法降價。

1866

你可以再便宜點。
You can make it cheaper than that.

(替換) You can do better than that.
You can go lower than that.

(範例) **A:** I'll sell it to you for $200. 我賣你兩百美元。
B: You can make it cheaper than that. 你可以再便宜點。

1867

你的價錢可以降低多少？
How much can you knock off the price?

(替換) What discount can you offer us?

(範例) **A:** How much can you knock off the price? 你的價錢可以降低多少？
B: 20%. 可以打八折。

1868	…美元可以嗎？ **How about...dollars?**
(替換)	Would you take...dollars? Would it be possible to sell it to us for...? Would you let me pay...dollars for it? Would you accept...dollars for it? Would you consider selling it to us for $...?
(範例)	**A:** We're asking 70 dollars. 我們要求的價錢爲七十美元。 **B:** How about 50 dollars? 五十美元可以嗎？

1869	如果你要價…美元，我們就成交。 **I'll buy it from you for $...**
(替換)	I'll buy it if you'll give it to me for $... I'll buy it if it's $...
(範例)	**A:** I'll buy it from you for $30. 如果你要價三十美元，我們就成交。 **B:** I'm sorry, $50 is as low as I can go. 十分抱歉，最低價爲五十美元。

1870	最高價爲…美元。 **No more than $...**
(替換)	We can't go higher than $... $...is our limit. $...is as far as we can go.
(範例)	**A:** What's your bottom line? 你的底價是多少？ **B:** No more than $1,000. 最高價爲一千美元。

1871	價格是主要問題嗎？ **Are the prices what you're worried about?**
(替換)	Are the prices the main problem? Are the prices troublesome?
(範例)	**A:** Are the prices what you're worried about? 價格是主要問題嗎？ **B:** Yes. 是的。

1872	我們可以降價一些。 **We could come down a little.**
(替換)	We could lower/reduce the price.

範例 A: What can you do for us? 你有何辦法？
B: We could come down a little. 我們可以降價一些。

1873 如果你能買…以上，就有…折扣。
You'll get...% off if you buy...or more.

替換 There'll be a...% discount on orders over...units.
If you buy...or more, you'll get a...% discount.
We offer a...% discount on orders over...
We give a...% discount for purchases of...and up.

範例 A: You'll get 10% off if you buy 1,000 or more.
如果你能買一千份以上，就有百分之十的折扣。
B: We'd like 1,200 units, please.
請給我們一千兩百份。

提示 purchase ['pɜ˞tʃəs] *n.* 買；購買

1874 只要你買…就可以。
It's OK if you buy...

替換 That's fine if you buy...
As long as you buy...

範例 A: Give us a bulk rate, will you? 有團體優惠嗎？
B: It's OK if you buy 1,000. 只要你買一千個就可以。

提示 bulk [bʌlk] *adj.* 大量的；大批的

1875 我們可以給予…優惠。
We can offer a better price on...

替換 We can mark down on...

範例 A: We can offer a better price on that model.
我們可以給予那型號優惠。
B: Then we have a deal.
那就成交。

1876 我們已經給你折扣了。
We already gave you a discount.

替換 We just gave you a price cut.
We just gave you a deal.

範例　A: Can you give me a better deal? 你能再給點優惠嗎？
B: We already gave you a discount. 我們已經給你折扣了。

1877　我們要求再降價。
We have to ask for another price reduction.

範例　A: We have to ask for another price reduction. 我們要求再降價。
B: That won't go over well. 那可不行。

1878　即使一點也可以。
Even a small amount would help.

替換　Even one percent would help.
1% would work.

範例　A: Did you have an amount in mind? 你想要多少？
B: Even a small amount would help. 即使一點也可以。

1879　百分之…的折扣就可以。
A...percent discount would help.

替換　We're asking for...% off current prices.
We need a...percent discount.

範例　A: A five percent discount would help. 百分之五的折扣就可以。
B: We can't go that far. 我們不能給那麼多優惠。

1880　百分之…的折扣對我們不利。
...percent would hurt us.

替換　...percent would make our business suffer.

範例　A: Five percent would hurt us. 百分之五的折扣對我們不利。
B: What about four percent? 那百分之四怎麼樣？

1881　這是我們的底價。
That's our final price.

替換　That's our final offer.
We can't go any lower than this.
This is the lowest we can go.
That's as low as we can go.
That's our limit.

範例　A: I hope you will reconsider. 希望你能再考慮一下。
B: That's our final price. 這是我們的底價。

1882	價格是固定的。 **We have a fixed price.**

替換	Our price is fixed.
範例	**A:** We have a fixed price. 價格是固定的。 **B:** You mean there's no room for negotiation? 你的意思是沒得商量囉？
提示	negotiation [nɪ͵goʃɪ'eʃən] *n.* 談判；磋商

1883	我們如果以成本價出售，就沒有利潤了。 **We won't make a profit if we sell it at cost.**

替換	We can't give it to you at cost.
範例	**A:** I was hoping for a better discount than that. 我希望價格再折扣一些。 **B:** We won't make a profit if we sell it at cost. 我們如果以成本價出售，就沒有利潤了。

1884	我們無法給你打八折。 **We can't give you a 20% discount.**

替換	A 20% discount is out of the question. A 20% discount is way too much.
範例	**A:** We can't give you a 20% discount. 我們無法給你打八折。 **B:** What about 10%? 那麼九折呢？

1885	不能再降價了。 **You can forget about another cut.**

替換	Another cut is out of the question.
範例	**A:** Could you lower the price? 價格可以再低些嗎？ **B:** You can forget about another cut. 不能再降價了。

1886	可以接受我們的付款條件嗎？ **Can you accept our payment terms?**

替換	Are our payment terms acceptable? Do you find our payment terms acceptable?
範例	**A:** Can you accept our payment terms? 可以接受我們的付款條件嗎？ **B:** They are a little too rigid. 條款訂得太死了些。
提示	rigid ['rɪdʒɪd] *adj.* 死板的；嚴苛的

1887	它們有天壤之別。 **They're totally different.**

(替換) They're as different as night and day.

(範例) **A:** Their selling prices are the same. 它們的售價完全一樣。
B: But they're totally different. 但是它們有天壤之別。

● 商談服務 About Service

1888	可以有折扣嗎？ **Can I have a discount?**

(替換) Would you give me a good deal?
Could you give me a deal?

(範例) **A:** Can I have a discount? 可以有折扣嗎？
B: We can't afford it. 我們無法做到。

1889	再追加一些吧。 **Let's add a few things.**

(替換) Let's add some extras.
Let's give them more incentives.

(範例) **A:** Let's add a few things. 再追加一些吧。
B: Great idea. 好主意。

(提示) incentive [ɪnˈsɛntɪv] *n.* 獎勵；鼓勵

1890	買三送一。 **Buy three, get one free.**

(替換) If you buy three, you'll get one free.
We offer one free with each purchase of three.

(範例) **A:** Buy three, get one free. 買三送一。
B: What a deal! 真划算！

1891	喜歡就買下吧。 **Please take it if you like it.**

(替換) You may have it if you like it.
Would you like to have it?

範例 A: I love it. 我太喜歡了。
B: Please take it if you like it. 喜歡就買下吧。

1892 可以拿一個嗎？
May I take one?

替換 May I have one?

範例 A: May I take one? 可以拿一個嗎？
B: Sure, it's free. 當然可以，是免費的。

1893 我們提供免費送貨。
We're offering free shipping now.

替換 We're giving free shipping now.
We have free shipping now.

範例 A: How much will the shipping cost be? 運費是多少？
B: We're offering free shipping now. 我們提供免費送貨。

1894 漲幅是多少？
What's the markup?

替換 Would you tell me the markup?
How much markup does it have?

範例 A: What's the markup? 漲幅是多少？
B: Seven percent. 百分之七。

1895 別擔心，公司會付帳的。
Don't worry. The company is paying.

替換 Don't worry. It's a company expense.
Don't worry about it. The company will pick up the bill.

範例 A: This will cost me a fortune. 這會花我很多錢。
B: Don't worry. The company is paying. 別擔心，公司會付帳的。

1896 我們不提供此項服務。
We don't offer that kind of service.

替換 We don't have that kind of service available.

範例 A: Do you have free shipping? 你提供免費送貨嗎？
B: We don't offer that kind of service. 我們不提供此項服務。

1897
你想多了解一些我們的服務項目嗎？
Would you like to know more about our services?

(替換)
Would you like some information about our services?
Can I inform you about our services?

(範例)
A: Would you like to know more about our services?
你想多了解一些我們的服務項目嗎？
B: Yes, what do you provide for long-term customers?
好，你們對長期顧客提供何種服務？

1898
你是否對此項服務感興趣？
Is this a service you'd be interested in?

(替換)
Are you interested in this kind of service?

(範例)
A: Is this a service you'd be interested in?
你是否對此項服務感興趣？
B: Maybe. Could you tell me more about it?
大概吧，可否請你提供更詳細的資料？

1899
我們為幾家大公司提供服務。
We provide service to some major companies.

(替換)
Several major companies use our service.

(範例)
A: We provide service to some major companies.
我們為幾家大公司提供服務。
B: You must be very successful.
你們一定做得很好。

1900
客戶對我們的服務十分滿意。
Our clients are pleased with our service.

(替換)
Our service has been well-received by our clients.
Our clients have no complaints with our service.

(範例)
A: Our clients are pleased with our service.
客戶對我們的服務十分滿意。
B: You should consider expanding.
你們可以考慮擴大規模。

1901
保固期是多久？
What warranties do you offer?

431

替換 | What are the warranties that you offer?
What type of warranties do you offer?

範例 | **A:** What warranties do you offer? 保固期是多久？
B: We offer five-year warranties. 我們提供五年保固。

提示 | warranty ['wɔrəntɪ] *n.* 保固

1902　我們提供免費的…維修。
We offer free repairs on...

替換 | We repair...free of charge.
We repair .. at no cost.

範例 | **A:** What's the cost for repairs? 維修費是多少？
B: We offer free repairs on computers. 我們提供免費的電腦維修。

● 確認事宜 Making Sure

1903　可以立即給我答覆嗎？
Can you give us your answer now?

替換 | Can you answer now?

範例 | **A:** Can you give us your answer now? 可以立即給我答覆嗎？
B: How about Friday? 星期五怎麼樣？

1904　希望你在…前答覆。
We'd like to hear from you by...

替換 | Could we hear from you by...?
Please be in touch by...

範例 | **A:** We'd like to hear from you by Friday. 希望你在星期五前答覆。
B: No problem. 沒問題。

1905　何時可以得到答覆？
When can we have an answer?

替換 | When can we expect an answer?
When can you get back to us?
When will we know?

範例 | **A:** When can we have an answer? 何時可以得到答覆？
B: By Friday. 星期五之前。

1906

給我一些時間考慮。
Give me a while to work it out.

(替換) Give me some time.
I need some time.

(範例) **A:** I need an answer. 我需要你的答覆。
B: Give me a while to work it out. 給我一些時間考慮。

1907

這次我們想保留選擇權。
We want to keep our options open at this time.

(替換) We'd like to keep our options open for now.
We'd prefer to keep our options open for now.

(範例) **A:** We want to keep our options open at this time.
這次我們想保留選擇權。
B: Let me know if you change your mind.
如果有變動，請讓我們知道。

(提示) option ['ɑpʃən] *n.* 選擇權；選項

1908

你需要立即獲得答覆嗎？
Do you need an answer right away?

(替換) Do you need my answer right now?
Do I have to answer you now?

(範例) **A:** Do you need an answer right away? 你需要立即獲得答覆嗎？
B: The sooner, the better. 愈快愈好。

1909

稍後再跟你談。
I'll get back to you about it later.

(替換) I'll have to get back to you later.

(範例) **A:** I'll get back to you about it later. 稍後再跟你談。
B: I'll be waiting for your response. 我等你的答覆。

(提示) response [rɪ'spɑns] *n.* 回答；回應

1910

我得先和總公司商討一下。
I must talk it over with the head office first.

(替換) I'll have to discuss it with the head office first.
I'll have to check with the head office first.

範例
A: I must talk it over with the head office first.
我得先和總公司商討一下。
B: When can we expect an answer?
何時可以得到你的答覆？

1911
我從不倉促做決定。
I never make snap decisions.

替換
I always take my time deciding things.
I never hurry when making decisions.

範例
A: Have you made up your mind yet? 你決定了嗎？
B: I never make snap decisions. 我從不倉促做決定。

提示
snap [snæp] *adj.* 突然的；迅速的

1912
你要再考慮嗎？
Would you consider changing your mind?

替換
Would you reconsider your decision?
Would you give your decision some more thought?

範例
A: Would you consider changing your mind? 你要再考慮嗎？
B: Sorry, I've made up my mind. 對不起，我已經決定了。

1913
請再考慮你的付款條件。
Please think about your payment terms.

替換
Please reconsider your payment terms.

範例
A: Please think about your payment terms. 請再考慮你的付款條件。
B: Let me talk to my boss about it. 我得與老闆商量一下。

1914
讓我們雙方都再考慮一下。
Let's both think it over again.

替換
Let's both give that more thought.

範例
A: Let's both think it over again. 讓我們雙方都再考慮一下。
B: I think that would be best. 那最好了。

1915
我們等不了那麼久。
That's too long to wait.

替換
We can't wait that long.

範例 | **A:** How about Monday? 星期一怎麼樣？
B: That's too long to wait. 我們等不了那麼久。

1916 感覺怎麼樣？
How did you like it?

替換 | How was it?
Did you like it?

範例 | **A:** How did you like it? 感覺怎麼樣？
B: It was great! 非常好。

1917 你決定了嗎？
Have you decided yet?

替換 | Have you decided on it?
Have you made up your mind?
Have you come to a decision?

範例 | **A:** Have you decided yet? 你決定了嗎？
B: Not yet. 還沒有。

1918 我已經重新考慮過了。
I've reconsidered my position.

替換 | I've thought it over again.
I've given it some more thought.

範例 | **A:** I've reconsidered my position. 我已經重新考慮過了。
B: I'm glad to hear that. 那太好了。

1919 它們不符合我們的標準。
They're not up to our standards.

替換 | They don't meet our standards.
The quality isn't good enough.
The quality is substandard for us.
We're disappointed with the quality of the goods.

範例 | **A:** They're not up to our standards.
它們不符合我們的標準。
B: We'll make all the necessary improvements.
我們會做必要的改進。

提示 | substandard [sʌbˈstændɚd] *adj.* 標準以下的

1920	我們各讓一步好嗎？ **Can we each give in a little?**

替換　How about some give-and-take then?

範例　A: Can we each give in a little? 我們各讓一步好嗎？
　　　B: OK. 好的。

1921	…是答覆的最後期限。 **...is the deadline for an answer.**

替換　They need an answer by...

範例　A: When do they want an answer? 什麼時候需要答覆？
　　　B: Friday is the deadline for an answer. 星期五是答覆的最後期限。

1922	價格我還沒同意呢！ **I haven't agreed on the price yet.**

替換　The price isn't set yet.

範例　A: So, you've decided to buy the machine? 那你決定買這台機器吧？
　　　B: I haven't agreed on the price yet. 價格我還沒同意呢。

● 達成協定或商談破裂
Reaching an Agreement or Negotiations Breaking Down

1923	不會有問題的。 **Everything will be fine.**

替換　There shouldn't be any problems.
　　　There should be no problem.

範例　A: Only a five-year warranty? 只有五年的保固期？
　　　B: Don't worry. Everything will be fine. 別擔心。不會有問題的。

1924	我們各讓一步好嗎？ **Can we meet halfway?**

替換　Why don't we meet halfway on this?
　　　How about splitting the difference?
　　　How about a compromise?
　　　Why don't we compromise on this?
　　　Let's find a happy medium.

範例　A: We can't agree to that. 我們無法同意。
　　　B: Can we meet halfway? 我們各讓一步好嗎？

提示　compromise [ˈkɑmprəˌmaɪz] *n. v.* 妥協；折中

1925　你有意購買嗎？
Would you like to buy it?

替換　Would you like to take/purchase it?

範例　A: This is an excellent product. 這個產品不錯。
　　　B: Would you like to buy it? 你有意購買嗎？

1926　我們同意你出的價格。
We'll take your offer.

替換　We accept your offer.
　　　We'll agree to your offer.

範例　A: We'll take your offer. 我們同意你出的價格。
　　　B: We're very happy to hear that. 很高興聽到你這樣說。

1927　我會接受你的要價。
I'll take your kind offer.

替換　I'll accept your kind offer.
　　　I'll take your generous offer.
　　　It sounds like an offer I can accept.

範例　A: I'll take your kind offer. 我會接受你的要價。
　　　B: I'm glad we've reached an agreement. 很高興我們達成一致。

1928　我們完全達成共識。
We're in complete agreement.

替換　We've arrived at a satisfactory agreement.
　　　We're in total agreement.

範例　A: We're in complete agreement. 我們完全達成共識。
　　　B: Well, let's get started. 好的，讓我們開始合作吧。

1929　感謝你的訂購。
Thank you for your order.

替換　I appreciate your business.

範例 | **A:** I'd like to order your products. 我想訂購你的產品。
| **B:** Thank you for your order. 感謝你的訂購。

1930　成交！
It's a deal!

替換 | You got a deal!
| Let's shake on it!

範例 | **A:** Is it a deal? 可以成交嗎？
| **B:** It's a deal! 成交！

提示 | shake on it【口】握手為定

1931　好的，我接受。
Okay, okay.

替換 | I give up.
| You win.
| I'll accept your offer.

範例 | **A:** Okay, okay. 好的，我接受。
| **B:** I knew you'd see it my way. 我知道你一定會同意我的看法。

1932　成交吧！
Let's shake hands on it.

替換 | Why don't we shake on it?
| Shall we shake on it?
| Let's close the deal.
| Let's shake on it.

範例 | **A:** It seems like we have a deal. 似乎可以成交了。
| **B:** Let's shake hands on it. 成交吧！

1933　我們能成交嗎？
Should we shake on it?

替換 | Do we have an agreement?

範例 | **A:** Should we shake on it? 我們能成交嗎？
| **B:** Of course. 那當然。

1934　我們有獨家經銷權。
We have exclusive rights.

| 替換 | It's an exclusive agreement. |

| 範例 | **A:** What type of agreement do you have? 你們有哪種合約？
B: We have exclusive rights. 我們有獨家經銷權。 |

| 提示 | exclusive [ɪk'sklusɪv] *adj.* 獨占的；唯一的 |

1935 你能擬一份合約給我嗎？
Can you write up a contract for me?

| 替換 | Could you prepare a contract?
Would you put together a contract? |

| 範例 | **A:** Can you write up a contract for me?
你能擬一份合約給我嗎？
B: Certainly. I'll have it ready by tomorrow, OK?
當然可以，我明天之前會準備好，好嗎？ |

1936 請仔細閱讀這份合約。
Please read the contract carefully.

| 替換 | Please make sure you read the contract carefully. |

| 範例 | **A:** Please read the contract carefully. 請仔細閱讀這份合約。
B: I certainly will. 我一定會的。 |

1937 我們會書面確認你的訂單。
Let's confirm your order in writing.

| 替換 | I'd like to confirm your order in writing.
I'll send you written confirmation of your order. |

| 範例 | **A:** That's all I need. 這是全部所需資料。
B: Let's confirm your order in writing. 我們會書面確認你的訂單。 |

| 提示 | confirmation [ˌkɑnfɚ'meʃən] *n.* 確認；批准 |

1938 你能現在簽字嗎？
Can you sign it now?

| 替換 | Are you ready/prepared to sign it? |

| 範例 | **A:** Can you sign it now? 你能現在簽字嗎？
B: Yes, right away. 可以，馬上就簽。 |

1939 請在虛線處簽字。
Sign on the dotted line, please.

範例
A: Anything else? 還有什麼？
B: Sign on the dotted line, please. 請在虛線處簽字。

1940
請把表格填好，再簽名。
Please complete this form and sign it.

替換
Please fill out this form and sign it.
Complete and sign this form, please.

範例
A: Please complete this form and sign it. 請把表格填好，再簽名。
B: Could you show me how? 請告訴我如何填寫好嗎？

1941
如果撤銷合約，後果會怎樣？
What will happen if we break the contract?

替換
What happens if we break the contract?
What happens if the contract is broken?

範例
A: What will happen if we break the contract?
　　如果撤銷合約，後果會怎樣？
B: You'll have to pay financial compensation.
　　你必須賠償。

提示
financial [faɪˈnænʃəl] *adj.* 財政的；金融的
compensation [ˌkɑmpənˈseʃən] *n.* 賠償

1942
我們改採投標制。
We're changing over to a bidding system.

替換
We're adopting a bidding system.

範例
A: How do you assign contracts? 你們如何給合約？
B: We're changing over to a bidding system. 我們改採投標制度。

1943
這是最好的價格了。
We cannot offer you a better deal.

替換
We cannot change/alter our offer.
We are not able to change our offer.

範例
A: What about an additional 10% off? 再降價百分之十吧？
B: We cannot offer you a better deal. 這是最好的價格了。

提示
alter [ˈɔltɚ] *v.* 改變
additional [əˈdɪʃənl] *adj.* 另外的；額外的

| 1944 | 此項不包含在内。
That isn't included. |

(替換) That's separate.
That's charged separately.

(範例) **A:** Is this part of the agreement? 合約中包含此項嗎？
B: That isn't included. 此項不包含在內。

| 1945 | 我認為你價錢過高。
I think you charge too much. |

(替換) Your prices are too high.
The prices you charge are unreasonable.

(範例) **A:** I think you charge too much. 我認爲你價錢過高。
B: Well, we have to make a living, too. 可是，我們也得過活呀。

● 商討付款 About Payment

| 1946 | 你何時能付款？
When can you pay us? |

(替換) When can you arrange payment?
When will we get paid?

(範例) **A:** When can you pay us? 你何時能付款？
B: Within two months. 兩個月之內。

| 1947 | 我們會立即付款的。
We'll remit the payment promptly. |

(範例) **A:** Payment is due within a month of delivery. 貨到一個月內付款。
B: We'll remit the payment promptly. 我們會立即付款的。

(提示) remit [rɪ'mɪt] v. 匯款
promptly ['prɑmptlɪ] adv. 迅速地

| 1948 | 我們會在每個月月底寄帳單給你。
We'll send you a bill at the end of each month. |

(替換) You'll get a bill at the end of each month.

(範例) **A:** We'll send you a bill at the end of each month.
我們會在每個月月底寄帳單給你。

B: I'd prefer paying for a year up front.
　　我希望年度預付。

提示　up front [ʌpˈfrʌnt] *adv.* 在前面；在最前面

1949　我希望一次付清，而不是每個月分期付款。
I'd like to make one payment instead of paying each month.

範例　**A:** I'd like to make one payment instead of paying each month.
　　我希望一次付清，而不是每個月分期付款。
B: I'd like to pay in full.
　　我也希望全部付清。

1950　我們希望能一次付清。
We want it paid in one lump sum.

替換　We want it in one payment.
　　We don't want you to pay in installments.

範例　**A:** How would you like me to pay? 你希望我如何付款呢？
B: We want it paid in one lump sum. 我們希望能一次付清。

提示　installment [ɪnˈstɔlmənt] *n.* 分期付款

1951　付現還是刷卡？
Will that be cash or charge?

替換　Cash or charge?
　　Would you like to pay by cash or charge?
　　Will you be paying by cash or credit card?

範例　**A:** Will that be cash or charge? 付現還是刷卡？
B: I'll put it on my credit card. 我用信用卡。

1952　你是指利率嗎？
Are you talking about the interest rate?

替換　Do you mean the percentage rate?
　　Are you referring to the loan interest rate?
　　Do you mean the amount of interest on the loan?

範例　**A:** Are you talking about the interest rate? 你是指利率嗎？
B: No, the payment schedule. 不，我指付款期限。

442

1953 我們想要以現金預付。
We'd like cash up front.

(替換) Please pay in cash up front.
We'd like the money up front, in cash.

(範例) A: How would you prefer payment? 你預備如何付款？
B: We'd like cash up front. 我們想要以現金預付。

1954 我需要付訂金嗎？
Do I need to make a deposit?

(替換) Do you require a deposit?
Is there a deposit required?

(範例) A: Do I need to make a deposit?
我需要付訂金嗎？
B: If you want us to order it for you, yes.
如果你想訂購的話，就得支付訂金。

(提示) deposit [dɪ'pɑzɪt] n. 訂金；押金；保證金

1955 我們需要百分之…的訂金。
We want...% down.

(替換) We ask for a...% down payment.
The terms include a...% down payment.

(範例) A: How much deposit is required? 需要多少訂金？
B: We want 15% down. 我們需要百分之十五的訂金。

1956 請用…支付。
Please pay us in...

(替換) Please use...currency for payment.
We'd appreciate the payment in...

(範例) A: How do you prefer to be paid? 請問要用何種貨幣付款呢？
B: Please pay us in US dollars. 請用美元支付。

(提示) currency ['kɜ˞ənsɪ] n. 貨幣

1957 我們會以…支付。
We'll pay in...

(替換) We'll pay for them in...

範例 | **A:** We'll pay in US dollars. 我們會以美元支付。
B: That will be fine. 那太好了。

1958　付款期限是個難題。
It's the payment schedule that bothers me.

替換 | I wish you'd change the payment schedule.

範例 | **A:** How do you feel about the loan?
你對這項貸款有何意見？
B: Well, it's the payment schedule that bothers me.
嗯，付款期限是個難題。

● 商討送貨 About Shipment

1959　你們何時送貨？
When can you ship it?

替換 | How soon can you ship it out?
When can you ship it?

範例 | **A:** When can you ship it? 你們何時送貨？
B: We can get it out by Thursday. 我們可以在週四之前交貨。

1960　我們希望貨物在…之前到達。
We need the goods by the end of...

替換 | We need the goods no later than...

範例 | **A:** We need the goods by the end of June.
我們希望貨物在六月底之前到達。
B: I don't think we can do that.
我想我們做不到。

1961　明天可以拿到貨。
You can have it tomorrow.

替換 | You'll have it tomorrow.
I'll get it to you tomorrow.

範例 | **A:** When can I have it? 什麼時候可以拿到貨？
B: You can have it tomorrow. 明天可以拿到貨。

1962	我們每天都有送貨。 **We make shipments every day.**

(替換) | Shipments are made every day.
We ship our orders out every day.

(範例) | A: When will my order be shipped? 我們的貨物什麼時候運送？
B: We make shipments every day. 我們每天都有送貨。

1963	我們會在一週內送貨。 **We will deliver it within a week.**

(替換) | We will have it delivered within a week.

(範例) | A: When can you deliver the product to me? 什麼時候送貨給我？
B: We will deliver it within a week. 我們會在一週內送貨。

1964	最早於下星期到貨。 **The earliest we can get it to you is next week.**

(替換) | The earliest delivery will be next week.

(範例) | A: The earliest we can get it to you is next week. 最早於下星期到貨。
B: I guess that will do. 我想那可以。

1965	我們將於…送貨給你。 **We can deliver the goods to you on...**

(替換) | ...is when we can deliver the goods.

(範例) | A: When can we expect them?
我們何時收到？
B: We can deliver the goods to you on May 10th.
我們將於五月十日送貨給你。

(提示) | expect [ɪk'spɛkt] v. 期待；預料

1966	你需要多少？ **How many do you want?**

(替換) | How many would you like?

(範例) | A: How many do you want? 你需要多少？
B: Ten will do. 十個。

1967
我們現在可以運送⋯。
We can ship...now.

(替換) We'd be able to ship...now.

(範例) A: How many can you ship? 你可以運送多少貨？
B: We can ship 5,000 now. 我們現在可以運送五千個。

1968
現在暫時缺貨。
We're out of stock now.

(替換) Those are out of stock.
We don't have any in stock now.
We don't have any of that in stock at this time.
We are currently out of stock.

(範例) A: We'd like to order five. 我們要預定五個。
B: I'm sorry. We're out of stock now. 對不起，現在暫時缺貨。

1969
我們目前無法滿足這麼多訂單。
The demand is more than we can handle.

(替換) Our factory can't satisfy the demand.
We can't keep up with the demand now.

(範例) A: The demand is more than we can handle.
我們目前無法滿足這麼多訂單。
B: I didn't realize you were so busy.
我不知道你們這麼忙。

1970
我們不久會制訂新的送貨時間表。
We'll have a new shipping schedule ready soon.

(替換) Our new shipping schedule will be set up shortly.
We're now in the process of setting up a new shipping schedule.

(範例) A: When can I expect delivery?
我什麼時候收到貨？
B: We'll have a new shipping schedule ready soon.
我們不久會制訂新的送貨時間表。

1971
下一批貨一定準時到達。
The next shipment will arrive on schedule.

(替換) The next shipment will be on time.
The next shipment will not be late.

(範例) A: The shipments have been arriving late. 這批貨遲到了。
B: The next shipment will arrive on schedule. 下一批貨一定準時到達。

1972 **請問你怎麼送貨呢？**
How do you distribute your products?

(替換) How will the products be distributed?
How are your products delivered?

(範例) A: How do you distribute your products? 請問你怎麼送貨呢？
B: We have a fleet of trucks. 我們有車隊。

(提示) distribute [dɪˈstrɪbjut] v. 分發；分配
fleet [flit] n. 船隊；車隊

1973 **我們無法準時交貨。**
We're going to miss the delivery deadline.

(替換) We can't make the delivery on time.
We can't deliver on schedule.

(範例) A: We're going to miss the delivery deadline. 我們無法準時交貨。
B: You will have to make it up to us. 你必須賠償我們。

1974 **將會晚⋯天出貨。**
The delivery will be...days late.

(替換) The delivery will be delayed by...days.
The deliveries will be delayed...days.
The delivery will take...extra days due to a delay.
The deliveries will be...days behind.

(範例) A: How long is the delay? 會晚多久？
B: The delivery will be two days late. 將會晚兩天出貨。

6.3 問題事故 Troubles and Accidents

　　商務工作中，出現問題與麻煩是很正常的事情，但能否處理問題卻顯示出個人的能力。例如，處理投訴就非常講究技巧。接到投訴時，要特別注意問題的性質及責任歸屬。如果指出的問題確實應由己方負責，就要接受，表達誠摯的歉意，承認對對方造成不便，不要推卸或轉嫁責任。如果可能的話，應該主動補償所造成的損失。另外，一旦發現有錯，應該立即道歉，不要一拖再拖，延誤道歉的最佳時機。道歉話語要恰當簡練，不要說一大串理由，讓人覺得你在推卸責任。承認所發生的一切並道歉，然後保證下不爲例。還有，多數情況下，你需要私下道歉，不要使其公開化，否則會造成負面影響。此外，有時還要感謝對方，並表示你會採取適當的行動及時處理問題。例如可以說：「謝謝你的指正，我會努力讓它不再發生。」(Thank you for pointing out those errors. I'll try hard not to let it happen again.) 如果別人的批評不對或不公正，也要平靜地解釋。如果對你們的批評很籠統，不做具體說明，你可以說：「除非你能具體告訴我，否則我很難接受你的批評。」(Unless you can tell me exactly what you mean, it's hard for me to accept your criticism.)。

● 投訴抱怨 Complaining

1975	你得賠償損害。 **You need to pay us for the damage.** (094)
(替換)	You need to cover the cost of the damage.
(範例)	**A:** You need to pay us for the damage. 你得賠償損害。 **B:** As long as we're responsible. 只要是我們該負責的，我們就負責。

1976	我要投訴。 **I have some complaints.**
(替換)	There are some things I'm not happy with.
(範例)	**A:** I have some complaints. 我要投訴。 **B:** I'm listening. 請講。

1977	如果合約是這樣的條件，我們不準備續約。 **We won't be renewing the contract under these conditions.**
(替換)	Some conditions must change before we renew the contract. We will not renew the contract under the same conditions.

範例　**A:** It's time for renewal.
該續約了。
B: We won't be renewing the contract under these conditions.
如果合約是這樣的條件，我們不準備續約。

提示　renew [rɪ'nju] *v.*（使）更新

1978　**操作起來有點困難。**
It's hard to operate.

替換　It's difficult to operate.
It's not easy to operate.

範例　**A:** It's hard to operate. 操作起來有點困難。
B: It'll get easier with practice. 多練習就會簡單些的。

1979　**誰負責這項工作？**
Who's in charge of this job?

替換　Who's responsible for this job?
Who is the person in charge of this work?

範例　**A:** Who's in charge of this job? 誰負責這項工作？
B: Jimmy. 是吉米。

1980　**我想和負責人談一談。**
Let me talk to the person in charge.

替換　Let me talk to the manager about it.
I want to see the manager about it.
I want to speak with the manager.

範例　**A:** I'm afraid I can't help you, sir. 對不起，先生，我無能為力。
B: Let me talk to the person in charge. 我想和負責人談一談。

1981　**你沒看到我有多生氣嗎？**
Can't you see how mad I am?

替換　Don't you know how upset I am?
Don't you realize how angry I am?

範例　**A:** Can't you see how mad I am? 你沒看到我有多生氣嗎？
B: Would you like to file a formal complaint? 你想正式投訴嗎？

1982

你不能處理一下嗎？
Can't you do something about it?

(替換) Isn't there anything you can do about it?
Can't you do something?

(範例) **A:** Can't you do something about it? 你不能處理一下嗎？
B: I'm sorry, but the machine is broken. 對不起，機器故障。

1983

百分之九十的貨物有瑕疵。
Nine out of ten were no good.

(替換) Nine out of ten were defective.
Nine out of ten turned out to be lemons.
They were almost all defective.

(範例) **A:** I hope the products were OK. 貨物沒問題吧！
B: Well, nine out of ten were no good. 嗯，百分之九十的貨物有瑕疵。

(提示) defective [dɪˈfɛktɪv] *adj.* 有缺陷的
lemon [ˈlɛmən] *n.*【美，非正式】無用之物；易出故障之物

1984

這些貨物的品質不好。
These goods are low quality.

(替換) These goods are inferior in quality.
These goods have a low standard of quality.
The quality of these goods is poor.

(範例) **A:** These goods are low quality. 這些貨物的品質不好。
B: How come? 怎麼會呢？

(提示) inferior [ɪnˈfɪrɪɚ] *adj.* 次級的；劣等的

1985

找錯零錢了。
This isn't the right change.

(替換) You gave me the wrong change.
This is the wrong change.
You didn't give me the correct change.
The change you gave me is wrong.
I'm afraid you gave me the wrong change.
You gave me the wrong amount back.

(範例) **A:** This isn't the right change. 找錯零錢了。
B: Oh, sorry. 噢，十分抱歉。

1986	支票有誤。 **The check isn't correct.**

替換	The check is wrong. There's a mistake on the check.
範例	**A:** The check isn't correct. 支票有誤。 **B:** Oh, let me have a look. 噢，讓我看一下。

1987	你有營業執照嗎？ **Do you have the necessary paperwork to do business here?**

替換	Do you have a license to do business here? Do you get a permit to do business here?
範例	**A:** Do you have the necessary paperwork to do business here? 你有營業執照嗎？ **B:** Yes, we do. 有，我們有。
提示	paperwork ['pepɚ,wɝk] *n.* （商貿所需的）資料；文件

● 發生問題 Having Troubles

1988	我不再跟你合作了。 **I will no longer do business with you.**

替換	I'm through doing business with you. I no longer wish to do business with you.
範例	**A:** You never returned my calls. 你一直沒有回我的電話。 **B:** I will no longer do business with you. 我不再跟你合作了。

1989	我要做最後的修正。 **I have to make a last-minute change.**

替換	Here's a late change.
範例	**A:** I have to make a last-minute change. 我要做最後的修正。 **B:** We don't want to make any changes now. 現在我們不想有任何改變。

1990	你得簽字。 **We need your signature.**

替換 | You have to sign it.
You have to sign your name.

範例 | A: We need your signature. 你得簽字。
B: Not until our lawyers have read it. 得等我們的律師讀過之後再說。

提示 | signature [ˈsɪɡnətʃɚ] *n.* 簽名

1991 不能有任何違法的事。
We want to keep it legal.

替換 | We don't want to do anything illegal.

範例 | A: We want to keep it legal. 不能有任何違法的事。
B: That's good for both sides. 這對雙方都好。

提示 | illegal [ɪˈligl] *adj.* 不合法的；違法的

1992 我不會放棄的。
I'm not going to give up.

替換 | I'm not about to give up.
I won't give up.

範例 | A: I'm not going to give up. 我不會放棄的。
B: Good for you. 很好。

1993 我的腦袋今天不管用。
My brain isn't working today.

替換 | My brain isn't functioning (right) today.
My brain doesn't seem to be working today.
My mind isn't very sharp today.

範例 | A: My brain isn't working today. 我的腦袋今天不管用。
B: Well, let's continue tomorrow. 那我們明天再接著談吧。

1994 計畫停滯不前了。
The project hasn't moved forward.

替換 | The project has been held up.
The project has been put on hold.
The project has been delayed.

範例 | A: Why aren't you working? 為什麼不進行下去？
B: The project hasn't moved forward. 計畫停滯不前了。

1995	計畫還沒有最後敲定。 **The project hasn't been finalized.**

(替換) The project is still being decided upon.

(範例) **A:** How is the project going? 計畫進展得如何？
B: The project hasn't been finalized. 計畫還沒有最後敲定。

(提示) finalize ['faɪnḷ‚aɪz] *v.* 把（計畫、稿件等）最後定下來；定案

1996	這是唯一選擇。 **It was the only choice.**

(替換) I had no other choice.
It was my only choice.
It was the only thing we could do.
There was nothing else we could have done.

(範例) **A:** Why did you do that? 為何這樣做？
B: It was the only choice. 這是唯一選擇。

1997	我們還沒有決定。 **We haven't made a decision yet.**

(替換) We haven't decided on anything yet.
We haven't reached any conclusions.
We haven't made up our minds yet.

(範例) **A:** What are the new rules? 新規定怎麼說的？
B: We haven't made a decision yet. 我們還沒有決定。

● 處理問題 Dealing with Troubles

1998	對不起。 **Sorry.**

(替換) I apologize.

(範例) **A:** Sorry. 對不起。
B: That's all right. 沒關係。

1999	我對…感到愧疚。 **I'm sorry about...**

範例 | **A:** I'm sorry about my mistake. 我對自己的錯誤感到愧疚。
B: That's all right. 沒關係。

2000

對你造成的不便，我們深感抱歉。
We're sorry for the trouble that this has caused you. We apologize for any inconvenience.

替換 | We're sorry for any inconvenience this has caused.
We apologize for the inconvenience.
We're sorry we caused you this trouble.

範例 | **A:** Your shipment came in late. 你的船期延誤了。
B: We're sorry for the trouble that this has caused you. We apologize for any inconvenience. 對你造成的不便，我們深感抱歉。

2001

對公司造成的商譽損害，我深表抱歉。
I'm really sorry for damaging the company's reputation.

替換 | I apologize for damaging the company's reputation.
I feel so bad about damaging the company's reputation.

範例 | **A:** I'm really sorry for damaging the company's reputation.
對公司造成的商譽損害，我深表抱歉。
B: Sorry can never be enough.
抱歉也無法彌補。

提示 | reputation [ˌrɛpjə'teʃən] *n.* 名譽；名聲

2002

我十分抱歉。
I'm really sorry.

替換 | I'm sincerely sorry for that.
I sincerely apologize.

範例 | **A:** You got it wrong. 你犯了個錯誤。
B: I'm really sorry. 我十分抱歉。

2003

是我的錯。
It's my fault.

替換 | My mistake.
I'm to blame.

範例 | **A:** It's my fault. 是我的錯。
B: Don't take it too much to heart. 不必太內疚。

454

2004	對不起，讓你失望了。 **I feel bad about letting you down.**

(替換) I'm sorry for not meeting your expectations.
I'm sorry I couldn't meet your expectations.

(範例) **A:** I feel bad about letting you down. 對不起，讓你失望了。
B: Perhaps I expected too much. 也許我們的期望過高了。

(提示) expectation [ˌɛkspɛk'teʃən] n. 期待；預料

2005	對不起，給你添麻煩了。 **Sorry to trouble you.**

(替換) I'm sorry to bother you.
Sorry to cause you trouble.
I'm sorry for the trouble.
I apologize for troubling you.

(範例) **A:** Sorry to trouble you. 對不起，給你添麻煩了。
B: It's no trouble at all. 一點也不麻煩。

2006	希望沒有給你帶來極大的不便。 **We hope it wasn't a big inconvenience for you.**

(替換) We hope we didn't cause you too much trouble.

(範例) **A:** Your shipment arrived late.
你們送貨晚了。
B: We hope it wasn't a big inconvenience for you.
希望沒有給你帶來極大的不便。

2007	我並不是有意讓你陷入窘境。 **I didn't mean to embarrass you.**

(替換) I didn't intend to embarrass you.

(範例) **A:** You made me feel so bad. 你們給我的感覺很糟。
B: I didn't mean to embarrass you. 我並不是有意讓你陷入窘境。

2008	請原諒我好嗎？ **Will you forgive me?**

(替換) Please forgive me.
I beg your forgiveness.

範例 A: Will you forgive me? 請原諒我好嗎？
B: This is the last time. 下不爲例。

提示 forgiveness [fɚ'gɪvnɪs] *n.* 寬恕；寬仁之心

2009
對不起，我沒有注意到。
I'm sorry, I didn't notice.

替換 I apologize for not noticing.

範例 A: You should follow the rules more closely. 你應該更嚴格遵守規定。
B: I'm sorry, I didn't notice. 對不起，我沒有注意到。

2010
我弄錯數字了。
I made a mistake in reading the number.

替換 I read the number incorrectly/wrong.
I mistook the number.

範例 A: I made a mistake in reading the number. 我弄錯數字了。
B: What should it have been? 那應該是多少？

2011
我加錯了。
I added it wrong.

替換 I made an error in calculation.
I made a math mistake.
I made a mistake in the calculation.

範例 A: I'm afraid you overcharged me. 恐怕你多收了。
B: Sorry. I added it wrong. 對不起，我加錯了。

提示 calculation [ˌkælkjə'leʃən] *n.* 計算

2012
我忘記了。
I forgot about it.

替換 I totally/completely forgot.
It must have slipped my mind.
It (just) slipped my mind.

範例 A: Did you call Mr. White? 你打電話給懷特先生了嗎？
B: Uh-oh. I forgot about it. 噢！我忘記了。

2013
我不是有意對你不敬的。
I didn't mean to be impolite.

(替換) I didn't mean to be rude.

(範例) A: You were very rude to me on the phone.
你在電話中對我十分不禮貌。
B: I didn't mean to be impolite.
我不是有意對你不敬的。

2014 這是口誤。
It was a slip of the tongue.

(替換) I'm sorry I said it.
I regret saying that.
It just slipped out.
I said it before thinking.
I shouldn't have said that.

(範例) A: You should never have said that. 你不應該那麼說。
B: It was a slip of the tongue. 這是口誤。

2015 請原諒我的粗魯。
I'm sorry for my rudeness.

(替換) Excuse me for my rudeness.
Please forgive my rudeness.

(範例) A: I'm sorry for my rudeness. 請原諒我的粗魯。
B: I can understand that. 我可以理解。

2016 我已經盡全力了。
I did everything I could.

(替換) My part is done.

(範例) A: Why won't you talk to him for me? 為什麼不替我和他談一談？
B: I did everything I could. 我已經盡全力了。

2017 我們會補償損失的。
We'll take care of the loss.

(替換) We'll make up for the loss.
We'll take responsibility for the loss.
We'll make the loss up to you.

(範例) A: Your company's mistake has cost us a lot of money.
你們公司的錯誤令我們損失慘重。

B: Don't worry. We'll take care of the loss.
別擔心，我們會補償損失的。

2018　**我已經得到教訓了。**
I've learned my lesson.

(替換)　I'll be wiser next time.

(範例)　**A:** I've learned my lesson. 我已經得到教訓了。
B: I'm happy to hear that. 我很高興聽到你這樣說。

● 調查原因 Investigating Reasons

2019　**出什麼事了？**
Is anything wrong?

(替換)　What happened?
Has anything happened?

(範例)　**A:** Is anything wrong? 出什麼事了？
B: There was just a serious accident. 是一起嚴重的事故。

2020　**究竟出什麼事了？**
What on earth happened?

(替換)　What (the hell) happened?

(範例)　**A:** What on earth happened? 究竟出什麼事了？
B: It's a long story. 說來話長。

2021　**怎麼回事？**
What was the trouble?

(替換)　What was the problem?
What problems did you have?
Was there a problem?
What were the problems you had?

(範例)　**A:** It didn't go well. 進展不順利。
B: What was the trouble? 怎麼回事？

2022　**怎麼了？**
What's up?

(替換) What's the problem?

(範例)
A: What's up? 怎麼了？
B: It's not working well. 不是很順利。

2023
你上次檢查存貨是什麼時候？
When did you last check the inventory?

(替換) When did you take inventory?

(範例)
A: When did you last check the inventory? 你上次檢查存貨是什麼時候？
B: About three months ago. 大約三個月之前。

(提示) inventory [ˈɪnvənˌtorɪ] *n.* 存貨清單；存貨盤存（報表）

2024
我們會查看一下。
We'll see what's going on.

(替換)
We'll look into it.
We'll check it out.

(範例)
A: You have a problem in accounting. 你們的會計方面有問題。
B: We'll see what's going on. 我們會查看一下。

2025
損失有多少？
How much was the damage?

(替換) What was the total damage?

(範例)
A: How much was the damage? 損失有多少？
B: $3,000. 三千美元。

2026
既然我已經知道事情的原委，那就不成問題了。
It's OK, now that I know the full story.

(替換)
Now that I know the whole story, I'm happy with the situation.
It's cool now, because I know the whole story.

(範例)
A: I hope you forgive him.
希望你能原諒他。
B: It's OK, now that I know the full story.
既然我已經知道事情的原委，那就不成問題了。

2027
他怎麼說？
What does he say?

替換　What's his story?

範例　A: What does he say? 他怎麼說？
　　　B: He said he's innocent. 他說他是無辜的。

2028 | 他不是有意的。
He didn't mean it.

替換　He didn't do it on purpose.

範例　A: Why did he do it? 他為什麼這樣做？
　　　B: He didn't mean it. 他不是有意的。

2029 | 我們無能為力。
We can't do anything about it.

替換　There's nothing we can do.

範例　A: We can't do anything about it. 我們無能為力。
　　　B: Sorry to hear that. 很遺憾聽到你這樣說。

2030 | 情況進展不順。
Things aren't going smoothly.

替換　We're having some problems now.

範例　A: Things aren't going smoothly. 情況進展不順。
　　　B: I'm sorry to hear that. 我很遺憾聽到你這樣說。

2031 | 每個人都已經筋疲力盡了。
Everyone is exhausted.

替換　Everyone is worn out.
　　　Everybody is tired.

範例　A: Everyone is exhausted. 每個人都已經筋疲力盡了。
　　　B: What a hard day! 這一天太忙了。

2032 | 情況非常緊急。
It's something that can't wait.

替換　It's something urgent.
　　　It's something very important.

範例　A: Why is the meeting so sudden? 為何要開緊急會議？
　　　B: It's something that can't wait. 情況非常緊急。

● 解決問題 Dealing with Troubles

2033
我們無意回避問題。
We have no intention of avoiding the issue.

(替換) We don't intend to avoid the issue.

(範例) A: We have no intention of avoiding the issue. 我們無意回避問題。
B: Neither do we. 我們也是。

2034
我打算縮小選擇範圍。
I'd like to narrow down the choices.

(替換) I'd like to eliminate some of the choices.

(範例) A: We've been given four ways to go. 我們有四種方法可行。
B: I'd like to narrow down the choices. 我打算縮小選擇範圍。

(提示) eliminate [ɪ'lɪmə,net] v. 排除；消除

2035
我們能做的只有等待了。
The only thing we can do about it now is wait.

(替換) All we can do now is play the waiting game.

(範例) A: I don't know if we got the order right.
我無法確認訂單是否正確。
B: The only thing we can do about it now is wait.
我們能做的只有等待了。

2036
我是這家公司的負責人。
I'm in charge of this company.

(替換) I'm the president, the highest ranking, most powerful person in this company.
There's no person more powerful than me in this company.

(範例) A: Let me talk to your boss. 我想與你的老闆談一談。
B: I'm in charge of this company. 我是這家公司的負責人。

2037
我們無能為力。
There is nothing else we can do.

(替換) We've done all that we can.

(範例) A: Is there anything else we can do? 我們能做些什麼？
B: There is nothing else we can do. 我們無能為力。

461

2038

希望一切都沒事。
I hope it will all work out.

(替換)
I want it to work out smoothly.
I want it resolved quickly.
I hope everything will be OK soon.

(範例)
A: I hope it will all work out. 希望一切都沒事。
B: I think everyone involved feels the same. 我想大家有同感。

2039

我絞盡腦汁，卻毫無成效。
I tried everything and it just didn't work.

(替換)
I tried every possible way, but nothing worked.
There's just no way it'll work.

(範例)
A: I tried everything and it just didn't work. 我絞盡腦汁，卻毫無成效。
B: There's always a solution. Give it time. 會有辦法的。等待時機吧。

2040

讓我解釋一下情況。
Let me explain the situation.

(替換)
Let me clarify the situation for you.

(範例)
A: Why was the contract cancelled? 合約為什麼取消？
B: Let me explain the situation. 讓我解釋一下情況。

(提示)
clarify [ˈklærəˌfaɪ] v. 澄清；闡明

2041

毫無希望。
It's hopeless.

(替換)
All hope is gone.
There's no hope.

(範例)
A: Can you save the company? 你可以救這家公司嗎？
B: It's hopeless. 毫無希望。

2042

我們不想捲入。
We don't want to get involved.

(替換)
We don't want any part of this.
We're not getting involved.

(範例)
A: You should intervene. 你們應該干預此事。
B: We don't want to get involved. 我們不想捲入。

| 提示 | involved [ɪn'vɑlvd] *adj.* 連累的；有關的
intervene [ˌɪntɚ'vin] *v.* 干涉；干預 |

2043 | 不會太久的。
It won't take long.

| 替換 | It shouldn't take long.
It should be finished shortly. |
| 範例 | **A:** How long will it take to fix the computer? 多久才能修好這台電腦？
B: It won't take long. 不會太久的。 |

2044 | 我們已經順利解決了。
We have it all worked out now.

| 替換 | We've got it straightened out now.
The problem's been taken care of.
We worked it out. |
| 範例 | **A:** Have you dealt with the problem yet? 問題解決了嗎？
B: We have it all worked out now. 我們已經順利解決了。 |

2045 | 隨你便。
I don't care what you do.

替換	You can do whatever you want.
範例	**A:** I'm going to sue you. 我要告你。 **B:** I don't care what you do. 隨你便。
提示	sue [su] *v.* 控告；向…請求

2046 | 那不是我的責任。
That is not my responsibility.

| 替換 | I cannot bear responsibility for that. |
| 範例 | **A:** The product was broken when we received it.
收到貨物時，商品已經破損。
B: That is not my responsibility.
那不是我的責任。 |

2047 | 我們只能訴諸法律。
We have to go to court to settle this.

替換 | Going to court seems the only way to settle this.
This will have to be settled in court.
The only way to settle this is in court.

範例 | **A:** Let's sit down and try to work this out. 我們坐下來好好協商。
B: We have to go to court to settle this. 我們只能訴諸法律。

提示 | settle ['sɛtl] *v.* 解決

第7章
海外生活

① ②

③ ④ ⑤

⑥ ⑦

7.1 問路 Finding the Way

　　在異地旅行時，往往對路不是很熟悉，因此要學會問路，聽懂別人的方向指示。隨身攜帶地圖是很必要的，有了地圖，你可以請對方指出你在地圖上的位置，了解前往目的地的路線。在此同時，也應熟悉基本的指路表達方式，對他人的相關提問，有所準備。

2048 請問…在哪裡？
Where is..., please?

替換　Can you tell me where...is?
　　　Would you like to tell me where...is?
　　　Do you mind telling me where...is?

範例　**A:** Where is the student dining hall, please? 請問學生餐廳在哪裡？
　　　B: It's the northeast corner of the campus. 在校園的東北區。

2049 請問去…的路怎麼走？
Which way is..., please?

替換　Can you direct me to...?
　　　Would/Could you please tell me how to get to...?
　　　Would/Could you please tell me the way to...?
　　　Would/Could you tell me which way...is?

範例　**A:** Which way is the gym, please?
　　　　請問去健身房的路怎麼走？
　　　B: Go straight ahead along this street, then turn left at the second traffic light. It's on the right.
　　　　沿著這條路一直直走，在第二個紅綠燈向左轉，然後就在你的右邊。

2050 請問一下，這附近有…嗎？
Excuse me. Is there a...near here?

替換　Excuse me. I wonder if you could tell me whether there is a...around here?

範例　**A:** Excuse me. Is there a public phone near here?
　　　　請問一下，這附近有公共電話嗎？
　　　B: Yes, it's just around the corner.
　　　　有，就在轉角處。

2051 對不起，我對這裡也不熟。
Sorry, I'm new here, too.

（替換）
I'm new around here, too.
I'm a newcomer here, too.
I'm not familiar with this area, either.
I haven't been here for long, either.

（範例）
A: Excuse me, do you know how to get to City Hall?
請問一下，你知道怎樣去市政廳嗎？
B: Sorry, I'm new here, too.
對不起，我對這裡也不熟。

2052 去⋯是走這條路嗎？
Is this the road to...?

（替換）
Is this the right way to...?
Am I on the right road to...?
Would you mind telling me if this is the right way to...?

（範例）
A: Is this the road to the airport? 去機場是走這條路嗎？
B: I'm not sure. I'm just passing through. 我不清楚。我只是路過。

2053 這條街到哪裡？
Where does this street lead?

（替換）
Where does this road go?

（範例）
A: Where does this street lead? 這條街到哪裡？
B: To the beach. 到海灘。

2054 從這裡能到⋯嗎？
May I get to...from here?

（範例）
A: May I get to the drugstore from here?
從這裡能到藥房嗎？
B: Yes. Just cut across the square and then turn left.
可以，你穿過廣場，然後左轉。

（提示）
square [skwɛr] *n.* 廣場

2055 這個地址離這裡很遠嗎？
Is this address far from here?

範例
A: Is this address far from here?
　這個地址離這裡很遠嗎？
B: No. Turn left here, and a short way along the left you'll see it.
　不遠，從這裡左轉，靠左邊走一點點路就會看到了。

2056
我是不是應該搭⋯去？
Should I take...?

範例
A: Should I take a bus?
　我是不是應該搭公車去？
B: No, you shouldn't. It's on the corner opposite the gas station. It's only a five-minute walk.
　不用。它就在加油站對面轉角處，你五分鐘之內就可以走到。

2057
到那裡要花很多時間嗎？
Will it take me long to get there?

替換
Will it take me a lot of time to get there?
Will I have to spend a lot of time getting there?

範例
A: Will it take me long to get there? 到那裡要花很多時間嗎？
B: No, it's only a few blocks away. 不用，那裡離這只有幾個街區。

2058
我怎樣才能到那裡？
How do I get there?

範例
A: How do I get there?
　我怎樣才能到那裡？
B: I'm going that way. I can drive you there.
　我正要去那裡，我可以送你到那邊。

7.2 搭公車 Taking a Bus

　　搭公車既經濟又實惠，還可以欣賞街景。搭車前，必須要了解路線。上車前要準備好零錢，上車後要自動投幣，下車時要按鈴或拉鈴通知司機。搭車時，還要注意搭車的行為規範：上車要排隊，適時禮讓座位，說話要有禮貌。

2059
請問一下，我要在哪裡搭⋯？
Excuse me, where can I get...?

096

範例 | **A:** Excuse me, where can I get the No. 23 bus?
請問一下，我要在哪裡搭 23 號公車？
B: Just half a mile ahead.
前方半英里遠的地方。

2060
我應該搭幾號公車去…？
Which bus should I take for...?

替換 | Which bus do I take to get to...?
Which bus must I take to...?

範例 | **A:** Which bus should I take for Lincoln Park?
我應該搭幾號公車去林肯公園？
B: No. 15.
15 號。

2061
這輛車是去…嗎？
Does this bus go to...?

替換 | Is the bus going to...?

範例 | **A:** Does this bus go to the park? 這輛車是去公園的嗎？
B: Yes, it does. 正是。

2062
這是開往…的車嗎？
Is this the bus for...?

替換 | Is this bus going to...?
Does this bus go to...?

範例 | **A:** Is this the bus for the zoo? 這是開往動物園的車嗎？
B: No, you should take bus No. 27. 不是，你應該搭 27 號公車。

2063
這輛車是不是經過…？
Does this bus go past...?

範例 | **A:** Does this bus go past the post office?
這輛車是不是經過郵局？
B: No, you have to change to bus No. 8 if you want to go there.
不，你要去郵局，得轉 8 號公車。

2064
到…有幾站？
How many stops are there to...?

範例 A: How many stops are there to downtown? 到市中心有幾站？
B: Five. 五站。

2065
這一線公車可到⋯嗎？
Does this bus line go to...?

範例 A: Does this bus line go to the Art Gallery?
這一線公車可到美術館嗎？
B: No, this bus goes only as far as the Botanical Gardens.
不，這公車只到植物園。

提示 botanical [bo'tænɪk]] *adj.* 植物的

2066
⋯號公車多久一班？
How often does the...bus run?

範例 A: How often does the No. 81 bus run? 81 號公車多久一班？
B: Every three minutes. 三分鐘一班。

2067
它會在⋯和⋯號公車銜接嗎？
Does it connect with the...bus at...?

範例 A: Does it connect with the No. 78 bus at the square?
它會在廣場和78 號公車銜接嗎？
B: No, at the stadium.
不，是在體育館的地方。

提示 stadium ['stedɪəm] *n.* 體育場；運動場

2068
請買票。
Fares, please.

範例 A: Fares, please. 請買票。
B: Here you are. 錢在這裡。

2069
到⋯多少錢？
What's the fare to...?

替換 How much is it to...?
範例 A: What's the fare to Fisherman's Wharf? 到漁人碼頭多少錢？
B: Fifty cents, please. 五角。

2070
請在車箱內投入⋯。
Please put...in the fare box.

範例 **A:** Please put two dollars in the fare box. 請在車箱內投入兩塊美元。
B: All right. 好的。

2071
月票可以嗎？
May I use my commuter's pass?

替換 Is this commuter's pass all right?

範例 **A:** May I use my commuter's pass? 月票可以嗎？
B: That's fine. 可以。

提示 commuter [kə'mjutɚ] *n.* 通勤者；經常往返者

2072
到⋯時，請告訴我一聲好嗎？
Please tell me when we get to...

替換 Would you please tell me when we arrive at...?
Would you please let me know when we get to...?
Would you announce when we get to..., please?

範例 **A:** Please tell me when we get to the museum.
到博物館時，請告訴我一聲好嗎？
B: Don't worry. I'll remind you when it's your stop.
不用擔心，到站時我會提醒你的。

提示 announce [ə'naʊns] *v.* 宣布；通知

2073
可以請你到⋯時，通知一聲嗎？
Would you announce it when we get to...?

範例 **A:** Would you announce it when we get to Times Square?
可以請你到時代廣場時，通知一聲嗎？
B: Sure.
當然可以。

2074
我要去⋯，應該到哪裡轉車呢？
Where should I change buses for...?

範例 **A:** Where should I change buses for the Double Tree Hotel?
我要去雙樹旅館，應該在哪裡轉車呢？
B: Change at the railway station, and get the No. 102 bus. Then get off at the third stop.
到火車站轉搭 102 號公車，在第三站下車。

| 2075 | 你搭錯車了。
You're on the wrong bus. |

替換 | You've got on the wrong bus.
I'm afraid you're on the wrong bus.

範例 | **A:** You're on the wrong bus. 你搭錯車了。
B: Thank you. 謝謝你。

| 2076 | …是不是在這站下車？
Is this the stop for...? |

替換 | Do I get off here if I want to go to...?

範例 | **A:** Is this the stop for Disneyland?
迪士尼樂園是不是在這站下車？
B: Yeah. Hurry up or you'll miss your stop.
是的。快點兒，不然就過站了。

7.3 搭計程車 Taking a Taxi

如果時間趕、事情急或經濟條件允許，搭計程車是很方便的。通常在街上就可以叫到車，但有時須到計程車停靠站（Taxi Stand）搭車。如果在旅館或飯店打電話叫車，需要給小費，小費約占車資的15-20%。國外叫車的計費有以下幾種：1）按時間與里程合併計費；2）按人數、行李、里程、夜間費用、市外費用計費；3）按街區和地區計費；4）按基礎費用加里程費用計費。為了防止司機敲竹槓，要先了解計費方法，打聽距離遠近，記住車牌號碼，聽懂司機的語言，因此學會相關的表達方法是非常必要的。

| 2077 | 請上車。
Get in, please. | 097 |

替換 | Hop in, please.

範例 | **A:** Taxi! 計程車！
B: Get in, please. 請上車。

2078

請派一輛計程車到…。
Please send a taxi to...

範例
A: Please send a taxi to the Central Hospital.
請派一輛計程車到中心醫院。
B: A taxi will be there in five minutes.
計程車五分鐘之後到。

2079

要去哪裡？
Where to?

替換
Where're you going?
Where will you be going, sir?
May I ask where you would like to go?
Where do you wish me to take you?

範例
A: Where to? 要去哪裡？
B: The Holiday Inn, please. 假日飯店。

提示
inn [ɪn] *n.* 小酒店；小飯店

2080

請送我到…。
Drive me to..., please.

替換
Please take me to...
Will you give me a ride to...?
Could you take me to...?

範例
A: Drive me to the mall, please. 請送我到商場。
B: All right. 好的。

2081

我必須…，你看我能趕上嗎？
I've got to...Do you think I can make it?

替換
I've got to...Can you make it?

範例
A: I've got to catch the 6:25 train. Do you think I can make it?
我必須趕六點二十五分的火車，你看我能趕上嗎？
B: Don't worry. I'll get you there within 10 minutes.
別擔心。我可以在 10 分鐘內把你送到那兒。

2082

如果…，我想我們能趕到。
I think we can make it if...

替換　We should be OK, if...

範例　**A:** Can I get to work on time?
　　　我能準時上班嗎？
　　　B: I think we can make it if we take a route without much traffic.
　　　如果路上不塞車，我想我們能趕到。

2083　應該沒有問題，除非⋯。
It should be OK, unless...

替換　It should be all right, unless...
　　　It should be no problem, unless...
　　　There shouldn't be any problem, unless...

範例　**A:** I won't miss the train, will I?
　　　我不會趕不上火車，對吧？
　　　B: It should be OK, unless there's a traffic jam.
　　　應該沒有問題，除非塞車。

2084　請在這裡停，我要下車。
Just pull up here and I'll get out.

替換　Will you stop here? I'll get off.

範例　**A:** Just pull up here and I'll get out. 請在這裡停，我要下車。
　　　B: OK. 好的。

2085　對不起，這裡不能停，有一個「禁止停車」的標誌。
Sorry. I can't stop here. There's a "No Parking" sign.

範例　**A:** Stop here, please.
　　　請在這裡停車。
　　　B: Sorry. I can't stop here. There's a "No Parking" sign.
　　　對不起，這裡不能停，有一個「禁止停車」的標誌。

2086　這是車費，這是給你的（小費）。
Here's the fare, and this is for you.

範例　**A:** Here's the fare, and this is for you. 這是車費，這是給你的（小費）。
　　　B: Thank you. 謝謝。

2087　這是⋯，不用找零。
Here's...Keep the change.

替換　Here's..., and you can keep the change.

範例　**A:** The fare is 18 dollars. 車費是十八元。
B: Here's 20 dollars. Keep the change. 這是二十元，不用找零。

| 2088 | 祝你有愉快的一天。
Have a nice day. |

替換　I hope you have a nice day.

範例　**A:** Have a nice day. 祝你有愉快的一天。
B: Thank you. Good-bye. 謝謝，再見。

7.4 搭火車 Taking a Train

　　搭火車旅行舒適安全，而且還可以飽覽沿途風光。在美國，列車的設備相當完備，餐車、浴室、理髮廳、洗衣店一應俱全。列車車廂有客車和臥車之分，座位有等級差別。在歐洲，列車有國內和國際兩類，列車多分為一等和二等。列車進入或離開某國國境，會有該國的出入境官員上車檢查證件。乘車前，如果要托運行李，必須先到行李托運處辦理托運手續，辦好後要妥善保管托運單。請搬運工幫忙要給小費。

● 詢問與提供資訊 Asking for & Giving Information about Trains

（098）

| 2089 | 我該搭哪班列車去…？
Which train should I take for...? |

替換　Which train will get me to...?

範例　**A:** Which train should I take for Boston?
我該搭哪班列車去波士頓？
B: No. 81.
81 次列車。

| 2090 | 從…到…有直達車嗎？
Is there a through train from...to...? |

範例 A: Is there a through train from Pittsburgh to San Francisco?
從匹茲堡到舊金山有直達車嗎？

B: Sorry, there isn't. You have to change in Denver.
對不起，沒有，你必須在丹佛轉車。

2091 這是直達車嗎？
Is this a through train?

範例 A: Is this a through train? 這是直達車嗎？
B: Sorry, it isn't. 很抱歉，不是。

2092 這是特快車嗎？
Is this the express train?

範例 A: Is this the express train? 這是特快車嗎？
B: Sorry, it's the local. 很抱歉，這是普通車。

2093 前往…的特快車…發車。
The express train for...leaves at...

替換 The express for...is due to depart at...

範例 A: The express train for New York leaves at 6:35.
前往紐約的特快車六點三十五分發車。
B: We'd better hurry.
那我們最好趕快了。

2094 我必須換車嗎？
Do I have to change trains?

替換 Should/Must I change trains?
Is it necessary to change trains?

範例 A: Do I have to change trains?
我必須換車嗎？
B: Yes. You'll have to change at Washington for New York.
是的，你必須在華盛頓轉搭開往紐約的列車。

2095 我必須改搭…嗎？
Do I have to change to...?

範例 A: Do I have to change to a local train? 我必須改搭普通車嗎？
B: No, you don't. 不用。

476

2096	從…來的那班列車什麼時候到達？ **What time does the train from...get in?**

(替換) When does the train from...arrive?
When's the train from...due?

(範例) **A:** What time does the train from Dublin get in?
從都柏林來的那班列車什麼時候到達？
B: It will be arriving in five minutes.
過五分鐘就到了。

2097	列車會準點抵達嗎？ **Will the train arrive on schedule?**

(替換) Is the train on time?

(範例) **A:** Will the train arrive on schedule? 列車會準點抵達嗎？
B: Yes, it will. 會。

2098	列車誤點了嗎？ **Is the train delayed?**

(範例) **A:** Is the train delayed? 列車誤點了嗎？
B: Yes, it's a half hour behind schedule. 是的，晚了半個小時。

2099	列車在這裡停多久？ **How long will the train be stopped here?**

(範例) **A:** How long will the train be stopped here? 列車在這裡停多久？
B: About 15 minutes. 約十五分鐘。

2100	這列火車上有餐車嗎？ **Is there a buffet car on the train?**

(替換) Is there a restaurant car on the train?

(範例) **A:** Is there a buffet car on the train? 這列火車上有餐車嗎？
B: Yes, there is. 有。

● 購票事宜 Buying & Selling Tickets

2101	去…的車票還有嗎？ **Are there any seats available for...?**

範例

A: Are there any seats available for the train to Chicago?
去芝加哥的車票還有嗎？

B: Yes, which kind?
有，要買哪一種？

提示 available [ə'veləbļ] *adj.* 可得到的；可買到的

2102

請給我一張去…的票。
I'd like a ticket for..., please.

替換

Give me a ticket for..., please.
I want/need a ticket for...
I'd like a seat for...
I'd like to buy a ticket for..., please.
May I have a ticket for...?

範例

A: I'd like a ticket for Edinburgh, please. 請給我一張去愛丁堡的票。
B: Cash or charge? 刷卡還是付現？

2103

去…的車票多少錢？
How much is a ticket to...?

替換

How much does a ticket to...cost?
What's the fare for a ticket to...?

範例

A: How much is a ticket to London? 去倫敦的車票多少錢？
B: 16 pounds. 十六英鎊。

2104

我可以在這裡訂去…的車票嗎？
Can I book a ticket here for...?

範例

A: Can I book a ticket here for Los Angeles?
我可以在這裡訂去洛杉磯的車票嗎？
B: Of course.
當然。

2105

我可以預訂…開往…的火車車位嗎？
May I reserve a seat on the...train leaving at...?

範例

A: May I reserve a seat on the New York train leaving at 8:30 this evening? 我可以預訂今晚八點半開往紐約的火車車位嗎？
B: Let me check. 讓我查一下。

提示 reserve [rɪ'sɝv] *v.* 預訂

2106	抱歉，…座位都訂滿了。 **Sorry, all the...seats are reserved.**

替換 I'm sorry, but all the...seats are reserved.

範例
A: Are there any window seats available right now?
現在還有靠窗的座位嗎？
B: Sorry, all the window seats are reserved.
抱歉，所有靠窗的座位都訂滿了。

2107	售票處通常提前幾天賣票？ **How far in advance does the booking office usually sell tickets?**

範例
A: How far in advance does the booking office usually sell tickets?
售票處通常提前幾天賣票？
B: One week.
一個星期。

2108	車票多少天之內有效？ **For how many days will the tickets be good?**

替換 For how many days will the tickets be valid?

範例
A: For how many days will the tickets be good? 車票多少天之內有效？
B: For three days. 三天之內有效。

提示 valid ['vælɪd] *adj.* 有效的

2109	如果我買來回票，會便宜一點嗎？ **Is it cheaper if I get a round trip ticket?**

替換 Can I save some money if I buy a round trip ticket?

範例
A: Is it cheaper if I get a round trip ticket?
如果我買來回票，會便宜一點嗎？
B: Yes, it is.
會。

● 出發與抵達時間 Departure & Arrival Times

2110	…點…分開往…的列車會準時出發嗎？ **Will the...train for...leave on time?**

479

範例　A: Will the 6:30 train for Washington leave on time?
六點三十分開往華盛頓的列車會準時出發嗎？
B: Sorry, it has been canceled.
對不起，這班列車已經取消了。

2111　那班列車什麼時候開出？
When is that train scheduled to depart?

替換　What time does the train leave?
What time is the train leaving?

範例　A: When is that train scheduled to depart? 那班列車什麼時候開出？
B: 7:00 p.m. 晚上七點。

2112　預訂什麼時候抵達？
What time is it due to arrive?

範例　A: What time is it due to arrive? 預訂什麼時候抵達？
B: 11:35 a.m. 上午十一點三十五分。

2113　如果我們搭這列⋯出發的火車，幾點會抵達⋯？
When will we arrive at...if we take the...train?

範例　A: When will we arrive at the Grand Canyon if we take the 4:30 train?
如果我們搭這列四點半出發的火車，幾點會抵達大峽谷？
B: It takes about three hours, so you'll arrive before 8:00 p.m.
要花三小時，所以你會在八點之前抵達。

提示　canyon ['kænjən] *n.* 峽谷

● 行李托運 Taking Baggage

2114　我可以帶多少行李？
How much baggage may I take with me?

範例　A: How much baggage may I take with me? 我可以帶多少行李？
B: Fifty pounds per person. 每人五十磅。

2115　能否把這行李送到⋯？
Can I have the luggage delivered to...?

（範例）　A: Can I have the luggage delivered to this address?
　　　　　能否把這行李送到這個地址？
　　　　B: All right. Please fill out this form.
　　　　　可以。請填這份表格。

2116　托運費是多少？
What's the charge for delivery?

（替換）　How much do I need to pay for the delivery?

（範例）　A: What's the charge for delivery? 托運費是多少？
　　　　B: The total is 27 dollars. 總計二十七美元。

2117　超重費多少？
What's the overweight charge?

（範例）　A: What's the overweight charge? 超重費多少？
　　　　B: 52 dollars. 五十二美元。

● 尋找月臺 Looking for the Platform

2118　到月臺怎麼走？
How do I get to the platform?

（替換）　Could you tell me how to get to the platform?

（範例）　A: How do I get to the platform? 到月臺怎麼走？
　　　　B: Go straight and you will see the sign. 直走，你就會看到標誌。

2119　請問前往…的…火車在哪個月臺搭車？
Which platform is for the...train to..., please?

（替換）　Do you know what platform the...train to...leaves from?
　　　　From which platform does the...train to...leave?
　　　　Which platform does the...train to...leave from?

（範例）　A: Which platform is for the 6:30 train to Paris, please?
　　　　　請問前往巴黎的六點半火車在哪個月臺搭車？
　　　　B: Platform 9.
　　　　　九號月臺。

2120　要搭…的火車，我應該要去哪個月臺呢？
For the...train, which platform do I need to go to?

範例 | **A:** For the 12:25 train, which platform do I need to go to?
要搭十二點二十五分的火車，我應該要去哪個月臺呢？
B: Platform 4.
第四月臺。

● 上下火車 Getting on & off the Train

2121
請上車了。
All aboard!

範例 | **A:** All aboard! 請上車了。
B: Let's hurry. 我們快點吧。

2122
這是⋯號車廂。我們上車吧。
This is Carriage...Let's get on.

範例 | **A:** This is Carriage 8. Let's get on. 這是八號車廂。我們上車吧。
B: All right. 好吧。

提示 | carriage ['kærɪdʒ] *n.*【英】（火車）客車廂

2123
我可以幫你拿行李嗎？
Can I help you with your luggage?

範例 | **A:** Can I help you with your luggage? 我可以幫你拿行李嗎？
B: I'd appreciate that. 謝謝。

2124
這裡有人坐嗎？
Is this seat taken?

替換 | Is someone sitting here?

範例 | **A:** Is this seat taken? 這裡有人坐嗎？
B: Yes, someone's sitting there. 是的，有人坐了。

2125
這是⋯號車廂，第⋯號舖位嗎？
Is this Carriage..., Berth...?

範例 | **A:** Is this Carriage 6, Berth 12? 這是六號車廂，第十二號舖位嗎？
B: Yes, please have a seat. 是的，請坐吧。

提示 | berth [bɝθ] *n.* 臥鋪

2126	我們把…放在行李架上吧。 **Let's put...on the rack.**
範例	**A:** Let's put our suitcases on the rack. 我們把皮箱放在行李架上吧。 **B:** The luggage rack is full. 行李架已經塞滿了。
2127	列車馬上就要開了。 **The train is leaving now.**
範例	**A:** The train is leaving now. 列車馬上就要開了。 **B:** Bye-bye. 再見。
2128	列車馬上就要到站了。 **The train will be stopping soon.**
範例	**A:** The train will be stopping soon. 列車馬上就要到站了。 **B:** Let's take our luggage down now. 我們現在把行李拿下來吧。

7.5 在海關 At Customs

　　搭飛機到他國時，空服員會在飛機上發給旅客入境登記卡（或表格）（Immigration Form 或 ED Card），在入境之前要先將登記卡填好。入境檢查時，要把登記卡和護照出示給入境管理人員。在入境櫃檯時，入境管理人員會檢查你的護照，在登記卡上註明你入境與預計離境的時間，並問一些問題。問題主要涉及旅行目的、停留時間及住宿情況等。通過入境檢查之後，如果有托運行李，就要到行李領取處領行李，接著就是過海關（customs clearance），這時要向海關人員出示報關單（Customs Declaration Form）。各國對海關免稅品和違禁品有一定規定，不符合規定的東西要補稅或沒收。個人隨身用品不用補稅，但水果、植物和肉類有可能被沒收。

● 海關手續 Asking about Customs Procedures

2129	我該在哪裡辦理通關手續呢？ **Where should I go through customs?**	

(替換) Could you tell me where I should go through customs?
Will you tell me where I should go through customs?

(範例) **A:** Where should I go through customs?
我該在哪裡辦理通關手續呢？
B: Go straight ahead to the counters over there.
直走到那邊的櫃檯處辦理。

2130 什麼東西要繳稅？
What do I need to pay a duty on?

(替換) What articles are subject to a duty?
What articles/things do I have to pay a duty on?

(範例) **A:** What do I need to pay a duty on? 什麼東西要繳稅？
B: You have to pay a duty on this CD player. 你的 CD 播放器要交稅。

(提示) article ['ɑrtɪkl] *n.* （物品的）一件；物品；商品

2131 …需要繳稅嗎？
Do I have to pay any duty on...?

(替換) Do I need to pay a duty on...?

(範例) **A:** Do I have to pay any duty on personal belongings?
個人物品需要繳稅嗎？
B: No, you don't.
不，你不用。

(提示) belongings [bə'lɔŋɪŋz] *pl. n.* 財產；所有物

2132 我得付…多少稅金？
How much is the duty I have to pay on...?

(替換) How much should I pay for the duty on...?

(範例) **A:** How much is the duty I have to pay on this laptop?
我得付這個筆記型電腦多少稅金？
B: About $50.
大約五十美金。

(提示) laptop ['læptɑp] *n.* 筆記型電腦

2133 允許帶…入境嗎？
Am I allowed to import...?

(替換) May...be imported?

(範例) A: Am I allowed to import this digital video camera?
允許帶數位錄影機入境嗎？
B: Yes, you are.
是的，可以。

2134 我需要填寫這份海關行李申報單嗎？
Do I have to fill out this customs baggage declaration form?

(替換) Do I need to fill out this customs baggage declaration form?
Am I required to fill out this customs baggage declaration form?

(範例) A: Do I have to fill out this customs baggage declaration form?
我需要填寫這份海關行李申報單嗎？
B: Yes, if you have checked baggage.
是的，如果你有行李要托運的話。

(提示) declaration [ˌdɛkləˈreʃən] n. 聲明

2135 我需要在報關單中填上這項嗎？
Do I have to include it on the declaration form?

(範例) A: Do I have to include it on the declaration form?
我需要在報關單中填上這項嗎？
B: I'm afraid so.
恐怕得如此。

2136 我可以走綠色通道嗎？
Can I go through the green line?

(範例) A: Can I go through the green line?
我可以走綠色通道嗎？
B: Go through the red line if you have something to declare.
如果你有需要申報的物品，就要走紅色通道。

2137 我可以拿走我的…嗎？
May I take my...?

(替換) May I have my...?

(範例) A: May I take my passport? 我可以拿走我的護照嗎？
B: Yes, please. 可以，請拿走吧。

| 2138 | 可以，請拿走吧。
Take them, please. |

(替換) Yes, please.
Please take them with you.
Yes, you may.
Go ahead, please.

(範例) **A:** May I have my entry documents? 我可以拿走我的入境證件嗎？
B: Take them, please. 可以，請拿走吧。

(提示) entry ['ɛntrɪ] *n.* 入境
document ['dɑkjəmənt] *n.* 證件；文件

● 常見問答 Basic Questions and Answers

| 2139 | 請出示…。
..., please. |

(替換) Show me your..., please.
May I see your...?

(範例) **A:** Passport, please. 請出示護照。
B: Right here. 給你。

| 2140 | 給你。
Here you are. |

(替換) Here it is.
Here they are.
Right here.
Here you go.

(範例) **A:** Show me your documents, please. 請出示你的文件。
B: Here you are. 給你。

| 2141 | 你要在…待多久？
How long are you going to stay in...? |

(替換) How long will you be staying in...?

(範例) **A:** How long are you going to stay in Sweden? 你要在瑞典待多久？
B: About half a month. 約半個月。

2142
你此行的目的是什麼？
What's the purpose of your trip?

(替換) Why are you taking this trip?
May I know the purpose of your trip?
Would you tell us what you are taking the trip for?

(範例) **A:** What's the purpose of your trip? 你此行的目的是什麼？
B: Academic exchange. 學術交流。

(提示) academic [ˌækəˈdɛmɪk] *adj.* 學術的

2143
你是出差還是度假？
Are you here on business or on holiday?

(替換) Are you coming here to study or to travel?

(範例) **A:** Are you here on business or on holiday?
你是出差還是度假？
B: Neither. I'm here to attend my son's graduation ceremony.
兩者都不是，我是來參加我兒子的畢業典禮。

2144
有需要繳稅的東西嗎？
Do you have anything dutiable?

(替換) Do you have anything to pay a duty on?

(範例) **A:** Do you have anything dutiable? 有需要繳稅的東西嗎？
B: Nothing that I'm aware of. 據我所知沒有。

2145
你有沒有帶什麼禮品入境？
Are you bringing any gifts into the country?

(範例) **A:** Are you bringing any gifts into the country?
你有沒有帶什麼禮品入境？
B: Yes. Some bottles of perfume for my friends.
有，我給朋友們帶了幾瓶香水。

2146
你帶多少外幣？
How much foreign currency are you carrying?

(範例) **A:** How much foreign currency are you carrying? 你帶多少外幣？
B: Eight hundred US dollars in bills. 八百美金現鈔。

(提示) currency [ˈkɝənsɪ] *n.* 貨幣；錢幣

2147

你帶的現金超過…了嗎？
Are you carrying more than...with you?

(替換) Does the money you have on you exceed...?

(範例) **A:** Are you carrying more than $10,000 with you?
你帶的現金超過一萬美元了嗎？
B: No. 沒有。
A: OK. Otherwise, you have to declare it. 很好。否則要報關。

(提示) exceed [ɪk'sid] *v.* 超過

2148

你有東西要報關嗎？
Do you have anything to declare?

(替換) Do you have anything particular to declare?

(範例) **A:** Do you have anything to declare?
你有東西要報關嗎？
B: Can you tell me what has to be declared?
可以告訴我什麼東西是需要報關的嗎？

2149

你去了…嗎？
Were you on...?

(替換) Did you go to...?
Would you please tell me whether you went to...?

(範例) **A:** Were you on a farm or on a ranch of any kind?
你去了農場或牧場之類的地方嗎？
B: No, I was not.
我沒去。

(提示) ranch [ræntʃ] *n.* 大牧場；農場

2150

你帶了什麼東西嗎？
Are you importing anything?

(範例) **A:** Are you importing anything? 你帶了什麼東西嗎？
B: No, I'm not. 沒有。

2151

你帶了什麼食品嗎？
Are you bringing any food items?

(範例) **A:** Are you bringing any food items? 你帶了什麼食品嗎？
B: No, I'm not. 沒有。

2152
請把你的包包放在桌上，讓我看看…裡面的東西。
Please place your bags on the table. Show me what's in...

(替換) Please put your bags on the table and let me see inside...

(範例) A: Please place your bags on the table. Show me what's in that suit-case. 請把包包放在桌子上，讓我看看手提箱裡面的東西。
B: OK. 好的。

2153
…裡面是什麼？
What's in the...?

(替換) Can you tell me what you have in the...?
Would you please tell me what there is in the...?

(範例) A: What's in the shoulder bag? 側背的包包裡面是什麼？
B: My personal clothing. 我個人的衣物。

2154
這些行李都是你的嗎？
Is all the luggage yours?

(範例) A: Is all the luggage yours? 這些行李都是你的嗎？
B: Yes, it is. 是的，都是我的。

2155
你所有的行李都檢查過了嗎？
Was all your luggage checked?

(替換) Has all your luggage been checked?

(範例) A: Was all your luggage checked? 你所有的行李都檢查過了嗎？
B: Yes, it was. 是的，已經檢查過了。

2156
你申報的是…，但是你實際上攜帶的是…。
...you declared was..., but you've got a...here.

(範例) A: The computer you declared was Toshiba, but you've got a Dell here. 你申報的是東芝電腦，但是你實際上攜帶的是戴爾的。
B: I'm very sorry. I wasn't careful. 非常抱歉，我不小心的。

2157
對不起，這些…不能帶往國外。
I'm sorry these...cannot be taken out of the country.

(範例) A: I'm sorry these curios cannot be taken out of the country.
對不起，這些古物不能帶往國外。

B: Then, what should I do with them?
那要怎樣處理它們呢？

提示　curio ['kjʊrɪ,o] *n.* 古董；古物

2158　你填完所有海關的表格嗎？
Have you filled out all your customs forms?

範例　**A:** Have you filled out all your customs forms?
你填完所有海關的表格嗎？
B: Yes, I have.
是的。

2159　這是你的收據。
Here's your receipt.

替換　Take your receipt, please.

範例　**A:** Here's your receipt. 這是你的收據。
B: Thank you. 謝謝。

2160　你已經辦完手續了。
You're finished now.

替換　The customs formalities are over.
You're through with the customs formalities.

範例　**A:** You're finished now. 你已經辦完手續了。
B: Thank you. 謝謝。

提示　formality [fɔr'mælətɪ] *n.* 正式手續

7.6　在旅館 At the Hotel

　　去國外自助旅行時，要注意提前預訂好旅館。預訂可以透過電話進行，在機場或車站，一般都有預訂旅館的免費電話。預訂時，要說出自己的姓名、預訂的時間和客房種類等。房間有 single room（單人房）、double room（雙人房間）。要了解是否有浴室時，要注意 bath（盆浴）和 shower（淋浴）的意思不同。到了旅館之後，要先填 registration card（登記卡），最好事先問清楚價目表。賓館計費有 European plan（費用不包括餐費，tax 和 service charge 另

算）、American plan full pension（費用包括三餐）和 half pension/semi-pension（早餐固定，午餐或晚餐任選其一）。

　　旅館的入住時間叫作入住登記時間（check-in time），在美國通常是中午或一點左右。你必須離開的時間叫作退房登記時間（check-out time）。通常是上午十一點左右或是中午。不過每個旅館都有自己的規定，所以你在訂房間時，需要確定一下這兩個時間。

● 預約訂房 Making Reservations

2161	這裡是訂房部。請問有什麼需要嗎？ **Reservations. How may I help you?**

(100)

替換　This is the reservations office. May I help you?
　　　　Reservations. How may I serve you?

範例　A: Reservations. How may I help you?
　　　　　這裡是訂房部。請問有什麼需要嗎？
　　　　B: I'd like to reserve a room.
　　　　　我想要訂房間。

2162	我要預訂一間⋯的⋯房。 **May I reserve a...room for...?**

替換　Can I book a...room for...?
　　　　I'd like to book a...room for...
　　　　I want to book a...room for...
　　　　Could you reserve a...room for me for...?

範例　A: May I reserve a double room for August 16?
　　　　　我要預訂一間八月十六日的雙人房。
　　　　B: I'm afraid we only have a single room available on that date.
　　　　　恐怕那天只有一間單人房。

2163	你什麼時候住？ **When do you need the room?**

範例　A: When do you need the room? 你什麼時候住？
　　　　B: May 21, next Monday. 五月二十一日，下週一。

2164

住多久？
For how long?

(替換) How long will you be staying?
How long do you expect to stay?
How long do you plan to stay here?

(範例) **A:** For how long? 住多久？
B: I'll be staying for five days. 我要住五天。

2165

你要什麼樣的房間？
What kind of room do you want?

(替換) What kind of room would you like?

(範例) **A:** What kind of room do you want? 你要什麼樣的房間？
B: A double room, please. 請給我雙人房。

2166

我能要一間有…的客房嗎？
Could I have a room with..., please?

(替換) Can you let me have a room with...?
Can I book a room with...?
I want (to have) a room with...
I'd like a room with...

(範例) **A:** Could I have a room with a good view of the sea, please?
我能要一間有海景的客房嗎？
B: Sure.
當然。

2167

我想要一間吸煙／非吸煙的客房。
I'd like a smoking/non-smoking room.

(替換) Could I have a smoking/non-smoking room, please?

(範例) **A:** I'd like a smoking room. 我想要一間吸煙的客房。
B: Sorry, but they are fully booked. 對不起，都被訂光了。

2168

對不起，面海的房間目前都已客滿了。
Sorry, the rooms facing the ocean are all full at present.

(替換) Sorry, the rooms facing the ocean are fully booked.

(範例) **A:** Sorry, the rooms facing the ocean are all full at present.
對不起，面海的房間目前都已客滿了。

B: What a pity! Could you please check again?
真遺憾，可以請你再查一遍嗎？

2169 你能不能幫我查一查…有沒有空房間？
Could you find out for me whether there are any vacant rooms for...?

（範例）**A:** Could you find out for me whether there are any vacant rooms for tomorrow?
你能不能幫我查一查明天有沒有空房間？
B: Sorry. We don't have any vacancies at the moment.
對不起，目前我們沒有空房。

（提示）vacancy ['vekənsɪ] *n.* 空缺；空房

2170 你能不能為我保留這房間？
Can you hold it for me?

（範例）**A:** Can you hold it for me? 你能不能為我保留這房間？
B: I can hold it for you until 6 p.m. 我可以為你保留到下午六點鐘。

2171 可以請你告訴我…的費用嗎？
Can you tell me the rate for..., please?

（替換）What does...cost?
What price would...be?
How much is...?
How much does...cost?
How much do you charge for...?

（範例）**A:** Can you tell me the rate for a double room, please?
可以請你告訴我一間雙人房的費用嗎？
B: It's 100 dollars per night, not including tax.
每晚一百美金，不包含稅金。

2172 含三餐嗎？
Are meals included?

（替換）Does that include meals?

（範例）**A:** Are meals included? 含三餐嗎？
B: It includes a full breakfast. 包括全套早餐。

2173

加床要加錢嗎？
Is there a charge for extra beds?

(替換) Do we have to pay for extra beds?

(範例) **A:** Is there a charge for extra beds? 加床要加錢嗎？
B: For each additional bed, there will be an extra charge of 8 dollars per day. 每增加一個床鋪，每天加收八美元。

(提示) extra ['εkstrə] *adj.* 外加的
additional [ə'dɪʃənl] *adj.* 另外的；額外的

2174

兒童要付全額嗎？
Do we have to pay full price for children?

(範例) **A:** Do we have to pay full price for children? 兒童要付全額嗎？
B: No, there is a discount for children. 不，兒童可以減價。

2175

市內電話要收費嗎？
Do you charge for local phone calls?

(替換) Do we need to pay for local phone calls?

(範例) **A:** Do you charge for local phone calls?
市內電話要收費嗎？
B: We charge 10 cents for each phone call.
每打一次電話我們收費十分。

2176

能用信用卡付帳嗎？
Can I put that on my credit card?

(替換) May I pay by credit card?

(範例) **A:** Can I put that on my credit card? 能用信用卡付帳嗎？
B: Of course. 當然可以。

2177

我打電話是要確認一下我預訂…的房間。
I'm calling to confirm my reservation for...

(範例) **A:** Reservations, may I help you?
訂房部，有需要我為你服務的地方嗎？
B: I'm calling to confirm my reservation for September 9.
我打電話是要確認一下我預訂九月九日的房間。

2178

請問大名是？
Your name, please?

(替換) What's your name, please?
May I have your name?
Would you please tell me your name?

(範例) **A:** Your name, please? 請問大名是？
B: William Smith. 威廉‧史密斯。

● 住房與退房 Checking In & Checking Out

2179

你在我們這裡訂房了嗎？
Do you have a reservation with us?

(替換) Have you reserved a room?
Have you had a room reserved here?

(範例) **A:** We'd like to check in, please. 我們要辦理住宿登記。
B: Do you have a reservation with us? 你在我們這裡訂房了嗎？

2180

我預訂了…。
I have a booking for...

(替換) I have reservations for...
I booked a room here for...
I've just made a reservation for...

(範例) **A:** I have a booking for tonight. 我預訂了今晚的房間。
B: Let me check. 讓我查一下。

2181

對不起，這裡沒有以這個名字預訂的客房。
Sorry, there is no reservation under that name.

(範例) **A:** My name is Henry Peter.
我的名字是亨利‧彼得。
B: Sorry, there is no reservation under that name.
對不起，這裡沒有以這個名字預訂的客房。

2182

請給我看一下證件？
May I see some identification, please?

(替換) Have you got any identification?
Show me some ID, please.

範例) **A:** May I see some identification, please? 請給我看一下證件？
B: Is my driver's license OK? 我的駕照可以嗎？

提示) identification [aɪˌdɛntəfəˈkeʃən] *n.* 身分證明

2183
你預訂的是…的一間單人房，對嗎？
You have a reservation for a single room for...Is that right?

範例) **A:** You have a reservation for a single room for tonight. Is that right?
你預訂的是今晚的一間單人房，對嗎？
B: Yes, that's right.
是的。

2184
請填上這份旅客登記表。
Fill out this traveler's form, please.

替換) Please fill out the traveler's form.
Could you fill out this traveler's form, please?
Will you please fill out/in this traveler's form?
Would you mind filling in this traveler's form, please?

範例) **A:** Fill out this traveler's form, please. 請填上這份旅客登記表。
B: Do we all have to do that? 我們每個人都必須登記嗎？

2185
我要結帳（退房）。
I'd like to check out.

替換) May I have my bill, please?
Get me the bill, please.
I'd like to have my bill now, please.
I'd like to pay my bill.
I'd like to settle my account.

範例) **A:** I'd like to check out. 我要結帳。
B: Yes, of course. 好，當然可以。

● 入宿與詢問其他資訊 Entering the Room & Asking for Other Information

2186
房間的鑰匙卡在哪裡？
Where is the key card?

替換) Where is the room key?
Where can I get a key to my room?

範例 │ **A:** Where is the key card?
房間的鑰匙卡在哪裡？
B: You can get a key to your room at the service counter on your floor.
你可以在房間樓層的服務台拿到鑰匙。

2187 我如何去房間？
How do I get to my room?

範例 │ **A:** How do I get to my room? 我如何去房間？
B: The porter will take you up. 行李員會帶你上去。

提示 │ porter ['portɚ] *n.* （飯店的）守門人；（車站的）行李搬運工

2188 電燈開關在哪裡？
Where are the light switches?

範例 │ **A:** Where are the light switches? 電燈開關在哪裡？
B: Right behind the door. 就在門後面。

2189 怎樣打開…呢？
How do I turn on the...?

範例 │ **A:** How do I turn on the heating? 怎樣打開暖氣？
B: Press the button, please. 請按那個按鈕。

2190 蒸汽室在哪裡？
Where's the sauna?

替換 │ Can you tell me where the sauna is?

範例 │ **A:** Where's the sauna? 蒸汽室在哪裡？
B: It's on the second floor. 在二樓。

提示 │ sauna ['saʊnə] *n.* 蒸汽室
在美式英語中，建築物的一樓叫作 first floor（一樓）；在英式英文中，叫作 ground floor（底層）。再往上一層，美式英文為 second floor（二樓）；英式英文為 first floor（二樓），以上以此類推。

2191 房間內有直撥電話嗎？
Is there a direct-dial phone in the room?

範例 │ **A:** Is there a direct-dial phone in the room? 房間內有直撥電話嗎？
B: Yes, there is. 是的，有直撥電話。

2192	你們提供哪些娛樂設施？ **What sorts of recreational facilities do you offer?**

替換　What kinds of recreational facilities do you provide?

範例　A: What sorts of recreational facilities do you offer?
　　　你們提供哪些娛樂設施？
　　　B: We offer many.
　　　我們提供很多種。

2193	早餐什麼時候供應？ **What time do you serve breakfast?**

範例　A: What time do you serve breakfast? 早餐什麼時候供應？
　　　B: From 6 a.m. to 9 a.m. 從早上六點到九點。

2194	如果你需要任何東西，就打電話給服務台。 **If you want anything, just call the front desk.**

替換　If there's anything you need, just ring Reception.
　　　If you need anything, please call the service counter.

範例　A: If you want anything, just call the front desk.
　　　如果你需要任何東西，就打電話給服務台。
　　　B: Thanks.
　　　謝謝。

7.7 在郵局 At the Post Office

　　在西方國家，儘管科技的發展使電子信件非常普及，但仍然有很多人對親筆書信情有獨鍾。他們喜歡在節慶、特殊的日子以及旅途中寄卡片或信件給親朋好友，以表達他們的情感。而對那些來自其他國家的移民、留學生們來講，在國外光顧郵局寄信或寄東西回國內是常有的事。考慮到時間的關係，通常人們會利用航空郵政。郵票可以在書攤、藥房、車站零售店和旅館的郵票販賣機買到，郵筒通常位於郵局、街角、旅館或大廈，有時我們也可以請旅館代寄信件和物品。寄包裹需要寫明內容，填寫關稅申報單。如果擔心包裹遺失，還可以加保險。

● 郵寄方式 Ways of Mailing Things

2195 我想寄…。
I'd like to send it by...

101

(替換) By..., please.
May I send/have it by...?

(範例) **A:** How would you like to send it? 你想以什麼方式郵寄？
B: I'd like to send it by surface mail. 我想寄平信。

2196 你要掛號嗎？
Do you want it registered?

(替換) Do you want to have it registered?
Would you like to send it registered?

(範例) **A:** Do you want it registered? 你要掛號嗎？
B: Yes, I'd like to have it registered. 是的，我要掛號。

2197 我可以寄航空郵件嗎？
May I send this letter by airmail?

(範例) **A:** May I send this letter by airmail? 我可以寄航空郵件嗎？
B: Sure. 當然可以。

● 郵寄時間 Delivery Time

2198 …要花多少時間？
How long does it take by...mail?

(範例) **A:** How long does it take by regular mail? 平信要花多少時間？
B: About a week at the most. 最多約一個星期。

2199 從這裡寄往…的航空郵件大約要花多少時間？
Approximately how long does it take for a letter to go by airmail from here to...?

(替換) How long does it take an airmail to reach...?

(範例) **A:** Approximately how long does it take for a letter to go by airmail from here to London?
從這裡寄往倫敦的航空郵件大約要花多少時間？

499

B: About one week.
大約一個星期。

提示　approximately [ə'prɑksəmɪtlɪ] *adv.* 大約

● 郵資費用 Postage

2200　請告訴我從這裡寄一封航空信到…要多少郵資？
Can you tell me how much it costs to send a letter by airmail from here to...?

範例　**A:** Can you tell me how much it costs to send a letter by airmail from here to Japan?
請告訴我從這裡寄一封航空信到日本要多少郵資？
B: I'll just make sure. Is there anything else?
我確定一下。還有其他需要嗎？

2201　寄往…的…費率是多少？
What's the...rate for...?

替換　What's the postage for a...letter to...?

範例　**A:** What's the airmail rate for Europe? 寄往歐洲的航空郵件費率是多少？
B: 40 cents per ounce. 每盎司四十分。

提示　ounce [auns] *n.* 盎司

● 郵寄與領取包裹 Sending & Claiming a Parcel

2202　我想把這包裹寄往…。
I want to mail this parcel to...

替換　I want to send this package to...

範例　**A:** I want to mail this parcel to Singapore. 我想把這包裹寄往新加坡。
B: Please fill out this form first. 請先填寫這張表格。

2203　請問這包裹寄往…需要多少郵資？
How much postage does it need for...?

替換　What's the postage for this parcel for..., please?

範例　**A:** How much postage does it need for Vancouver?
請問這包裹寄往溫哥華需要多少郵資？

B: Let me weigh it first.
讓我先稱一下重量。

2204

請快遞這個包裹。
Please send this parcel by special delivery.

範例 **A:** Please send this parcel by special delivery.
請快遞這個包裹。

B: You have to pay a surcharge on this express-mail parcel.
快遞包裹要付額外郵資。

2205

用海運寄一個包裹到…要多久時間？
How long will it take to deliver a parcel to...by...?

範例 **A:** How long will it take to deliver a parcel to Hong Kong by surface mail? 用海運寄一個包裹到香港要多久時間？

B: Less than two months. 兩個月內。

2206

印刷品的郵寄費比較便宜嗎？
Is the rate for printed matter cheaper?

範例 **A:** Is the rate for printed matter cheaper?
印刷品的郵寄費比較便宜嗎？

B: Yes, but it's not as fast as ordinary mail.
是的，但是不如一般信件那麼快。

2207

郵寄包裹的大小及重量限制是多少？
What's the size and weight limit for a package?

替換 What's the maximum size and weight allowed?

範例 **A:** What's the size and weight limit for a package?
郵寄包裹的大小及重量限制是多少？

B: Just a moment. I'll look it up.
等一會兒，我查一下。

2208

要保險嗎？
Do you want it insured?

替換 Do you want to get it insured?
Do you wish to insure it?
Would you like to buy insurance for it?

範例 **A:** Do you want it insured? 要保險嗎？
B: Yes. Please insure it for 40 dollars. 是的，請保四十美元。

2209
我要領取包裹。這是通知單。
I'd like to pick up a package. Here is the notification.

替換 This is a parcel arrival notice. May I have my parcel?

範例 **A:** I'd like to pick up a package. Here is the notification.
我要領取包裹。這是通知單。
B: Sign here, please.
請在這簽名。

提示 notification [ˌnotəfəˈkeʃən] *n.* 通知單

● 匯款與兌現匯票 Sending & Cashing a Money Order

2210
我要一張郵政匯票。
I need a postal order, please.

替換 I'd like a postal order, please.
May I have a postal order?

範例 **A:** I need a postal order, please. 我要一張郵政匯票。
B: Here you are. 在這裡。

2211
匯…到…要多少費用？
What's the cost for...remittance to...?

替換 What's the cost to send...to...?

範例 **A:** What's the cost for a 2000-dollar remittance to Boston?
匯兩千美元到波士頓要多少費用？
B: About 40 dollars.
大約四十美元。

提示 remittance [rɪˈmɪtṇs] *n.* 匯款

2212
匯款金額上限是多少？
What's the limit for wiring money?

範例 **A:** What's the limit for wiring money?
匯款金額上限是多少？
B: You can wire up to $5000 with this money order.
用這張匯票，最多可以匯五千美元。

2213
…要多久才能收到這筆錢？
How long will it take for the money to get to...?

 A: How long will it take for the money to get to my son in Australia?
我在澳洲的兒子要多久才能收到這筆錢？
B: At least three working days.
至少三個工作天。

2214
我在等匯款，不知匯到了沒？
I'm expecting some money. Has it arrived?

(範例) **A:** I'm expecting some money. Has it arrived?
我在等匯款，不知匯到了沒？
B: May I see some ID?
給我看一下身分證好嗎？

2215
請幫我把這張匯票兌現。
I want to cash this money order, please.

(替換) Can I have this money order cashed, please?

 A: I want to cash this money order, please.
請幫我把這張匯票兌現。
B: OK.
好。

● 其他資訊 Other Information

2216
為什麼這封信被退回來了？
Why was the letter returned?

(替換) Why did the letter get returned?

(範例) **A:** Why was the letter returned? 為什麼這封信被退回來了？
B: It needs more postage. 需要補郵資。

2217
郵差上午什麼時候來收信？
What time does the postman pick up the mail in the morning?

(替換) When does the postman come to collect the mail in the morning?

範例　A: What time does the postman pick up the mail in the morning?
郵差上午什麼時候來收信？
B: Around 9 o'clock.
九點鐘左右。

2218
我能趕上今天的末班郵件嗎？
Am I in time for the last mail today?

替換　Is it possible for me to catch the last post today?

範例　A: Am I in time for the last mail today?
我能趕上今天的末班郵件嗎？
B: I'm afraid the last post has been dispatched.
恐怕末班郵件已經發出了。

提示　dispatch [dɪ'spætʃ] *v.* 分派；派遣

2219
這裡有傳真服務嗎？
Is fax service available here?

範例　A: Is fax service available here? 這裡有傳真服務嗎？
B: Yes, it's over there. 有，在那邊。

2220
傳真到…要多少費用？
What's the rate for a fax to...?

範例　A: What's the rate for a fax to my hometown?
傳真到我家鄉要多少費用？
B: About one dollar per page.
每頁近一美元。

2221
請幫它保…美元。
Please insure it for...dollars.

範例　A: Do you want it insured? 你要投保嗎？
B: Yes. Please insure it for 200 dollars. 要。請幫它保兩百美元。

2222
保費是多少？
What's the insurance fee?

範例　A: What's the insurance fee? 保費是多少？
B: 58 marks. 五十八馬克。

7.8 在銀行 At the Bank

銀行的最重要功能就是收款和發款,而幾乎所有的銀行都設有自動提款機(Automatic Teller Machine, ATM),以方便顧客使用。我們在銀行門口、主要街道、超級市場、車站等,隨處都可以見到 ATM。

在美國,checking account 指「支票存款戶頭」。辦理 checking account 後,銀行會把印好的正式支票簿寄給你。上面一般會有姓名、地址,用的時候要在支票上簽名。開了支票,對方拿去銀行兌現,這個動作就叫 clear。checking account 一般沒有利息,而且每當你開出一張支票,銀行還要扣服務費(service charge)。

在旅行時,使用旅行支票(traveler's check)是比較安全方便的作法,但是買旅行支票要付手續費。在使用時,要當著對方的面簽名,簽名樣式要與支票上已有的簽名樣式相同無誤(再加上有照片的身分證件,如護照或國際信用卡),對方才收。如果不簽名,支票是無效的,所以不怕被偷。

● 開戶與結清 Opening & Closing an Account

2223	我可以開個…戶頭嗎? (102) **Can I open a...account here?**
替換	I'd like to open a...account. I want to open a...account.
範例	**A:** Can I open a savings account here? 我可以開個儲蓄戶頭嗎? **B:** You can open a savings account at any time with an initial deposit of 50 dollars. 你隨時都可以用開戶金額五十美元來開立一個儲蓄帳戶。
提示	initial [ɪˈnɪʃəl] *adj.* 開始的
2224	我的…存摺…到期了。 **My...deposit certificate matured...**
範例	**A:** My fixed deposit certificate matured yesterday. 我的定期存摺昨天到期了。 **B:** Let me check. 讓我看一下。

505

2225 我想請你幫我結清戶頭。
I'd like to close my account with you.

(替換) May I close my account here?

(範例) **A:** I'd like to close my account with you. 我想請你幫我結清戶頭。
B: All right. 好的。

● 存款與放款 Depositing & Withdrawing from an Account

2226 第一次存款有最低限額嗎？
Is there any minimum for the initial deposit?

(替換) What is the minimum original deposit?

(範例) **A:** Is there any minimum for the initial deposit?
第一次存款有最低限額嗎？
B: Our minimum deposit is $30.
最低存款金額是三十美元。

(提示) minimum ['mɪnəməm] *n. adj.* 最低；最小值

2227 這種戶頭有利息嗎？
Do you pay interest on this account?

(範例) **A:** Do you pay interest on this account? 這種戶頭有利息嗎？
B: Yes, you will earn a little interest. 有。你可以賺到一點利息。

2228 年利率是多少？
What's the annual interest rate?

(範例) **A:** What's the annual interest rate? 年利率是多少？
B: The account carries an interest of 4.5%. 利息是百分之四點五。

(提示) annual ['ænjʊəl] *adj.* 一年一次的；每年的

2229 你希望戶頭裡存入多少錢？
How much do you want to deposit in your account?

(替換) How much do you wish to put into your account?
How much money do you want to place to your credit?
How much cash do you plan to deposit in your account?

範例
A: How much do you want to deposit in your account?
你希望戶頭裡存入多少錢？
B: 1,000 dollars.
一千美元。

2230
你想從戶頭提領多少錢？
How much would you like to withdraw from your account?

範例
A: How much would you like to withdraw from your account?
你想從戶頭提領多少錢？
B: I want to take out 800 dollars from my savings account, please.
我想從我的儲蓄帳戶中提領八百美元。

提示
withdraw [wɪð'drɔ] *v.* 提領；撤銷

2231
你要多少面額的現金？
How do you want it?

替換
How would you like it?
In what denominations?
Do you want large or small bills?

範例
A: How do you want it? 你要多少面額的現金？
B: Give me some small bills, please. 請給我一些小面額的紙幣。

提示
denomination [dɪˌnɑmə'neʃən] *n.* 單位；幣值

2232
請給我十美元的。
In tens, please.

替換
Please give me ten dollar bills.
Would you give me ten-dollar bills, please?

範例
A: In tens, please. 請給我十美元的。
B: OK. Wait a moment, please. 好的，請稍等。

2233
請告訴我我的餘額。
Please tell me my balance.

替換
Could you tell me my balance?
I'd like to know my balance, please.

範例
A: Please tell me my balance. 請告訴我我的餘額。
B: Your balance in the bank is 600 dollars. 你在銀行的餘額是六百美元。

提示
balance ['bæləns] *n.* 餘額；結餘

● 兌現與找零 Cashing Checks & Changing Money

2234	我想把…兌換成現金。 **I want to cash..., please.**
(替換)	Can I cash...here? Could you cash..., please?
(範例)	A: I want to cash this money order, please. 我想把這張匯票兌換成現金。 B: Please fill out this form. 請填這張表格。

2235	今天…匯率是多少？ **What's...going for today?**
(替換)	I'd like to know the rate for... Would you please tell me the current rate for...? What's your selling rate for...today? What's your buying rate for...? Could you tell me the current rate for..., please?
(範例)	A: What's the dollar going for today? 今天美元的匯率是多少？ B: Please wait a moment. Let me check. 請稍候。讓我查一查。

2236	換成…是多少？ **How much will it be in...?**
(替換)	How much would I get for...? How much in Foreign Exchange Certificates can I get for...? What would you give me for my...?
(範例)	A: How much will it be in German marks? 換成德國馬克是多少？ B: Please wait a minute. I'll check the exchange rate between marks and dollars. 請等一下，我查查德國馬克和美元的兌換率。

2237	你要兌換什麼貨幣？ **What currency do you want?**
(替換)	What do you wish to exchange? What kind of currency do you want (to change)?
(範例)	A: What currency do you want? 你要兌換什麼貨幣？ B: Euro, please. 我想換成歐元。

| 2238 | 我可以兌換價值…的…嗎？
Can I have...worth of...? |

(替換)	Can you give me...in...? Give me...worth of... I'd like...worth of... I want to change...to... I want to convert...into...
(範例)	**A:** How much do you want to exchange? 　你想兌換多少錢？ **B:** Can I have 200 dollars worth of NT Dollars? 　我可以兌換價值兩百美元的新台幣嗎？
(提示)	convert [kən'vɝt] *v.* 使轉變；轉換

● 其他服務 Other Services

| 2239 | 我想買一些旅行支票。
I'd like to buy some traveler's checks. |

| (替換) | I'd like some traveler's checks, please. |
| (範例) | **A:** I'd like to buy some traveler's checks. 我想買一些旅行支票。
B: How many do you want? 你需要多少？ |

| 2240 | 能不能請你幫我查查是否有一筆來自…的匯款？
Could you find out whether there's a remittance for me from...? |

| (範例) | **A:** Could you find out whether there's a remittance for me from Taiwan?
　能不能請你幫我查查是否有一筆來自台灣的匯款？
B: Sorry, your remittance hasn't arrived yet.
　對不起，匯款還沒有到我們這裡。 |

| 2241 | 我能不能租用一個保險箱？
Can I rent a safe/safety deposit box? |

| (範例) | **A:** Can I rent a safe deposit box? 我能不能租用一個保險箱？
B: Sure. 當然可以。 |

| 2242 | 我能不能用普通支票支付旅行支票的款項？
Can I pay for the traveler's checks with an open check? |

範例
> **A:** Can I pay for the traveler's checks with an open check?
> 我能不能用普通支票支付旅行支票的款項？
> **B:** Let me confirm that.
> 讓我確認一下。

7.9　在戲院 At the Cinema

　　電影已經成為人們日常生活的話題。電影的熱門話題，有助於人際關係的發展。但有一點要特別注意：根據影片內容，英美電影院上映的影片有分類標記，如 "X" 表示「限制級」，"U" 表示「普通級」，"15" 表示「輔導級，十五歲以下不得觀賞」，"18" 和 "X" 相同，表示「十八歲以下不得觀賞」。

● 談論電影 Talking about Movies

| 2243 | …上演什麼電影？
What's playing...? | 103 |

範例
> **A:** What's playing this week? 這個星期上演什麼電影？
> **B:** *Titanic* is on. 上演《鐵達尼號》。

| 2244 | 電影幾點開始？
When does it start? |

範例
> **A:** When does it start? 電影幾點開始？
> **B:** It's on at 7 o'clock. 電影七點開始。

| 2245 | 你…願意跟我一起去看電影嗎？
Would you like to go to the movies with me...? |

替換
> Can you go to the movie with me...?

範例
> **A:** Would you like to go to the movies with me tonight?
> 你今天晚上願意跟我一起去看電影？
> **B:** Sorry, I have an appointment then.
> 對不起，我有約了。

2246	電影的內容是什麼？ **What's the movie about?**

(替換) Can you tell me something about the movie?

(範例) **A:** What's the movie about? 電影的內容是什麼？
B: It's a story of a Roman emperor. 講的是羅馬皇帝的故事。

(提示) emperor [ˈɛmpərɚ] *n.* 皇帝；君主

2247	這是一部什麼樣的電影？ **What kind of movie is it?**

(範例) **A:** What kind of movie is it? 這是一部什麼樣的電影？
B: It's a science fiction film. 這是一部科幻片。

2248	男女主角都很有名。 **The leading actor and actress are both very famous.**

(範例) **A:** The leading actor and actress are both very famous.
男女主角都很有名。
B: Yes, you're right.
對呀。

2249	…還有座位嗎？ **Have you got any seats for...?**

(替換) Are there any tickets left for...?

(範例) **A:** Have you got any seats for *Star Wars* at 3 o'clock?
三點鐘開始的《星際大戰》還有座位嗎？
B: The tickets were sold out three days ago.
三天前就已經銷售一空了。

2250	請問票價多少錢？ **How much is that, please?**

(替換) How much are the tickets, please?

(範例) **A:** How much is that, please? 請問票價多少錢？
B: Five dollars per person. 每人五美元。

● 觀後感想 Commenting on the Movie

2251　這個故事太…了。
The story was too...

（替換）　It's too...!

（範例）　**A:** The story was too sentimental. 這個故事令人傷感了。
　　　　B: I agree with you. 我跟你的想法一樣。

（提示）　sentimental [ˌsɛntə'mɛntl] *adj.* 感傷性的；感情脆弱的

2252　你覺得電影怎麼樣？
How did you like the movie?

（替換）　What did you think of the film?

（範例）　**A:** How did you like the movie? 你覺得電影怎麼樣？
　　　　B: I just couldn't see the point of it. 我看不出有什麼意義。

2253　電影的…如何？
How is the...in the movie?

（替換）　What do you think of the...in the movie?

（範例）　**A:** How is the music in the movie? 電影的配樂如何？
　　　　B: Quite excellent! 非常棒！

2254　你最喜歡哪個片段？
Which part did you like best?

（範例）　**A:** Which part did you like best? 你最喜歡哪個片段？
　　　　B: The part when they met each other. 他們相遇的那一段。

7.10　在餐廳 At the Restaurant

　　西方國家的餐館服務趨向多元化。人們可以在餐館用餐，也可以叫外賣，把食品帶到辦公室或公園裡吃。在美國「外賣」叫作 "take-out" food；在英國則叫作 "take-away" food。在速食店用餐，如果把食物帶走要說 "Take out." 或 "Food to go."；如果在店裡用餐要說 "I'll have it here." 或 "For here."，而速食店不需要支付任何服務費或小費，但若是在一般的餐館用餐，就要付小費（大約 15%）。在美國，餐廳服務人員的收入大部分來自小費。餐廳也許只付他們很少的時薪，所以大部分的服務人員期望至少獲得 15% 的小費。如果服務確實很糟糕，你付的小費可以少於 15%。但如果只留一點小費，或什麼都不留，餐廳老闆也許會過來問服務是否有問題，這可能會令人很尷尬。不幸的是，許多到美國的遊客不了解付小費的文化，因而產生一些誤會。這是因為亞洲國家基本上是不付小費的。美國餐廳現在正努力讓外國旅客熟悉這個文化。一些餐廳會用幾種外語說明需付小費。如果用信用卡付帳，信用卡帳單上通常有一行寫著 "Tip"。他們甚至會根據不同的比率算出小費，比如 15% 和 20% 的小費比率。在美國，有時小費也包括在帳單中，比如一些餐廳會對大型團體收取 15% 的服務費。

● 接待客人與帶位 Greeting Customers & Ushering Them In

2255
(104)
歡迎光臨！已訂位嗎？
Welcome to our restaurant! Do you have a reservation?

替換 | Welcome to our restaurant! Have you made a reservation?

範例 | **A:** Welcome to our restaurant! Do you have a reservation?
歡迎光臨！已訂位嗎？
B: Yes, I do.
是的。

2256
我訂位了。我的名字叫…。
I have a reservation. My name is...

替換 | We've got a reservation. I'm...

範例 | **A:** I have a reservation. My name is Jim Pitt.
我訂位了。我的名字叫吉姆‧彼德。
B: Let me check.
讓我查看一下。

2257
你們一共幾個人？
How many of you are there altogether?

替換 | How many (persons) are there in your party?
How many people?
How many in your group?

範例 | A: How many of you are there altogether? 你們一共幾個人？
B: There are five of us. 我們一共五個人。

2258 | 這邊請。
This way, please.

替換 | Would you follow me, please?
Could you come with me, please?
I'll show you to your table.

範例 | A: This way, please. 這邊請。
B: Thank you. 謝謝。

2259 | 這裡是你的桌子。可以嗎？
Here's your table. Is it all right?

範例 | A: Here's your table. Is it all right? 這裡是你的桌子。可以嗎？
B: It's fine. We'll sit here. 還不錯。我們就坐這裡。

2260 | 請問我們可以換桌子嗎？
Could we change tables?

替換 | Is it possible to change tables?

範例 | A: Could we change tables? 請問我們可以換桌子嗎？
B: Where would you like to sit? 你們想坐哪裡呢？

2261 | 你願意坐…嗎？
Would you like to sit...?

替換 | Do you want to sit...?
Would you rather sit...?

範例 | A: Would you like to sit near the dance floor? 你願意坐在舞池附近嗎？
B: I suppose that will do. 我想可以。

2262 | 有空位嗎？
Is there an available table?

替換 | Do you have any tables free?
Do you have any seats available?

範例 | A: Is there an available table? 有空位嗎？
B: Not at the moment I'm afraid. 恐怕目前沒有空位了。

2263	你們現在有⋯的座位嗎？ **Do you have any tables for...available at the moment?**

替換　Do you still have tables by...free?

範例
A: Do you have any tables for five available at the moment?
你們現在有五個人的座位嗎？
B: Sorry. I'm afraid all those tables are taken.
對不起，恐怕桌子都滿了。

2264	那裡有一張⋯個人的桌子。你們想要嗎？ **There's a table for...over there. Would you like it?**

範例
A: There's a table for seven over there. Would you like it?
那裡有一張七個人的桌子。你們想要嗎？
B: Yes, we would.
是的，我們要。

● 出示菜單與點菜 Presenting the Menu & Ordering

2265	請給我們菜單好嗎？ **We'd like a menu, please.**

替換　Could we see the menu, please?
Please show me the menu.
Let's have a look at the menu.

範例
A: We'd like a menu, please. 請給我們菜單好嗎？
B: Here's the menu, sir. 先生，這是菜單。

2266	有商業午餐的菜單嗎？ **Is there a set menu for lunch?**

範例
A: Is there a set menu for lunch? 有商業午餐的菜單嗎？
B: Yes, we have a set menu. 有，我們有套餐。

2267	不好意思！我現在可以點菜了嗎？我的時間有點趕。 **Excuse me! Could I order now? I'm in a little bit of a hurry.**

範例
A: Excuse me! Could I order now? I'm in a little bit of a hurry.
不好意思！我現在可以點菜了嗎？我的時間有點趕。
B: What would you like?
你要吃什麼？

2268

我推薦你點…。
I can recommend...

(替換)
I would suggest...
Why not try...?
How about...?
I think...is worth trying.

(範例)
A: What do you recommend? 你看我們點什麼好？
B: I can recommend the fried oysters. 我推薦你點炸牡蠣。

(提示) recommend [ˌrɛkə'mɛnd] *v.* 推薦；介紹

2269

你們的招牌菜是什麼？
What's your specialty?

(替換)
What are your specialties?
What's the specialty of the house?
What's the chef's specialty?

(範例)
A: What's your specialty? 你們的招牌菜是什麼？
B: Roast duck's the specialty here. 烤鴨是這裡的招牌菜。

2270

今天的特餐是什麼？
What's today's special?

(替換) What's special for today?

(範例)
A: What's today's special? 今天的特餐是什麼？
B: Today's special is fried sliced squid. 今天的特餐是炸魷魚片。

2271

要點…嗎？
Any...?

(替換) Do you want any...?

(範例)
A: Any vegetables? 要點蔬菜嗎？
B: I think I'll have potatoes. 我想要馬鈴薯。

2272

今天有什麼湯？
What soup do you have today?

(範例)
A: What soup do you have today?
今天有什麼湯？

B: We offer many kinds of soup. You can choose from oyster soup, beef soup, gold carp soup, clear soup, and shrimp soup.
我們提供很多種類的湯。有牡蠣湯、牛肉湯、鯽魚湯、清湯和蝦湯，任君選擇。

2273

我可以為你點菜了嗎？
May I take your order?

(替換)
Are you ready to order?
Can I take your order now?
Would you like to order now?

(範例)
A: May I take your order? 我可以為你點菜了嗎？
B: You order first, Bill. 比爾，你先點。

2274

你選好了嗎？
Have you chosen something?

(範例)
A: Have you chosen something? 你選好了嗎？
B: I'd like an order of chicken curry. 我要一份咖哩雞。

2275

要沙拉嗎？
Any salad?

(範例)
A: Any salad? 要沙拉嗎？
B: I'd like a chicken salad, please. 請來點雞肉沙拉。

2276

你要什麼沙拉醬？
What kind of dressing would you like on your salad?

(範例)
A: What kind of dressing would you like on your salad?
你要什麼沙拉醬？
B: What are my choices?
有什麼選擇？

(提示) dressing ['drɛsɪŋ] *n.* （沙拉的）調料

2277

你的牛排要三分熟、五分熟或全熟？
Would you like your steak rare, medium, or well-done?

(範例)
A: Would you like your steak rare, medium, or well-done?
你的牛排要三分熟、五分熟或全熟？
B: Medium, please.
請給我五分熟的。

2278

吐司要不要抹…或…？
Would you like...or...with your toast?

範例　A: Would you like butter or jam with your toast?
　　　　吐司要不要抹奶油或果醬？
　　　　B: I'd like it plain.
　　　　我喜歡白吐司。

2279

我們換換口味來點海鮮吧。
Let's have seafood for a change.

替換　Shall we have seafood for a change?

範例　A: Let's have seafood for a change. 我們換換口味來點海鮮吧。
　　　　B: All right. 好的。

2280

吃…好嗎？
Would...be alright?

替換　How about...?
　　　　Perhaps you might like...
　　　　Will...be to your taste?

範例　A: Would fried crab meat be alright? 吃炒蟹肉好嗎？
　　　　B: That will be great! 好極了！

2281

甜點要什麼？
How about dessert?

替換　What would you like for dessert?

範例　A: How about dessert? 甜點要什麼？
　　　　B: I'd like strawberry cake. 我要草莓蛋糕。

2282

要喝點什麼？
Anything to drink?

替換　What can I get you to drink?
　　　　What would you like to drink?
　　　　Would you like something to drink?

範例　A: Anything to drink? 要喝點什麼？
　　　　B: A large coke, please. 請給我一杯大杯可樂。

2283	你喜歡怎麼樣的咖啡？ **How would you like your coffee?**

範例 | A: How would you like your coffee? 你喜歡怎麼樣的咖啡？
B: With milk, but without sugar, please. 請加牛奶，但不要加糖。

2284	你的茶要濃一點還是淡一點？ **Do you like your tea strong or weak?**

範例 | A: Do you like your tea strong or weak? 你的茶要濃一點還是淡一點？
B: Strong, please. 請給我濃一點的。

● 用餐與應酬 Having a Meal & Expressing and Responding to Hospitality

2285	不要客氣，請隨便。 **Don't stand on ceremony. Make yourself at home.**

替換 | Help yourself to anything you like.

範例 | A: Don't stand on ceremony. Make yourself at home.
　不要客氣，請隨便。
B: Thank you.
　謝謝。

2286	請嘗嘗這個。 **Have some of this, please.**

範例 | A: Have some of this, please. 請嘗嘗這個。
B: All right. 好的。

2287	你想再來一點嗎？ **Don't you want to have any more?**

替換 | Would you care for another serving?
Wouldn't you like some more?
Do you want another piece?

範例 | A: Don't you want to have any more? 你想再來一點嗎？
B: With pleasure! 非常樂意！

2288	我再給你斟點酒好嗎？ **May I pour you some more wine?**

替換 | Let me get you some more wine.
Shall I get you another glass of wine?
Would you like a refill?

範例 | A: May I pour you some more wine? 我再給你斟點酒好嗎？
B: No more, thanks. 夠了，謝謝。

2289 要再來一點嗎？
Would you like some more?

替換 | Some more?
Do you want any more?

範例 | A: Would you like some more? 要再來一點嗎？
B: No. I've never been much of an eater. 不了，我食量不大。

2290 請把⋯遞給我，好嗎？
Pass me..., please.

替換 | Please pass me...
Give me..., if you can.
Could you hand me...?
Could I trouble you for...?
Would you give...to me?
Would you please pass me...?
May I trouble you for...?

範例 | A: Pass me the pepper, please. 請把胡椒粉遞給我，好嗎？
B: Here you are. 給你。

● 處理抱怨 Dealing with Complaints

2291 我們還得等多久才能用餐呢？
How much longer are we going to have to wait for our food?

範例 | A: How much longer are we going to have to wait for our food?
我們還得等多久才能用餐呢？
B: I'm sorry. I'll try to hurry things up.
對不起，我會設法催他們快點。

2292 服務太慢了。
The service is too slow.

範例
A: The service is too slow. 服務太慢了。
B: I'm sorry, sir. We're terribly busy. 對不起，先生。我們實在很忙。

2293
我看你搞錯了。這不是我點的菜。
I think you've made a mistake. This isn't what I ordered.

範例
A: I think you've made a mistake. This isn't what I ordered.
　 我看你搞錯了。這不是我點的菜。
B: Oh, I'm sorry. I made a mistake.
　 哦，對不起。我弄錯了。

2294
有什麼問題嗎？
What's the problem?

替換
Can you tell me what's wrong?
Could you tell me what's the matter?

範例
A: What's the problem, ma'am? 夫人，有什麼問題嗎？
B: The lobster is badly cooked. 這份龍蝦做得很差。

2295
能不能請你換一份？這個太…。
Could you bring me another one? This one's too...

範例
A: Could you bring me another one? This one's too salty.
　 能不能請你換一份？這個太鹹了。
B: I'll tell the kitchen to exchange it for you.
　 我會叫廚房幫你換掉。

2296
這肉是生的！我告訴過你，我的肉要全熟。
This meat's raw! I told you I wanted it well-done.

範例
A: This meat's raw! I told you I wanted it well-done.
　 這肉是生的！我告訴過你，我的肉要全熟。
B: I'm terribly sorry, sir. Would you like it cooked a little more?
　 非常對不起，先生。你願意再煮一下嗎？

● 結帳付款 Settling the Bill

2297
請把帳單拿來。
The bill, please.

替換
The check, please.
Give me the bill, please.

May I have the check, please?
Can I have the bill, please?
Could we have the bill, please?
Would you please bring us the check?
Can you bring us our check, please?

範例 A: The bill, please. 請把帳單拿來。
B: All right. Just a minute. 好的，馬上就來。

2298
今天我請客。
Be my guest.

替換 I'm going to pay.
It's my treat (today).

範例 A: Be my guest, I insist. 我堅持今天我請客。
B: OK. I'll pay next time. 好吧。下回換我請。

2299
讓我付帳。
It's on me this time.

替換 It's all on me.
Let me get it.
This one's mine.
Let me pay this time.
Let me have the check.

範例 A: It's on me this time. 讓我付帳。
B: How about splitting the bill? 各付各的怎麼樣？

2300
我們各付各的吧。
Let's go Dutch!

替換 Let's go fifty-fifty!

範例 A: Let's go Dutch. 我們各付各的吧。
B: I agree. 我同意。

2301
能不能把帳單分開？
Can we have separate checks?

替換 We'd prefer separate bills.

範例 A: Can we have separate checks? 能不能把帳單分開？
B: Yes, of course. 當然可以。

2302
你們接受… ?
Do you accept...?

(替換)
Do you accept...?
Will...do?

(範例)
A: Do you accept personal checks? 你們接受私人支票嗎？
B: Yes, we do. 可以，我們接受。

7.11 在醫院 At the Hospital

　　在英美等國看病，一般都要預約（make an appointment），一般的小病不經預約的話，連醫生的面都見不到。什麼時候看到醫生，得視醫生而定。有時一、兩天內可以看成，有時則要一星期以後才行。當然如果是急診，就可以直接送醫院接受治療。

　　在美國，一般可以在藥房（drugstore/pharmacy）或超市（supermarket）購買到成藥，處方箋的藥品則不能隨便買到，一定要有醫生簽了名的處方簽（prescription）才能到藥房購買。有些超市也有設立藥房。

● 掛號登記 Registration

2303
請告訴我掛號處在哪裡。
I'd like to know where the registration office is, please.

(105)

(替換)
Would you show me where the registration office is?

(範例)
A: I'd like to know where the registration office is, please.
請告訴我掛號處在哪裡。
B: Go straight and you'll see the sign.
直走，你就會看見牌子。

(提示)
registration [ˌrɛdʒɪˈstreʃən] *n.* 掛號

2304
我和…醫生…點有約。
I have an appointment with Dr...at...

(範例)
A: I have an appointment with Dr. George at two.
我和喬治醫生兩點有約。

B: May I have your name, please?
請問你叫什麼名字？

2305　你來過嗎？
Do you have a record?

（範例）**A:** Do you have a record? 你來過嗎？
B: Yes, it's here. 有。

2306　你有保險嗎？
Do you have insurance?

（替換）Are you insured?

（範例）**A:** Do you have insurance? 你有保險嗎？
B: Yes, here is my insurance card. 有，這是我的保險卡。

● 詢問與陳述病情 Asking about & Describing Symptoms

2307　我不舒服。
I don't feel well.

（替換）I feel so ill.
I feel poorly.
I feel very bad.
I feel a bit off-color.
I feel rather unwell.
I really feel terrible.
I'm under the weather.

（範例）**A:** Are you feeling well? 你感覺還好嗎？
B: I don't feel well. 我不舒服。

（提示）under the weather【非正式】身體不大舒服

2308　你覺得怎麼樣？
How are you feeling?

（範例）**A:** How are you feeling? 你覺得怎麼樣？
B: I feel absolutely rotten. 我覺得非常不舒服。

（提示）rotten ['rɑtṇ] *adj.* 不舒服的

2309	你的頭很痛嗎？ **Do you have a bad headache?**

(替換) Does your headache hurt you very much?

(範例) **A:** Do you have a bad headache? 你的頭很痛嗎？
B: It hurts terribly. 痛得很厲害。

2310	我的…痛。 **My...hurts.**

(替換) I feel a dull pain in my...
I've got a sore...
I've got a pain in my...
My...has been sore.

(範例) **A:** What's wrong with you? 你怎麼啦？
B: My left foot hurts. 我的左腳痛。

2311	你什麼時候開始覺得不舒服？ **When did you begin feeling sick?**

(替換) When did the pain start?
How long have you been feeling like this?
When did you start feeling the pain?

(範例) **A:** When did you begin feeling sick? 你什麼時候開始覺得不舒服？
B: About a month ago. 大約一個月前。

2312	有沒有咳嗽？ **Do you have a cough?**

(範例) **A:** Do you have a cough? 有沒有咳嗽？
B: Yes, I cough a lot at night. 有，我晚上咳得很厲害。

2313	你有咳血嗎？ **Are you coughing up blood?**

(範例) **A:** Are you coughing up blood? 你有咳血嗎？
B : I did once. 有過一次。

2314	你會呼吸困難嗎？ **Do you have difficulty breathing?**

範例 A: Do you have difficulty breathing? 你會呼吸困難嗎？
B: Sometimes. 有時候會。

2315 我得了肺炎嗎？
Do I have pneumonia?

替換 Is it pneumonia that I have?

範例 A: Do I have pneumonia? 我得了肺炎嗎？
B: It sounds like bronchitis. 聽起來像是支氣管炎。

提示 pneumonia [nju'monjə] *n.* 肺炎
bronchitis [brɑn'kaɪtɪs] *n.* 支氣管炎

2316 你有發燒嗎？
Do you have a fever?

替換 Have you got a fever?

範例 A: Do you have a fever? 你有發燒嗎？
B: Yes. I've got a temperature. 我發燒了。

2317 我發燒了。
I've got a fever.

替換 I feel feverish.
I'm running a fever.

範例 A: How do you feel? 你覺得怎麼樣？
B: I've got a fever. 我發燒了。

提示 feverish ['fivərɪʃ] *adj.* 發燒的

2318 為什麼我總是頭暈，沒有胃口？
Why do I always feel dizzy and have no appetite?

範例 A: Why do I always feel dizzy and have no appetite?
為什麼我總是頭暈，沒有胃口？
B: It sounds like you've caught a cold.
聽起來你似乎感冒了。

提示 appetite ['æpə,taɪt] *n.* 食欲；胃口

2319 你的胃口怎麼樣？
How is your appetite?

替換 | What's your appetite like?
Do you have any appetite?

範例 | **A:** How is your appetite? 你的胃口怎麼樣？
B: I've got a bad appetite. 我的胃口很差。

2320
我的風濕病嚴重嗎？
Is my rheumatism serious?

範例 | **A:** Is my rheumatism serious?
我的風濕病嚴重嗎？
B: Your rheumatism will need to be treated for about a month.
你的風濕病要進行一個月左右的治療。

提示 | rheumatism ['rumə‚tɪzəm] *n.* 風濕；風濕病

2321
你有藥物過敏嗎？
Are you allergic to any medication?

範例 | **A:** Are you allergic to any medication? 你有藥物過敏嗎？
B: Not as far as I know. 據我所知沒有。

提示 | allergic [ə'lɝdʒɪk] *adj.* 過敏的

2322
看上去像⋯。
It looks like...

範例 | **A:** It looks like measles. 看上去像麻疹。
B: It's inflammation of the skin. 這是皮膚發炎。

提示 | measles ['mizl̩z] *n.* 麻疹；風疹
inflammation [‚ɪnflə'meʃən] *n.* 炎症；發炎

2323
我一直失眠。
I'm suffering from insomnia.

替換 | I've been losing sleep.
I'm having trouble sleeping.

範例 | **A:** Do you sleep well? 你睡得好嗎？
B: I'm suffering from insomnia. 我一直失眠。

提示 | insomnia [ɪn'sɑmnɪə] *n.* 失眠；失眠症

2324
你的牙齒哪顆不好？
Which tooth is troubling you?

527

範例
A: Which tooth is troubling you?
你的牙齒哪顆不好？
B: One of my upper teeth is loose and it hurts.
我的一顆上齒鬆動而且疼痛。

2325
我必須拔牙嗎？
Do I have to have my tooth pulled?

替換
Will I have to have my tooth extracted?

範例
A: Do I have to have my tooth pulled? 我必須拔牙嗎？
B: I'm afraid so. 恐怕得如此。

提示
extract [ɪk'strækt] *v.* 拔出

2326
我的腿怎麼了？
How is my leg?

範例
A: How is my leg? 我的腿怎麼了？
B: It has a compound fracture. 你有複雜性骨折。

提示
compound ['kɑmpaʊnd] *adj.* 混合的
fracture ['fræktʃɚ] *n.* 骨折；折斷

2327
我的…近來一直不對勁。
My...have not been right lately.

範例
A: My legs have not been right lately. 我的腿近來一直不對勁。
B: Don't worry. It's nothing serious. 不用擔心。不嚴重。

2328
你眼睛以前有問題嗎？
Have you had any problems with your eyes before?

範例
A: Have you had any problems with your eyes before?
你眼睛以前有問題嗎？
B: Never.
從來沒有。

2329
除了眼睛痛和發炎之外，還有什麼不舒服的嗎？
Are you having any other problems besides your red and sore eyes?

範例
A: Are you having any other problems besides your red and sore eyes?
除了眼睛痛和發炎之外，還有什麼不舒服的嗎？

B: It feels like there's something in them. There are a lot of secretions and they are sensitive to light.
我感覺眼睛裡有異物,分泌物很多,還對光敏感。

提示 secretion [sɪ'kriʃən] *n.* 分泌;分泌物

2330 我的視力正在衰退。
My eyesight is failing.

替換 My eyesight is becoming worse.

範例 A: My eyesight is failing.
我的視力正在衰退。
B: These eye drops may improve your eyesight.
這種眼藥水可以增進你的視力。

● 體檢、醫生建言和處方箋
Medical Examinations & Doctor's Advice & Prescriptions

2331 讓我量一下你的體溫/血壓吧。
Let me take your temperature/blood pressure.

替換 May I take your temperature/blood pressure?

範例 A: Let me take your temperature. 讓我量一下你的體溫吧。
B: Is it normal? 正常嗎?

2332 最近我的胸口一直痛。
I've been having pains in my chest recently.

範例 A: I've been having pains in my chest recently. 最近我的胸口一直痛。
B: We'll take an X-ray. 去照個 X 光。

2333 我們要為你⋯。
We'll give you...

範例 A: We'll give you a routine blood test.
我們要為你做一次例行性的血液檢查。
B: All right.
好的。

提示 routine [ru'tin] *adj.* 例行的;常規的

2334

我先給你打一針。
I'll have to give you a shot.

(替換) I'll give you an injection first.

(範例) A: I'll have to give you a shot. 我先給你打一針。
B: OK. 好吧。

(提示) injection [ɪnˈdʒɛkʃən] *n.* 注射

2335

你會開藥給我嗎？
Are you going to give me a prescription?

(範例) A: Are you going to give me a prescription?
你會開藥給我嗎？
B: Yes, I'll prescribe a bottle of cough syrup for you.
是的，我要給你開一瓶止咳糖漿。

(提示) prescription [prɪˈskrɪpʃən] *n.* 處方（藥）；處方（簽）
syrup [ˈsɪrəp] *n.* 糖漿

2336

如何服用這藥？
How do I take this medicine?

(範例) A: How do I take this medicine?
如何服用這藥？
B: Take this mixture three times a day, one dosage each time.
一天服用三次，每次一格。

(提示) mixture [ˈmɪkstʃɚ] *n.* 混合劑
dosage [ˈdosɪdʒ] *n.* （藥的）劑量

2337

恐怕你得立刻動手術。
I'm afraid you need an emergency surgery.

(替換) I'm afraid an urgent operation is necessary.
I'm afraid you need to be operated on.

(範例) A: Is my illness serious?
我的病嚴重嗎？
B: It's acute. I'm afraid you need an emergency surgery.
這是急性病。恐怕你得立刻動手術。

(提示) acute [əˈkjut] *adj.* 急性的；劇烈的

2338	我必須立即住院嗎？ **Must I be hospitalized right now?**

範例　A: Must I be hospitalized right now?
　　　　我必須立即住院嗎？
　　　　B: Yes. You must have your appendix removed.
　　　　是的，你必須動盲腸手術。

提示　hospitalize ['hɑspɪtḷ͵aɪz] v. 住院治療
　　　　appendix [ə'pɛndɪks] n. 闌尾

2339	我什麼時候可以出院？ **When will I be discharged?**

範例　A: When will I be discharged?
　　　　我什麼時候可以出院？
　　　　B: If your recovery goes well, you can leave in a couple of days.
　　　　如果康復情形良好，過幾天你就可以出院了。

提示　discharge [dɪs'tʃɑrdʒ] v. 允許…離開醫院
　　　　recovery [rɪ'kʌvərɪ] n. 恢復；痊癒

2340	我還需要做什麼？ **What else do I need to do?**

範例　A: What else do I need to do?
　　　　我還需要做什麼？
　　　　B: Take the medicine I prescribed and get plenty of rest.
　　　　服用我開的藥，好好休息。

7.12 在校園 On Campus

　　校園是學生接受教育與文化薰陶，並為就業做準備的重要場所。專業學習、出國留學等是學生日常會話的重要話題。掌握特定的表達方法有助於學生之間的交流和與老師的溝通，從而獲得更多有用的資訊。

● 課程主修 Courses and Majors

| 2341 | 你主修什麼?
 What's your major? | 106 |

替換　What's your field of study?

範例　**A:** What's your major? 你主修什麼?
B: My major is history. 我主修歷史。

| 2342 | 我主修…。
 I'm majoring in... |

替換　...is my major.
I'm a...major.
...is my field of study.

範例　**A:** I'm majoring in computer science. 我主修電腦科學。
B: You must like it very much. 你一定很喜歡吧!

| 2343 | 你打算修什麼課?
 What courses are you planning to take? |

替換　What are you going to study?
What subjects are you going to take?

範例　**A:** What courses are you planning to take? 你打算修什麼課?
B: Applied linguistics. 應用語言學

提示　linguistics [lɪŋˈgwɪstɪks] *n.* 語言學

| 2344 | 你現在正在修什麼課?
 What course(s) are you taking? |

範例　**A:** What course(s) are you taking? 你現在正在什麼課?
B: I'm taking anthropology. 我在修人類學。

提示　anthropology [ˌænθrəˈpɑlədʒɪ] *n.* 人類學

● 念研究所 Post-graduate Study

| 2345 | 你拿到研究所的獎學金嗎?
 Did you get a grant to go to graduate school? |

替換 | Have you got a grant for graduate study?

範例 | A: Did you get a grant to go to graduate school?
你拿到研究所的獎學金嗎？
B: Not yet.
還沒有。

2346
你打算到哪裡讀…研究所？
Where are you going to do post-graduate work in...?

範例 | A: Where are you going to do post-graduate work in medicine?
你打算到哪裡讀醫學研究所？
B: UCLA.
加州大學洛杉磯分校（University of California at Los Angeles）。

2347
你已經開始攻讀博士學位嗎？
Have you started your doctorate?

範例 | A: Have you started your doctorate?
你已經開始攻讀博士學位嗎？
B: I'm going to start my doctorate in biochemistry next year.
我準備明年開始攻讀生物化學博士。

提示 | doctorate ['dɑktərɪt] *n.* 博士頭銜
biochemistry ['baɪo'kɛmɪstrɪ] *n.* 生物化學

2348
…對我來說是個更合適的領域。
...is a much better field for me.

範例 | A: Human Resources Management is a much better field for me.
人力資源管理對我來說是個更合適的領域。
B: It sounds more interesting, too.
聽起來也更有意思。

2349
你畢業之後打算做什麼？
What do you plan to do after you graduate?

範例 | A: What do you plan to do after you graduate? 你畢業之後打算做什麼？
B: I haven't decided yet. 我還沒有決定。

● 出國留學 Studying Abroad

2350 聽說你要去⋯了。
I hear you're going to...

範例
A: I hear you're going to Australia. 聽說你要去澳洲了。
B: Yes. I will go there for graduate study. 是的，我要去那裡唸研究所。

2351 你已經向大學提出申請了嗎？
Have you applied to any university?

範例
A: Have you applied to any university?
　　你已經向大學提出申請了嗎？
B: Yes, I have.
　　是的。

2352 你收到那所學校的招生簡章了嗎？
Have you received a catalog from that university?

範例
A: Have you received a catalog from that university?
　　你收到那所學校的招生簡章了嗎？
B: Yes, I received it last week.
　　是的，我上個星期就收到了。

提示
catalog ['kætəlɔg] n. 【美】目錄；一覽表（= catalogue）

2353 英語的要求如何？
What's the English requirement?

範例
A: What's the English requirement?
　　英語的要求如何？
B: An IELTS overall band score of at least 7.0.
　　雅思平均分數要達到 7.0 以上。

提示
requirement [rɪ'kwaɪrmənt] n. 要求；必要條件

2354 你找到擔保人了嗎？
Have you found a sponsor?

範例
A: Have you found a sponsor? 你找到擔保人了嗎？
B: My friend in Canada is willing to be my guarantor during my stay
　　there. 我加拿大的朋友願意當我的保證人。

| 提示 | sponsor ['spɑnsə·] *n.* 保證人
guarantor ['gærəntə·] *n.* 保證人 |

| 2355 | 你唸書時住在哪裡？
Where will you stay during your studies? |

| 範例 | A: Where will you stay during your studies? 你唸書時住在哪裡？
B: I will live in a students' apartment with other international students on campus. 我和其他留學生一起住在校園裡的學生公寓。 |

| 2356 | 留學生的學費是多少？
What's the tuition for international students? |

| 範例 | A: What's the tuition for international students? 留學生的學費是多少？
B: That depends on the major. 看主修來決定。 |

| 2357 | 一拿到學位，我就立即回國。
I'll come back as soon as I get my degree. |

| 範例 | A: Will you settle down permanently in France?
你打算長住在法國嗎？
B: I'll come back as soon as I get my degree.
一拿到學位，我就立即回國。 |
| 提示 | permanently ['pɝmənəntlɪ] *adv.* 永久地；不變地 |

| 2358 | 我獲得了全／半額獎學金。
I have been granted a full/half scholarship. |

| 範例 | A: Did you get any kind of scholarship? 你拿到獎學金了嗎？
B: I have been granted a full scholarship. 我獲得了全額獎學金。 |
| 提示 | scholarship ['skɑlə·ˌʃɪp] *n.* 獎學金 |

| 2359 | 你拿到護照了嗎？
Did you get your passport? |

| 範例 | A: Did you get your passport? 你拿到護照了嗎？
B: Yes. I got my passport last week. 是的。我上週拿到了。 |

| 2360 | 你拿到財力證明了嗎？
Have you got your bank statement notarized already? |

| 範例 | A: Have you got your bank statement notarized already?
你拿到財力證明了嗎？ |

B: Yes.
拿到了。

提示　notarize [ˈnotəˌraɪz] *v.* 證明；確認

2361
你的簽證下來了嗎？
Did you get your visa approved?

替換　Has your visa application been granted?

範例　**A:** Did you get your visa approved? 你的簽證下來了嗎？
B: Yes. I'm lucky. 下來了。我很幸運。

7.13 在圖書館 At the Library

　　圖書館是智慧的寶庫，也是傳播知識的地方。它是求知者的伴侶，探索者的助手。善用圖書館的人就如同擁有一座無窮的智慧寶藏。要想充分、有效地利用圖書館，就必須了解借閱手續、圖書分類法、目錄編排、圖書的分布情況等。當然，首先應該聽懂圖書管理人員的語言，掌握借閱時的語言表達方法。

● 借閱規則 Library Regulations

2362
我想申請一張借書證。　　　　　　　(107)
I'd like to apply for a library card.

範例　**A:** I'd like to apply for a library card. 我想申請一張借書證。
B: Please show me your student ID. 請出示你的學生證。

2363
一次可以借多少本書？
How many books can I check out at a time?

範例　**A:** How many books can I check out at a time?
一次可以借多少本書？
B: As many as you want, but remember to return or renew them when they are due back.
想借多少就借多少，只是一定要記得到期要歸還或續借。

2364
這本書什麼時候到期？
When is it due back?

替換 | When do I need to return this book?

範例 | **A:** When is it due back? 這本書什麼時候到期？
B: It's due four weeks from today. 四個星期之後。

2365 | 如果我沒及時辦理續借這本書呢？
What if I fail to renew the book?

範例 | **A:** What if I fail to renew the book?
如果我沒及時辦理續借這本書呢？
B: Well, you'll be fined for each day it's overdue.
那麼你就得按過期天數付罰款。

● 查閱書目 Finding a Book

2366 | 我在找…。請幫我找一下好嗎？
I'm looking for...Would you help me find it?

範例 | **A:** I'm looking for *The Scarlet Letter*. Would you help me find it?
我在找《紅字》。請幫我找一下好嗎？
B: Sure.
好。

2367 | 能不能請你幫我找一本…方面的書？
Can you find me a book about...?

替換 | Could you find me a book on...?

範例 | **A:** Can you find me a book about Buddhism?
能不能請你幫我找一本佛教方面的書？
B: Do you know the title of the book?
你知道書名嗎？

提示 | Buddhism ['budɪzəm] *n.* 佛教

2368 | 請推薦…方面的書好嗎？
Could you recommend some books on...?

替換 | What would you suggest on...?

範例 | **A:** Could you recommend some books on biology?
請推薦一些生物學方面的書好嗎？
B: How about this book? It's very popular.
這本書怎麼樣？它現在很熱門。

2369	我可以在卡片目錄中找到這本書嗎？ **Can I find this book in the card catalog?**
範例	**A:** Can I find this book in the card catalog? 　　我可以在卡片目錄中找到這本書嗎？ **B:** I think so. 　　我想可以的。

2370	如果我只知道作者，怎樣使用卡片目錄找到這本書呢？ **If I only know the author's name, how can I find the book in the card catalog?**
範例	**A:** If I only know the author's name, how can I find the book in the card catalog? 如果我只知道作者，怎樣使用卡片目錄找到這本書呢？ **B:** You may look it up in the author catalog. 你可以查作者目錄。

2371	能不能請你告訴我怎樣在…上找到一篇…發表的文章？ **Can you tell me how to find an article that was published...in...?**
範例	**A:** Can you tell me how to find an article that was published last year in *Fortune*? 　　能不能請你告訴我怎樣在《財富》雜誌上找到一篇去年發表的文章？ **B:** You can look it up in the *Fortune* Index. Find the volume for last year and check the title or author. 　　你可以查《財富》雜誌的索引，找到去年的那一期，再用標題或作者目錄查詢。

● 借閱資料 Borrowing Books or Magazines

2372	我想借…方面的書。 **I'd like to check out a book on...**
範例	**A:** I'd like to check out a book on computer technology. 　　我想借一本電腦科技方面的書。 **B:** Do you know the author's name or the title of the book? 　　你知道作者的姓名或書名嗎？

2373	你們有最新一期的…嗎？ **Do you have the latest issue of...?**

Has the latest issue of...come out yet?

A: Do you have the latest issue of *Reader's Digest*?
你們有最新一期的《讀者文摘》嗎？

B: Here's the latest one.
這是最新的一期。

2374

我能把這本書借出圖書館嗎？
May I check this book out of the library?

 A: May I check this book out of the library?
我能把這本書借出圖書館嗎？

B: You can't take it out, but you can photocopy any article in it that you want.
你不能借回家，但是可以影印你要的那一篇文章。

2375

我想再續借…。
I'd like to renew it for...

I want to keep it for...
May I renew it for...?

A: I'd like to renew it for another week.
我想再續借一個星期。

B: I'm sorry. Your books are two days overdue.
對不起，你借的書已經過期兩天了。

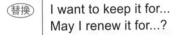

2376

你要續借多久？
How long do you want to renew it for?

A: How long do you want to renew it for? 你要續借多久？

B: For another two weeks. 再續借兩個星期。

2377

你要的書已經借出了。
The book you want has been checked out.

 The book you want has been taken out.
The book you want is on loan.

A: I'm sorry. The book you want has been checked out.
對不起，你要的書已經借出了。

B: Will you please get it back as soon as possible?
請你儘快把這本書取回，好嗎？

2378	你可以在圖書館預約登記那本書。 **You can reserve that book at the library.**

範例
A: You can reserve that book at the library.
　　你可以在圖書館預約登記那本書。
B: All right.
　　好吧。

7.14 在美容院 At the Barber's and Hairdresser's

隨著人們的觀念變化和美髮業的蓬勃發展，人們對髮型提出愈來愈多的要求，以便充分展示自己的個性。同時，關於美容院的語言表達也變得愈來愈豐富。我們有必要掌握各種表達方法，以便清楚、準確地表達自己要提供或期望獲得的服務。

● **詢問與說明髮型 Asking about & Requesting a Hair Style**

2379	你想要什麼樣的髮型？ **How do you want it?**	(108)

替換
How would you like it?
How do you want it cut?
What kind of hairstyle do you want?
What would you like me to do with your hair?

範例
A: How do you want it? 你想要什麼樣的髮型？
B: Shoulder length, with long bangs. 到肩膀的長度，長的劉海。

提示
bang [bæŋ] n. 劉海

2380	我只是想把頭髮修一修。 **I just want to have it trimmed a little.**

替換
I just want a trim, please.

範例
A: I just want to have it trimmed a little. 我只是想把頭髮修一修。
B: All right. 好的。

2381	兩邊的鬢角請不要剪。 **Leave the sideburns, please.**
(替換)	Please don't cut off my sideburns.
(範例)	A: How shall I cut it, sir? 先生，我應該怎麼剪？ B: Leave the sideburns, please. 兩邊的鬢角請不要剪。
(提示)	sideburns ['saɪd͵bɝnz] *n.* 鬢角（= sideboards）

2382	頭頂處請不要剪去太多。 **Don't take too much off the top, please.**
(範例)	A: Don't take too much off the top, please. 頭頂處請不要剪去太多。 B: OK, I'll do as you say. 好的，我會按照你說的去做。

2383	兩邊剪短一點，但後面別剪那麼短。 **Cut the sides a bit short, but not too much at the back.**
(範例)	A: Do you want to cut the sides short? 兩邊剪短一點嗎？ B: Cut the sides a bit short, but not too much at the back. 兩邊剪短一點，但後面別剪那麼短。

2384	保持原來的樣子。 **The same as before, please.**
(替換)	Just the same as always. Leave it as it is, please.
(範例)	A: Would you like to keep the same style? 你要保持原來的髮型嗎？ B: Yes. The same as before, please. 是的，保持原來的樣子。

2385	…的頭髮請稍微修掉一些。 **Trim a bit off the..., please.**
(範例)	A: Trim a bit off the back, please. 後面的頭髮請稍微修掉一些。 B: All right. Do you also want your hair layered? 好的。你的頭髮也要打層次嗎？

2386	我頭髮要中分／旁分。 **I'd like my hair parted in the middle/on the side.**

範例 | A: On which side do you want to part your hair? 你的頭髮要怎樣分？
B: I'd like my hair parted in the middle. 我頭髮要中分。

● 清洗與護理頭髮 Washing & Conditioning Hair

2387 | 我要洗頭。
A shampoo, please.

替換 | Give me a shampoo, please.
I want a shampoo.
I'll have a shampoo.
I'd like it washed.

範例 | A: What can I do for you? 有什麼需要我服務的嗎？
B: A shampoo, please. 我要洗頭。

2388 | 你喜歡什麼洗髮精？
What shampoo do you prefer?

替換 | What shampoo do you like?

範例 | A: What shampoo do you prefer?
你喜歡什麼洗髮精？
B: Whatever. I don't use any particular brand.
都可以，我沒有特殊的喜好。

2389 | 請整理一下就好。
Just tidy it up a bit, please.

範例 | A: Do you want me to put some highlights in your hair? 你要挑染嗎？
B: No. Just tidy it up a bit, please. 不用，請整理一下就好。

提示 | hightlight ['haɪt‚laɪt] n. 挑染

2390 | 請抹一點髮膠。
A little hair gel, please.

替換 | I'd like some hair gel on my hair, please.

範例 | A: Would you like me to apply anything? 要抹些什麼嗎？
B: A little hair gel, please. 請抹一點髮膠。

提示 | gel [dʒɛl] n. 凝膠

2391	要…嗎？ **Any...?**
(替換)	Shall I put some...on? Do you want/like some...?
(範例)	**A:** Any conditioner? 要護髮嗎？ **B:** Just a little. 一點點就行了。
(提示)	conditioner [kən'dɪʃənɚ] *n.* 護髮劑；潤髮乳

● 燙髮定型 A Perm or Cold-Wave

2392	你要燙髮，還是上髮捲？ **What will you have, a perm or a set?**
(範例)	**A:** What will you have, a perm or a set? 你要燙髮，還是上髮捲？ **B:** A permanent wave, please. 請燙髮。
(提示)	perm [pɝm] *n. v.* 燙髮；電燙頭髮

2393	我想要普通燙髮。 **I'll have an ordinary perm.**
(範例)	**A:** Do you want a cold wave? 你想要冷燙嗎？ **B:** No, I'll have an ordinary perm. 不，我想要普通燙髮。

● 其他服務 Other Services

2394	請幫我把頭髮吹乾。 **Please dry my hair.**
(範例)	**A:** Please dry my hair. 請幫我把頭髮吹乾。 **B:** OK. 好的。

2395	我希望染一下頭髮。 **I'd like to have my hair dyed.**
(替換)	I want to dye my hair.
(範例)	**A:** I'd like to have my hair dyed. 　　我希望染一下頭髮。 **B:** OK. Please have a look at this hair-color chart. 　　好。請看一下這個髮色表。

2396	請把我的頭髮染成…。 **Please dye my hair...**
範例	**A:** What color would you like it dyed? 你要染什麼顏色？ **B:** Please dye my hair brown. 請把我的頭髮染成咖啡色。

2397	你要修臉嗎？ **Would you like a shave?**
替換	Do you want a shave?
範例	**A:** Would you like a shave? 　你要修臉嗎？ **B:** No. But I'd like my moustache trimmed, please. 　不，但我想修一修鬍子。
提示	moustache [məs'tæʃ] *n.* 八字鬍

2398	請把我的鬍子剃掉。 **Shave off my beard, please.**
範例	**A:** Would you like your beard trimmed? 你要修鬍子嗎？ **B:** Shave off my beard, please. 請把我的鬍子剃掉。

2399	我想要把鬢角剪短些。 **I'd like my sideburns cut short, please.**
範例	**A:** I'd like my sideburns cut short, please. 我想要把鬢角剪短些。 **B:** All right. 好的。

2400	你要修指甲嗎？ **Do you want a manicure?**
範例	**A:** Do you want a manicure? 你要修指甲嗎？ **B:** No, thank you. Just leave them as they are. 不，謝謝。就這樣。
提示	manicure ['mænɪˌkjʊr] *n.* 修指甲

7.15 在加油站 At the Gas Station

　　加油站有多種叫法，如：a service station、a filling station、a gas station 或 a petrol station。一般而言，加油站除了賣汽油之外，也兼賣其他物品。顧

客可以根據自己的需要，選擇不同口味的熱咖啡（hot coffee）或者冷飲（cold drink），也可以買到零食（snack）和其他日常用品。例如：郵票、報紙、地圖以及明信片等等。人們在加油的同時，自己也可以得到休息和放鬆。這對那些疲憊的駕駛而言，尤其重要。有的加油站還提供洗車和修車服務。

● 加油 Fueling the Car

2401 我的車快沒油了。請加滿它。 (109)
My car's almost out of gasoline. Fill it up, please.

(替換) There isn't any petrol in the tank. Please fill it up.

(範例) A: My car's almost out of gasoline. Fill it up, please.
我的車快沒油了。請加滿它。
B: What kind of gasoline do you want?
你要哪種汽油？

2402 請加…汽油。
..., please.

(範例) A: What kind of gasoline do you want? 你要哪種汽油？
B: Regular, please. 請加普通汽油。

2403 你要多少汽油？
How much gasoline do you want?

(範例) A: How much gasoline do you want? 你要多少汽油？
B: 10 gallons, please. 請加十加侖。

(提示) gallon ['gælən] *n.* 加侖

2404 加無鉛汽油嗎？
Unleaded?

(替換) Do you want unleaded gas?
Is that unleaded gas that you want?

(範例) A: Unleaded? 加無鉛汽油嗎？
B: Yes, please. 是的。

(提示) unleaded [ʌn'lɛdɪd] *adj.* 無鉛的；不含鉛的（汽油）

● 其他服務 Other Services

2405

請你也檢查一下機油和水，好嗎？
Would you also check the oil and water?

（範例）
A: Would you also check the oil and water?
請你也檢查一下機油和水，好嗎？
B: Your oil's fine, but you need some water.
你的機油足夠，但是要加點水。

2406

能不能請你檢查一下我的蓄電池？
Could you check my battery?

（替換）
I'd like my battery checked.
Could you have a look at the battery, please?

（範例）
A: Could you check my battery?
能不能請你檢查一下我的蓄電池？
B: The battery's quite low, and it needs some distilled water.
電瓶水位相當低了，需要加些蒸餾水。

（提示）
distilled [dɪ'stɪld] *adj.* 蒸餾的

2407

我希望檢查一下車胎。
I'd like to have the tires checked.

（範例）
A: I'd like to have the tires checked. 我希望檢查一下車胎。
B: Your tires are worn quite smooth. 你的輪胎磨損得很平了。

2408

我的輪胎破了。
I've got a flat tire.

（範例）
A: How about your tires? 你的輪胎怎麼樣？
B: I've got a flat tire. 我的輪胎破了。

2409

…有問題。
Something is wrong with the...

（替換）
The...has a problem.
The...doesn't work.

（範例）
A: What's the problem? 什麼問題？
B: Something is wrong with the carburetor. 汽化器有問題。

（提示）
carburetor ['kɑrbə,retɚ] *n.* 汽化器

| 2410 | 你什麼時候有空可以檢查一下我的車子？
When do you think you'll have time to look over my car? |

範例 A: When do you think you'll have time to look over my car?
　　你什麼時候有空可以檢查一下我的車子？
B: Just leave it with us. Is that OK for you?
　　就把它放在我們這裡吧。可以嗎？

| 2411 | 請你清洗一下…好嗎？
Could you clean the...? |

範例 A: Could you clean the windshield? 請你清洗一下擋風玻璃好嗎？
B: Yes, of course. 當然。

提示 windshield ['wɪnd.ʃild] *n*.【美】擋風玻璃（=【英】windscreen）

| 2412 | 你要洗車嗎？
Do you want your car washed? |

替換 Would you like a car wash?

範例 A: Do you want your car washed? 你要洗車嗎？
B: No, not this time. 不，這次不用了。

| 2413 | 這裡有賣飲料嗎？
Do you sell drinks here? |

替換 Are drinks sold here?

範例 A: Do you sell drinks here? 這裡有賣飲料嗎？
B: Yes, inside. 有，在裡面。

7.16　在裁縫店 At the Tailor's

　　隨著人們生活水準的提高和服裝業的發展，購買成衣的人愈來愈多，但有時由於自己的特殊需要，我們還是要光顧裁縫店。在裁縫店，我們難免要談到做工、式樣、衣料、尺寸、價格等，而要清楚明白的表達這一切，就必須掌握一些特定的表達方法。

● 做工與布料 Workmanship and Materials

2414　你們的做工怎麼樣？
How's your workmanship?

110

範例　A: How's your workmanship? 你們的做工怎麼樣？
B: Our workmanship's the best in the city. 我們的做工是全市最好的。

提示　workmanship ['wɝkmənˌʃɪp] *n.* 手藝；作工

2415　我想做…。要多少錢？
I'd like to have a...made, please. How much do you charge for the tailoring?

替換　I'd like to have a...made. How much money do I need to pay for the tailoring?

範例　A: I'd like to have an autumn suit made, please. How much do you charge for the tailoring? 我想做一套秋裝。要多少錢？
B: Our price for a suit is 180 dollars. 我們一套服裝是一百八十美元。

2416　你有什麼布料？
What do you have in the way of materials?

範例　A: What do you have in the way of materials? 你有什麼布料？
B: How about this, sir? 這塊怎麼樣，先生？

2417　你有好的布料嗎？
Do you have any material of good quality?

範例　A: Do you have any material of good quality?
你有好的布料嗎？
B: What do you think of these woolen fabrics?
你認為這塊羊毛織品怎麼樣？

提示　fabrics ['fæbrɪks] *n.* 織物；織品

2418　可以用這塊布料替我做…嗎？
Can you make me...from this length of cloth?

範例　A: Can you make me two dresses from this length of cloth?
可以用這塊布料替我做兩件衣服嗎？
B: A three-piece suit can be made from this length of cloth.
這布的長度可以做三件式的套裝。

2419	請你用…給我做…吧。 **I'd like...made from...**

替換　Would you make me...out of...?
Would you make a...from...for me, please?

範例　**A:** I'd like a shirt made from linen. 請你用亞麻布給我做件襯衫吧。
B: All right. 好的。

提示　linen ['lɪnən] *n.* 亞麻布；亞麻製品

● 服裝式樣 Patterns

2420	請給我看些紙樣好嗎？ **Would you show me some patterns?**

範例　**A:** Would you show me some patterns?
　　 請給我看些紙樣好嗎？
B: Here's the pattern book. You might find something you like here.
　　 這是紙樣本，你也許會在其中找到喜歡的樣式。

提示　pattern ['pætən] *n.*（服裝裁剪的）紙樣

2421	請做成…。 **Please make it...**

範例　**A:** I wonder if you like this style. 我不知道你是否喜歡這個樣式。
B: No. Please make it loose. 不喜歡。請做成寬鬆的樣式。

2422	你想要在肩膀放墊肩嗎？ **Do you want any padding in the shoulders?**

範例　**A:** Do you want any padding in the shoulders? 你想要在肩膀放墊肩嗎？
B: No padding, please. 請不要放墊肩。

提示　padding ['pædɪŋ] *n.* 塞墊；填料

2423	你這服裝要單排扣還是雙排扣？ **Do you want the suit to be single- or double-breasted?**

範例　**A:** Do you want the suit to be single- or double-breasted?
　　 你這服裝要單排扣還是雙排扣？
B: Please make it single-breasted.
　　 請做單排扣的。

2424	我希望把我的⋯做成⋯。 **I'd like my...**
範例	**A:** I'd like my jacket to have wide lapels and three buttons in the front. 我希望把我的外套做成寬翻領，胸前有三個鈕扣的樣子。 **B:** You can leave all that to us. 你可以完全交給我們。
提示	lapel [ləˈpɛl] *n.* 翻領

2425	你的上衣要什麼樣的領口？ **What kind of neckline do you prefer in your coat?**
範例	**A:** What kind of neckline do you prefer in your coat? 你的上衣要什麼樣的領口？ **B:** A round neckline, please. 請做成圓領。

2426	我可以量一下你的尺寸嗎？ **May I take your measurements?**
範例	**A:** May I take your measurements? 我可以量一下你的尺寸嗎？ **B:** Definitely. 當然。

● 試穿與領取衣物 Fitting and Picking up Clothes

2427	可以請你⋯來試穿嗎？ **Can you come for a fitting...?**
替換	The fitting will be... It'll be ready for trying...
範例	**A:** When will it be ready to try on? 什麼時候可以試穿？ **B:** Can you come for a fitting in three days? 可以請你三天以後來試穿嗎？

2428	我希望你們能馬上開始做。 **I hope you can do it right away.**
範例	**A:** I hope you can do it right away. 我希望你們能馬上開始做。 **B:** OK. When would you like to pick it up? 好的。你想什麼時候來取？

2429	這是你的收據。 **Here's your receipt.**
範例	**A:** Here's your receipt. 這是你的收據。 **B:** Thank you. 謝謝。

● 修改衣物 Alterations

2430	天哪！這個我沒辦法穿。 **My goodness! I can't wear this!**
範例	**A:** My goodness! I I can't wear this! I had something slim and elegant in mind. 天哪！這個我沒辦法穿。我本來想要的是苗條而優雅的衣服。 **B:** Yes, it should be taken in here. 是的，這裡應該要收進來一點。

2431	腰部有一點太緊了。 **It's a little too tight around the waist.**
替換	The waist is too tight. I'm afraid the waist seems a bit too tight.
範例	**A:** It's a little too tight around the waist. 腰部有一點太緊了。 **B:** All right, we'll take care of it. 好的，我們會處理。

2432	請把…改一改可以嗎？ **Could I have...altered, please?**
替換	Would you please alter...for me?
範例	**A:** Could I have this skirt altered, please? 請把這條裙子改一改可以嗎？ **B:** I'll be glad to do any minor alterations for you. 我很樂意為你做任何細微的修改。
提示	alteration [ˌɔltəˈreʃən] *n.* 變更；修改

2433	你可以把…改成…嗎？ **Can you make this...into a...?**
範例	**A:** Can you make this dress into a skirt? 你可以把這件衣服改成一條裙子嗎？ **B:** We can reset the seams and take in some of the material. 我們可以重新安排縫口，並收進一點衣料。
提示	seam [sim] *n.* 接縫；線縫

2434	你打算怎麼改？ **How do you plan to fix it?**

範例　A: How do you plan to fix it? 你打算怎麼改？
B: We can take it in an inch at the sleeves. 可以在袖子這裡收進一英寸。

7.17　逛街購物 Shopping

購物是日常生活中的重要活動。常見的購物地方有：百貨公司（department stores）、專賣店（specialty shops）、商場（malls）、超市（supermarkets）等等。商店一般允許顧客持發票退換，退換期為 7-10 天，但食品或廉價品不可退換，購買時需要精心挑選。

在西方國家，人們通常喜歡在週末開車，帶著全家大小一起去購物，購買全家人一週的生活用品。因此，西方國家的購物車（shopping cart）尺寸很大，小孩子還可以在裡面或坐或站，形成一幅溫馨的畫面。

● 服務顧客 Attending to a Customer

2435	有人招呼你了嗎？ **Are you being helped?**	111

替換　Are you being served?
Are you being attended to?
Have you been taken care of?
Is anybody looking after you?
Is someone taking care of you?

範例　A: Are you being helped? 有人招呼你了嗎？
B: I'd just like to have a look around. 我只想隨便看看。

提示　attend to、see to、take care of、look after 都有「照料」、「看照」的意思。

2436	我能為你服務嗎？ **Can I help you?**

替換 | May I help you?
What can I show you?
What can I do for you?
Is there anything I can do for you?
Can I help you in any way?
Could I be of service to you?
Could I be of any assistance to you?

範例 | **A:** Can I help you? 我能為你服務嗎？
B: Can I see the ring, please? 可以把那戒指給我看看嗎？

提示 | assistance [ə'sɪstəns] *n.* 協助

2437　你在找…嗎？
Are you looking for...?

替換 | Do you want to buy...here?

範例 | **A:** Are you looking for lamps? 你在找燈具嗎？
B: I'll buy one if they're nice. 如果不錯的話，我會買一盞。

2438　你們有賣…嗎？
Do you sell...?

替換 | Do you carry/stock...?

範例 | **A:** Do you sell flashlights? 你們有賣手電筒嗎？
B: Yes, we do. 有。

2439　你喜歡什麼樣的？
What kind would you like?

替換 | What style do you prefer?
What style would you like to have?

範例 | **A:** What kind would you like? 你喜歡什麼樣的？
B: I'm not too particular. 我沒特別想要的樣式。

2440　還要什麼別的嗎？
Can I get you anything else?

替換 | Will there be anything else?
Is there anything else I may show you?
Is there anything else you might need?
Is there anything else you'd like?

553

範例　A: Can I get you anything else? 還要什麼別的嗎？
B: No, thanks. 不用了。謝謝。

2441　你想要什麼材質的？
What material do you have in mind?

替換　What material do you prefer?

範例　A: What material do you have in mind? 你想要什麼材質的？
B: Do you have it in cotton? 你們有棉做的嗎？

2442　這材質耐穿嗎？
Will this material wear well?

範例　A: Will this material wear well? 這材質耐穿嗎？
B: It's the most durable. 它是最耐用的。

提示　durable ['djʊrəbl] *adj.* 持久的；耐用的

2443　你們還會進貨嗎？
Will you be getting any more in?

範例　A: Will you be getting any more in? 你們還會進貨嗎？
B: I'm afraid not. 恐怕不會了。

2444　這正是我要的東西。
This is just what I'm looking for.

替換　It's just what I wanted.
It's the right one I need.

範例　A: Will this do? 行嗎？
B: This is just what I'm looking for. 這正是我要的東西。

2445　對不起，賣完了。
Sorry, we're all out now.

替換　Sorry, we're out of them today.
Sorry, but we're sold out.
I'm sorry we don't have this in stock.
I'm sorry we haven't got that in stock at the moment.

範例　A: Do you have any scanners? 你們有沒有掃描器？
B: Sorry, we're all out now. 對不起，賣完了。

● 談論價格 Talking about Prices

2446	請問這個多少錢？ **How much is this, please?**

(替換)
How much does this cost?
How much did you say it is?
How much are you asking for it?
How much are you selling it for?
How much do you want for it?
How much shall I pay for it?
What does it cost?
What does it sell for?
What do you charge for it?

(範例)
A: How much is this, please? 請問這個多少錢？
B: They're 16 marks per kilo. 每公斤十六馬克。

2447	一共多少錢？ **What does it come to?**

(替換)
How much is it altogether?
How much will that be altogether?

(範例)
A: What does it come to? 一共多少錢？
B: It comes to 69 dollars, sir. 先生，總共六十九美元。

2448	正常價格是多少？ **What's the regular price?**

(範例)
A: What's the regular price? 正常價格是多少？
B: It's normally 100 dollars. 一般是一百美元。

2449	這是特價嗎？ **Is this the sale price?**

(範例)
A: Is this the sale price? 這是特價嗎？
B: Yes. 是的。

2450	…的最低價是多少？ **What's the lowest price for the...?**

(範例)
A: What's the lowest price for the watch? 這手錶的最低價是多少？
B: $19.99, plus tax. 十九‧九九美金加稅。

2451	這比我想付的價錢高了些。 **That's a bit more than I wanted to pay.**

範例
A: 40 dollars. Is that alright? 四十美元吧。可以嗎？
B: That's a bit more than I wanted to pay. 這比我想付的價錢高了些。

2452	真是搶錢呀！ **It's highway robbery!**

替換
That's too much.
That's outrageous!
That's a fortune!
The price is too steep!

範例
A: What do you think of this price? 你認為這個價錢怎麼樣？
B: It's highway robbery! 真是搶錢呀！

提示
outrageous [aʊt'redʒəs] *adj.* 無法無天的；令人吃驚的
steep [stip] *adj.*【口】（價錢）過高的

2453	這價格不合理。 **The price is not reasonable.**

範例
A: The price is not reasonable. 這價格不合理。
B: It's almost cost. 這幾乎是成本價了。

2454	這東西不錯，但是我覺得太貴。 **This is nice, but I think it's quite expensive.**

範例
A: This is nice, but I think it's quite expensive.
　　這東西不錯，但是我覺得太貴。
B: That's our rock-bottom price.
　　這是我們的最低價了。

2455	你可以算便宜一點嗎？ **Can you come down a bit?**

範例
A: Can you come down a bit? 你可以算便宜一點嗎？
B: The price is reasonable enough. 這價格夠不錯了。

2456	有沒有可能再便宜一點？ **Is there any chance of getting a lower price from you?**

範例 | A: Is there any chance of getting a lower price from you?
有沒有可能再便宜一點？
B: We're practically giving it away.
我們簡直是用送的了。

2457
我最多只能出…美元。這個價錢你肯賣嗎？
I'll give you no more than...Will you sell it for that?

範例 | A: I'll give you no more than $50. Will you sell it for that?
我最多只能出五十美元。這個價錢你肯賣嗎？
B: OK, it's a deal.
好吧，成交。

● 談論式樣 Talking about Fashions and Designs

2458
給我看一些樣品好嗎？
Can you show me some samples?

範例 | A: Can you show me some samples? 給我看一些樣品好嗎？
B: Here're some samples. 這些是樣品。

2459
這是最新款式嗎？
Is it the latest?

範例 | A: Is it the latest? 這是最新款式嗎？
B: It's the latest thing, and it's very popular. 這是最新款式，非常流行。

2460
這圖案有點太複雜了。
The design is a bit too complicated.

範例 | A: Do you like this design? 你喜歡這個設計嗎？
B: The design is a bit too complicated. 這圖案有點太複雜了。

提示 | complicated ['kɑmplə,ketɪd] *adj.* 複雜的；難解的

2461
我需要一件條紋／圓點／格子的。
I need one with stripes/polka dots/checks, please.

範例 | A: What type do you want? 你想要什麼樣的？
B: I need one with stripes, please. 我需要一件條紋的。

● 談論顏色 Talking about Colors

2462	想要什麼顏色呢？ **Any particular color?**
替換	Do you have any preference for color? What color do you prefer?
範例	**A:** Any particular color? 想要什麼顏色呢？ **B:** I want something light. 我要淺色的。

2463	這個太花俏／樸素。 **It's too loud/plain.**
替換	That looks a bit too loud/plain.
範例	**A:** How about the color? 這顏色怎麼樣？ **B:** It's too loud. 這個太花俏。

2464	你們有…的嗎？ **Do you have this in...?**
替換	Do you have the same design in...?
範例	**A:** Do you have this in pink? 你們有粉紅色的嗎？ **B:** We have that color, but not in that size. 我們有這顏色，但沒有這尺寸了。

● 談論尺寸 Talking about Size

2465	請問你穿什麼尺寸？ **What size?**
替換	What size do you want/take?
範例	**A:** What size? 請問你穿什麼尺寸？ **B:** Size 34. 三十四號。

2466	這件…是我的尺寸嗎？ **Is this...my size?**
範例	**A:** Is this red dress my size? 這件紅色洋裝是我的尺寸嗎？ **B:** No. It's a bit too small on you. 不是，你穿有點太小了。

2467	我想買一件…號的…。 **I'm looking for a size...**

範例	**A:** I'm looking for a size 40 evening dress. 我想買一件四十號的晚禮服。 **B:** I'm afraid we haven't anything in your size. 恐怕我們沒有你的尺寸。

2468	這個尺寸怎麼樣？ **How about this size?**

替換	What do you think of this size?
範例	**A:** How about this size? 這個尺寸怎麼樣？ **B:** It's a bit too big for me. 這個我穿太大了一點。

● 試穿與決定 Trying on Clothes & Deciding

2469	試試這個。 **Try this one on.**

替換	Perhaps you'd like to try this one on.
範例	**A:** Try this one on. 試試這個。 **B:** Thank you. 謝謝。

2470	我可以試穿一下嗎？ **May I try it on?**

替換	Could I try it on?
範例	**A:** May I try it on? 我可以試穿一下嗎？ **B:** Of course. 當然。

2471	這件如何？ **How about this one?**

替換	Does this one suit you?
範例	**A:** How about this one? 這件如何？ **B:** It's a good fit. 很合適。

2472	你打算要買嗎？ **Do you want to buy it?**

Will you take it?

範例 **A:** Do you want to buy it? 你打算要買嗎？
B: Not this time. Thank you just the same. 這次先不要。謝謝。

7.18 觀光旅遊 Sightseeing

　　西方人熱愛旅遊，旅遊是西方人生活的重要部分。在西方，很少人不外出旅遊的。旅遊之前，他們樂意談論自己的計畫；旅遊之後，則喜歡和他人分享自己的經歷，甚至向朋友展示自己的照片，或者播放自己拍攝的影片，所以與西方人談旅遊經歷，是一個很合適的話題。

● 談論計畫 Discussing Sightseeing Plans

2473	我們去…旅行吧。 **Let's go to...**

範例 **A:** Let's go to Africa. 我們去非洲旅行吧。
B: I think we'd better take a tour of Europe. 我想我們最好去歐洲旅行。

2474	我們打算去…。 **We plan to...**

替換 We're going/planning to...
We would like to...

範例 **A:** We plan to go mountain-climbing. 我們打算去登山。
B: Can I go with you? 我可以跟你們去嗎？

2475	我們可以改去…嗎？ **Can we go to the...instead?**

範例 **A:** Can we go to the beach instead? 我們可以改去海灘嗎？
B: We'll go there some other time. 我們改天再去那裡吧。

● 詢問與提供觀光資訊 Asking about & Offering Sightseeing Information

2476
請你告訴我這裡的一些風景名勝好嗎？
Would you please tell me about some of the attractions here?

範例
A: Would you please tell me about some of the attractions here?
請你告訴我這裡的一些風景名勝好嗎？
B: I'll start with the historical sites.
讓我先從歷史古蹟開始介紹吧。

2477
…有什麼東西可看？
What's there to see...?

替換
Is there anything interesting to see...?
What interesting places are there...?

範例
A: What's there to see in the city?
市內有什麼東西可看？
B: You should visit the Golden Gate Bridge.
你應該去遊覽一下金門大橋。

2478
…以什麼著名呢？
What is...famous for?

範例
A: What is this street famous for? 這條街以什麼著名呢？
B: It's famous for its museums. 這裡的博物館很有名。

2479
我們比較喜歡跟團的套裝行程。
We'd prefer a package tour with a group.

範例
A: Will you go there alone or in a group?
你們自己去，還是跟團去？
B: We'd prefer a package tour with a group.
我們比較喜歡跟團的套裝行程。

● 觀賞風景 Sightseeing

2480
它們是我見過最…的…。
They are the most...I've ever seen.

範例
A: Now, we're approaching the waterfalls.
現在我們接近瀑布了。
B: They are the most beautiful waterfalls I've ever seen.
它們是我見過最美麗的瀑布。

2481
你看到那…了嗎？
Do you see that...?

範例
A: Do you see that tall building? 你看到那座高大的建築物了嗎？
B: It must be the castle. 那一定是城堡了。

2482
你以前…嗎？
Have you ever...before?

範例
A: Have you ever felt a wind like that before?
你以前感受過這樣的風嗎？
B: I've never felt the wind so gentle.
我從來沒有感受過這樣輕柔的風。

2483
太美了！
What a place!

替換
How beautiful!
What a beautiful place this is!
This is really fascinating.

範例
A: Let's enjoy the wonderful view of the lake.
我們來欣賞湖泊的美麗風光吧。
B: What a place!
太美了！

2484
快過來看看這裡的壯麗景色。
Come here and check out this magnificent view.

範例
A: Come here and check out this magnificent view.
快過來看看這裡的壯麗景色。
B: It's really worth seeing.
這確實值得一看。

提示
magnificent [mæg'nɪfəsənt] *adj.* 華麗的；宏偉的

2485
他們非常令人心動。
They are very impressive.

A: Do you like these buildings? 你喜歡這些建築物嗎？
B: They are very impressive. 他們非常令人心動。

7.19 吸煙行為 Smoking

雖說「吸煙有害健康」（Smoking is hazardous to health.），但是香煙卻具有一定的社交功能。一根香煙能拉近對話雙方的距離；一句 "Have you got a light?" 能使交談自然開始。

● 提供香煙與應答 Offering a Cigarette & Responding to the Offer

2486	要抽煙嗎？ **Cigarette?**	113

替換
Do you smoke?
Will you have a cigarette?
Have a smoke, will you?
Would you like a cigarette?
Would you care for a cigarette?
Would you like one?
Won't you have a smoke?

範例 A: Cigarette? 要抽煙嗎？
B: No, thanks. I'm trying to quit. 不，謝謝。我正在戒煙。

2487	老實說，我現在不想抽。 **Actually, I don't feel like having one at the moment.**

範例 A: Please have a smoke.
請抽煙。
B: No, thanks. Actually, I don't feel like having one at the moment.
不，謝謝。老實說，我現在不想抽。

2488	請抽一根我的煙。我似乎老抽你的。 **Please have one of mine. I always seem to be smoking yours.**

(範例) **A:** Please have one of mine. I always seem to be smoking yours.
請抽一根我的煙。我似乎老抽你的。
B: OK, I'll have one.
好，我抽一支。

2489 對不起，借個火可以嗎？
Excuse me. Can you give me a light?

(替換) Excuse me. Could I trouble you for a light?
Excuse me. Do you have a match?
Excuse me, but have you got a light?

(範例) **A:** Excuse me. Can you give me a light? 對不起，借個火可以嗎？
B: Sure. 當然。

● 談論吸煙 Talking about Smoking

2490 我是個老煙槍。
I smoke like a chimney.

(替換) I'm a chain smoker.
I'm a heavy smoker.

(範例) **A:** Are you smoking a lot? 你抽很多煙嗎？
B: Yes, I smoke like a chimney. 是的，我是個老煙槍。

(提示) chimney ['tʃɪmnɪ] *n.* 煙囪

2491 你會抽出病的。
You'll smoke yourself sick.

(替換) Smoking is harmful to your health.

(範例) **A:** You'll smoke yourself sick. 你會抽出病的。
B: I'm really hooked on these cigars. 我真的離不開這些雪茄。

(提示) hooked [hʊkt] *adj.* 服用…上了癮（+ on）

2492 你現在比較少抽煙了嗎？
Are you smoking less?

(範例) **A:** Are you smoking less? 你現在比較少抽煙了嗎？
B: Yes, I am. 是的。

2493	你抽這種…嗎？ **Do you smoke this kind of...?**

範例 A: Do you smoke this kind of cigar? 你抽這種雪茄嗎？
B: I prefer cigarettes. 我更喜歡香煙。

7.20 體育運動 Talking about Sports

　　體育運動包括競技比賽和鍛鍊身體的各種活動。與體育運動相關的語言極其豐富，有時描述起來像戰場廝殺，有時像欣賞藝術傑作，有時講的是外行人聽不懂的行話，有時則是老少皆知的會話。很多人都愛好體育運動，也常常成為話題。原因很簡單，因為體育運動容易引起談話的興趣，且不涉及隱私。體育運動本身的刺激和難以預測的結果也增添了話題的魅力。談論體育運動時，有了共同話題，加上得宜的表達，談起來不僅投機，而且還能幫助建立友誼。

● 觀賞田徑比賽 Watching Track and Field Events

2494	現在正在進行…半準決賽／準決賽／決賽。 (114) **Now, the quarterfinals/semifinals/finals...are underway.**

範例 A: Now, the quarterfinals of the track and field events are underway.
現在正在進行田徑項目的半準決賽。
B: Let's hurry.
我們快點吧。

提示 quarterfinal [ˌkwɔrtɚˈfaɪn!] *n.* 半準決賽
semifinal [ˌsɛmɪˈfaɪn!] *n.* 準決賽

2495	他們起跑了嗎？ **Are they off?**

範例 A: Are they off? 他們起跑了嗎？
B: Yes, they are. 是的。

2496	他正遙遙領先。 **He has a safe lead.**

| 範例 | A: How is Peter? 彼德怎麼樣？
B: He has a safe lead. 他正遙遙領先。 |

| 2497 | …已經超過…個人了。
...has overtaken...others. |

| 範例 | A: Bill has overtaken three others. 比爾已經超過三個人了。
B: He's so great! 他太棒了！ |

| 2498 | 第…條跑道上的運動員居領先地位。
The man in lane...has taken the lead. |

| 替換 | The one in the...lane is in the lead now. |
| 範例 | A: Who is in the lead?
領先的是誰？
B: The man in lane 5 has taken the lead.
第五條跑道上的運動員居領先地位。 |

| 2499 | 誰第一個抵達終點？
Who was the first to break the tape? |

| 範例 | A: Who was the first to break the tape? 誰第一個抵達終點？
B: A runner from England. 一位來自英格蘭的跑者。 |

| 2500 | 他締造了一個新的全國紀錄。
He has set a new national record. |

| 範例 | A: The referee is reporting the time. 裁判員正在報時間。
B: He has set a new national record. 他締造了一個新的全國紀錄。 |
| 提示 | referee [ˌrɛfə'ri] *n.* 裁判 |

● 談論選手 Talking about Athletes

| 2501 | …，是…年…冠軍。
... the...champion. |

| 範例 | A: Can you tell me who that person is?
你能告訴我那個人是誰嗎？
B: Peter Harris − the 1995 all-American champion.
彼德‧哈裡斯，是一九九五年的全美冠軍。 |
| 提示 | champion ['tʃæmpɪən] *n.* 冠軍 |

2502	他的狀態很好／差。 **He's in good/bad form.**

範例　**A:** Is he in good form? 他的狀態好嗎？
　　　B: Yes, he's in good form. 他的狀態很好。

2503	他今天的狀態不如從前。 **He's not in form today.**

範例　**A:** How is Ted? 泰德怎麼樣？
　　　B: He's not in form today. 他今天的狀態不如從前。

2504	她肯定有機會奪得金／銀／銅牌。 **She sure has a chance at a gold/silver/bronze medal.**

替換　She has got a good chance of getting a gold/silver/bronze medal.

範例　**A:** Your sister is the most experienced athlete on the field.
　　　你姐姐是場上最有經驗的運動員。
　　　B: She sure has a chance at a gold medal.
　　　她肯定有機會奪得金牌。

● 談論比分 Talking about Scoring

2505	比賽（以二比二）打平。 **The game ended in a tie (of 2-2).**

替換　The game was tied.
　　　The game ended in a draw.
　　　Both teams tied (at two-all).
　　　They leveled the score (at two-all).

範例　**A:** What is the result? 比賽結果怎麼樣？
　　　B: The game ended in a tie of 2-2. 比賽以二比二打平。

2506	他們以…的成績贏了…。 **They enjoyed a...win over...**

替換　They've won by a score of...

範例　**A:** Did they win?
　　　他們贏了嗎？
　　　B: Yes. They enjoyed a 5-2 win over the Tigers.
　　　贏了。他們以五比二的成績贏了老虎隊。

2507	比賽成績是多少？ **What's the score of the game?**

範例 A: What's the score of the game? 比賽成績是多少？
B: 2-1 in favor of our team. 二比一，我們領先。

2508	以…輸給了…。 **They were beaten...by...**

替換 They have lost...to...

範例 A: How did the Roses do? 玫瑰隊如何？
B: They were beaten 1-0 by the Wolves. 以零比一輸給了狼隊。

2509	…在第…輪比賽中被淘汰。 **...was down and out in the...round.**

替換 ...was knocked out in the...round.

範例 A: Why didn't I see Bob?
為什麼沒有見到鮑伯？
B: He was down and out in the second round.
他在第二輪比賽中被淘汰。

2510	主隊在…賽中以…比…輸給了客隊。 **The local team lost to the visiting team...in the...**

範例 A: The local team lost to the visiting team 7-12 in the semifinals.
主隊在準決賽中以七比十二輸給了客隊。
B: What a pity!
太遺憾了！

7.21 電視節目 Talking about TV Programs

在現代社會中，電視已經非常普及，電視節目也愈來愈豐富，成為人們百談不厭的話題。如今，電視頻道眾多，節目豐富，其趣味性以及觀眾的參與性都日漸增強，這為人們的日常會話提供了豐富的內容。談論電視節目時，人人都可以發表自己的評論，或喜或惡，或褒或貶，只要有利於人與人之間的溝通，沒有什麼特別的限制。

● 談論電視機 Talking about TV Sets

2511	它是一台 56 英寸的平面落地式電視機。 **It's a console model with a 56-inch flat screen.**

115

範例	A: What's your TV like? 你的電視機是什麼樣子的？ B: It's a console model with a 56-inch flat screen. 它是一台 56 英寸的平面落地式電視機。
提示	console [kən'sol] *n.* 落地式（電視機等）

2512	你的電視機是什麼牌子的？ **What make is your TV?**

範例	A: What make is your TV? 你的電視機是什麼牌子的？ B: It's a Sony. 是索尼的。

2513	這台電視機情況良好。 **It works very well.**

替換	It's in good condition. There is nothing wrong with it.
範例	A: How does your TV work? 這台電視機狀況怎麼樣？ B: It works very well. 這台電視機情況良好。

2514	我的電視機影像總是⋯。 **I always get a...image on this TV.**

範例	A: Do you get a clear picture on your TV? 你的電視機影像清晰嗎？ B: I always get a blurred image on this TV. 我的電視機影像總是模糊。
提示	blur [blɝ] *v.* 把（界線、視線等）弄得模糊不清

2515	電視機的螢幕壞了。 **The TV screen is wearing out.**

範例	A: Can you make the image on the television a little clearer? 你能不能把電視影像再調清楚一點？ B: The TV screen is wearing out. 電視機的螢幕壞了。

2516

對不起。我的電視音量不夠大。
Sorry. My TV doesn't have enough volume.

範例

A: Make it louder, please.
　　請把音量開大聲一點。
B: Sorry. My TV doesn't have enough volume.
　　對不起。我的電視音量不夠大。

2517

收訊情況良好。
The reception is good.

替換

It gets good reception.

範例

A: How is the reception? 收訊情況怎麼樣？
B: The reception is good. 收訊情況良好。

提示

reception [rɪ'sɛpʃən] *n.* 接收；收訊

2518

你們如何接收…的電視節目？
How do you receive telecasts from...?

範例

A: How do you receive telecasts from the capital?
　　你們如何接收首都的電視節目？
B: Through relay stations.
　　通過轉播站。

提示

telecast ['tɛlə,kæst] *n.* 電視廣播
relay [rɪ'le] *n.* 轉播

● 節目資訊 Information about TV Programs

2519

…有什麼電視節目？
What's on TV...?

替換

What's on channel...?

範例

A: What's on TV this evening? 晚上有什麼電視節目？
B: A Korean TV series. 韓劇。

2520

什麼時候播？
When's it on?

替換

What time does it start?
When does the show begin?

範例 A: When's it on? 什麼時候播？
B: Around nine. 大約九點。

2521 你通常看什麼電視節目？
What television shows do you usually watch?

範例 A: What television shows do you usually watch?
你通常看什麼電視節目？
B: I often watch the news.
我經常看新聞報導。

2522 你知道下一個節目是什麼嗎？
Do you know what's on next?

範例 A: Do you know what's on next? 你知道下一個節目是什麼嗎？
B: A mystery movie. 一部偵探電影。

2523 在…之後是什麼節目？
What's on after the...?

範例 A: What's on after the news and weather?
在新聞氣象之後是什麼節目？
B: A football match between France and Germany.
法國和德國的足球賽。

2524 你有電視節目表嗎？
Do you have a TV guide?

範例 A: Do you have a TV guide? 你有電視節目表嗎？
B: I don't have one, either. 我也沒有。

2525 …在哪個頻道播出？
What channel is the...on?

範例 A: What channel is the movie on? 電影在哪個頻道播出？
B: It's on channel 28. 在二十八頻道。

● 收看電視 Watching TV

2526 你想看這個電視節目嗎？
Do you want to watch this TV program?

範例　A: Do you want to watch this TV program? 你想看這個電視節目嗎？
　　　B: No. Let's find something else. 不想，我們找別的節目吧。

2527 | 我們可以換一個頻道嗎？
Can we change the channel?

替換　Shall we switch to another channel?

範例　A: Can we change the channel? 我們可以換一個頻道嗎？
　　　B: Let's switch to 5. 轉到第五頻道吧。

2528 | 不知道這是不是實況轉播的節目。
I wonder whether this is a live program.

範例　A: I wonder whether this is a live program.
　　　　不知道這是不是實況轉播的節目。
　　　B: Yes, it's a live broadcast.
　　　　它是實況轉播的。

2529 | 節目中斷了。
The program's been interrupted.

替換　The program's off the air.

範例　A: The program's been interrupted. 節目中斷了。
　　　B: What a pity. 太可惜了。

● 評論節目 Discussing TV Programs

2530 | 你覺得⋯怎麼樣？
What did you think of...?

範例　A: What did you think of *Dialogue*? 你覺得《對話》這個節目怎麼樣？
　　　B: It lacked involvement from the audience. 這個節目缺乏觀眾的參與。

提示　involvement [ɪnˈvɑlvmənt] *n.* 參與

2531 | 現在電視節目裡的⋯太多了。
There's too much...on TV nowadays.

範例　A: There's too much violence on TV nowadays.
　　　　現在電視節目裡的暴力太多了。
　　　B: You can say that again!
　　　　你說得真對！

2532	我覺得…不怎麼樣。 **I don't think much about...**

範例	**A:** Do you like soap operas? 你喜歡電視連續劇嗎？ **B:** I don't think much about them. 我覺得那些東西不怎麼樣。

2533	我不喜歡這個頻道。 **I don't like this channel.**

替換	This channel is not my cup of tea.
範例	**A:** Do you like the sports channel? 你喜歡體育頻道嗎？ **B:** No, I don't like this channel. 不，我不喜歡這個頻道。

7.22 求職面試 Having a Job Interview

得到理想的工作是實現自我價值的第一步，但並不是所有具備工作能力的人都能順利得到理想的工作；獲得人才是事業發展的基礎，但並不是每個公司都能如願獲得自己所需要的人才。在某種意義上講，面試的過程是雙方工作能力和交際能力的展示過程，也是個人特質和語言能力的展示過程。

● 申請工作 Applying for a Job

116

2534	你們公司有職缺嗎？ **Are there any vacancies in your company?**

替換	Are there any positions vacant in your company?
範例	**A:** Are there any vacancies in your company? 你們公司有職缺嗎？ **B:** I'm sorry, there are no vacancies at present. 對不起，目前沒有空缺。
提示	vacancy ['vekənsɪ] *n.* 空缺

2535	你們有…工作嗎？ **Have you got any jobs for a...?**

替換	Have you got any vacancies for a...? Do you have any job for a...? Do you have openings for a...? I was wondering if you have any openings for a...?

範例 A: Have you got any jobs for a typist?
你們有打字員的工作嗎？

B: There are no typist jobs at the moment, but check back next week.
目前沒有打字員的工作，不過下個星期再來看看吧。

2536 我對…廣告上的…職位很感興趣。
I'm interested in the...position you advertised in...

範例 A: I'm interested in the sales manager position you advertised in yesterday's newspaper. 我對昨天報紙廣告上的銷售經理職位很感興趣。

B: The position has been filled. 這職位已經有人了。

2537 你能不能為我安排一個…工作？
Can you arrange a...job for me?

範例 A: Can you arrange a part-time teaching job for me?
你能不能為我安排一個兼職教師的工作？

B: OK. There is an opening here.
好的，現在正好有個空缺。

2538 我急需就業。這裡有職缺嗎？
I'm badly in need of employment. Is there an opening here?

替換 I need a job badly. Is it possible for me to work here?

範例 A: I'm badly in need of employment. Is there an opening here?
我急需就業。這裡有職缺嗎？

B: Do you have any special skills?
你有什麼專長嗎？

提示 employment [ɪmˈplɔɪmənt] n. 工作；職業

2539 你有什麼工作經驗呢？
What experience do you have?

範例 A: I'd like to know if you need a bartender.
我想知道你們是否需要酒保？

B: What experience do you have?
你有什麼工作經驗呢？

提示 bartender [ˈbɑrˌtɛndɚ] n. 酒保

● 詢問與說明資格 Asking & Answering about Qualifications

2540

請告訴我你從事這個工作所具備的資格吧。
Tell me about your qualifications for the job, please.

(替換) Would you like to talk about your qualifications for that job?

(範例) A: Tell me about your qualifications for the job, please.
請告訴我你從事這個工作所具備的資格吧。
B: I've been doing the same job at another company for 10 years.
我在另外一家公司做同樣的工作已經有十年了。

(提示) qualification [ˌkwɑləfəˈkeʃən] *n.* 資格

2541

貴公司的聲譽不錯。
Your company has a good reputation.

(範例) A: Tell me, why you are applying for work at our company?
告訴我，為何申請我們公司的工作？
B: Your company has a good reputation.
貴公司的聲譽不錯。

(提示) reputation [ˌrɛpjəˈteʃən] *n.* 名譽；名聲

2542

我覺得我適合做…的工作。
I think I'm quite suited for a...job.

(範例) A: Why did you apply for the position?
你為什麼要申請這個職位？
B: I think I'm quite suited for a sales job.
我覺得我適合做業務的工作。

2543

你受過什麼樣的教育？
What kind of education do you have?

(替換) What kind of education have you received?

(範例) A: What kind of education do you have? 你受過什麼樣的教育？
B: I got my MBA in 2001. 我於二○○一年獲得了 MBA 學位。

2544

你已經辭去…的工作了嗎？
Have you quit working at...?

(替換) Have you vacated your post at...?

A: Have you quit working at that organization?
你已經辭去在那個機構的工作了嗎？

B: No, not yet.
不，還沒有。

2545
你的條件非常適合這份工作。
Your qualifications for the job are excellent.

 You seem to be very qualified.

 A: Your qualifications for the job are excellent.
你的條件非常適合這份工作。

B: Then, when may I start work?
那麼，我什麼時候可以開始上班呢？

● 說明期望 Stating One's Expectations

2546
你要找什麼樣的工作？
What kind of job are you looking for?

 What kind of job are you seeking?

 A: What kind of job are you looking for? 你要找什麼樣的工作？
B: A managerial job of some kind. 管理方面的工作。

 managerial [ˌmænəˈdʒɪrɪəl] *adj.* 管理的

2547
我想要一個薪水不錯，有正常假期的工作。
I'd like a good-paying job with regular vacation time.

 A: What job would you prefer?
你比較喜歡什麼樣的工作？

B: I'd like a good-paying job with regular vacation time.
我想要一個薪水不錯，有正常假期的工作。

2548
我很希望在外商找到一份工作。
I was hoping to find a job in a foreign company.

 A: What kind of job would you like?
你喜歡什麼樣的工作？

B: I was hoping to find a job in a foreign company.
我很希望在外商找到一份工作。

2549

這工作有假期嗎？
Is there vacation time with this job?

（範例）　**A:** Is there anything you would like to ask about the job?
關於這份工作，你有什麼想知道的嗎？
B: Is there vacation time with this job?
這工作有假期嗎？

● 其他資訊 Other Information

2550

能否請你告訴我你期望的薪水？
Could you tell me what kind of salary you're expecting?

（範例）　**A:** Could you tell me what kind of salary you're expecting?
能否請你告訴我你期望的薪水？
B: Around $3,000 a month.
月薪三千美元左右。

2551

謝謝你的到訪。…之內，我們會通知你。
Thank you for coming. We'll call you within...

（替換）　Thank you for coming. We'll let you know within...
Thank you for coming. You'll hear from us within...

（範例）　**A:** Thank you for coming. We'll call you within a week.
謝謝你的到訪。一週之內，我們會通知你。
B: Thank you.
謝謝。

2552

很高興和你談話。
I've enjoyed talking with you.

（替換）　It's been a pleasure to talk with you.

（範例）　**A:** I've enjoyed talking with you. 很高興和你談話。
B: The feeling is mutual. 我也是。

（提示）　mutual ['mjutʃʊəl] *adj.* 共同的；共有的

577

7.23　電話溝通 Talking on the Telephone

隨著現代通訊技術的發達，打電話愈來愈方便。在國外還存在 station-to-station call（不指定某一個人接電話，只要有人接就計費）、person-to-person call（指定人接電話，人不在不計費，但費用較高）和 collect call（指定電話費由對方來付）。打國際長途電話時，如果有接線生轉接，要講明對方國名、居住地區、區號和電話號碼、電話種類、自己的姓名、號碼和對方的姓名；打國際直撥電話時，要記清楚需要的各種代碼及電話號碼。打國際長途電話時，還要注意地區的時差。此外，通話完畢後，要放好電話，以免繼續計費。不知道電話號碼時，可以查電話號碼簿或求助於接線生。和親朋好友通話時，西方人通常做非正式的自我介紹；打電話給陌生人時，通常要做正式的自我介紹。中英文的電話用語差別很大，切勿用中式英文來表達。

● 請求接線生服務 Asking the Operator for Help

2553	你的電話要轉到哪裡？ **How may I direct your call?**	117
替換	Who are you trying to reach? What's the name of the party you're trying to reach?	
範例	**A:** How may I direct your call? 你的電話要轉到哪裡？ **B:** Please connect me with 5369, please. 請接 5369。	

2554	請轉分機…。 **Extension..., please.**
替換	Get me extension..., please. Put me through to extension... Could I have extension...? Could you get me extension..., please?
範例	**A:** Extension 5652, please. 請轉分機 5652。 **B:** OK. 好的。
提示	extension [ɪk'stɛnʃən] n. 分機

2555

請幫我接⋯好嗎？
May I have...?

(替換)
Connect me with..., please.
Can you put me through to...?
Can you connect me with...?
Please put my call through to...
I want to talk to..., please.
I'd like to place a call to..., please

(範例)
A: May I have the White Swan Hotel? 請幫我接白天鵝大酒店好嗎？
B: Just a moment, please. 請稍候。

2556

我想打對方付費的電話給⋯。
I'd like to call collect to...

(替換)
I'd like to make a collect call to...

(範例)
A: I'd like to call collect to the headquarters.
我想打對方付費的電話給總部。
B: All right.
好的。

(提示)
collect [kə'lɛkt] adv. 對方付費地 adj. 對方付費的
headquarters ['hɛd,kwɔrtəz] n. 總部

2557

電話忙線中。
The line is busy.

(替換)
The line is engaged.

(範例)
A: Put me through to the HR Department, please.
請幫我接人力資源部。
B: The line is busy.
電話忙線中。

(提示)
「電話忙線中」通常說："The line is busy."。等到分機可以接通了，總機
會告訴你："The line is free."。
HR 為 Human Resources（人力資源）的縮略字。

2558

我想要⋯的電話號碼。
I'd like the number for...

(替換)
Do you have the number for...?
Can you give me the number for...?

Could you tell me the number of...?

範例 **A:** I'd like the number for the Double Tree Hotel.
我想要雙樹酒店的電話號碼。
B: The number is 539-5529.
號碼是 539-5529。

2559　接線生，我的電話斷了。
Operator, I was cut off.

替換 Operator, I've been cut off.
Operator, I've been disconnected.

範例 **A:** Operator, I was cut off. 接線生，我的電話斷了。
B: You're connected now. Go ahead. 現在接通了。說吧。

提示 disconnect [ˌdɪskəˈnɛkt] *v.* 切斷（電話、電源等）

2560　電話現在接通了。
You're connected now.

替換 Your call is ready.
The line is through now.
Your call has gone through.

範例 **A:** You're connected now. 電話現在接通了。
B: Thank you. 謝謝。

● 打電話 Starting a Phone Call

2561　喂？我是…。
Hello?...here.

替換 Hello? My name's...
Hello? (This is)...speaking.
Hello? This is...(here).

範例 **A:** Hello? John Smith here. 喂？我是約翰‧史密斯。
B: Who're you calling? 你要找誰？

2562　我就是。
Speaking.

替換 That's me.
It's me.

This is he (speaking).
You are speaking to him.

範例　**A:** Hello? Is Bob in? 喂？請問鮑伯在嗎？
　　　B: Speaking. 我就是。

2563　喂？我想請⋯聽電話。
Hello?..., please.

替換　Hello? I'd like to speak to...
　　　Hello? Get me...on the phone, please.

範例　**A:** Hello? Mr. Clark, please. 喂？我想請科拉克先生聽電話。
　　　B: Just a minute. 請等一下。

2564　你是哪位？
Who is this?

替換　Who's calling/speaking, please?
　　　May I ask/know who's calling?
　　　May I have your name, please?
　　　Who can I say is calling?
　　　Who's this calling, please?
　　　Who's that speaking, please?

範例　**A:** Who is this? 你是哪位？
　　　B: Bruce Hill. 布魯斯・希爾。

2565　我去找⋯。
I'll go get...

替換　I'll see if...is in.
　　　I'll just find out if...is in.
　　　Let me check and see if...is available.

範例　**A:** Hi, is Susan in? 嗨！蘇珊在嗎？
　　　B: I'll go get her. 我去找她。

2566　這裡沒有這個人。
There is no one here by that name.

替換　There's nobody here by that name.
　　　No one lives here by that name.

範例　**A:** Hello! Is Mary in? 嗨！瑪麗在嗎？
　　　B: There is no one here by that name. 這裡沒有這個人。

581

2567

對不起，你打錯了。
Sorry, wrong number.

（替換）
I'm sorry, but you must have the wrong number.
Sorry, you've got the wrong number.
Sorry, but I think you have the wrong number.

（範例）
A: Is this the Baseball Club? 是棒球俱樂部嗎？
B: Sorry, wrong number. 對不起，你打錯了。

2568

請稍候。
Hang on, please.

（替換）
One moment/minute, please.
Just a moment/second, please.
He'll be right with you.
Hang on a moment/second, please.
Don't hang up, please.
Hold the line, please.
Hold on a moment/second, please.
Would you like to hold, please?
Would you hold the line a moment?
Would you wait a moment, please?

（範例）
A: Hello. May I talk to Mr. Smith? 哈囉，我可以和史密斯先生談話嗎？
B: Hang on, please. 請稍候。

● 不接電話 Not Answering the Call

2569

對不起，她不在。
Sorry, she is out now.

（替換）
Sorry, she is not in.
Sorry, she is not here how.
Sorry, she is out of the office right now.
Sorry, she has stepped out.
Sorry, she is not in right now.
Sorry, but she is not here at the moment.

（範例）
A: Hello, Mrs. Hans, please. 喂，請找漢斯夫人。
B: Sorry, she is out now. 對不起，她不在。

2570	他現在不能接電話。 **He is tied up right now.**

(替換)	He is unable to take your call right now. He is not available right now. He is not able to take your call at the moment. He cannot come to the phone right now.
(範例)	A: He is tied up right now. 他現在不能接電話。 B: When would be a good time to reach him? 什麼時候找他最好？

2571	他正在講電話。 **He's on another line right now.**

(替換)	He is with someone right now.
(範例)	A: Hello. May I talk to Mr. Kidman? 你好，我要找吉德曼先生？ B: He's on another line right now. 他正在講電話。

2572	…，你的電話。 **..., your phone call!**

(替換)	..., you're wanted on the phone. ..., telephone. ..., it's for you. ..., a phone call for you. ..., someone wants you on the phone. ..., somebody's asking for you on the telephone. There's a phone call for you, ...
(範例)	A: Jenny, your phone call! 珍妮，你的電話。 B: I'm busy. 我現在很忙。

● 留言 Leaving a Message

2573	你要留言嗎？ **Would you like to leave a message?**

(替換)	May/Can I take a message? Can I leave him a message for you? Can I tell him something for you? Do you want to leave a message? Do you have a message that I can pass on to him?

Do you want to leave word for him to call you?
Is there any message I can give him?
Would you like me to tell him something?
Would you like me to relay a message for you?

範例　A: Would you like to leave a message? 你要留言嗎？
B: No, thanks. I'll just call back. 不，謝謝。我待會再打。

2574

我可以留言嗎？
May I leave a message?

替換　Can I leave a message?
I'd like to leave a message.
Could you take a message?

範例　A: May I leave a message? 我可以留言嗎？
B: Sure. 當然可以。

2575

我會轉告他的。
I'll give him the message.

替換　I'll see that he gets the message.
I'll make sure that he gets the message.

範例　A: Please tell him the meeting has been cancelled.
請你告訴他會議取消了。
B: I'll give him the message.
我會轉告他的。

2576

有電話嗎？
Are there any messages for me?

替換　Did I get any calls?
Did anyone call me?
Any phone calls for me?
Do I have any messages?
Who called while I was out?

範例　A: Are there any messages for me? 有電話嗎？
B: There were a few calls for you. 有幾通電話找你。